Copyright ©2025 by Jude Barnes

All rights reserved.

No part of this publication may be reproduced, distributed, or transmitted in any form or by any means, including photocopying, recording, or other electronic or mechanical methods, without the prior written permission of the publisher, except as permitted by U.S. copyright law.

The story, all names, characters, and incidents portrayed in this production are fictitious. No identification with actual persons (living or deceased), places, buildings, and products is intended or should be inferred. Elements of the story are dramatized and are not a reflection of the standards of the organizations, teams, or brands depicted.

Racing Hearts
Jude Barnes

For Emma,
my editor and Diego's original ride-or-die.
This book wouldn't have been possible without you.
I love you always! <3

Contents

1. PART ONE — 1
2. Chapter One — 2
3. Chapter Two — 11
4. Chapter Three — 21
5. Chapter Four — 33
6. Chapter Five — 47
7. Chapter Six — 55
8. Chapter Seven — 71
9. Chapter Eight — 79
10. Chapter Nine — 93
11. Chapter Ten — 99
12. Chapter Eleven — 115
13. Chapter Twelve — 129
14. Chapter Thirteen — 139
15. Chapter Fourteen — 145
16. Chapter Fifteen — 151

17.	Chapter Sixteen	167
18.	Chapter Seventeen	181
19.	PART TWO	197
20.	Chapter Eighteen	199
21.	Chapter Nineteen	211
22.	Chapter Twenty	221
23.	Chapter Twenty-One	235
24.	Chapter Twenty-Two	247
25.	Chapter Twenty-Three	259
26.	Chapter Twenty-Four	273
27.	Chapter Twenty-Five	284
28.	Chapter Twenty-Six	289
29.	Chapter Twenty-Seven	295
30.	Chapter Twenty-Eight	305
31.	PART THREE	316
32.	Chapter Twenty-Nine	317
33.	Chapter Thirty	324
34.	Chapter Thirty-One	338
35.	Chapter Thirty-Two	347
36.	Chapter Thirty-Three	360
37.	Chapter Thirty-Four	365
38.	Chapter Thirty-Five	376

39.	Chapter Thirty-Six	381
40.	Chapter Thirty-Seven	388
Acknowledgements		395
About the author		397

PART ONE

FIND A WAY OR MAKE ONE

Chapter One

June didn't know what she had done to piss off the universe, but if one more thing went wrong tonight, she'd have to file a formal complaint with God.

June downed another drink. Whiskey. Not champagne. Champagne was for celebration. For a job well done. But June had started her season at absolute rock bottom. Might as well drink herself stupid when she couldn't get any lower.

A shit round on a green horse warranted a night alone in her hotel room, watching *Mamma Mia!* and drinking herself to sleep in true pity-party fashion.

Instead, she got overpriced whiskey at a shitty party meant for networking, music blasting loud enough to make her ears bleed, and a restlessness thrumming deep in her chest.

Lotus Energy had built their drink brand on sponsoring extreme athletes, which meant their events were packed with leagues of people who all thought they were a gift from God, and their underlings. June couldn't stand them, even though she was technically one of them.

At least she delved low enough to remember her mortality.

Now, she was surrounded by drunk versions of the assholes, grinding on each other, shotgunning beers, and doing keg stands. She had begged Charlene not to make her go, but here she was anyway. As if things weren't bad enough, her partners in crime—both of her PR girls—were missing, preoccupied with work.

June loved a good party, but as she watched a pretty boy drown his Armani suit in liquor, she wondered if she was in hell. That wasn't partying. That was just sticky and gross.

June wandered through the expanse of the club, feeling a bit lightheaded. June loved whiskey; whiskey did not love her back. Still, she insisted on drinking it. It soothed her mind, even if it made her sick to her stomach. Soothed the loneliness and the ache for home. She turned, disappearing into the women's restroom in an attempt to escape the chaos.

None of these people could possibly understand what any of this was like. June wasn't a rookie anymore. She had her first year in the Global Champions Tour under her belt. Hardly a veteran but no longer the new kid. She'd been riding horses as long as she could remember—though in Texas rather than all over the world and in a western saddle with a slew of cowboys rather than the tiny slip of leather English riders deemed a saddle.

It was impressive enough to go from a brand-new English rider to a professional jumping 1.60 meters in a matter of three years, but to nearly win the Longines Global Champions Tour her rookie year? June had earned every bit of her reputation, including the fact that she was a poor girl from Texas, rough around the edges, and impossible to control.

She missed her jeans and boots. She missed line dancing, Brooks & Dunn, and *manners*.

She made her way into a stall, sinking to sit on the floor with her knees tucked up to her chest as she fumbled with her phone. Her manager's contact beamed up at her on the glaringly bright screen, and June texted her with clumsy, drunken fingers.

JUNE: i wannnaa go homeeeeee

She was way too drunk for this shit. She leaned against the bathroom wall, her head pounding. Her phone buzzed.

CHAR: Behave for twenty more minutes and I'll send Lola and Liv. Swear it.

June groaned. She had fought so hard for this life. Early mornings and late nights. Hours upon hours. Blood, sweat, bruises, and tears. And she loved jumping. Loved her horses. She lived for those moments in the arena. But this? Being dressed up as her sponsor's doll? She was hardly pageant material, and it showed.

June forced herself out of the stall, bracing her arms on the bathroom counter as she stared at herself in the mirror, the bass from the music reverberating through the walls. She was not weak. She had accomplished things she hadn't thought possible three years ago, jumped nearly as high as she was tall in massive arenas with thousands of people watching. She could handle twenty more minutes in a shitty club.

Finally, June shoved the door open.

And collided with a solid chest.

She drew in a sharp breath through her teeth, wincing at the frigid liquor. Tequila. All down the front of her dress. Cold and foul-smelling.

For a moment, she contemplated lying on the floor, screaming, and hopefully getting trampled.

"*¡Mierda!*" the man cursed in a heavy Spanish accent. It was Pretty Boy. His Armani suit coat had been discarded, leaving him in a white button-up with the sleeves rolled over his elbows. He grabbed her by the shoulder, big brown eyes blown wide, and lips parted in surprise. "*Dios mío,* I am so sorry—"

June shook her hands, flinging the liquor off. She gritted her teeth, reminding herself to be nice as she stared up at the Spaniard. "It's fine."

He took her by the arm, now-empty glass still in hand as his eyes searched the crowd. "Let me help you clean up."

June grimaced. "I'm good, thanks. I was just leaving anyway." Everything was far too much. She was leaving this stupid club, and she was going to sit in an alley and sulk for the next—she glanced at her phone—seventeen minutes.

She wrung out the front of her dress, leaving the fabric disheveled and wrinkled.

"*Por favor, Hermosa.* Let me help you—"

She yanked out of his grasp, stepping away from him. "Fuck's sake, it's fine!"

The man drew his hand back, looking at her like a kicked puppy. June was swarmed with guilt immediately. Damn those big brown eyes. He was beautiful. Even in her drunken haze, she knew that. Soft skin, soft lips, and kind eyes. She wanted to apologize. He wasn't the one she was angry at. It was just a drink. An accident. Nothing more.

Besides, she hated this dress.

She opened her mouth to speak, only to be interrupted by another drunken man stepping between the pair. "Don't fucking talk to him like that!"

Pretty Boy groaned, grabbing the Drunkard gruffly by the back of the neck. *"Cabrón—"*

Drunkard shoved Pretty Boy's hand off, surging forward to push June. Any sympathy or apology died in her throat. She was angry, and irritated, and drunk, and pissed. In that order.

She could almost immediately hear Charlene's scoldings in the back of her mind. *Don't do it. Stay calm. Stay composed. Rage is temporary. Your image is forever.* Don't do it.

June threw her hands up in surrender, turning away from the pair, headed for the side door exit. It was Qatar, for fuck's sake, she wouldn't freeze to death. At this point, that sounded like the better option. Behind her, she could hear Drunkard lean over to his friend. "That bitch is in a mood."

June stopped dead in her tracks and whispered a silent apology to Charlene.

She whirled, snagging a drink from someone's hand, and hurled the contents across them both. The liquor hardly hit its target before Drunkard surged forward and caught her by the front of her dress, dragging her toward him and yelling something at her in Spanish.

June's adrenaline spiked at the promise of the impending fight. She threw a punch before she'd even registered what she was doing, landing it right in his face. He went sputtering off to the floor, and Pretty Boy laughed out loud, pointing at him as he crashed to the ground.

Everything went to hell all at once. A short girl stepped up, throwing a punch that caught June in the nose, and instantly, it was pouring blood. June whirled, landing a solid blow to the girl's gut that left her doubled over and gasping for air before June shoved her back into the crowd.

Drunkard ran to the girl's side, and June turned to bolt.

Pretty Boy caught her by the back of the neck, slamming her back against the wall. She beamed up at him with a shit-eating grin as he pinned her in place and stuck a finger in her face, shouting at her in a mix of English and Spanish that she didn't understand. A crowd had gathered to watch, phones pulled out and pointed toward the duo.

The bouncer grabbed Pretty Boy by the arm, dragging him off

of her. Then, his friend grabbed the bouncer, a mix of patrons and security quickly spiraling out of control.

June turned to slip away when another bouncer met her eyes over the crowd. "Hey!" he called, cutting through the mass.

She knew she was in deep shit when she heard it. June turned and bolted into the crowd, slipping through the throng of onlookers into the blissfully unaware partiers and dancers.

People turned to watch as she ran, shouting to each other in words she couldn't hear or understand through the loud thrumming of music. June darted through the crowd, not paying them a moment of attention as she hurried for the exit. Somebody caught her by the elbow. She didn't ask questions. She turned and swung, landing a blow right to Pretty Boy's pretty face. He yelped, staggering back, his hand immediately flying to his nose.

June's jaw dropped, clapping a hand over her mouth as she watched blood cover the Spaniard's pretty face, a slew of curses falling from his mouth. She hadn't meant to. It was instinct. She shouldn't have—

She took a step forward and reached out for him when she saw the bouncers rushing toward them. *Shit*.

There was no time for apologies or excuses. June turned and ran.

Right into the chest of a policeman. He caught her gruffly, glowering down at her, and she offered him an apologetic smile. *Fuck*. He wrenched her arms behind her, slamming cuffs on her wrists.

Sometimes, she wondered if believing in God would make him kinder to her, because this shit was getting ridiculous.

The man marched her out of the club and into the night, throwing the door of the police car open and shoving June in. The girl from the fight was already there—a pretty, petite Spaniard with dark hair in a blue dress and blood on her knuckles. She didn't say a word, head fixed carefully forward, hands placed delicately in her lap despite the handcuffs on them. June let her head fall back against the headrest. And then the door was opened again, and the policeman shoved her into the middle seat; Pretty Boy promptly filled her seat. He shouted a slew of Arabic, arguing with the officer up until he slammed the door on Pretty Boy.

He grumbled to himself in Spanish as he glanced to see his newfound accomplices, and immediately, his rage softened. Honeyed brown eyes focused on her as his lips parted in surprise, blood staining his pretty face. The blood she put there.

June puffed up, immediately ready for another fight. *"You—"*

"Me?!" he exclaimed in utter disbelief, throwing his hands up in innocence the best he could in a pair of handcuffs. "You're the one who started this!"

"Me?" June was almost offended. "You spilled a drink on me, and then your friend shoved me and called me a bitch!"

Pretty Boy spluttered like the words had gotten halfway out of his throat, then his brain recomputed and tried for three different answers at once before he settled on one. "My *friend*?!" His jaw hung open, appalled at the implication.

The woman reached over her and smacked Pretty Boy straight across the chest. "He is trying to be your friend, but you're stuck up!"

"Tell him to quit being such a stupid bastard, and I'll consider it!"

They exploded in a slew of angry Spanish.

June understood all at once. The pair were siblings. The odd man out was the girl's boyfriend.

June was in yet another public scandal. Family drama of a family she didn't know. And didn't want to know.

Pretty Boy threw his hands up, using them to the full extent his cuffs would allow. The woman, so well-mannered before, whirled and began shouting back, both of them raising their voices over the other until they were screaming across June, or rather through her.

June kept her eyes carefully trained forward as the officer threw the car into gear and escorted them to the police station.

Chapter Two

June could have cried from relief the moment she saw them—Charlene, Lola, and Olivia. Her manager and PR team.

It had been two hours since she'd been discarded in the holding pen, and she was beginning to wonder if Charlene was going to leave her there for a week just to teach her a lesson.

It was far from the first instance in which June had taken things a little too far. Just that most of the time, she was partying hard enough to end up in the hospital rather than in jail. In a single season, she had sprained her wrist after tumbling off a crowd surf, had to have stitches after she hit her head while being pushed in somebody else's bar fight, and drank enough to convince herself she had alcohol poisoning and was rushed to the ER just for it to be a panic attack.

She had a reputation—harassing paparazzi who tried to sneak pictures, heckling rude journalists. Fans loved her for her fire.

But to turn it on a random citizen?

Charlene blamed every gray hair she'd ever had on June.

June was still in her tequila-soaked dress. Her makeup was smeared over both eyes, her hair a mess, and she'd never needed to brush her teeth more in her life.

Pretty Boy and his sister had argued in vehement Spanish for half an hour before the girl broke into tears, and Pretty Boy wrapped her up in handcuffed arms. They'd been silent since, asleep against the far end of the cell. Others had come and gone, but June couldn't bother to pay them any mind, picking at her fingers until they bled. Finally, *finally*, her team had come to her rescue.

Charlene marched into her line of sight, giving her one of her signature *'Mom'* looks—hands on her hips, head cocked to the side, foot tapping impatiently. Charlene was the human personification of a Barbie Doll, nothing short of perfect at any given moment. Even now, at nearly four in the morning, she wore an ironed gray pencil skirt and a matching blazer with her makeup done and her dirty-blonde hair flawlessly straight.

Olivia and Lola, June's PR team, were a stark difference on either side of Charlene. Lola wore a pastel pink sweatsuit, her hair tucked under a bonnet; Olivia wore a pair of boys gym shorts and a graphic T-shirt triple the size of her.

June was escorted out of the cell, and Pretty Boy offered her a beaming grin and a wave, still handcuffed.

Olivia immediately shot June a look at the sight of her unbearably attractive cellmate. She elbowed June in the ribs the moment she was cut loose and they were walking down the hall. "Awooga."

"Shut up."

They didn't exchange another word the entire walk to the car. Charlene was deadly quiet as she took the front seat. The kind of quiet that was typically followed by her making someone beg for their life. June clambered into the back seat between Olivia and Lola, readying for the beatdown of her life.

Charlene took a deep, terrifyingly composed breath. "Have you eaten anything?"

It was a trick to get her to eat poison; June was sure of it. "... No."

Charlene nodded gingerly to the driver, and he threw the car into gear. It was all of five incomprehensibly drawn-out minutes before they pulled into the nearest convenience store. Charlene went inside. She returned with a bag filled to the brim with breakfast sandwiches and burritos in one hand and a drink carrier in the other.

She passed the food and drinks off wordlessly, and the girls immediately dug in. June got all of two bites into breakfast burrito before Charlene drew a deep breath. *There it is.* "Twenty minutes . . . I said I would get you in *twenty minutes*!"

June swallowed hard, allowing a few moments of silence as she tried to gather a response. "In my defense—"

Charlene whirled, grabbing for June, and she screamed, clambering over the seat in an attempt to flee the attack. She dropped hard into the trunk of the SUV, fumbling for her bearings. "It's not that bad!"

"Not that—*Not that bad*?" Charlene grabbed a burrito from the bag, chucking it at her head. Two more followed in rapid succession.

June ducked just in time to avoid them, using the seat as a war trench. "It was just a bar fight! We can just say I drank too much or something—"

"Just a bar fight?" Charlene turned fully around in her seat. "It was a bar fight with Diego Cabrera!"

June perked up, eyeing her over the edge of the seat. She had never heard the name in her life. He couldn't have been another equestrian. She knew all of those. "Who?"

Charlene buried her face in her hands to muffle the scream she let out instead of socking June in the face. "Girls, deal with her."

Olivia looked up from her breakfast sandwich like a deer in headlights until Charlene turned to funnel her rage into aggressively chugging her coffee. "Oh. Yeah. Girl, you're fucked."

"What do you mean?"

Lola shrugged. "He's a driver for Lotus's Formula One team."

June blinked. Formula One were the most prissy of the prissy—and that was coming from an equestrian—millionaires funneled into the sport from the time they were old enough to drive toy cars. Go-kart racing that gradually increased until they were zipping around elaborate tracks at speeds over two hundred miles an hour. Paid enough to buy companies like Lotus Energy, not be sponsored by them. No wonder he didn't care about an Armani suit.

Clearly, June's prayers that they could sweep this all under the rug had gone unanswered. Another point for agnosticism! Pictures and videos of the fight were probably—inevitably—all over the internet.

She was itching for some sleep and water.

All June could say was, "Oh."

Charlene whirled on her. "*Oh*? That's all you've got?"

June rubbed at her temple. This sort of thing happened, especially in racing. Guys got into brawls; they made out with strangers or each other after. There were scandals. It wasn't a new headline. "What do you want me to say, Char?"

"Say you know this is a huge mess!" Charlene shouted. "You're lucky he and his sister aren't pressing charges! Lotus is talking about dropping your sponsorship or his, and *he* has a seat on a team."

June swallowed hard. She'd done a lot of stupid shit before, but this one took the cake. "Shit," she said. Better than *'Oh'*, at least.

Charlene wasn't satisfied, as if she had to smack June upside the head to get through to her. "It's all any media outlet has been talking about. You punching Lotus's Golden Boy in his money maker is big news."

June threw her hands up in innocence. "He started it!"

"Don't even." Charlene held up her hand, cutting her off. "We have to fix this. The two of *you* are going to fix this."

Uh-oh.

June sat up, alerted by her tone. Charlene had gone manager mode, any lightheartedness fleeing as June became her client rather than her friend. "Charlene Mayfair, what did you do?"

Charlene whirled on her, throwing her hands up in the air. "Saved your career! Like always!"

June shot forward, hanging over the edge of the seat as she looked to the girls for help. "What did she do!"

Lola shrugged, opening her mouth to speak through a bite of breakfast sandwich, but Charlene spoke first.

"Lotus is doing a Petal Event. You show up, you walk a red carpet, you drink a Lotus. You make it look like you're friends."

June's mouth dropped open, her voice raising two octaves. *"Another one?!"*

A Petal Event. An invite-only event where you walked a red carpet into the lamest party you'd ever seen. To walk it with Diego? To smile, hold onto his arm, and joke about a little incident involving too much liquor and the bruises on his face? Nothing could have sounded worse to her.

"Lotus is trying to expand international business, which means you're going to go kiss ass."

June groaned louder, clapping herself on the forehead. Karma was such a bitch. She didn't even like energy drinks. She was certain by the time she was done with this bullshit, her heart was going to be fried. "When is this?"

Charlene's hand fell to the radio, turning up the music as if she hadn't heard June's question at all.

June groaned, "Charlene!"

"Tomorrow."

"Tomorrow?!" She shot up, smacking her head on the roof of the car before she dropped back down, rubbing her newly earned goose egg to add to her already pounding headache.

"You're going," Charlene told her. "Distract Lotus with smiles and apologies, and maybe, just *maybe*, you get through this without them dropping you."

Jumping out of the car sounded more pleasant. It was the only way she was getting out of this. The rest of the trek to the hotel was made in complete silence, aside from the girls whispering amongst themselves about something on Lola's phone. June lay down in the trunk and stared out the window at the mix of the night lights and the beginnings of a lightening sky. She burrowed herself against the seat, spiraling deeper and deeper until she was brimming with anxiety and the need to run.

When had she let herself get so lax? So stupid? A phenomenal rookie year secured her sponsors because she wasn't a problem. At least, not big enough of a problem to warrant any real reprimands. But having a reputation for calling out paparazzi and rude reporters was a lot different than assaulting her main sponsor's racing driver.

She had made a habit of playing it cool. If she kept her head on straight and her eyes on the fight for the Longines Global Champions Tour season title, everything else would be fine. June was loved by fans for how unapologetic she was in such an elitist sport. Her team had done a wonderful job of marketing it. Carefree and easy-going June Walker who did what she felt like.

The truth was this: June cared more than she could ever voice. It ate her alive. Haunted her in the dead of night. She hated being around her sponsors because she was not good with them. She wasn't good at the line of what was an acceptable level of confrontation, and what was vigilantism. That was why she had the girls.

June Walker was a hard pill to swallow. A hard person to tolerate. A hard woman to love. So, she let the girls handle it. Make her charming and admirable. But all the fun social media posts in the world couldn't cover the fact that wasn't her. A train wreck was a closer equivalent. The kind that got too drunk in bars, punched people in the face, and lost her main sponsor over it. The kind that worked her entire life away for her dream career just to fumble it all. The kind who couldn't face her own stupidity, so she bitched about a PR event instead of acknowledging that she had truly, genuinely fucked up.

At the hotel, the girls bailed out. Olivia rushed to pop the cargo trunk before she said something about breakfast and went scampering off towards the hotel. Lola chased after her, shoving her the moment she caught up. Olivia reached out and promptly tripped Lola, nearly dropping her on her face before she caught herself at the last second before they disappeared through the doors of the hotel.

Clearly, they'd forgotten the fact Charlene had already fed them in the car. Any excuse to escape what was about to come was good enough for them.

June lingered in the trunk, legs dangling off the back of the SUV when Charlene stepped into her sights. She didn't say a word, just crossed her arms and met June with a set of squared shoulders and a clenched jaw. Exasperation bubbled up in June's chest, refusing to be the first to look away from her. She hated letting Charlene down, but it seemed all she was capable of most days. Finally, June sighed. "Char, say something."

June could take the yelling. She could take the lectures. She could take anything other than this wretched silence.

Charlene drew the skin of her cheek between her teeth, biting it mercilessly the way she always did when she was irritated. June had become mighty familiar with it. "I can't force you to care, June."

Any argument died on June's tongue immediately.

"It's your career. Your life."

The implications weighed heavily. Her career. Her life. To fuck up however she pleased. June chewed on her bottom lip, turning her gaze toward the car so she wouldn't have to see Charlene's disappointment. No arguing this time. No downplaying that she was destroying herself from the inside out because she couldn't help but push the limits in all things—in the arena, in her career, and to the bottom of a bottle.

The guilt ate her alive.

June finally sighed her exhaustion, and Charlene took it as defeat.

"Shower. Sleep. Make it happen."

Her favorite phrase. It didn't matter what June wanted so long as she could make it happen. And she could make this happen.

June nodded shortly, and a moment later, Charlene turned on her heel and marched back into the hotel. June drew a deep breath, cursing loudly as she hopped out of the trunk and slammed it shut.

All of this could have been avoided if she'd just ridden Midus.

June had competed combinations and courses just like this one hundreds of times. It should have been infallible. *She* should have been infallible, and yet, she had managed to fuck it up. Severely. Or rather, her choice to ride Hades had.

Hades was nine. He'd only been jumping 1.60 meters for a few months. He was still green to this level of competition. She was supposed to be schooling him consistently in the lower level classes while she actually won points on Midus in the Tour.

Attempting to compete in the LGCT on Hades right now was just ignorant.

She didn't blame the fact she had a minimal number of sponsors. She didn't exactly make the best choices in her career. But if there was one thing June could do, it was ride.

Amelia Santiago had been the first to see it. Though, in a western saddle as far in the middle-of-nowhere Texas as you can get.

While traveling from Ocala, Florida, to Austin, Texas with a load full of showjumping horses, the woman's rig had broken down. Amelia and her crew found the nearest barn, where June was working client horses.

June had spent the last four years as Amelia's mentee and groom after she convinced June to move to Italy for a real profession in horses. Working the woman's horses, grooming for her across the world, taking lesson after lesson from her.

Amelia saw talent. Or she took pity. June still wasn't sure which.

The first half of her rookie year, June hadn't even thought of the title. It was only a new round, in a new country, and a horse that was all hers. Doing it with Midus. Now, the title loomed over her head. The only chance for her to prove herself.

There were five levels of competition in international showjumping, ranging from 1* all the way to 5*, gradually increasing in height and difficulty until they reached 1.60 meters. June had spent the last four years diligently working her way up those ranks until she was finally playing with the big dogs.

The Longines Global Champions Tour.

The ultimate individual challenge. Only the best for the best.

The rules were simple: a two-round style competition. A qualifying ride, followed by the competition. The fastest ride with the fewest faults won. Though expected to compete in all fifteen Grand Prix, only points from the best eight scores counted towards the championship battle.

June had earned the nickname The Sensational Rookie after nearly taking the LGCT season win her first year. She was the runner-up to only her coach, mentor, and biggest advocate of her career: Amelia.

She owed her life to that woman. She owed a lot to a lot of people.

She just wished the spotlight wasn't so bright all the time.

Back in her hotel room, June stumbled into the shower and then collapsed in bed for a solid nine hours of hangover-induced misery.

Chapter Three

The next day brought the ridiculous luncheon and, with it, a much-needed excuse to get dolled up. June wore a simple baby blue midi dress with a square neckline and a cut-out back tied up with a bow. Just enough to be scandalous while maintaining a modicum of class. That seemed to be June's forte. Her hair remained down most of her life, far too short to draw back into anything other than a hairnet to stuff under her helmet, so dark red curls it was, with gold earrings protruding from behind the ringlets and a simple matching necklace resting in the divot of her throat.

June sat in the back corner of the Michelin-starred restaurant, vaguely listening as Charlene rattled on about the importance of this meeting. Gourmet seafood and steakhouse. Lots of good eats. A distraction to keep her from more trouble. She waited for Pretty Boy and his manager to arrive, drumming her fingers across her jaw in boredom. It wasn't like she had expected anything different. Of course they were late. What must it be like to be the kind of person so full of yourself to disrespect others' time?

Diego Cabrera sauntered into the restaurant, his manager a few steps ahead of him. He looked even more handsome now than he had in the club—the light catching the gorgeous tones of his skin kissed by the Spanish sun, a pleasant shade of brown, silky black curls that always seemed to rest perfectly, dark, honeyed eyes that landed on her and left her immediately reeling for another drink.

Diego dressed semi-casually, though she knew his entire outfit must cost more than her house. She couldn't imagine Diego wearing anything other than designer. He wore beige linen pants and a collared, short-sleeved sweater that she would have bullied him for if he didn't wear it so well. She suspected he got away with a lot of things on account of his beauty.

No Armani today, then. The watch on his wrist seemed to make up for that. A gold Longines, she recognized. The main sponsor of the Global Champions Tour. A peace offering.

She hadn't seen him since the holding cell two nights earlier. Since he'd spilled a drink on her, and she'd punched him right in the face.

Diego's mouth quirked up into a smirk at the sight of June, giving her a small wave as he and his manager found their seats. He pulled out her chair before he extended a hand to Charlene across the table. She beamed and shook it, clearly pleased by his gentlemanly manners. June turned her head away so they couldn't see her roll her eyes.

Pretty Boy extended his hand to June. She shook it. A firm, solid handshake that she'd learned from the cowboys she'd trained horses with, rather than the dainty handshake he'd clearly been expecting.

Her hands were more calloused than his.

That was a point in her book.

She was an athlete, too, she wanted to remind him. Her sport was arguably the more dangerous of the two. When his eyes flicked up to hers, he raised a brow a little, clearly amused. She dropped her grip.

His honey-brown gaze remained locked with hers as he took his seat. *"Hola,"* he greeted.

"Howdy," she returned, plainly unamused.

Diego's manager and Charlene clearly understood the gravity of their situation and jumped to each other's every whim—far more willing to cooperate than the pair they were sent to manhandle.

If June could swallow her pride enough to be Amelia's bitch for the last four years just to get this opportunity, she could be Diego's bitch long enough to save it.

Diego had been sponsored by Lotus since his debut in Formula Three, one of the lesser leagues that eventually led to Formula One. Now, at twenty-four years old and chasing his first World Driver's Championship, Lotus had supported him for nearly a decade. If she could make nice with Lotus's poster child, she could sate them.

Her career meant more to her than any arrogant boy ever could.

She kept Diego carefully out of her line of sight as she listened to their managers discuss the impending red carpet. Diego opened his mouth to speak—seemingly to her—when the waiter came to her rescue, ready to take orders.

"Chef's favorite," she said simply. Ordering at fancy restaurants stressed her out. She only recognized a sixteenth of what was on the menu, and when she ordered something she knew, it never came out how she expected. Chef's Special had become her safeguard instead. She knew how to say that, at least.

Diego, on the other hand, seemed to be a seasoned customer at upscale restaurants, having traveled and raced all over the globe. He simply gave the waiter a charming smile and rattled off in Arabic. He leaned back in his seat, his gaze drifting back to June, who sat decidedly uncomfortable.

A tinfoil dinner would probably kill the poor guy. She kept her gaze fixed on their managers as the waiter retreated with their orders.

"Come on," Antonia—as Diego's manager had introduced herself—said as she grabbed Charlene by the arm. "They have a lovely salad bar up front."

June paled, shooting Charlene a pleading look. *Don't leave me alone with him!*

Charlene shot her a glare equivalent to a death threat before she flashed a smile at Antonia and followed her away from the table.

June sank into her chair, staring down at her glass of wine. She'd promised Charlene not to drink too much, but the glass was looking more and more tempting.

She could feel Diego's eyes on her, watching her from his peripheral. His gaze flickered to her hands. The moment their managers had slipped away, Diego leaned toward June, a smirk playing on his lips. *"'Chef's favorite'?"* he mused, his voice filled with mockery.

She shrugged, no shame in it. "I'm too focused on winning to care about what they feed me." Of course, not the truth. June was an athlete. She had meal plans carefully curated by her personal trainer, but one random meal here and there was worth the extra time in the gym to save her pride.

"How very practical." His voice betrayed his amusement. "I'll make sure to bring pictures to match the menu next time."

She refused to take the bait, leaning forward on her hand in boredom. She wasn't stupid, but she didn't care enough to convince him of that. She'd heard the scorn plenty. She was in one of the most prestigious sports in the world. She knew how people talked about people like her. Like they were royalty, and anyone else were mere peasants. "How kind of you. I expect it all to be as disappointing as your personality."

"The food here is not up to your standards?" He sat back in his chair, making a show of examining the ridiculously extravagant restaurant.

June offered him a tight-lipped smile that didn't reach her eyes. "It's more the company that's not up to par."

A mix of emotions fluttered across his face in rapid succession. Amusement, annoyance at her refusal to give him a reaction, and then intrigue with each passing comment she threw at him. He was a nepotism baby, with a father retired from Formula One after his godfather was killed in an accident. He'd been raised on a silver spoon and then funneled into his dream life.

She could hardly fault him for being rattled at the first time he'd even been told no.

A muscle jumped in his jaw, and he had to take a deep breath before he spoke again. "Are you always this charming, or is this all for me?"

June couldn't help the smug feeling growing in her chest from materializing as a smirk. "All for you, baby." She knew the answer would be enough to rile him. The pet name was just the cherry on top, and it seemed to have its desired effect.

Diego's eyes widened a bit before returning to their usual size, grinning absentmindedly at the table. "First, you punch me in the face, then you call me pet names." He leaned in a little closer, his voice dripping with false sweetness. "Careful, June. Keep acting like this and you might just make me fall in love with you."

It was the last comment she'd been expecting, and she struggled to keep a straight face. June was good at making people feel uncomfortable. In fact, she reveled in it. A question she didn't want to answer from a rude journalist? Sheer bluntness. Another degrading comment from a competitor? Ruthlessness.

She wasn't quite sure what to do with someone who matched her at full force. "What can I say? You're so likable I can't help myself. It's like my fist is drawn to your face."

His lips betrayed him, quirking into a semblance of a smile. Annoyed but amused. "You sure do know how to make a guy feel special." He crossed his arms on the table, leaning forward on his elbows.

She rolled her eyes at him, wishing Charlene would sweep in and save her, but she was so entranced with Antonia she didn't so much as glance in her charge's direction.

Finally, he sighed—not in surrender, but rather a truce—and stuck his hand halfway across the table for her to shake. "Let's try this again, hm? Diego Cabrera. Formula One driver for Bugatti Lotus Racing." June wanted to shudder. Even the way he spoke was obnoxiously rich.

She eyed his hand, making no move to meet him halfway. "I know who you are."

He didn't budge, unfazed by her refusal. "In a world where I cannot leave my house without someone knowing my name, I have to do something to keep it sacred. So, I introduce myself."

She blinked, rubbing her lips together before she finally sighed and extended her hand to him across the table. ". . . June. June Walker."

He lit up, shaking her hand firmly. "Mm, not June 'Rider'?"

June offered him her best attempt at a deadpan stare, the corner of her mouth turning up in amusement as she let go of his hand. "How long have you been sitting on that joke?"

"Since you gave me this." He beamed, pointing at the remnants of the bruise that peeked through the makeup on his cheek.

"It wasn't funny," she grinned.

"Oh, I know. But it is a once-in-a-lifetime joke. How can I not make a name pun when it suits so well?"

"Oh please," June scoffed. "You're a racer, and your name is Die-*go*."

He barked out a surprised laugh, drawing the attention of other patrons. "Ah. I did not expect you to be funny."

June sat back in her chair, raising a brow at him. "Because I'm a woman? Or because I'm poor?"

Diego's face dropped in absolute horror, holding his hands up in innocence. "No—No! I only meant . . . the horse riders I've seen are so serious, and I—"

She bit her lip to suppress her growing amusement at having

rattled him, and his panic turned to irritation. "Ah. I did not expect your teasing, either. Or for you to punch me in the face. I suppose I should expect the unexpected from you."

"Equestrians aren't serious," she said simply. "The ones I know aren't, at least. Most have at least a decent sense of humor."

"Hm," Diego hummed. "And do they find your situation as funny as you seem to?"

June's smile fell. She glowered at her fork, half-tempted to pick it up and stab him with it. Thankfully, years of training under Amelia had taught her lovely restraint. She clenched her hand around her glass instead.

He shifted uncomfortably in his seat, seeming to realize he'd touched a nerve, and he quickly changed the subject. "Where are you from? I cannot place your accent."

She hesitated. *The slums of Texas.* "Everywhere and nowhere."

"Everywhere and nowhere?" Diego repeated, raising a brow at June's vague response. "And here I thought you were an open book."

June clenched her jaw. It was a line from an interview several months ago, a reporter questioning how much of her life June kept private, to which she had replied, *'None. I'm an open book.'*

A lie, of course. June was known for secrecy in her private life. Mainly because she didn't have one. She had her apartment, her team, and her horses. Occasionally, she texted her younger sister. Still, it was more than she'd ever had, and it was all hers. She protected it with her life.

She didn't want to give Diego another reason to dig in. Still, he had called her out, and June could never look away from a challenge. ". . . Texas," she said softly.

Diego's lips twisted into a satisfied smile at her answer. "Ah, Texas," he drawled, his Spanish accent drawing out the word. June winced, readying for a blow. She was familiar with the way Europeans spoke about Americans.

"The Lone Star State. You are a cowgirl then, *Vaquera*?" He leaned in closer, his eyes glinting with challenge and never wavering from her own.

June blinked. No teasing. No backhanded comments. Only mere curiosity. "Yes," she admitted.

He sat back, seeming to ponder for a moment before a waiter walking by snagged his attention, and whatever he had meant to say was swept away. He spouted off to the boy in what sounded like Arabic before the waiter nodded knowingly and hurried off for the kitchen.

For some reason, it irritated her. The fact he could speak other languages with such ease. "You speak Arabic," she said. She'd heard it last night, but it bothered her more now, knowing who he was. Why shouldn't he know other languages? With access to tutors and time, he should know them all.

"Arabic, Spanish, Italian, and French. The latter three are so similar they hardly count. Oh, and English." He smiled. "Sometimes, it is a mix of the five. I never know until it comes out. Learning a bit of German and the basics of Mandarin, but I am hardly fluent."

Okay, so he didn't know them all. Just most. June's brows shot up in surprise. "Smart cookie."

"That is flattery." Still, he beamed.

Charlene and Antonia returned, chattering amongst themselves, and June could have cried out in relief, saved from Diego and his prying eyes and questions. June nursed her drink and watched out the window, ignoring Pretty Boy and the way he was egging her on from her peripherals, trying to get her to speak to him.

The waiter brought their food promptly, and June was grateful for another excuse to keep Diego out of her sights.

Her plate was filled with an expanse of seafood—almost like the crawfish boils Mama Odie served at the diner but plated better with fancier cuts, though June would never mention that to Mama. Her mouth watered. It took every ounce of restraint and Southern Manners in the world not to dig in until everyone's plates were settled and wine glasses refilled. The first bite was heaven, flavor melting in her mouth. Charlene and Antonia filled the silence with happy chatter. They'd clearly hit it off, and June was just grateful that meant she didn't have to talk to the Spaniard.

It wasn't until several bites in that she noticed her red wine glass had been replaced with a white chardonnay. And Diego's had too, as a matter of fact. Her brow furrowed, casting a glance at his plate. Sure enough, it was the same as her own, and he dug into it with a coy grin.

She sat back, an odd mix of irritation and gratitude settling in her stomach.

He had switched her plate without telling her. Sure, it was delicious and somehow exactly what she'd been craving, but he had switched her plate. *Without telling her.*

She bit her tongue and choked down the delicious food, trying to ignore how bitter the wine seemed when sharing it with Diego. June kept herself on a tight leash the entire luncheon. She made pleasantries with Antonia and kept Diego carefully out of her gaze, even when he attempted to play footsies with her under the table. She knew the chances of pictures from this meeting getting leaked were high, so she flashed bright smiles at Diego and acted almost as if they were friends. If she could handle today, she could definitely handle tonight.

Diego didn't let the others get a word in when the waiter asked about a check, shoving a credit card into the boy's hand before ushering him off. He wouldn't hear a word of argument. "My treat," he insisted to their managers.

Charlene was charmed, and June knew it. She hated it. She sat back in her chair as Diego excused himself to send for their car. If he thought he was getting thanks from her, he had another thing coming. Especially because he made the mistake of leaving his wallet on the seat.

Wordlessly, June snagged her purse from the back of her chair, grabbing a handful of cash—more than enough to cover both her and Charlene's lunch—before she tucked it neatly into his wallet alongside the stack of other foreign currency. Would he notice? Probably not. Did it immediately absolve her of any feeling of debt toward the man? Absolutely.

People didn't buy her things.

If the others disapproved of her actions, they didn't voice it. Not even Charlene, who merely shot her an irritated look. Diego returned, and they all offered pleasant goodbyes, promising to see each other soon at the impending event as though it were some kind of class reunion rather than their charges' punishment for being stupid.

The moment they stepped out of the restaurant and away from her punishment and his caretaker, June's body deflated with exhaustion and relief. She survived. She didn't punch him. Didn't even kick him under the table. There had been some moments, she could admit only to herself, where their conversations had been almost enjoyable. *Almost.*

The moment they were in the car, June braced for a lecture the way she always did.

It never came.

Charlene sat in the backseat beside June, offering her a suspicious side-eye.

"What?" June asked, and then after several more moments of silence, *"What?"*

Charlene squinted at her. "You almost looked like you were having fun when Antonia and I were gone."

June tried not to cringe at being on a first-name basis with his manager. "I know, right? I missed my calling on the stage." She slouched in her seat, a frown on her lips.

Charlene raised a brow at her, clearly expecting more, and June cocked her head to the side. "What? You thought I forgot how to be charming?"

"It's just rare to see you play nice with someone like him." She shrugged, reaching into her bag to retrieve her lipstick. Charlene couldn't have been any more perfect. Always put together. Always organized. June was the exact opposite.

Her expression darkened, and she shifted her focus to picking at her cuticles instead.

June had worked for every penny and every opportunity she'd ever had. Watching people be handed everything she'd ever wanted made her sick.

People like Diego made her sick. So blissfully unaware of his own station in life.

How much further along could she have been with that kind of direction? She damn sure wouldn't be riding borrowed horses, scrambling for sponsors, and schooling Amelia's horses in exchange for having her in June's corner.

"I owe it to you." She did her best to appear unbothered. "I don't care about him."

Charlene studied June's expression for a moment, almost sympathetically. She put a hand on June's thigh. "I know you don't."

June looked out the window as the car sped down the road. She wanted to believe in the bullshit all those self-help books spewed—that money couldn't buy happiness—but deep down, she knew the truth. Maybe money wouldn't fix her problems, but it would sure as hell make life easier. Her blood boiled at the thought of what she might have accomplished if she had been born into wealth, or at least a supportive family. She would take either-or. She wasn't picky.

And there was Diego Cabrera with both.
Of course he was successful. What else could he be?
It made her want to punch him all over again.

Chapter Four

Standing in a secluded corner of the hotel lobby, Antonia and Charlene recited the plan for the millionth time. Arrive at the event separately: Diego first, then June. June would walk up to Diego, say anything at all, and Diego would laugh and offer her his arm. They would go down the red carpet together like old friends, enter the party together, and then do whatever it took *not to cause a scene.*

June had too much resting on Pretty Boy for her liking. June did things alone to ensure they were done right. Relying on him felt like a bullet to the chest. Both Diego and June's PR teams had released statements saying that the pair were close friends and it was merely an accident after too much to drink. The public wasn't buying it, and Lotus wasn't happy.

Finally, deciding they'd gone over the very *complicated and elaborate plan* enough times, Antonia and Charlene rushed off to call for the drivers. Diego leaned against the wall, watching out the window with his arms crossed over his chest. He was so gorgeous it hurt, in an all-black suit tailored to perfection, a white-and-gold pocket square peeking out. The Lotus colors. June had to clench her teeth to keep from drooling. She avoided looking at him altogether.

Diego cleared his throat, nodding toward her simple dress as he straightened his cufflinks. "Which H&M did you get that from?"

June spared him a single glance. Some people couldn't see the class in simplicity. "Suck my dick," she said, entirely classlessly.

Diego choked, clearly not anticipating the crude response, but he didn't argue.

She looked lovely and she knew it. A royal-blue maxi slip dress with a slit up the side, hair pulled up into an elegant updo, simple gold jewelry: a delicate chain around her neck, a pair of large earrings shaped like longhorns, and a white and gold bracelet—a hint back to the company paving the way for her career.

Her dress was fine, her hair was lovely, her body looked *great*—but she still wanted to shrink back into the wall. Sometimes, all she wanted was to pack her bags and disappear back to Texas.

Amelia was not the first trainer June had studied with—Mama Odie held that title. A field separated June's childhood trailer park from the vast expanse of Odie's home: a large, two-story white house with shutters and a wrap-around porch. Whenever June imagined Texas, her mind conjured Odie's place. She would spend hours in that field catching mice, snakes, and spiders. It wasn't until years later June realized how dangerous that was. Everything was bigger in Texas. And poisonous.

She was seven years old when she found the horse, a black and white paint that found her in the field and lowered it's head for June to pet. She'd seen horses around—it was rural Texas, she couldn't throw a stone without spooking one—but she'd never seen one so close.

She fashioned a halter out of twine she had found in the field and made a mounting block out of a tree stump and an old rusty bucket. Looking back, it was a wonder that June wasn't shot. A miracle that the horse was broke.

When Odie found her, June's first thought was that she hadn't realized the horse had an owner. The second was that she was going to jail.

She walked out with her hand on her hips, a stern look on her face. "What ya' got there?"

June blinked at the woman, words dead on her tongue. The woman raised an eyebrow, eyeing the tiny girl on the back of the horse she owned. That June had no right to. "Where'd ya' get that from?" She nodded to the attempt at a halter.

June went bright red. ". . . Made it."

Odie nodded, eyeing her handiwork. "How'd ya' get up there?"

June swallowed over the lump in her throat. ". . . Stacked a bucket on a log."

A beat of silence. And then, the woman reeled back and howled with laughter, smacking her leg. It was the first time June's antics had been met with anything other than screaming or a slap.

Mama Odie was her name, known for taking in the stray children that a small town in Texas generated.

In exchange for doing chores, Mama Odie would let her ride the mare and tell her stories. The mare had belonged to the woman's daughter before a car accident took her life. Odie held such melancholy. So did the mare.

What a trio they made, each missing pieces of their souls, stolen by someone leaving.

From that moment on, the attachment was formed. June's best friend in the whole world was a fifty-year-old woman and her dead daughter's horse.

She taught June the basics. Walk, trot, lope. Stop. Back. Balance.

June spent hours riding under Odie's guidance. And then, she turned June loose. A hundred acres of farmland and a horse that was all June's. She'd never known anything like the freedom a set of hooves under her could bring. Despite her age, the paint loved speed almost as much as June. She called the mare Lightning. They tore across the property, always pushing for more—faster speeds, longer stretches in between the thick of the wooded areas.

Lightning lived two more years before cancer, and an inability to afford its removal led to the kinder fate of a bullet and a backhoe.

June was nine.

Diego's voice drew her from her thoughts. "It was you who put the money in my wallet, then."

Shit.

He took a seat in the arm chair directly across from hers, drawing his hands together in front of him. Not a question, but an accusation he dared her to refute. He said it casually, as though he were merely commenting on the weather forecast, but June still felt like she'd wound up in the principal's office after a fight. She said nothing, hoping he'd drop it, but if there ever were her equal in hardheadedness, it would be Diego Cabrera.

"I said it was my treat. It was my invitation."

Had it been? Charlene hadn't told her—had merely put it on the schedule. Probably because she knew June would never go had it been phrased as an invitation. Especially one from him.

"I have my own money," she said rather shortly, probably rude according to his standards, but she had only meant it matter-of-factly. June bought everything she owned. From her horses, to her tack, to the shoes on her feet, to the deodorant on her armpits—it was *hers*. No one could ever take anything from her if nobody had even given it to her in the first place. She earned it.

She looked down into her hands, picking at her fingers as she attempted to soften the blow. "Don't take it personally. I just . . . don't let people buy me things."

"No?" he challenged, raising an inquisitive brow. It felt an awful lot like him peering into her soul and dressing her down. "If I had offered to buy you a drink after I spilled on that pretty dress, you would not have obliged me?"

An uncomfortable weight settled in the center of her chest at the thought of him that night—drenched in champagne, flushed, and unbearably gorgeous. Would she have? Would they have talked at the bar until Charlene came to rescue her? Would she have been absolved of this mess entirely?

She didn't like to dwell on *what-ifs*. That sounded too much like *'regrets,'* and June didn't have those. So, she shrugged.

Diego threw his head back with what looked an awful lot like exasperation, his fingers gripping the arms of the chair. "Very forthcoming, aren't you?"

She shrugged again. "I don't let people buy me things."

Diego shook his head at the ceiling, muttering under his breath. *"Mujer testaruda."*

She shot a glare at him. "Just because you say it in Spanish doesn't mean I can't tell it's an insult."

He shrugged with a cheeky grin, determined to return the silent treatment she'd so graciously offered him. June bit her tongue, wishing she could wipe that smugness right off his face.

Diego's driver arrived before hers, and he hustled into his car and off toward the event center.

The moment he left, June's defenses disappeared with him. At least when he was here, she could deflect her nerves into hatred for him. Now, the anxiety threatened to ravage her.

Instead, as June stepped into the car, she thought of competing. She thought of the horses. Thought of the roar of a crowd. Thought of soaring over the jumps. The adrenaline rush. This feeling was similar enough. She could pretend.

June was great at pretending.

The car rolled to a stop at the center of the chaos, and she stepped out, steeling herself against her raging nerves. The flash of cameras had her seeing spots, and the roar of the crowd was nearly as deafening as her thundering heart. At the front of the carpet stood Diego, already chatting with reporters and photographers, his charming demeanor captivating the crowd. He was gorgeous and he knew it. He reeked of old money—like he was born to be the prince of some kind of car empire. Every step he took was sheer elegance. She wanted to throttle him.

As she approached, a group of reporters swarmed her, eager to hear the tale of their drunken scuffle. She put on a smile, fumbling for an answer. Their lie. That Diego and June were friends and it was merely an accident. "Diego and I have been in the same circle for ages. We were celebrating our beginning weekends in Qatar and got caught up in a rowdy bar."

The reporter paused for a second, and June could see the disbelief on her face. "But . . . you punched him?"

June fumbled for a moment. This was not how this was supposed to go. She wasn't even supposed to talk to the press tonight, but here she was. She forced a laugh, hoping it came out far more natural than it felt. "Friendly fire. He grabbed me to pull me out of the way, and I didn't realize it was him."

Diego carved his way through the crowd to get to her. He took her side, his hand grazing her arm. The touch of his fingertips against her bare skin sent a wave of heat across her arm, and her mind ran directly into a brick Diego-shaped wall, whatever the reporter was saying quickly forgotten. Diego offered June his arm, and she took it gratefully. The camera flashes were dizzying, and June took a moment to steady herself. Diego said something to the reporter that seemed to sate her, and Diego instantly whisked June away from the stack of journalists.

Four years of the showjumping and she still couldn't shake the feeling of being the new kid. Forever the rookie.

"Weren't you supposed to laugh at something I said?"

Diego grimaced. "I do not fake laugh."

Great.

Okay, so they still managed to somehow fuck up the plan. But at least she hadn't punched him this time! Progress!

Diego carried himself with the easy confidence she had been trying to muster for the last hour. He had been born into this—his father was a mid-tier retired Formula One racer, his mother the CEO and founder of a multi-billion-dollar fine art trading business.

The spotlight felt natural on him, lit him up where it washed her out.

The voices in her head only grew louder.

Fraud, fraud, fraud.

She never looked more out of place than on the arm of a man who belonged in this world with his every breath.

They waited in line behind a stack of brand-covered boards to proceed after the other athletes, June maintaining a vise grip on Diego's arm. He chatted casually with the other athletes in a low tone. June just tried to focus on her breathing. Hot, white stars branded on the back of her eyelids from the cameras.

If this didn't go well, her entire career might as well be over. She needed sponsors. She couldn't afford to be dropped by Lotus. June shook off her nerves one final time and then dropped her grip on him, strutting out onto the carpet without him. The cheers went up immediately, fans in their designated areas clamoring for her attention as she made her way up the line. Diego must have been alerted by the sound of the screaming because moments later, he was at her side, arm slipping around her waist.

The moment he joined her, her ears could've bled. She had never heard a crowd so loud. Diego grinned, clearly pleased with the reaction. He angled his head toward her, wiggling his eyebrows.

One thing was for certain—Diego Cabrera had his fair share of fangirls.

June maintained a calm smile despite her urge to repeat the bar incident and punch that smug smile right off his face. "Ah, I knew I was missing something. My accessory."

Diego laughed as if she had told him a world-class stand-up routine, flashing her an award-winning smile. The onlookers went wild, screaming and pushing each other to get a glimpse of the unexpected duo. He played the crowd nearly as well as he controlled his car.

June bit back a grimace. "I thought you didn't fake laugh."

He leaned back to take a look at her, allowing his eyes to roam across each curve and divot of her body as though he hadn't already insulted her dress. "Who said it was fake?" His fingertips grazed her neck, touching her gold longhorn earrings. "These are cute."

Diego's cologne swarmed over her in a dizzying fog, leaving her feeling a bit tipsy. June flinched, her stomach tensing with traitorous desire at his touch.

Ugh. Why was it even possible to get butterflies over a man she despised? This was her payback for not getting properly laid in ages.

The crowd practically exploded around them, but she kept her focus on him and his big brown doe eyes. "What do you think you're doing." More of an accusation than a question.

He smiled softly, his fingertips grazing the curve of her neck. "Changing the headlines."

He was right. Search June and Diego; him laughing at something she said or playing with her earring would be a top article.

Hopefully, over the one of her socking him in the face.

June just smiled brighter, reaching up to push a dark curl out of his face. "Fine."

Diego's smile faltered, his eyes widening slightly as though he hadn't expected the returned touch. Then, he was right back to it, leading her down the line of cameras with a hand on the small of her back. It was quick enough that she could have imagined it. But even if just for a second, she had seen Diego's confidence fail. She made him nervous.

She loved it. She leaned in closer to him, letting her hands wander a little further. Let her gaze linger on his a bit longer than necessary.

Anything to make him squirm.

June relished in every reaction she stirred from him. He kept his gaze focused strictly on the cameras and the crowd clamoring for his attention, even when she leaned in and lowered her voice, turning on every ounce of Southern Charm she could muster. "What is it, baby? Crowd got ya' nervous or is it just me?"

A muscle tensed in his jaw, but it was the only reaction she drew from him. She had to hand it to him; his self-control was impressive.

She allowed him to guide her down the rest of the carpet in weighted silence. His skin was warm even through his suit, making her feel flushed and a bit irritable. It seemed like a decade later when she'd finally made it through the line and out to mingle with the other athletes in the conference center. She split away from him instantly. Paparazzi weren't allowed inside the event. There was no one to entertain here.

She slipped off to get a drink before she found refuge from the others in a corner tucked under the stairs. She was getting antsy, and the crowded room was driving her mad. The music was too loud, and the clash of expensive, designer perfumes made her nauseous. June swallowed hard, tugging at her dress and taking deep breaths to remind herself she wasn't, in fact, suffocating. She wished Lola were here. Or Liv. She was not good at these kinds of things. She liked watching people far more than being among them.

Diego found her tucked under the stairs, his own drink in hand. He reached above him to hold onto a step as he eyed her from top to bottom. "What are you doing over here?"

June shrugged, reeling her irritation back in to some level of agreeableness. "There was a wounded child in this corner that I had to save and now I'm processing everything."

He snorted at her blatant sarcasm, finding his way next to her where he propped his leg against the wall and nursed his drink. It was the most relaxed he had looked all night. He nodded out over the crowd. "I have never seen a hairline recede to the back of someone's neck before."

June immediately caught sight of the man and choked on her drink, clapping a hand over her mouth. His hair was practically gone on the top, and the parts that he did have were matted to his head with sweat and grease.

Diego chuckled, watching the baseball player chat with a very disinterested woman.

"It's sad, really," he said, not very convincingly.

June leaned in mischievously, bumping his shoulder with her own. "Not everyone's hair can be as perfect as yours, Diego," she teased. The truth. Every picture she had ever seen of him included hair so perfect it could have been a shampoo commercial. Fresh out of the shower? Perfect. After a hard workout? Perfect. Helmet freshly off after two hours zipping around a track at 200 miles an hour? Perfect.

Diego merely sighed as if it were the greatest tragedy on earth. "A shame, really. I could not survive without my perfect hair. But it is so much pressure—" his voice was entirely serious despite his ridiculous words: she would have thought he was talking about the pressures of the media or his ridiculously difficult job, "—being so beautiful all the time."

June snorted, rolling her eyes at him. "Oh, you poor thing."

"You have no sympathy." His eyes twinkled with amusement and he scrunched his nose.

The very first time June went horse shopping, Mama Odie told her to look in the eyes. It was easy to get distracted by flashy coats or fancy tricks, but those things didn't matter. Sometimes, a horse was just a horse looking for an owner. Sometimes, they were a soul looking for refuge.

Diego's eyes were a bit like that. Everything Pretty Boy felt was reflected in the ebony of his gaze. Joy, irritation, amusement. All at

RACING HEARTS

once, those eyes narrowed in on her, glinting with mischief. "What are you looking at so intensely?"

June could feel her cheeks redden, turning away from him. She focused her attention on her cocktail, speaking into the drink. "Nothing."

He leaned into her line of sight, raising a brow at her. "You were staring at me," he accused, his accent making the words twist in a pleasing manner. His English wasn't always perfect, but the way it rolled off his tongue sure was. His brows shot up as if he understood all at once. "You were thinking about what I look like when I'm naked, weren't you?"

June could have died of embarrassment then and there. She smacked his arm, cheeks flaming. "I was not!"

He beamed, clearly pleased with her reaction. He tutted, shaking his head at her, his finger braced on his chin. "A pervert and a liar. What are we going to do with you?"

She huffed, turning her back to him again before she took a long drink from her glass. She was so accustomed to being the one who got under someone's skin. Diego got to her in a way no one else ever had. His boldness was riveting.

She hated it.

"I'm going to go get a drink." She nodded once and then turned, rushing off to the bar. Alarms were ringing in her head, screaming *BAD IDEA, BAD IDEA*. June made so many stupid decisions that if her own brain had deemed it dumb, it was downright atrocious.

She ordered a whiskey shot and downed it in one gulp. Only one. The last thing she needed was another whiskey fiasco involving Diego Cabrera.

It was like she was a magnet and Diego a paperclip, trailing her over to the bar. He slid up beside her, leaning against the counter. "I have a proposal."

Okay, so not one shot. June ordered a Lotus-vodka. At least that way, she could have it in a Lotus can and give people less to talk about. "Eager much? Take me to dinner first."

He remained entirely unfazed. "We should keep doing this. This is good publicity for both of us, no?"

June shrugged as the bartender slid the concoction across the counter to her. She stuck a straw in it, raising her drink. The last thing June needed was to be around him more. She despised him. Even worse, she despised that her anger towards him was starting to dull. "Don't exactly want my reputation associated with a douchebag, but sure."

Despite her best efforts, she couldn't seem to insult Diego. He merely met her distasteful comments with amusement. "Don't pretend like you aren't enjoying our little game," he retorted. "You love the push and pull, don't you?"

She shrugged, trying her best to look unaffected.

His amusement doubled. "You're a terrible liar, *cariño*."

She turned around, meeting his gaze as she raised the straw to her lips. "You got a crush on me or something?"

He didn't even blink, his face uncharacteristically deadpan. "Lotus is not renewing my contract."

June choked on her drink.

Diego was entirely unfazed. "I am not supposed to know yet. My manager overheard a private meeting. There's a young Italian driver in F2, their own little protégé with family ties to Lotus. Which means my future is in the air. I need eyes on me. You ensure I get that."

That explained the flirty attitude at least. A stranger punching him in the face one night, and laughing at his jokes on his arm the next gave a very enchanting view for potential teams.

June shrugged, peering at him over her drink. "Sounds to me like I'm good then. If Lotus is already dropping you, I don't have to worry about them kicking me over that bar fight. Problem solved.

Good luck to you, though—" She moved to walk past, only for him to catch her by the arm and drag her back.

He trapped her between the bar and his own body. His hand rested casually on one side of her, a bar stool on the other, effectively caging her while ensuring it didn't look too much like a hostage situation. "Not so fast. You need me, too."

June eyed him, schooling her face into one of indifference as she attempted to reel herself in. Scared dogs ran. Cornered dogs bit. And right now, he had her cornered. "Sure don't."

"No?" he challenged. "You don't want sponsors? I have plenty of those."

He took a small step closer, and June sucked in a breath that didn't quite fill her lungs. She raised a brow at him, pretending his proximity didn't affect her. "What are you saying?" She couldn't deny that her curiosity had been piqued.

"I am saying we have much to gain from each other. If we keep eyes on us, I get to stay with Lotus next year; you get more sponsors. It is a win-win."

There was a beat of silence as she pondered the proposal, her heart hammering in her chest. She had to admit, it was a perfect ploy. It wouldn't be difficult on her end either. Diego had a natural way of drawing eyes to him. Still, a tiny voice in the back of her head warned her to be careful. To keep her distance from pretty boys with charming smiles.

Diego leaned forward on his elbow, cocking his head to the side. "Racing isn't just about what you do on the track. It's in the field, too. Who's smarter? Who's one step ahead? Who has what it takes to push further? I won't be held back, June."

June met his gaze, his speech lighting a ridiculous fire of determination under her. Securing her place at Lotus wasn't just about her performance.

"People won't bat an eye seeing you with a woman," June reasoned.

Diego had a very specific kind of reputation. He was a true blue playboy, and yet he was so gorgeous that nobody cared to stop him. There was a new woman on his arm every week, and June had no interest in the unique kinds of STDs he could give her.

"No," he admitted with a chuckle. "But they will seeing me with the same woman multiple times."

June frowned at him in disgust, but she knew he was right. It could be good for her reputation. The Sensational Rookie who tamed the wild heart of the F1 Playboy. And then, when he inevitably *'cheated'* on her, he would be eaten alive by the public while fans flocked to support her.

The silence stretched on a moment too long before he dropped his grip on her elbow and reached into his pocket, opting instead to grab her hand, pressing a piece of paper into it. "Just . . . think about it, no?"

June bit the inside of her cheek, pinning him in place with her eyes. She didn't have to look at the paper to know it was his number scribbled on it. She could sell that bad boy on eBay and save herself the trouble of all of this. "Sure." She shoved the paper down the front of her dress.

Diego huffed out a laugh. *"Buena suerte diciéndome que no."*

Whatever that meant. June really needed to commit to her Babbel lessons. Diego tipped his head in dismissal before he turned and disappeared into the crowd.

She hated how her eyes lingered on the empty space where he'd just been, her eyes still trailing after his dark hair and his annoyingly sexy smile.

June downed the rest of her drink, the alcohol burning her throat and sending her mind swirling. She needed to step back, to think this through, but that man made all rational thought evade her.

She was completely and royally screwed.

Chapter Five

Amelia formally owned the small studio apartment—one she charged June only taxes and utilities to stay in. Another part of their deal. One that began with a seventeen-year-old from America with nowhere to stay. Amelia owned a small apartment right next to the barn specifically for her groom.

June's apartment was a quaint little thing, but it was fairly new, and it was all hers. It was just big enough for a kitchen, some excuse of a living room, a bedroom, and a small office. She was rarely home anyway. She got to decorate it and paint it however she chose. She could collect all the books and knick-knacks in the world.

When Olivia and Lola were first hired on as June's team, they got an apartment together just down the hall from June.

Their neighbors hated them.

Despite the comfortable pull of unconsciousness, the sound of banging on her door yanked her harshly out of it. She blinked blearily for several moments before the sound came again. *Bang. Bang. Bang.*

June groaned. Lola or Olivia, no doubt. "Just come in!" she shouted, her voice gravelly from sleep.

"You locked it, you idiot!" Olivia. "And I don't have my key!"

June groaned loudly the entire time as she got to her feet and moped over to the door, pulling it open. In an instant, Olivia burst in, practically screaming in delight. She kicked the door stopper out, leaving it propped open in a way that signified Lola would soon follow. June groaned, flopping on her bed and hiding her face under a pillow. Her body ached, and she was too tired for this.

Olivia flounced over to land on June's bed beside her. "Look at how cute this picture is." She shoved her phone into June's face, forcing her to look at the picture of her and Diego from the red carpet last night. Diego's fingertip grazed her earring, staring down at her like she was the only person there. June's surprise was evident but shockingly well-worn, lips parted, cheeks lightly flushed.

Well, his plan had worked at least.

June shrugged, fighting to maintain her nonchalance. "Cute." June shoved Olivia off, standing up and heading for her coffee pot. Olivia opted to hug a throw pillow instead.

Olivia grew up in Mexico, less than ten hours away from June's hometown. They had bonded over their close proximity. Over their love of Mexican food.

Lola was Pakistani, but she was raised in London. The three of them bonded over religious guilt and a shared hatred of flavorless food. June maintained the stance that she had the world's most gorgeous team. Lola was nearly as tall as June, with smooth, dark skin, a hooked nose, deep brown hair, and a smile that could knock any woman off her feet. Olivia was as classic Latina as June had ever seen—light brown skin, short, curvy, and fiery.

Olivia deemed June an *'honorary Latina'* and she clung to her badge of honor fiercely.

"Where's Lola?" June yawned, dumping enough grounds into the coffee filter that Olivia eyed her in disgust.

"Off praying."

June nodded shortly. "I don't stand a chance of getting into Heaven against someone with a prayer schedule."

"I mean, you're praying to different gods," Olivia reasoned. "Maybe yours doesn't mind inconsistent communication. Like your dad."

June opened her mouth to defend herself, but all she could come up with was a shrug. *Touché*.

Olivia dragged her phone closer to stare at the picture, groaning. "Ugh. He is so sexy it like actually hurts."

She rolled her eyes, turning back to the coffee pot. "He is okay at best." A lie. She called him Pretty Boy for a reason. Even if there was nothing going on behind those big brown eyes, they were still gorgeous.

"When's your next eye doctor's appointment?" Olivia asked.

She shrugged, dumping a copious amount of sugar and cream into her coffee. "I don't know, ask Charlene."

"I'll just make you one," Olivia concluded, "'cuz that boy is finer than a motherfucker."

June turned around, mug in hand as she leaned back against the counter. "Now, how fine is a motherfucker? Because I was under the impression sleeping with someone's mother was rude—"

From the doorway came a massive sigh, Lola strolling in a moment later. "I don't even want to know what I just walked into."

Olivia turned on June with a skeptical brow raised. "Girl, *Lola* thinks he's hot, and she doesn't even like boys."

That piqued Lola's interest. "Who?"

"Diego."

Immediately, Lola nodded in agreement. "Oh yeah, I'd let him hit."

June drew a heavy breath to sigh like her life depended on it. To think, a mere ten minutes ago, she had been peacefully sleeping. "Y'all are going to give me an aneurysm."

"Lesbians can still think guys are hot," Lola reasoned, leaning against the back of her couch. "It's like being a vegetarian. You don't have to eat it to admire a good piece of meat."

June almost dropped her mug as she choked on her coffee.

Olivia had no reservations about her appreciation of Diego, nodding in agreement with a far too eager grin on her face. "Exactly! We're just being objective."

June shook her head in mock disapproval and rolled her eyes. "And what part of him are you admiring from an objective standpoint?"

"I'm admiring him from any and all standpoints I can possibly get my hands on," Olivia argued, zooming in on her screen, and June groaned, rolling her eyes.

June very pointedly did not look through the rest of the photos, instead shoving Olivia's shoulder, desperate to think about anything other than Diego. Olivia had been assigned to her by Lotus; Lola had been hired by Charlene. They became a dynamic duo almost instantly, kicking ass in marketing June as some lovable firecracker. Social media brought sponsorships— the more sponsorships, the more things to make content on. June was popular, even by Lotus Athlete standards. All credit to that fact belonged to Lola and Olivia.

Siegfried Vaun was the only other equestrian Lotus sponsored. She was nineteen and in her second year competing in the lower divisions that he informed her if she ever wanted to grow her career, she should have a manager. He gave her Charlene's card. Charlene was the one who secured the Lotus contract for her. An energy drink company that had made their brand by marketing to extreme athletes.

Now, she wasn't sure why they had gambled on her so young, only that Siegfried must have put a good word in for her.

June's life never really slowed down. It was the only thing she could count on. Well, that and the people on her payroll. If she was done with work, there was more work. And then some work. And some more. Competitions, Lotus interviews, brand deals, sponsorship packages—sometimes, she wondered if she could ever take a break. Most of the time, June was exhausted.

But being exhausted was better than being anxious. Burnt out was better than lonely.

If she wasn't competing, she was training. If she wasn't schooling horses, she was at the gym. If she wasn't smiling for sponsors, she was smiling for the ridiculous challenges Olivia made her do.

Amelia enjoyed producing horses. She had anywhere from three to five horses in her program at a time. When June joined on, that number skyrocketed to nearly ten. People would pay good money for a horse trained by Amelia Santiago. With June, she could make the number of horses a lot higher.

June didn't know where that money went, only that it dulled the odd guilt she still packed around at how much Amelia had done for her. Bringing her into this mad world she now lived in. Giving her a chance.

It was one such morning—readying to compete in the 1.25 meter on one of Amelia's junior horses that June had trained up—that Siegfried had found her in the arena.

The clock on the wall inside the arena showed 5:32 a.m., but June was in the saddle. Sleep very rarely knocked at her door, and when it did, it didn't stay long.

June was trotting circles on a seven-year-old chestnut when a groan of utter disgust came from the other end of the arena. She nearly jumped out of her skin, whirling to find Siegfried standing in the door. June broke into a smile immediately.

She would never tell Amelia, but Siegfried had always been her favorite of the other LGCT riders. The others didn't like him much, but they didn't like her either. He was grumpy, stuck to himself, and remained thoroughly irritated at all times. June had made it her personal mission to befriend the man, and to her luck, she had succeeded.

There wasn't a time she asked *'how are you'* that he didn't reply with *'terrible'*, even after a perfect round. June was familiar with grumpy old men from her time waitressing at Mama Odie's Cafe. Truthfully, he was only sixty, and June didn't really consider that to be *old,* but that wouldn't stop her from making every old man joke in the book.

She adored him, and he tolerated her.

Siegfried's mare, Frieda, was his other half. Grey, grumpy, and horribly unimpressed. They were fond only of each other and good rounds—both the competitive and alcoholic kind. She was the only horse June knew of that would drink beer straight from the can. A testament to Siegfried's German heritage, she supposed.

June beamed at Siegfried as he came strolling into the arena. "Morning, Siggy."

He'd told her a million times to stop calling him that, but June was persistent, and at some point he had accepted his fate.

"Morning." A gruff grumble of acknowledgement was delivered in a thick German accent. As always, he looked the epitome of unimpressed. The man was athletic, with broad shoulders and a barrel of a chest. Still, his age was evident in his weathered skin, and the silver streaked through his hair and beard. All the man ever did was talk about how badly he wanted to retire. Still, he never could seem to convince himself.

A scoff escaped him as June approached. "What are you doing here so early, hm? I haven't even had my coffee."

She nodded to her own cup perched on a fence post rail. "It's iced, but you're welcome to it," she offered. She knew he'd never take it. The man would rather die than touch iced coffee. Even during the hottest days of the Italian summer, Siegfried took his coffee hot and black.

"I'd rather get frostbite on my balls," the man retorted with that familiar deadpan look. A joke. Everything he said that was a little too ridiculous was a joke, she'd come to understand. Or at least, she took it as one.

"When are you finally going to retire and coach me, Grandpa?" June asked.

Siegfried didn't flinch, leading his mare to the mounting block. "When you stop being such a pain in the ass."

She stuck her tongue out at him, and he returned the gesture, a ridiculous look on such a serious man. He knew as well as she did that she was trouble. But for as stubborn, reckless, and impulsive as she was on the ground, she was talented and ambitious in the saddle.

Still, Siegfried wasn't the coaching type.

They rode in silence, each focused on their own rides, Siegfried only stopping momentarily to give her tips as short and precise as the man himself. Siegfried was a master in the saddle, and he was strict. Those facts made him intimidating to many riders, June included. The difference was that June welcomed his critiques.

"People are eating up this June-Diego thing," Olivia chided, drawing June from her thoughts. She wiggled her eyebrows. "I guess there's just something people like about a little horsepower."

June huffed her amusement. Then, she swallowed hard, thinking back to his proposal. To the slip of paper she had tucked in her nightstand with his number scrawled across it. She shook her head to herself, and returned to drinking her coffee.

Chapter Six

From the back of a horse, everything made sense. With a roaring crowd in the center of Monaco, everything had to be perfect. On Midus, it was. The bell sounded, and they were off like a rocket, Midus's long stride propelling them through and over the first jump in a matter of seconds before they locked onto the next like clockwork. There was a reason June had been a contender for the season title in her rookie year, and it wasn't just her talent or her sponsors, even her trainer or her team.

Horses like Midus only came along once in a lifetime.

Each jump rushed up quicker than the last, Midus launching them both into the air as easy as breathing, the crowd clamoring for more. Sometimes, she wondered if he loved jumping even more than her. The adrenaline. The thrill. Soaring through the air light as a feather, only for a twelve-hundred-pound animal to land hooves first and remind her of the sheer power behind it all.

They cleared the oxer with ease, just as they had in the qualifying round. Just as they had jump after jump the year before. June was here for a reason. The high of the chase—it was better than anything waiting at the bottom of any bottle. Midus's feet hit the ground at the other end of the final jump. June didn't need a timer to tell her it was the fastest time—the crowd did that well enough.

She collapsed forward on Midus's neck, beaming with relief. After such a poor opening round with Hades, this was precisely what she needed. Midus tucked his head back into a pretty canter, the hard breathing and sweat the only indicators that moments prior they had spent the last—73.4 seconds, according to the timer on the big screen—leaping over five-foot intervals.

The only thing that could match the exhilaration of a good round was celebrating it. The lap of victory had long been June's favorite, galloping around the arena decorated in sashes and a riding blanket pulled over Midus with *'Longines Global Champions Tour'* embossed on the side.

Midus loved the celebration even more than her. He loved the roar of a crowd, tucked his head up and his ears back, strutting out in a fancy extended trot. He enjoyed putting on a show just as much as she did.

After four years of jumping together, from the lower-levels, all the way up to the Tour, they had become one and the same. The moment she sat in the saddle, their minds and goals became one.

Midus was her horse. The one she'd spent her entire life dreaming of.

Cooldown was immediately met with a swarm of squealing girls. Lola chased after Olivia, who reached her first. Their fingers lodged anywhere they could get hands on, dragging her off her horse and into a chorus of screaming praises. Midus didn't balk at their ridiculousness. After a full season of wins, he was well used to it.

June had never cared for champagne before, far more familiar with cheap beer or box wine, but after an entire season of washing it from her hair and clothes, it became an acquired taste. It was even better from the second step of the podium, Amelia the only one above her. June didn't mind being in a shadow so long as it was Amelia's. Her mentor. The only reason she was here. She would beat her one day. It was the nature of mentor and mentee. But she was more than satisfied at second.

June had fallen in love with the Global Champions Tour from the first second. There was nothing like it. Their motto was *only the best for the best*, and June clung to it fiercely. A plethora of sand-filled arenas bursting with color, life, and promise waiting around every corner. It was her calling in life. She was good at it, too—one of the greats.

Amelia doused her in champagne and June reveled in it, returning the spray before she chugged straight from the bottle. By the time they made it into the car, June couldn't be sure if the flushed skin, buzzing veins, and giddy smile were from the adrenaline or the champagne.

Five shots later in a club with the girls, it was definitely the alcohol. The night was just getting started, and June's head was already swimming enough to make her absolutely sick. The buzz of a club was second only to the buzz of a crowded arena—whiskey second to only champagne. And June, second only to Amelia.

This was the life she had known last season. Taking the showjumping world by storm. Podiums. Talent. Hard work. Harder parties.

She jammed contentedly to the foreign party music, only yearning for Texas, country music, and boots on hardwood honky-tonk floors a little bit. Yet another improvement from last year. Nothing made her miss home quite like her highest highs and lowest lows. She downed another shot of liquor, not caring what was in the glass or that mixing liquors was going to make her sicker than a dog.

The girls swarmed her, dancing around her, their picks of poison in hand. Everything was perfect. Just like this. Of all the places to do well in a jump-off, Monaco was one of the best. The nightlife was incomparable—an entire country catering to the highest social class around. In theory, it sounded like June's worst nightmare. But for a night, the best of the best was great for a party.

June was giddy, a mix of champagne, liquor, and the delight of the dancing going to her head.

June sauntered off to the bar for another drink, humming along to the music that she didn't really know the tune of at all.

The bartender passed the drink to her, and June raised the straw to her lips, happily buzzed.

"Not whiskey this time, hm?"

June's eyes shot up and then widened in horror.

Diego.

She blinked, shaking her head as if that would rid her of the illusion, but the Spaniard stood before her clear as day. "What are you doing here?"

Diego grinned, clearly pleased at having surprised her. "I live in Monaco, *Vaquera*. I heard you were in town and came to congratulate you."

June shook her head in disbelief before she caught him by the arm and pulled him to a secluded corner of the club where the lights were dimmer and the music softer. She eyed him up and down, trying to make sense of him in her inebriated brain. "You can't just show up here uninvited."

Diego pressed his lips together in a thin line, glancing off to the side as though in thought before he spoke. "Well, I do sponsor this club. So, *technically*, I can do whatever I like."

June gritted her teeth. Okay. Fine. She hated Monaco, actually. And she wanted nothing more than to march out to her hotel, pack her bags, and hop on the next flight to Italy.

Hiding her disdain for him was much more difficult while intoxicated.

Gold flashed on his wrist, catching her eye, and a flash of rage washed over her. That thing could pay for the single-wide she'd grown up in three times over—maybe more. Could have paid for riding lessons. Could have changed her entire life. The worst part?

She knew it wasn't his only one.

Perhaps that was why Diego drove her so mad. He was so blissfully unaware of his station in life. Never having to worry about his next sponsor or his next meal. June was envious, as much as she hated to admit it. He was arrogant. He'd never been told no. She made it her mission to tell him no every time she saw him.

Pretty, rich, and talented. What more could a person want?

June jerked her eyes away from him. There was no world in which that was her life. All the money in the world could not turn back the clock. And she was here now, wasn't she? Living the life so many dreamed of. Money couldn't buy luck, either. Still, that wouldn't keep her from despising him. She huffed, turning away from him, only for Diego to step in front of her. "What is your problem?" He asked it as if he genuinely wanted to know the answer.

So, June answered him. "Nothing." A lie, but an answer.

"You really can't stand me, can you?"

June said nothing, staring down at her hands as she popped her knuckles, purposely keeping him out of her line of sight.

Diego let out a single humorless laugh. "Mature, aren't you?"

She clenched her fist into a ball. Cocky, arrogant, little rich boy. "You think you have the answer to everything, don't you?"

"But don't I?" he challenged. "Don't I have the answer to your little dilemma?"

And he did. It was a simple answer, really. Team up. Display a partnership. Garner attention using one another and open themselves up to a whole new world of fans and sponsors.

But that meant dealing with him. That meant swallowing her pride and letting him be right, and she wasn't sure if she could stand that.

Diego scoffed through his nose, shaking his head. "You know, they say this thing about horse riders—"

June almost groaned, rubbing her hands over her face. "If I have to hear *'what else can you ride'* one more time—"

His dark eyes locked on hers, his voice harboring a seriousness she hadn't heard from him before. "They say that the best ones never stop learning."

She paused. She'd heard it before. It was something that she had drilled into her head. She strived to be that kind of horseman. Learning every day. Soaking in information like a sponge. Correcting, fixing, learning.

He tutted. "You are not that kind, are you?"

She would have preferred that he stabbed her. Or broke her fingers one by one. Or shot her in the gut. It would have hurt less than hearing his words, stated as a simple observation when they felt far more like grounds for a war.

Anger coursed through her, and her hands landed square against his chest, shoving him backward. "You think you can tell me more about riding? Come on, Coach Diego! Let's see—"

He grabbed both of her hands in his own, yanking her against him. "You don't care to learn in *life*." His eyes blazed with pure fire despite the darkness of the club, his face set and brows scrunched in exasperation, as though he wanted nothing more than to grab her by the shoulders and shake her until something clicked. "So young and so set in your ways. You don't care enough to try this for fear of getting it wrong. But every time you are wrong, you learn. And you are wrong about me."

She laughed at that, utterly devoid of any humor. "I'm wrong about you? How much did you pay for that watch on your wrist?"

Diego's eyes flicked up, alight with the thrill of a challenge. "What? This old thing?" He dropped his hold on one of her hands and held it up for display. Gold and detailed and polished. And he wore it with a simple white button-up and a pair of linen pants.

June bit the inside of her cheek, turning her gaze away. His eyes scanned across her face, taking in her every small expression. It was

RACING HEARTS

as though he lived to get under her skin. June had the unfortunate disposition of being entirely readable. She could never hide what she felt, and her envy was on full display. She had sworn to herself being granted this life would not be in vain. She would make a difference. She gave back everything that she could. And here he was, wearing his wealth in an ugly watch just to tell the others, *'See? Look. I'm one of you.'*

She kept her eyes averted, but he was relentless, dropping his grip on her to step further into her space.

"So there it is," Diego said. "The real reason you can't stand me. That's it, isn't it? You're envious. Your *papá* couldn't pay for your fancy horses?"

June actually laughed at that. Her father could hardly pay the bills. She'd bargained for every lesson she ever got. Midus was the first horse she'd ever bought to keep rather than to train and sell.

She said nothing to him.

"Oh? What's the matter, you don't like it when someone else dishes it out?" he said, his tone laced with venom. "That doesn't change the truth, does it? You can mock me all you'd like, but you're envious of my money and my success."

"Your success?" she snapped. "You were fed to Formula One on a silver platter. Don't act like you're where you are because you earned it. Pay credit where it's due: Coach Daddy, doing whatever it takes to get his son to the top. All you had to do was drive."

"And you would have that, would you?" Diego laughed bitterly, his hands clenched into fists at his side. "A coach over a father?"

Yes, her instinct screamed, but least she was able to love her sport free of tainted memories. She had her horses. Horses were only ever hers. They were her safe haven, her ticket out.

She had never even considered the idea that Diego and his father were not on good terms.

He smirked, leaning in closer. "Your ego seems to be just as big as mine, *Vaquera*. Your pride just as sharp." The air between them crackled with tension. "Do you know what I think?" he challenged, taking a step forward. "I think that you're just mad because you're not me."

She gritted her teeth, glowering up at him. He wasn't that far off. What must it be like? Money where it's needed? Chance after chance? A mother and father pushing you further? *Anyone* pushing you further?

June got a father glued to a whiskey bottle and a mother who left. She got nothing. No one at her shows, no one to cheer her on, no good job texts. Nothing.

"Don't act like you know me," June spat.

"Don't I?" Diego challenged, cocking his head to the side. She wanted to punch him square in the face. She wished so desperately that she'd really savored that first night in the bar where she'd made his nose bleed. But he didn't stop there. "You can't stand that I have everything you want. Because if I fail, I go home to my *mamá*. I join her company. I wind up . . . what, CEO? What happens if you fail, *Cariño*?"

She clenched her fist. "Shut up."

"I'm right," he said confidently. "So focused on my *papá* and his money. You can't stand that you don't have anything you didn't work for. I've never had to beg for anything in my life." He leaned in closer, his breath hot on her cheek. "All you've ever done is beg."

He might as well be reading from her diary. She swallowed hard, unable to speak. What was there to say? She felt like a kicked dog begging for scraps.

"I'm right." He was.

He reached place a hand on her cheek, and June lurched back, swatting his hand away. "Who's the one begging here?" she challenged. "Chasing me down in a club? Cornering me? You're the one who reeks of desperation."

Diego froze blinking at her in disbelief. He let out a shocked huff of air. She had hit the mark, and she knew it. He tsked, meeting her gaze. "Would you look at that. June has a clever response."

She merely scoffed "Is it hard for you? That I don't just lie down and take whatever you dish out?"

Diego stepped forward, his arms outstretched like he was begging as he spoke. "I've tried, June. I've tried kindness, bargaining, flirtation, and now this, and you don't budge. What does it take to crack you?"

She stayed silent a long while, fumbling for the right words. "Honesty."

Diego stepped back, running his hands through his hair before he braced one on his hip, gesturing wildly with the other. "You want honesty? I am fucking disgusted. I've worked my entire life to get a seat in Formula One. I've been nothing but loyal to my team. I've done well, brought home points, kept the team in the running for a Constructors Championship all three years, and what do I get in return? Replaced the moment someone with better family ties comes waltzing in. We can play their game, but they will deal us a losing hand every time. This time, we are dealing the cards."

June swallowed hard, watching him carefully. She hadn't expected the raw passion. Hadn't expected him to sound so much like her. "Why me?" she whispered.

"Because you get it," Diego returned. "Your life may not be perfect, but at least yours is real."

He turned, shaking his head at her like she was committing some moral offense. She nearly felt like she was. Diego wasn't just proposing playing the fans—he was proposing playing all of them. Sponsors and teams alike. Make themselves popular enough, and it would be a lot harder to stomp them out.

But this deal with Diego meant risk. It meant putting herself out there. Meant opening herself up to a world of motorsport—a world

June hated.

"Give me your phone."

June stepped back, suddenly possessive. "What? No—"

"Give it."

June glowered up at him, detesting his demanding tone, but she unlocked her phone and passed it to him. He typed for a moment before he powered it off and handed it back. He'd texted his own number from her phone. She wondered vaguely why he didn't just add his number to her contacts until she remembered he'd already given her his number on a slip of paper she promptly threw out.

June swallowed hard. "Let me think about it." It was the only answer she could give. The only answer that existed.

Diego bowed his head in a truce. *"Buenas noches, cariño."* Without another word, he turned and slipped back into the crowd, disappearing into the throng of partygoers. And just like that, she could breathe again.

She blinked once, then twice. Shook her head. Turned her thoughts. But the ghost of his presence remained.

June woke the next morning to her phone pinging with a text message from an unknown number. Her heart leaped into her throat, and she quickly opened it to find a screenshot of an article from last season. A picture of June on a table, bottle of whiskey in hand. *"June Walker's Night Out Ends in €10,000 in Damages"*.

June grimaced. She knew Charlene had already handled it. Knew she'd already written the check. Knew it had come out of June's earnings from the last year, but it still made shame burn deep in her gut. The article detailed it all: broken tables and chairs, how the club had gone from rowdy to out of control with June at its head. The girls had been thrown from the club and blacklisted.

UNKNOWN: i thought we had something special :((((((

June's eyes narrowed toward it, her lip curling in disgust as the second text rolled in.

**UNKNOWN: it's diego btw since i
know you didn't save my number**

*JUNE: why would i
save your number??*

**UNKNOWN: you're heartless.
i deserve a cute
nickname and contact picture**

June immediately sent him a screenshot of his updated contact—"*Punching Bag*" with a stock image of a punching bag

PUNCHING BAG: that's just mean

The banter exacerbated from there, constantly barraged by a slew of texts from the Spaniard. June couldn't make it through more than a few hours without Diego sharing a new thought. She tried to convince herself that it was annoying, but Diego's messages were a welcome distraction from the monotony of her daily life. He knew exactly how to get a response out of her, whether it be a laugh or an eye roll.

She was beginning to doubt he actually slept at all. No matter when she messaged, it was hardly a matter of a few minutes before he was texting her back—from any country, any time zone. He was the one person she could count on for an automatic response.

**PUNCHING BAG: how come there are
no pictures of you with your family?**

JUNE: you're such a stalker.

**PUNCHING BAG: i've looked at every single picture
on your instagram.
are your horses your only friends?**

JUNE: yes.

It was a long moment before the next text lit up her phone.

**PUNCHING BAG: sorry i was just picturing you crying
in a horse stall in some ugly plaid pajamas,
while watching Spirit and eating cheez-its**

**JUNE: first of all, i eat goldfish
like a sophisticated adult.**

PUNCHING BAG: sofishticated :D

**JUNE: -_-
JUNE: second, if you don't cry at Spirit,**

you're fucking heartless.
the music is phenomenal

PUNCHING BAG: yet you don't deny the ugly pajamas.
i've got you all figured out
PUNCHING BAG: i've never seen it.
we should watch it sometime

JUNE: you just want to see me cry
to see if i actually have emotions

PUNCHING BAG: you have plenty of emotions.
you're angry at me all the time and
every now and then i get a solid 'lol' so . . .
i know you have a heart in there somewhere

JUNE: whatever helps you sleep at night

PUNCHING BAG: oh you could definitely
help me sleep at night ;)

Diego sent her memes and videos. Pictures of his day-to-day or his nights out with the rest of the Formula One grid. He loved to mess with her. Getting a rise out of her seemed to be his favorite hobby. She blocked him several times, only to unblock him again by the morning. He was absolutely shameless. There was not a question that passed through his mind that he didn't ask.

She hated that his attempts to befriend her were working. June caught herself reaching for her phone several times, intent on sharing her own stupid thoughts, only to realize what she was doing and set her phone back down. It didn't matter, though; within a few hours, her phone lit up with a text from him anyway.

PUNCHING BAG: why aren't you riding that other horse?

JUNE: stop interrogating me
JUNE: he's still young.
not ideal for earning points

PUNCHING BAG: why'd you ride him the first show then?

June frowned at her phone, thinking of a million responses before she finally settled on the truth.

JUNE: people spent my whole rookie year saying i was only good because of Midus.
i wanted to prove them wrong.
guess they were right, lol

PUNCHING BAG: as if i don't hear i'm only good because of the car 100x a race.
people like to talk out of their asses.
don't listen to them.

June was so touched she couldn't think of a single thing to say, staring down at the blinking cursor on her phone. The others had told her the same thing a million times, but it felt different coming from someone who got it. Felt genuine. Because Diego was a talented driver, and if he received the same comments, maybe she was a talented rider, too.

JUNE: thank you.
that actually means a lot
JUNE: if it's coming from someone
as talented as you it must
mean something, right? :)

PUNCHING BAG: omg were you just
nice to me???? i'm framing that and
hanging it on my wall

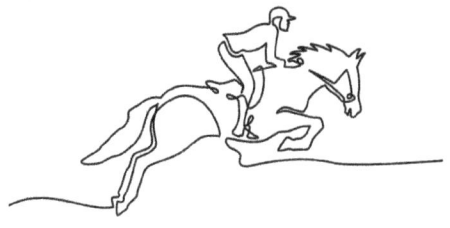

Chapter Seven

The trip to the Miami Grand Prix went without a hitch. They flew their horses out of Rome, which meant a three hour drive, followed by a twelve hour flight, and then the rest of the day and night to let the horses settle in before the competition.

The venue was built specifically for the event, an arena directly on the beach and surrounded with bleachers that would be packed. Miami always was.

It was still early in the day, but June was at the stables. With a temporary venue, the horses had to be stabled nearby and transported back and forth.

All the grooms and riders scrambled about, nervous energy filled the air. This was always the worst part—the waiting.

"June," her groom called from down the aisle, "come here!"

The tone in Isa's voice set June into motion, jogging over to her. "What is—"

She led Midus forward. He hobbled on his front right leg, trying his best to keep off of it. June's heart dropped. "Fuck."

"*Fuck* is right," Isa confirmed. "He's lame."

June swallowed hard, staring down at the afflicted limb when a voice sounded from behind her. Amelia.

"He's probably just sore from traveling," Amelia insisted, crossing her arms over her chest. "Ice him and get him tacked up. He'll be fine in the soft dirt."

June's jaw dropped. "... Amelia—"

Her coach snapped at her, eyes flaring with irritation. "You have fifteen chances to score points. So get out there and do it."

With a hard nod, Amelia headed out. June bit the inside of her cheek, watching as her trainer retreated down the hall. The season was off to a great start, ya' know, if great meant *really fuckin' shitty*. She needed Midus.

He was the only horse that could get her close to that title. The only one she wanted to win with. They'd chased after that victory full throttle last year. She needed his steady heart to guide hers.

She grit her teeth in resignation, turning to look at her gelding.

"June . . . ?" Isa asked.

June nodded. "I'm out this round." She had no other choice. Maybe she could get away with it. Maybe Amelia was right. She moved to Midus's side, rubbing gently over his eyes and he leaned into her touch. "I'll ice him. Go find a vet, please."

If June could trust Midus not to hurt her when it counted, he could expect the same.

He was just sore from travel. He was fine. He was going to be fine.

June had never really been the type to fuss about her health. Sure, being sick was inconvenient, but she never fretted about herself. As far as she was concerned, she was immortal. But one of her horses being injured? It may as well have been the end of the world. She'd always been this way, ravaged with a savage anxiety that assumed the absolute worst-case scenario. It worsened tenfold when she began competing. It wasn't just emotional attachment now. Her entire livelihood rested on her horses.

Midus's stall had been converted into a makeshift vet's office, the vet and her assistant hustling about to take X-rays and run diagnostic tests. Amelia returned after her round, clearly judging June's decision, but she'd brought a vet with. The woman explained to Amelia in Italian as she went, words flying right over June's head as she held Midus's head close to her chest. Midus wasn't exactly the affectionate type, and yet he nuzzled into her, seeking comfort. Something was wrong, and they both knew it. Amelia and the woman spoke in hushed, tense Italian. June tuned them out, holding Midus close.

Amelia cleared her throat, and June perked up immediately, looking at her expectantly. "What?" she demanded. "What is it?"

Amelia shook her head, pursing her lips into a thin line. "June . . ."

"Just say it!"

"It's navicular."

June felt the exact moment her heart stopped and dropped to her stomach. And then, as if by magic, it started again, pounding with a renewed, panicked fervor. June wanted to laugh. Not because it was funny but because it was stupid. He'd taken second in a Grand Prix a week ago. Navicular wasn't even a possibility.

But, of course, it was.

Navicular was the worst-case scenario, every equestrian's nightmare—right up there with kissing spine and colic. A degenerative disease that wore a horse from the inside out. The deterioration of the bone in his foot. Each case was different, but there was always a chance the horse would never be sound again. Definitely not for this level of competition.

Midus's career would be over.

The vet shook her head sadly, speaking English in a heavily Italian accent. "I am so sorry, Miss Walker."

June whirled on her ferociously. "Don't be. You're wrong."

Amelia stepped between June and the woman, quickly thanking her, and a moment later, the woman gathered her things and went scampering off, her assistant in tow. Amelia nodded toward Isa, and the girl hustled to care for Midus as June was ushered away. "Walk with me."

June was going to puke. The panic was setting in. Amelia recognized the symptoms well, well versed in beating them back whenever they arose until June could deal with her feelings in private. Amelia wasn't good with emotions. Blame her upbringing. Blame years in a high-stress sport. Whatever the case, she never handled it well. But she tried for June.

June clutched her hands close to herself, staring down into them, focusing on the feeling of her fingernails digging into her palm. The pain. Replacing Midus wasn't a possibility. He had carried her all the way to the Global Champions Tour. They'd competed four years together. "Can't we get a second opinion?"

"Do you know how many vets I had to go through to get one with this level of expertise?"

June swallowed back her own ungratefulness. "I know, I just—"

Amelia stopped, turning to face her. "You don't want it to be the truth."

She bit her bottom lip until it stung, squeezing her eyes shut as she willed herself not to cry.

Amelia reached forward, setting a hand on June's shoulder. "This is the result, June. A million different vets won't change that."

The truth was a knife to the gut. And yet, it was still the truth.

"What do I do?" A desperate plea.

"You retire him."

June swallowed back her emotion. It wasn't supposed to be like this.

"I don't have another horse, Amelia. I mean, if I get the right sponsors, maybe I can swing another horse, but—"

"You will ride Oviatt for the rest of the season."

June paused, clenching her teeth. She'd ridden Oviatt before—she couldn't have imagined a horse more insane. "... What?"

Amelia frowned, tapping her foot. "You have to replace him." Of course, she had to replace him. But it was the last thing she wanted. A last-minute replacement for her most reliable horse at the beginning of the season was a bullet to her title race and her career.

June dug her nails into her palm, hating that Amelia was right. It didn't matter that June didn't want to accept it—this was reality.

"Oviatt is your best option. He has the scope. He's a talented horse. You don't have another option at this point."

June stared at her in disbelief. No fucking way was she trading her Saint of a gelding for the Devil that was Oviatt.

"I have Hades," June argued.

Amelia scoffed. "You have more talent than Hades can keep up with. You need a horse who can jump."

June bit her tongue. They were Amelia's favorite lines: *he's too slow, he's lazy, he doesn't try hard enough.* But she wasn't the one riding him. Hades had heart. June just had to learn how to direct it.

As far as horses went, he was sensitive. The slightest shift in her hips had him changing leads. The tiniest bit of pressure, and he collected. The simplest bit of leg pressure and he would bend his body in half to please her. The slightest hesitation? No chance.

He knew her. He could feel her. Could sense the terror. The doubt. Could see that she was a fraud. She might be able to fool the rest of the world, but Hades saw right through her. That was hardly his fault. Amelia set a hand on her shoulder, gave it a squeeze—the closest thing to comfort she'd supply—and left.

June had spent most of her life at a loss. She couldn't remember a time she'd felt secure. Even when she was consistently bringing home money in her rookie year. Even when she'd been great, she didn't focus on it. The happiness success brought was a plush rug under cold feet, liable to be yanked from under her at any given moment. Sure, it was nice while she had it, but the last thing she wanted was to get used to it. To need it. To rely on it.

She spent so long waiting for the other shoe to drop. Sure enough, like clockwork, here it was. She should've known better than to get comfortable. All alone, she leaned against the inside of the stall door and watched Midus as he ate, content as could be with one leg cocked up. For a minute, June could pretend everything was normal, that he was merely sore. That they were gearing up for the next competition the way they always were. And then he shifted—his weight uncomfortable to bear—and grunted with the effort, tensing from the pain.

The tears came, a steady, vehement stream she was powerless to stop. She let them fall silently down her face, staining her cheeks and her shirt. She bit back a sob, reaching out to touch him. Midus held her heart. He'd carried her through two years in the Global Champions Tour. He'd nearly won her the title her rookie year. He'd earned enough to pay himself off in a single year competing in the pros. He took a small girl with small dreams of ribbons and turned her into a champion.

Well, nearly.

June collapsed against his chest, wrapping her arms around his neck as she sobbed against him. She couldn't say how long it'd been when a clatter sounded behind her, and June nearly jumped out of her skin, turning to face Lola entering the stall behind her. She was crying, too.

June wasn't brave the way Lola was. She wasn't able to cry when something hurt and smile when she was happy. She pushed it all down, covered it up with some cocky persona and bravado, and let it suffocate her until she was falling apart.

But June could fall apart in front of her. Lola always knew how to help pick up the pieces. She fell forward into Lola's arms, letting herself be comforted by the embrace as they watched Midus continue eating as though everything was fine. June swallowed hard, stroking his forehead. "Do you think he knows?" she whispered. "Do you think he knows we're never going to jump again?"

A shuddering breath escaped June. She slipped out of Lola's arms to lean forward and place her forehead against his own. It was so rare he allowed her such levels of affection. Maybe he really did know. She wondered if that made it better or worse.

"We were supposed to win this year," she choked out, a sob wrecking her sentence halfway through, and she clung tighter to him. "We were supposed to win together."

Lola's hand landed on her back. The comfort only made her break.

"Did I do this?" June choked out. The guilt had been eating her ever since she'd heard the diagnosis. "Did I ride him too hard?"

Lola shook her head, eyes laced with sympathy. "June, I've never known anyone who cares for their horses like you do. This wasn't neglect. Sometimes it's just bad luck."

Bad luck. She wasn't sure which was worse—the guilt or the terror of the unknown. The truth that she was completely and utterly powerless.

"What do I do, Lola?"

"You let it hurt." She stepped forward, one hand rubbing small circles against June's back, the other reaching forward to stroke Midus. He hadn't only given June her career, he'd given her entire team one. He'd lifted them all.

"He's been so good to us, June. He deserves a carefree retirement. Even if it's sooner than we wanted." Lola choked on the end of her words, her own tears flowing freely. June buried herself in Lola's arms and let her heart break under the grief.

Chapter Eight

When June didn't know what to do, she worked. It was the only thing that made sense. Sad? Gym. Confused? Media day. Exhausted? More horses. When everything went to shit, June needed a full schedule. She had two weeks until the next jump-off in Mexico City. There was no time to dick around.

June had ridden Amelia's stallion before as part of their deal. Amelia coached June in exchange for June keeping her horses rode down. She started and schooled horses for Amelia so she could sell them—money June never saw, but that was the price of having Amelia Santiago as your coach. She was the best. June needed the best to become the best.

Isa's jaw dropped when June asked her to catch and saddle Oviatt. The stallion was an asshole, plain and simple. No ground manners—no manners at all, as a matter of fact. But that asshole could clear the building if he wanted to. He knew his job, and he was dead set on it—with or without you.

At least he was pretty. 17.2 hands tall, light, dun-red color with a nearly brown mane and tail and a perfectly symmetrical white blaze down the center of his face. June wanted to like him. Too bad he was evil.

Lunging Oviatt was an ordeal. A minimum of thirty minutes

running him in circles from the ground in an attempt to blow off some steam. It just made him more amped up and in better shape, but Amelia insisted on it, and June was in no position to refuse. By the time she stepped on, he was electric. He terrified her. When he set his sights on a jump, it was the only thing in the world that existed to him.

Riding Oviatt felt a lot like what she would imagine sitting in an idling race car would—if said race car could make bad decisions.

Even at a walk, his power was palpable; the chestnut stallion was ready to explode into motion the moment June stopped holding him back. She warmed him up the same way she warmed up all her horses—checking flexion, yielding to pressure, focusing on movement, and stringing the connection between her thoughts and his own. Oviatt cared for only two things—forward and up.

June made up her mind very quickly that she wasn't going to compete on him. She'd ride him to appease Amelia, but if she had to compete the entire season on Hades, so be it.

Extra care, extra cooldown, the highest performance feed available. Hades was loyal and tough. If she took care of him, he'd take care of her.

Or at least she hoped that was the case.

The demand of her sport never lessened. It was something June reveled in. Fuck up? Fix it the following weekend. And then do it again the next. And the next. And the next. Even the off-season didn't slow for her. The hustle was the only thing that made June feel whole. Horses and ribbons and trophies and her career. That was all that mattered. That was all she had.

June stared down Hades neck in Mexico City and felt as a cavern opened in her stomach and threatened to swallow her whole. She was supposed to be on Midus.

She found herself in the warm-up arena, the pattern of it all familiar to her. As soon as Hades moved, nothing else existed outside

RACING HEARTS

of the feeling of her horse beneath her.

A simple circle, then two. All June had to focus on was herself and the animal. Not Oviatt or her lack of sponsorships. Not her family or her empty bank account. Hades and June. That was all that existed.

She could have spent her entire life like this, perfect warm-ups in the back arena, her heart thrumming with a mix of anticipation and dread. Such a horrific feeling, and yet, so, so addicting.

She wondered if this was what the bottles were like for her dad.

She crushed that thought immediately.

June waited for her turn, watching as her competitors flowed in and out of the arena. She glanced at the scoreboard and then back at the gate.

"June."

The moment she heard Amelia's voice, June's mouth went dry. She swallowed hard, feeling a bit like a student about to get smacked with a ruler as she stared down the neck of the brown horse that should have been a chestnut. Amelia didn't always pay close attention to June, and she'd hoped to be through before Amelia could say confront her about riding Hades again. But of course, here she was, waiting for her turn alongside June on her own horse.

Amelia eyed Hades, clearly displeased. "You are not riding Oviatt?"

As if this could get any worse.

How to tell a two-time title winner that her horse was a dickhead? "I need more rides on Oviatt before I take him in the ring—"

"Hm," was all Amelia had to say.

June stilled. She could never decide if Amelia admired her or wanted her dead, always silent and deadly against June's ability to talk the ears off of anyone horse related.

Amelia nodded towards her in acknowledgment. "Your family is not here?"

June flinched like she'd been shot. She supposed Mexico and

Texas were close enough. A normal family would have been there.

Her family?

"They couldn't make it," she lied. Amelia nodded knowingly, clicking her tongue against the roof of her mouth almost pityingly. "I see. Break a leg, then. Not literally, of course." Amelia forced an eerie smile that looked far more like baring her teeth to sink them into someone's throat before she turned and left without another word.

June stared after her. Her heart ached in her chest. Amelia didn't know the whole story of June's life—no one did—but she knew enough.

June didn't talk about her family. It was the unspoken rule. Nobody who wanted to keep their eyes mentioned June's family. Except for Amelia, who always seemed to find the most inconvenient times she possibly could.

Lola and Olivia came bolting up to her.

June stared after her coach. "Sometimes I think she's going to pull out a gun and shoot me right off my horse."

Lola didn't flinch. "That's an American thing, June."

Olivia surged up onto the fence. "What? What did she say? Did she say something about Hades?"

Finally, June turned to look at them properly. "She asked why I wasn't riding Oviatt."

"That bitch," Oliva swore.

Lola shrugged. "Probably because Hades is an angel, and Oviatt eats small children."

Hades swung his head back and forth, ripping the reins out of her hands. June gritted her teeth and squeezed her eyes tightly shut, snagging the reins again. "Don't compliment him! It makes him an asshole!"

The tension in the arena was palpable as the jump-off got underway. June could practically feel Amelia staring her down. Her stomach was in knots. June nodded in resignation, staring down Hades' neck. "I'm gonna puke."

"Oh, quit," Olivia scolded. "You're making him nervous."

She whirled on them. "He's making me nervous! I was supposed to be on Midus!"

Lola shrugged. "We can always throw you on Oviatt."

"Not funny." June stood at the gate, her heart hammering in her throat hard enough to choke her. Her entire body shook with adrenaline as she heard the screams and cheers from the other side of the arena.

Your family is not here?

June shook it off one last time, gathering her reins and locking onto the first jump before she spurred Hades in.

June started working full time the moment she looked old enough not to be gawked at as a waitress at Odie's Cafe. Which, as it happened, was a few days after she turned thirteen. She was tall and knew how to act mature. She wore her hair, and applied what little makeup she wore in such a way that made her look like a high schooler, rather than the seventh grader she was. She hated the idea of Ava ever knowing how poor they were.

The racked-up bills, the shittily patched-up holes in clothes, the scrounged-up linens in the house that never matched. Dad bought beer. June kept the lights and AC on. Ava was still young—nine years old—and though she would have been fine home alone, the idea of her in that shitty house all by herself was enough to make June sick. So, she enrolled her in dance classes after school.

Not even the easy, cheap kind that parents send their kids off to for an hour of silence. She paid hundreds every month. Odie, or one of the other waitresses, would take Ava to dance after school. June picked her up when she got off work.

Sure, she could have cut out the classes and halved her workload, but this way was kinder.

Neither of them wanted to be in that house.

As it turned out, Ava was quite good at dancing. Passionate, rhythmic, athletic. She progressed quickly.

It came as no surprise when Ava received an offer from The Hive, the most prestigious school for dancers under twenty-one in all of the South. The kind that made the Rockettes, professional ballerinas, and background dancers for pop artists. The kind that made dancing into a career.

The expensive kind.

June picked up a second job—barn hand at a local show barn. Her schedule was as follows:

Wake up at 3:30 in the morning.

Wish she were dead.

Feed and water twenty horses.

Waitress at Odie's Cafe from 6:30 until 2 in the afternoon.

Go to the barn, clean twenty stalls, put horses on walkers, saddle, and ride for clients until eight.

Pick Ava up from dance.

Home. Dinner. Online school. Sleep.

Repeat. Repeat again.

Again.

And again.

And again.

She didn't care what it was going to take to get Ava out of there, she was going to that damn school.

In the end, Ava got a scholarship. Her tuition was covered. All June had to pay was for her dorm and a meal card. A measly $2,000 of the $15,000 she'd saved.

Ava left for Austin when she was fourteen years old.

And June lost everything. She moved in with Odie, desperate to be out of her father's house. Her entire life had been raising Ava, and now she had $13,000 to her name and nothing to do with it.

She could have weaned back, should have. Worked twelve-hour days instead of sixteen, eight-hour days instead of twelve. But it was routine. And routine was all she had now. It was one such morning, just as June was starting her day that a woman stumbled upon her in the middle of feeding. It was four-thirty in the morning when the woman walked in, scaring June out of her skin. Her horses, however, didn't budge.

They bonded over the demand of a lifestyle such as theirs. Amelia told her she was a showjumper for a global league. "Have you heard of them?"

Of course, June hadn't. She laughed in amazement and, mostly jokingly, asked if she was hiring.

Three weeks later, she was on a flight to Florence with nothing more than a carry-on, a slew of exchanged cash, and an expedited passport. At seventeen, she wasn't legally allowed to leave the country, but small towns were great for tight-knit communities willing to help pull one over for the right kind of people. She managed to get her dad to sign a permission to travel form one night when he was too drunk to argue, claiming it was something for school.

By the time her father realized she had been gone for nearly three months, June had already turned eighteen. There was nothing he could do to bring her back to Texas.

Maybe it was God. Maybe it was fate. Maybe it was a coincidence.

But June was determined not to waste the opportunity. She did not get this far to squander it now.

Hades came into the arena like a trainwreck, his attention grounded on the crowd and their slew of shade umbrellas rather than the task ahead of them. *Please no.*

He nearly jumped out of his skin at the sight of the cameraman. Hundreds of arenas, but he was still a horse. Still young. She could feel the crowd's cautious energy—could practically hear what the commentators would be saying. *'She's on the young horse again, a bad call considering what a rough start they had.'*

GET OUT OF YOUR HEAD!

They circled and Hades shot out beneath her, headed for the first jump. *Don't flinch, don't tense, don't—*

He surged up and over the jump. She felt the moment his front feet clipped the top pole, fumbling to find his footing. She landed hard, Hades catching himself at the last moment before they were propelling to the next. She swore sharply. The first fence and they'd already fucked it up.

They pushed toward the next jump.

She met Hades halfway as he soared over the oxer, hunting down the next.

Focus.

Everything felt wrong. Her saddle too far back, her own body and her horse's out of time. They leaped over the next jump a stride too early, knocking a pole. The crowd sighed their disappointment all around her, and she swore sharply, gathering him beneath her as they sped to the next fence. *Please, please, please, please—*

They approached the wall jump, Hades locking onto it too late. He slid on his hind end, attempting to refuse, but the jump was already there. He lurched upwards at the last second, taking half the fence with him. June barely managed to hang on as he came down on the other side. The force of the landing nearly knocked her out of the saddle.

A shit show. A complete and utter shit show.

June hadn't jumped clear in the first round, and therefore wouldn't progress to the next. June was done. A small-town girl out of place in a world-class Grand Prix.

Your family isn't here?

No. They never were. She clenched her jaw until it ached, and she was certain her teeth would crack.

She heard the pity applause.

She grimaced, petting along Hades' neck and making her way out of the arena.

June was nine when Mama Odie's paint horse died—in all ways except paper, that horse was hers. Losing her broke June's heart in half.

June and Mama Odie had nothing tying them together then. Odie could have walked away. She had already done more than her share. But Odie ran a cafe, and people couldn't say no to the woman who served them coffee and breakfast in the morning, including the manager of BlackJack Stables. A deal was struck on June's behalf. In exchange for cleaning five stalls, June was given a thirty-minute lesson. June cleaned ten stalls and convinced them to make the lesson forty-five minutes. Perhaps not a fair trade, but one June was willing to make.

Odie's Cafe staff adopted June into their ranks, the waitresses and cooks taking it upon themselves to care for Mama Odie's cute little horse-obsessed neighbor. Someone drove her to the barn every day. When she was twelve, Odie let her borrow the farm truck. The bus dropped her off from school, and June headed straight to the barn.

By the age of fourteen, June had studied with four different instructors. She cleaned twenty stalls a day and was even paid to ride a few people's horses.

Somewhere along the line, caught up in the idea that she had made it, she forgot how many kind strangers it took to build June

Walker. How many people were rooting for her to strike it big.

How many people she was disappointing.

Sitting on the floor in Hades' stall, June picked up her phone. She didn't know what to say. She typed a text, only to delete it and try again. And again. And again. And again. They hadn't seen each other since that club in Monaco.

So, she pressed call before she could back out. And then immediately hung up, eyes wide as she stared down at her phone.

Fuck.

Mere seconds later, her screen lit up with the picture of a punching bag. Diego. She swore under her breath, picking up the phone.

"Hello." The word sounded foreign, like she'd been practicing it for a very long time, and now it came out forced.

"Vaquera," Diego greeted shortly. "How are you feeling?"

"Like shit," she said honestly.

"Still honest as ever. I thought you chose not to ride that horse this year?" June swallowed hard. So, he had been watching.

"Not supposed to be," she mumbled bitterly. "Midus came up lame."

She could sense his confusion from a continent away. "He . . . what?"

She huffed, amused and bitter. "He—He hurt his leg before the competition in Miami."

Diego hummed thoughtfully, a tinge of sympathy in his voice. "You see, this is why cars are easier. You have a bad tyre, you just change it."

She pursed her lips into a thin line, gritting her teeth. "Right. Thanks."

Immediately, Diego tried to rectify his words. "I just—cars are a lot more . . . replaceable. You're upset over a hurt horse. I don't get upset over a blown-out tyre. I get upset because I didn't win."

She let out an amused groan. "Do you always make everything

RACING HEARTS

Your family isn't here?

No. They never were. She clenched her jaw until it ached, and she was certain her teeth would crack.

She heard the pity applause.

She grimaced, petting along Hades' neck and making her way out of the arena.

June was nine when Mama Odie's paint horse died—in all ways except paper, that horse was hers. Losing her broke June's heart in half.

June and Mama Odie had nothing tying them together then. Odie could have walked away. She had already done more than her share. But Odie ran a cafe, and people couldn't say no to the woman who served them coffee and breakfast in the morning, including the manager of BlackJack Stables. A deal was struck on June's behalf. In exchange for cleaning five stalls, June was given a thirty-minute lesson. June cleaned ten stalls and convinced them to make the lesson forty-five minutes. Perhaps not a fair trade, but one June was willing to make.

Odie's Cafe staff adopted June into their ranks, the waitresses and cooks taking it upon themselves to care for Mama Odie's cute little horse-obsessed neighbor. Someone drove her to the barn every day. When she was twelve, Odie let her borrow the farm truck. The bus dropped her off from school, and June headed straight to the barn.

By the age of fourteen, June had studied with four different instructors. She cleaned twenty stalls a day and was even paid to ride a few people's horses.

Somewhere along the line, caught up in the idea that she had made it, she forgot how many kind strangers it took to build June

Walker. How many people were rooting for her to strike it big.

How many people she was disappointing.

Sitting on the floor in Hades' stall, June picked up her phone. She didn't know what to say. She typed a text, only to delete it and try again. And again. And again. And again. They hadn't seen each other since that club in Monaco.

So, she pressed call before she could back out. And then immediately hung up, eyes wide as she stared down at her phone.

Fuck.

Mere seconds later, her screen lit up with the picture of a punching bag. Diego. She swore under her breath, picking up the phone.

"Hello." The word sounded foreign, like she'd been practicing it for a very long time, and now it came out forced.

"Vaquera," Diego greeted shortly. "How are you feeling?"

"Like shit," she said honestly.

"Still honest as ever. I thought you chose not to ride that horse this year?" June swallowed hard. So, he had been watching.

"Not supposed to be," she mumbled bitterly. "Midus came up lame."

She could sense his confusion from a continent away. "He . . . what?"

She huffed, amused and bitter. "He—He hurt his leg before the competition in Miami."

Diego hummed thoughtfully, a tinge of sympathy in his voice. "You see, this is why cars are easier. You have a bad tyre, you just change it."

She pursed her lips into a thin line, gritting her teeth. "Right. Thanks."

Immediately, Diego tried to rectify his words. "I just—cars are a lot more . . . replaceable. You're upset over a hurt horse. I don't get upset over a blown-out tyre. I get upset because I didn't win."

She let out an amused groan. "Do you always make everything

RACING HEARTS

about you?"

"That's not—That's not what I—" he huffed. "Ugh. *June* . . . I just meant your sport is far more emotionally draining. It isn't just cogs and motors and tyres."

She smiled softly. She knew what he meant. But it was nice to fluster him. "How'd things go in Bahrain?"

"P4."

Fourth place. Salt in the wound. When she was doing shit, he was just shy of the podium in a team he'd helped rebuild from the ground up. "Good work."

"Thank you," he said genuinely.

"Shouldn't you be out partying?"

"Ah, yes. I . . . am," he admitted. "I had to go outside to call you, but I saw your missed call, and I just had to talk to you."

June blinked, imagining him outside a club in Bahrain, tucked in an alleyway to call her because he *had to talk to her*. He must have been a few drinks in because he wouldn't have admitted it otherwise. Or maybe he would. They didn't exactly know each other well. And Diego was an open book.

". . . I had to retire him." She didn't know why she said it. It felt like a confession for a confession. Each speaking what weighed on their minds.

"What?"

"Midus. He has a bone disease. I'll never be able to ride him again." She hoped she didn't sound as close to tears as she felt.

"*Dios mío*, June. I am so sorry." For what it was worth, he sounded genuine. The two were silent on the phone for a while, neither exactly sure what to say.

"You shouldn't be."

". . . What?"

She drew in a sharp breath and let out a heavy sigh. Her voice came out softer than she'd meant. ". . . I need sponsors." She may be able to suffer a single season with a green horse, but she had to get ahead of this. To win. *Winning isn't just what you do on the track.*

"Ah. I see." She could hear the smug grin in his voice. One day, when everything went to shit in her life enough to just give up, she was going to punch his lights out and savor it.

"I'm not blindly jumping into whatever you think this deal is supposed to be."

A laugh came from the other line. "You blindly jump all the time. Isn't that your job?"

June hated that his joke was almost funny. She bit the inside of her cheek, tracing the patterns in the wood grain of the stall door with her eyes. "Are we pretending to date then?"

"No, no, no. If we date, we take away the intrigue. We look at each other too long, and we touch each other a bit too much, and wind up in the same place too often. We give them something to *talk* about, *cariño*." She could almost see him gesturing with his hands the way he did in that stupid way of his. "There is an event this weekend in Valencia. You'll come with me."

Valencia. He said it so casually, as if she were the type of person to simply hop on a plane over to Spain for shits and giggles.

She caught his omitted details immediately. "An *'event'*? Really?"

She could practically see him throwing his hands up in exasperation. "What? It does not matter! Wear an evening gown. Who cares?—"

"I care!—"

"I'll put everything on my tab!"

June paused.

Diego caught her hesitation and ran with it. "Whatever you want, *Vaquera*. You come to a charity event with me. We are photographed together. People love it. It's all on me. I'll buy you a new dress, pay for the travel, and everything goes on me, hm?"

June was quiet for a long time. Thinking. Valencia, Spain. Another appearance with Diego. She needed the attention. Needed something positive. Needed a distraction. "... *Fine.*"

His voice was smug. "I knew you'd see things my way."

June clenched her fist. She needed him, she reminded herself. But he needed her, too. "I'm ordering a thousand-euro bottle of wine the second I touch down."

Diego actually laughed at that. "Oh, *Vaquera*, you need to set your ambitions higher. You act like I can't afford to spoil you."

June scrunched her nose in irritation. *Ugh*. Why did him being a cocky bastard have to be hot? "Asshole."

"You love it."

A few beats passed in silence, simply listening to him breathing on the other line before she spoke. "Diego?"

"Mhm?"

"Congrats. Seriously."

A long pause. Then, the first words that came out of that stubborn man's mouth that weren't some form of sarcastic jest or smartassery.

"... *Gracias.*"

She smiled softly. "Goodnight, Diego."

"*Buenas noches,* Junebug."

Chapter Nine

June wasn't exactly an evening gown and charity event kinda gal. Probably because there was nothing quite as embarrassing as a bunch of rich people trying to out-charity each other... But damn would it look good to sponsors. So, here she was, in Valencia on a Friday night, dragging her girls with her. He could afford to spoil her, after all.

The girls had screamed in utter delight when she told them. Diego Cabrera had invited them all to an event in Valencia, Spain. Not exactly the truth, but close enough. The room filled with shouts of, *'I knew he was into you!'* and *'You two are so getting married.'* June said nothing. Sooner or later, she was going to have to face the fact that she was stuck with him.

"You like him." Lola poked at her side, and June grimaced, flinching away from her touch.

"I like sponsors," June snapped back. "Sponsors want to see something they can sell. Something they can put on a t-shirt and make promotions about, and if that is a romance with Diego Cabrera, then for fuck's sake, let's sell it. Give people something to talk about and get me more sponsors. Yes?"

Lola and Olivia exchanged a weighted glance. ". . . Yes."

"If Diego is the price to secure myself in this sport, I'll pay it."

June had hoped the information would settle the girls' appetites. Instead, it only seemed to make them hungrier, as though determined to push June and Diego even closer together.

All June could do was ignore them, like antagonizing siblings. The more she reacted, the worse they'd behave.

Diego had booked them a private jet, a favor from one of his sponsors, and she wondered if the girls were going to keel over in amazement. A private driver took them from the tarmac to their hotel.

June had never even set foot in such an exquisite place, let alone stayed in one. Everything screamed luxury: massive windows, a cacophony of white, black, and gold with towering ceilings and massive chandeliers. Her room came with silk sheets and a bottle of tequila. June sighed at the sight, setting down her bag as she eyed the room. When he said it was on his tab, she'd expected a Hilton. Instead, each girl had been granted their own suite, a wholly unnecessary luxury. They'd all end up crowded together in one anyway.

Lola exited her room, holding a towel folded up like a little monkey. "Oh yeah, I'm taking him home."

June raised a brow. "Diego or the monkey?"

Lola shrugged. "Yes."

Olivia darted down the hall in a silk bathrobe with a bottle of champagne in her hand, twirling around for June. "I'm moving in."

For June, champagne was for podiums, and podiums only. Diego seemed to understand this. Her room had a bottle of tequila, the same drink he'd spilled on her that night in the club.

The girls piled into her room, lounging across the settee and the extravagant bed, pouring drinks, and flipping through the room service menu. June stared out the window, her room overlooking the gorgeous city. "He's ridiculous."

"*Ridiculous*," Olivia repeated with a scoff as she kicked her legs up on the coffee table, still bundled up in her robe. "He's everything you've ever needed."

June had to bite back a groan.

Olivia huffed, leaning into her hand braced on the armrest. "Is it so bad I want you to find someone? I've never seen anyone make it to the third date."

June tugged the curtain open further, irritation blooming in her chest. What time did June have for dates? "Yes, it is that bad. It's going to be the three of us, single, forever. And then we're going to have a three-way marriage and run an orphanage. Or a cafe."

Lola perked up from the couch. "A combination cafe-orphanage."

"Yes, exactly."

The phone set off from its place on the nightstand, and June whirled to glare at Olivia, lounging next to it. She threw her hands up in innocence. "I didn't even touch it!"

June crossed the room in two strides, picking up the phone to be greeted by a kind Spanish accent. "Miss Walker, *Señora María Cortez* is here for your fitting."

"Fitting?"

"For your dresses."

Dresses. Not dress. *Dresses*.

June cleared her throat.

When Diego had promised her a new dress, she'd expected him to foot the bill for whatever she picked out from a shopping trip. Not whatever this was.

"Of course," June said, as though she'd know exactly what the receptionist was speaking of. "Send her up."

The girls glanced between themselves in confusion, sharing shrugs as June dropped the phone back on the receiver. "What was tha—"

"I have no idea."

In a matter of minutes, a knock came at the door. Olivia jumped up to get it, rushing to invite the strange new woman inside as though she were some foreign curiosity that belonged in a museum or on a stage.

María Cortez was in her mid-60s, tiny and stoic with a surprisingly sturdy air about her. A small man hustled behind her, not saying a word as he carried in a stack of trunks, slamming the door behind them, and the girls exchanged another glance.

"*Señora* Walker and her girls." Her accent was so thick with Spanish that Diego barely had an accent at all in comparison.

María's eyes raked over the trio of women, lingering on their forms as though they were animals in a zoo, and she was trying to assess exactly what kind they were. "Come," she said, making a gesture for the girls to come forward, and they did as instructed without an ounce of protest. She flicked her wrist out with a dramatic embellishment, and the man set to prying open trunk after trunk, pulling dress after dress from the oak chests as though they were some kind of Mary Poppins bag. "Pick your dresses. Never mind the sizes."

June's jaw went slack, blinking in utter confusion as the gowns were dragged out for display. Olivia stared at June as though she were supposed to know what to do, Lola's hand coming up to cover her mouth in surprise. None of them moved for a long while, unable to do more than sit and stare until the woman clapped her hands together sharply. "You are trying to catch a fly in your mouths? *Vamos, Chicas!*"

Any hesitation was thrown to the wind. The girls rushed forward eagerly, peering into the trunks, pulling dresses at random before they held them up to themselves in front of the mirrors. June stood off to the side, watching as though this were some strange dream, and at any given moment, she'd wake up.

Olivia, however, could hardly get one dress into her hands before she was drawn to the next, her eyes shining with unbridled excitement. "Oh my God . . ." she said, her voice nearly a whisper. "Oh my *God* . . ."

Her assistant hustled about, taking measurements and fussing about with each of the girls as they selected their dresses. A dusty orange tulle for Lola, a bright pink sparkly one that reminded June of a cupcake for Olivia.

June could do little more than stare at the trunks, so overwhelmed by the options she wanted to simply wear something she already had. Diego had surprised her. With every chance she had to rattle him—to demand more, to act like a brat— he fulfilled her request tenfold. It irritated her, and she couldn't put a name to why.

She reached for a plain dark blue dress and called it good.

The woman tutted behind her. "So many beautiful dresses, and you pick the ugliest one, hm?"

June flushed bright red, fumbling for an answer. The woman sighed as though June were entirely helpless, swatting her hand away from the dress she'd been reaching for and shooing her down the line of gowns hung about the room.

The woman snapped her fingers at her assistant and sent him scampering to fetch something from a far trunk. He brought the dress to her, hanging it beside June and removing the plastic covering on the dress.

"Oh," June whispered, unable to stop her awe. She reached forward to run her hands over the silky black fabric. "Oh, that's wonderful."

"Try it," María ordered, with no room for argument. June nodded shortly, unhooking the dress from the rack and making her way to the divider that had been unfurled in one corner of the room. June could hardly stand to look in the mirror, too entranced by the sight of the gorgeous dress. Too afraid to be disappointed by the sight of it on herself. But the moment she looked, she fell in love all over again. The dress was floor length, with a long slit up the flowing, loose fit of the fabric that stopped mid-thigh. The back was cut out, slits that started in the middle of the ribcage and ended in a bow that sat at the small of the back, a gorgeous straight neckline that highlighted the divots in her collarbones.

She stepped out from behind the divider, and María's stoic face cracked a sliver of a smile. "*Señor Cabrera* has good taste, no?"

June froze as the words clicked in her head.

This dress was Diego's pick.

Fuck.

The girls squealed in utter delight, their own dresses pinned on. "Oh my God, June!" Lola exclaimed. June flushed, but she couldn't stop her growing smile as she cast another glance in the mirror.

Chapter Ten

Part of June had been doubtful the dresses would be ready in time for the gala, but the woman disappeared as quickly as she had come, and the dresses were delivered three hours before the venue's doors even opened.

María provided a selection of accessories she expected to be paired with the dresses, and the girls practically exploded. Diamond earrings. Elaborate jewels. June picked a pair of gold tassel earrings so long they brushed her collarbone, and a simple, delicate gold necklace with a dainty opal pendant resting in the hollow of her throat. She hadn't known it was possible to feel so beautiful.

The girls made their way down to the lobby with a bustle of excitement to await their ride. June had received a single text from Diego to inform her that their driver would be there at 7:00 p.m. sharp. It was the only thing she'd heard from him all day.

At seven, there was a limousine waiting outside their hotel. The driver opened the door for them, and June realized Diego was showing off to her crew. Trying to win them over while he had the chance. Irritation bloomed in her chest as June clambered in.

The girls filed into the car behind her, chattering like they were going to a school dance rather than a stuffy snob-off. Lola and Olivia were huddled together over a phone screen. June leaned against the opposite window, watching as the driver put the car into gear and began to speed down the streets of Valencia.

The ride was a short one, the driver speaking to the security guards in hurried Spanish, and a moment later, they were parked in front of a grand building, all white stone and towering spires.

The venue had been entirely privatized for the event, turned into a mix between a Museum for Fine Spanish Art, a cocktail bar, and an auction hall.

The girls traveled up the long stone steps together, making their way in. Gold chandeliers hung from the arched ceiling, light reflected across the walls like diamonds. The room itself was filled with elegant chairs and tables, a circular bar, and a floor already filled with people in their finest tuxedos and glittering dresses. The trio of girls stopped dead center to gawk with unbridled fascination. From ceiling to floor, the building screamed pure luxury, dripping with gold and glamor, fine art on the walls. The room was already packed to the brim, women in sparkling jewelry and fine dresses, their men with their coattails and polished shoes. Even in their fancy clothing, June couldn't help but feel out of place with her ragtag group.

Of all the things June expected from this deal with Diego—calling paparazzi on themselves just to 'sneak around' or sitting through each other's events to be spotted in the crowd—she hadn't expected this.

June shook her head. "Holy shit."

Olivia linked her arm through June's with a beaming grin.

"Come on," Lola urged. "Let's go get drinks."

They weaved and darted their way toward the bar, a strange sort of confidence growing between the girls as they made it through each minute without being thrown out, slowly assimilating into the ranks of the kinds of people who attended these sorts of things on the regular. Cocktail in hand, June wandered the museum, peering up at the art, the girls in tow behind her. They seemed far more interested in the slew of gorgeous people than the displays.

Across the masses, June spotted him. Diego's eyes dragged across the expanse of people in utter boredom, vaguely listening to a dirty blond boy tell an animated story. If June and her girls stuck out, Diego's crew were on the other end of the spectrum, far too perfect for a place like this.

On Diego's arm was the most beautiful girl June had ever seen. She was model-pretty—tall and lanky with high cheekbones and a soft face, silky black hair in perfect waves. She was Spanish.

A strange sense of possessiveness coiled in June's stomach at the sight.

She wasn't just on Diego's arm; she looked like she *belonged* there.

It enraged June. She'd never even heard of this woman before. Why was she here? Why would Diego bring her? To introduce June to his real girlfriend while they put on a show for sponsors? Rage coiled in her veins, and June swallowed hard, moving to turn away when Diego's eyes landed on her. Immediately, a handsome smile lit up his face, pulling out of the woman's grasp and abandoning the pack. He crossed the distance between them before June could blink.

He reached forward, fingertips grazing over one earring before his hand traced down her neck and shoulder to her hand. He drew it into his grasp, raising her fingers to his lips to press a gentle kiss. His eyes met hers from his half-bowed position. ". . . Just as exquisite as I envisioned."

June found herself inexplicably frozen, her heart choking her in her throat. She fumbled for something to say, coming up short before she was saved as his group migrated to swarm the pair.

"Oh!" The girl June had seen before now stood behind Diego. "Miss Walker."

The woman beamed, extending her hand forward for June to shake. "Catalina Cabrera." Her soft skin and the coolness of her golden rings were a stark contrast to June's own hands.

June's brows shot up. "Cabrera?" She felt horribly stupid. Now that she was looking, she could see the resemblance.

"His cousin. Don't hold it against me." She flashed a bright smile, the same perfect teeth as Diego. She even scrunched her nose the same way he did when he was amused.

She swallowed back the shame rising in the back of her throat at the odd jealousy. June didn't want anything to get in the way of this agreement. That was all.

They were exquisite—Catalina, Diego, and the boy with them.

Diego saw her eyeing them and set to introductions immediately, one hand tucked away in his pocket, the other holding a wine glass that he gestured about with. "Oscar."

Oscar, she knew of, familiar with the sight of him in Lotus white and gold. Diego's teammate. The Australian driver was a charmer outside of the track, but on the asphalt? He was as brutal as Diego himself. They made for quite the competitive duo—and a handsome one at that. Their hiring had spurred the joke that one must be a model first to join Lotus Racing.

The moment June saw him, she knew she was going to have a reason to give Olivia as much hell as she'd been giving June the last few weeks. He was exactly Olivia's type, all long, lean limbs and charming mischief in his dark eyes that lit up when he smirked at her. Oh, how she loved teasing Olivia about her love of white boys.

They were each their own planet, holding their own weight and ability to draw awe, but Diego was the sun—the bright, beaming force the other's orbited around.

Catalina flashed a bright smile at the girls. "And who are these lovely ladies?"

Olivia practically threw herself at Catalina. "Olivia. June's Social Media Manager."

Catalina smiled at her excitement, shaking hands with her before she turned to Lola.

She cleared her throat, extending a hand to her. "Lola. I manage sponsors for June."

Catalina shook her hand, but her brows furrowed. She was just like her cousin, unable to hide a thought from the world. Diego murmured something to her in Spanish and her face lit up with understanding.

It was odd how genuine Catalina seemed. Her eyes were kind as they flashed over the group, looking her up and down with a glimmer of interest that was far less predatory than the others they'd met at the venue thus far. Catalina knew they didn't quite belong and found it endearing rather than disgusting.

Lola was locked onto Catalina like a dog to a bone, eyes wide and a light blush dusted across her brown skin at the mere sight of the woman. Catalina swooped forward, grabbing onto her arm. "Come now! Let's get drinks!" Catalina ushered Lola off, Olivia in tow with Oscar trailing behind until June and Diego were left alone.

June watched Diego bite back a snicker as the pair interacted, immediately catching on to Lola's flustered expression despite Catalina's apparent obliviousness.

June whirled, whispering a hushed scolding to Diego. "She's shy! Don't ruin this!"

Diego threw his hands up in innocence. "I didn't say a word!"

"You didn't have to! Lola can sense it!"

"It is not my fault you travel with a bloodhound—"

June pinched him. Diego yelped and batted her hand away, just in time for Catalina to look back. He assumed a perfectly casual position, slinging an arm around June before Catalina turned her gaze back to Lola and the others.

Diego watched them go for a moment before his sharp gaze landed back on her, his arm trapping her against him. "You look beautiful tonight, *amor*. I don't know why anyone else bothers to show up when you put them all to shame." It was all June could do to not squirm under the intensity of his gaze. Every interaction felt like one of his races—a competition to leave the other more flustered. A challenge to win. It was hard to tell where her ally ended and her competitor began.

"You're blushing, *Vaquera*," he teased, giving her a smirk that made her stomach flip.

"I am not," she hissed, prying herself out from under his arm. But, of course, she was. She cleared her throat.

He chuckled, crossing his arms across his broad chest and regarding her with a playful look. "You don't do compliments well. Noted." He tapped the side of his head as though he were cataloging that information for later.

June bit the inside of her cheek, promptly turning away from him before he could embarrass her further. She stared at the rounded stage at the center of the room, loaded with the exact opposite of fine art, a stark contrast to the beauty that surrounded them.

"What is it, *chica*? You are frowning."

"I don't understand it."

"What don't you understand?"

"This," she gestured vaguely between her girls that had darted off to the bar, and then between her and Diego. "Any of this. Why go to all the trouble? All the expense? There aren't even reporters here."

"Oh, *mi amor*," he sighed. "You must learn to set your ambitions higher. Every notable person in Valencia stays at that hotel. Every notable person knows you were there. Knows I put you there. Knows I sent *Señora Cortez* right to you. You look around to all these people here tonight, and all you see is importance. And right now, the only thing they are talking about is me and you. You think that won't get tipped off to reporters?"

June blinked up at him. With all his beauty and over the top charm, it was easy to forget how genuinely smart he was.

"It is so much better to feed it down the line from the higher-ups than to expect the higher-ups to believe the bottom fish."

The bottom fish. Like her. Of course, her ambitions were too low for him.

It was hard to stay angry at the condescension of his comment when his eyes were so warm and intense upon her. He was right, of course. Diego, much to her annoyance, always was. He grinned, resting a hand on her shoulder, his thumb tracing the delicate slope of her neck with a light touch that sent shivers up her spine. "Besides, this way, I get to see you. Your company makes these events far more tolerable, *Vaquera*."

It wasn't even his hand at the junction of her shoulder and neck that she despised. Not his warm eyes or the intensity of his gaze. She hated that he said these things. She knew what this charade was. She knew what it was to put on a show for the cameras.

It was his words, which only the two of them could hear with any real clarity, that drove her to anger. They held no weight to the public who could not hear them, and so they were said only to her. Were they meant for her? Meant to be true? More ridiculous charm meant to seduce her? It flattered her as much as it irritated her. She was not naive enough to trust it.

She drew back, raising her glass to her lips as a woman made her way to the stage at the center of the room and began her welcome speech. She spoke Spanish, the words a little too fast for June to understand, but everyone seemed to hang on to her every word. June didn't take her eyes off the speaker. Diego on the other hand paid her no mind, instead opting to lean forward into June's frame of vision.

She knew he could tell she was annoyed, her entire demeanor betraying an air of irritation. That didn't dissuade his pestering. He leaned down toward her, speaking in a hushed tone. "What are you so mad about, *chica*?"

She crossed her arms firmly. "Hush. I'm listening."

Diego's lips twisted upwards in a coy grin. "Since when do you know Spanish?"

June didn't answer him, scowling in the vague direction of the stage. The woman's words flowed easily as she entertained the crowd, and with a few embellishments, the first piece of art was brought on stage. The auctioneer made his way to the stage, said a few words about the organization, and the bidding began.

Diego and June watched together as artwork went up to the auction block, one after another, the numbers mounting higher and higher. Diego leaned down to her, whispering about each piece. The breadth of his art knowledge was impressive. He was familiar with each of the artists' work and their history. He was a knowledgeable man, and it irritated her to no end. The paintings may have been ugly, but at least she wasn't bored. He could make pencils sound interesting.

June found herself actually listening, her eyes glued to the artwork as the auctioneer at the center of the room rattled off prices.

And then, Diego's hand went up.

June's head snapped to the side, eyeing him as he bid twenty thousand euros for the next piece. It was a simple thing—a canvas splattered in ugly, brightly colored paint blobs. Her jaw went slack.

Diego raised a brow at her in amusement. "Why the surprise?"

June blinked at it in absolute horror. "That's the ugliest thing I've ever seen."

Diego shrugged, thinly veiled glee painted on his face. Had he bid on the ugliest piece he could find just to rile her? She wouldn't put it past him. But then he bid on the next, and the next, and the next, and June wondered if he was starting some kind of local art collection for finger paintings done by toddlers.

"Not feeling charitable tonight, *Hermosa*?"

She cleared her throat. "I don't donate to these kinds of things."

"Bullshit," Diego said, turning to face her. "What about that animal sanctuary in Texas you give very sizable donations to?"

Her brows shot up. No one was supposed to know about that. To her knowledge, there was only even one picture of her there. A post on the sanctuary's page, not even her own. She'd gone back to Texas for all of a day to hand them a check. She hadn't been able to stomach going to visit home. She hopped on a plane back to Italy that night. "How much *have* you stalked me?" Her eyes remained on the stage as painting after painting made the rounds. "I prefer to help without slapping a logo on it. If I can't see where they put my money, they don't get my money."

"You really don't trust anything, do you?" He leaned in, peering into her soul even as he raised his hand for the next bid. Then the next. And the next. She wondered if he was listening to the price at all. It didn't even seem to matter to him in the slightest.

She eyed him, refusing to be the first to look away. "Pass."

He cocked his head to the side playfully. "On the painting or charity?"

His gaze narrowed in on her, sliding over her from top to bottom. The intensity of his deep brown eyes was nauseating, and finally, June had to look away. "The trusting. But thanks."

She cursed the girls for abandoning her with him. It didn't take *that* long to get drinks. They were probably hunkered down in the crowd, commentating on June and Diego's every interaction the way they did for all of their corny reality TV.

The others in the crowd were beginning to grow irritated, watching as each painting hit the stage just for Diego's hand to be in the air the next second.

"What do you even do with all this art?"

He shrugged. "I find a place for it."

She sighed in frustration, clutching her hands together in front of her to keep from forcing his arm down. The others around them gave him dirty looks, but it hardly seemed to matter to him. His attention was focused only on her and her growing irritation at his behavior. He was a cocky, self-assured show-off. He wasn't being charitable. He was just being a prick, trying to get a rise out of her.

"Pick your favorite." He gestured to the wide expanse of art across the stage. "I will buy it for you. As a thank-you for coming all this way."

That managed to pull a scoff from her. She eyed him from her peripherals. "That's not how this bargain works."

He turned entirely to face her, with no care for the caution she had shown in keeping him out of her line of vision. "No? You are as bad with thank-yous as you are with compliments?"

Diego had a special talent for knowing just what to say to leave her feeling pinned in a corner and grasping for straws. She shifted uncomfortably. "I told you, I don't want to give money to these kinds of things."

Diego bit back a grin, nodding knowingly. "I can vouch for this one, *Vaquera*. Swear it."

She bit her bottom lip, watching as another poor excuse for art went for an outrageous amount of money. "What is this supporting, anyway? Underclothed purse puppies?"

Diego didn't miss a beat. "Survivors of domestic violence."

June's lips pressed into a thin, embarrassed line, her eyebrows shooting up as she turned away from Diego. "Oh my God."

Another painting was brought to the stage and immediately, Diego's hand was up, answering the call for first bid and saving her from her own shame. "You should see it," he said, almost dreamily. "Women's shelters—men's too. So very rarely are there men's shelters. They pay for counselors, legal fees, and prosecutors. Anything to help people get away and on their feet. It's incredible. I know right where my money goes."

The worst part of it all was the way Diego's eyes lit up as he spoke. Such a reverent belief in the cause he supported. How could she fault him for that?

Despite herself, June's eyes began to wander over the stage. Something for everyone, she supposed, sculptures and handmade pottery and canvases of what she was certain was supposed to look like art. And then, a genuine painting.

An orange-hued wooden table sat in the center of a kitchen, just like the table from her childhood back when things were good. In fact, most of it looked the same, taken directly from her memory and put to canvas, or maybe her memory had become warped to the scene in front of her: dishes in the sink, paint peeling off yellowing walls, calendar with days X'ed out hung beside the door. Everything except the fruit bowl in the center of the table where the stack of bills should have been, and a carton of orange juice in place of a whiskey bottle.

It should have comforted her—the idea of what her childhood could have been without that bottle. Instead, it made her sick to her stomach.

Diego's hand fell to the small of her back, following her line of sight onto the stage. "You like that one?"

June flinched, startled from her thoughts. She blinked up at him. *I hate it.*

She shrugged. "At least that one looks like art." She'd half expected him to argue considering the plethora of non-art he'd just bought, but he just smiled into his drink.

The moment the painting touched the stage, Diego's hand was in the air. June had half a mind to protest, but she knew it would make no difference.

Fifteen rounds of shooting back and forth between him and the same platinum-blond fellow in a pinstripe suit, and the price had been dragged outrageously high.

"Diego," she warned, shaking her head, but his hand was in the air again.

"Diego, I don't want it!" She grabbed onto his arm, trying to counsel reason through clenched teeth. "He clearly does, let him have it—"

"Don't be so naive, *Vaquera*. That's Will Astor, he's been bidding against me all night. He doesn't give a shit about art, he just doesn't want me to win."

June blinked, stepping forward into his line of sight, "That's why you've been buying so much tonight?"

Diego's face lit up with a mischievous grin. "Hush, *querida*. I've got an auction to win."

The numbers kept going higher and higher until finally, Will dropped out with a scowl and the gavel came down. The art was going to go home to Diego. For fifty thousand euros.

June stared at him open-mouthed, still struggling to wrap her brain around that many zeros for a canvas.

Diego turned to her, clearly pleased as they carted yet another piece off to his growing collection. "Expensive taste, *Hermosa*."

Her shock turned into disdain, her lip twitching as she glowered up at him. "Right," she said, no humor in her voice. "Put it in one of your shelters. I don't want it."

Diego's cocky smile faltered, just for a moment, giving way to something else. Maybe a hint of hurt, or disappointment. But it was gone as quickly as it formed. "Ah, I see. Well, pick another then."

June blinked, her jaw set tightly. The whole ordeal. Again. What difference did that kind of money make to him?

His voice hardened with frustration. "Pick another, or I will."

June set her jaw stubbornly, refusing to give a single inch. She knew she was being difficult and childish, but the thought of allowing him to spend that much money on her, even for a good cause, made her sick to her stomach. "No, Diego." Her voice was firm. "I'm done playing your game."

Diego's jaw tightened, annoyance flashing in his eyes. He let out an abrupt huff of air, his fingers clenching around his wine glass. "You are infuriating." His usual charming tone was replaced by a sharp, irritated edge.

They stood beside each other in silence, and Diego offered no more bids for the rest of the night. At least, so long as the blond man in the pinstripe suit kept his hand down.

Uncomfortable silence settled between them, tense and irritable with one another. Whispers went up around the pair, pointing out the way Diego had stopped bidding. One woman near them in a horrifically ugly yellow dress bumped her friend's hip, jutting her gaze toward them.

June grimaced. Despite every nerve in her body begging to sucker punch him in the gut, she stepped closer to him, and looped her arm through his. It didn't matter that he was a pompous asshole. This was the exact wrong kind of attention. Diego shot her a confused look, brows furrowed in question. She answered him with absolute silence, and ignorance. Still, he simmered, and the talk quickly turned back to the auction.

The final three paintings were auctioned off in ease, June's hand nestled in the crook of Diego's arm even through the auctioneer's final words.

"And now a few words from the founder of Artists Against Family Violence."

A burst of applause gave way to a woman on stage. She was middle-aged, possibly fifty, and impeccably beautiful—tall, regal, and somehow still impossibly kind-looking, with dark brown curls and light brown skin. She wore a three-piece suit, the same deep shade as red wine with an oversized blazer. The exact kind of woman who ran a charity out of the goodness of her heart. She took the stage with impeccable grace, speaking in perfect English despite the lilt of Spanish in her accent. "Thank you all for showing up tonight and putting your money toward such an important cause. I am sorry you all had the misfortune of bidding against my son."

All at once, the woman's eyes found her own, and she raised her glass in June's direction. June froze. This was the preface of at least nineteen of her nightmare hell rotations.

And then, Diego raised his glass and everything made sense all at once. Her eyes weren't on June, they were on her son. On *Diego*. The crowd turned their attention back to the woman on the stage, continuing with her explanation for the expense and what the AAFV had managed to accomplish this year. June whirled on Diego, her plastered-on, falsified smile quickly giving way to absolute shock and horror. "That's your *mother*?"

He gave her no answer, only smiled at the stage, clearly pleased.

She swallowed hard, swarmed with embarrassment over the implications that his mother's charity was a scam. "You didn't tell me it was your family's organization."

He shrugged. "You didn't ask."

Asshole.

He hadn't told her on purpose. Because he knew she'd never come. How many of these rich snobs were family? Catalina should have been her first clue. No, *Spain* should have been her first clue. An art auction in Spain, and somehow that hadn't clued her in. Was he truly deceptive enough to hide this from her, or was she really just that dense?

June sat through the rest of the speech in utter silence, staring up at the woman in amazement. Reyes Cortez, as she introduced herself.

"Cortez?" She asked, shooting a look at Diego.

He shrugged. "*María* is my aunt."

June gulped. How many of the people he had surrounded her with had been family?

She stared up at the stage, feeling the blood drain from her face.

Diego's mother. For some reason, she had thought he simply

spawned into existence, like from those ancient tales. Some god carved him out of gold, or he walked out of a painting, a deity's hand-carved creation come to life. But there stood his mother, with the same handsome curls, honeyed eyes, and proud Spanish nose. They were identical.

The woman—Diego's mother—said something about dancing and music and drinks, and June came to understand the auction was over. With another round of applause, music rang out from a string sextet in the corner, and the crowd began to mingle, dispersing to the bar to network.

Diego opened his mouth to say something, but June's eyes were already on a door in the corner. She dropped his arm and turned for it, leaving him and whatever he was about to argue about planted firmly in place as the venue turned into a dance floor.

Chapter Eleven

June had no idea where she was going, only that she had to get away from this stuffy, snobby mess. She found her way into the hallway and to a set of stairs leading away from the conglomeration of gaudy show ponies on the first floor.

She hiked up her skirts, following the trail until it opened up to a rooftop terrace and the intoxicating coolness of the night. Still humid, and warm—this was Spain, after all—but a more welcome heat than the one caused by Diego breathing down her neck. Cities in Europe were different from those in America, so often focused on art rather than industry, and Valencia was no different. It was enchanting. Like those fae traps in storybooks. Dazzling lights, endless parties, constant food and wine. Great until you realize you've danced your feet bloody and there is no stopping. She didn't trust it. She didn't trust *him*.

As if sensing her contentment without him, the door flew open and the Spaniard rushed through, searching wildly. The moment he found her, he visibly relaxed, letting out a huff of breath and running his hands through his perfectly quaffed hair. Perhaps the action would have made her cringe on someone else, ruining perfection, but Diego's hair somehow always managed to fall to frame his face, and this new adornment only served to make him twice as handsome.

She turned away from him, bracing herself against the railing, feigning sudden interest in architecture in hopes it would drive him to leave. It did not.

He found his way beside her, forcing himself into her peripherals and the line of sight she so desperately attempted to keep him out of. "What was that?"

June's answer was immediate. "Go back inside."

"No." His voice was firmer than she'd ever heard, downright angry against his usual playful demeanor. "Not until you tell me what I've done to make you so angry with me."

June clenched her jaw, refusing to so much as look at him. "I said go inside, Diego."

He caught her by the arm, pulling her to face him. "I don't get it. The best hotel, the best designer, best drinks, and dresses, and restaurants, not to mention that painting—"

She whirled on him, shoving him back and away from her. Diego stumbled back, clearly caught off guard as he lost his grip on her. "I'm not just something for you to throw money at!" She marched forward, closing the space she had put between them as she dug her pointer finger into his chest. "*Your* girl, in the hotel *you* booked, in *your* limo, at *your* family's so-called 'charity event'. That painting was the cherry on top! This was all some ego trip and we both know it!" She forced her hands to her sides, clenching her dress in her fists as she stepped back, forcing her voice and breathing to calm.

The only accompaniment to their silence was the ever-flowing noise of the city below. The air between them went cold and quiet.

Diego's eyes narrowed toward her dangerously. "Ego trip?" he repeated with a humorless chuckle. "You act as if not participating does anything other than stroke your pride."

June opened her mouth to argue, but decided against it. Was he really that far off? Didn't it please her to set herself apart from these people?

Diego took a step back, hands wide open as though offering himself up to her chopping block. "You know me so well, fine. Answer this: who is Will Astor?" When she couldn't provide an answer, he stepped forward, lowering his voice to an icy tone. "Why does my mother run an organization against domestic violence?"

There was a bitter twinge to his voice that left her mouth feeling dry, her mind trying to conjure any other answer than the one he was insinuating. June swallowed hard, staring up at him through stubborn brows.

"This version of me that you've conjured in your head, he sure has it good, doesn't he?" He shook his head, letting out a humorless laugh. "You know nothing of my family. Nothing of my mother. Of the sacrifices she has made. So forgive me if I want her to see my face front and center while I pay some of it back, but I have no reason to apologize."

June could do nothing more than stop and stare. Of all the excuses she had been expecting—of poor people in need of money, and charity, and ends justifying means—this had been the last one she would have imagined.

Diego drew a deep breath, closing his eyes as he let it out and rubbed his hands over his face—like a reset before once again offering her the same Diego she had known all along. The kind smile. The playful mischief bottled up in the package of the competitive racer. "I don't want to fight, June. Let's forget this," he offered, accompanied with an outstretched hand. "Come dance with me."

Diego had an incredible talent for smoothing her ruffled feathers. For easing her worries. Putting her back in her place without wounding her pride and causing her to throw up walls. He made her better. She hated it.

She shook her head, not in rejection, but in disbelief. She took his hand and let him lead her off the terrace, down the stairs and to the dance floor. Silence passed between the two, a careful understanding in the hands clasped together.

Only when she was tucked safely against his chest, with the swell of a string sextet and a piano, did she finally let the words slip. "I'm sorry."

His answer was immediate, rumbling through her with her head so close to his chest. "Don't be."

"But I am." She pulled back, just enough to meet his eyes. To make sure he knew how genuine the words were.

He offered her a soft smile, any frustration with her slowly melting into gentle affection as he dropped his hold on her lower back, raising one hand to stroke her cheek. "Apology accepted."

He drew her back into his embrace, her head placed against his chest softly.

"... Who is Will Astor?"

Diego grimaced, tensed immediately, swore under his breath in Spanish. He took a deep breath before he spoke again. "My family got in a rough spot when I was growing up. My mom sold her favorite collection of art to get us out. Easily worth five million euros. He bought it for two million. My mom took it so she could keep me going in Formula Three. When I signed in Formula One, I tried to buy it back. Offered him ten million for the collection. He sold each painting individually to anyone who would buy it. I've spent eight million just to get half of the collection back."

Rough spot? June raised an eyebrow, still tucked against his chest. "I thought your dad was a millionaire."

He shrugged casually. "He had plenty of money. He just chose gambling and parties with it. My *mamá* left him and took Bianca and I with. Taking care of us was her punishment."

"Didn't she divorce him? Take half?"

Diego let out a bitter laugh at the sentiment. "There was nothing left to take when she left. He lost everything. Every cent. The house, the cars. My *mamá* had put money away for Bianca and me, but . . . when you're underage, you have to have a parent on your bank account."

June's heart dropped to her stomach. "He . . . he gambled *your* money?"

Diego merely shrugged, like he'd come to terms with it. Like it was merely a plot point in some movie rather than his own life. "All we had left was my mother's jewelry and art. She sold everything. For us."

She nodded, allowing him to slowly lead her, swaying across the dance floor. She thought of all his fancy things. Of his nice cars and expensive watches and luxurious suits. She found herself staring down at the gold watch and rings on his hand, and he laughed, catching her line of thinking. "Yes. I prefer to wear it now."

June flushed at having been caught, but he paid no mind to it at all as he gazed down at the watch on his wrist. "Numbers in an account mean nothing. But there is no losing it all so long as you never keep it all in one place."

A strange fondness washed over her so intensely that she had to look away. When she was seventeen, Mama Odie found all her cash in a coffee can and taught her never to store it all together. Some in an old pair of shoes, some under the mattress, some in her sock drawer. She hadn't expected someone like Diego to care about that kind of thing.

She swallowed hard, willing herself to speak. It seemed to be another part of their game—a truth for a truth. ". . . My dad was a real peach, too."

A beat passed in silence as Diego seemed to process. "Was? He's no longer with us?"

"God, I wish." The words were out before she could stop them.

Then, upon remembering that was not a thing normal people wished on their parents, she quickly backpedaled, embarrassment fanning her cheeks. "I mean—That's not—"

But Diego didn't flinch at her brutal honesty, only laughed at her bluntness. "I know what you mean. Sometimes I think it would be easier to love him if I could regret hating him so much. Now, there is only the hate."

It was the last thing she had expected from Diego. Something so harrowingly true to her own soul that he could have read it from her own diary.

"And your mother?" he asked, smoothly leading the conversation as if he had not just put words to a feeling June could never name.

She stared at him for a moment, still in disbelief as she simply shook her head at the hope in his open-ended question. "They were a pair for a reason."

"Ah," he said simply. "I know they hadn't supported you much financially, but I had . . . hoped otherwise as far as being supportive."

June offered a tight-lipped smile, hoping her bitterness didn't show. She'd always thought she would have been perfectly content with just one decent parent. How unfair that some people got two.

"Thank you . . . for telling me about him. I'm sorry for all the shit I said about Daddy's money and all that. I never would have had I known."

He softened, pleased with her response as he held her closer to him. "I know. Maybe that's why I wanted you here so badly this weekend. To show a bit of truth. What do we have in this agreement if not trust? No contract, no papers signed, no NDAs . . . but I can trust you. Can't I?"

Could he? It wasn't as if they were friends. It was publicity. A chance to further her career. A chance for him to further his. They were using one another. That was all. She was sure she could sell his secrets to a journalist for a mighty fine price, but they were safe with her. Secrets were worth a lot more than money, and Diego's trust couldn't be bought. Slowly, June nodded.

Diego smiled down at her. "And you can trust me."

June blinked. In that single moment, he caught her hesitation, his smile faltering as he leaned in closer. "You *can* trust me."

She knew that. But she didn't. She wouldn't. She wasn't that naive. She forced a smile, clearing her throat and changing the subject. "I still don't want that painting."

Diego barked out a laugh, and several people turned to glare at them. He paid them no mind. "Oh, me neither. Modern art is horrendous."

June stumbled in her confusion, and Diego caught her with a gentle laugh, grinning down at her when she turned to look him in the eye to see if he was joking. "But—you—"

"Bought a million euros worth? I know." He leaned in closer, lowering his voice as though he were letting her in on the secret of a lifetime. "It wouldn't be called a charity event if the art was good. That's what benefits are for, *Vaquera*."

This time, it was June who laughed, and when the crowd turned to glare daggers at the pair, she stifled her giggles in his chest and let him lead her through the dance.

The night dissolved in a blur. Their friends paired off, clearly pleased with each other's company. As much as she wanted to scold the girls for disappearing on her, they were happy. Despite her wariness, Diego's friends actually seemed decent. Olivia and Lola had happily picked their poison, and she nearly felt bad about it. They were all hung up on the idea of June and Diego. The idea that this ragtag group would be the new normal. She wished she could make it so, just for them. But it didn't change the fact that these people were not her friends outside of this facade. As the crowd waned, their crew rushed back to the bar for more drinks before the bar closed, and Diego grabbed her hand, eyeing their friends over her shoulder before he led her through the museum and away from the party.

Diego supplied her with another glass of wine he snagged from a waiter's tray before he held a door open for her. June had become familiar with the way he moved enough to understand this was more a demand than a request, but it was one June was happy to oblige. The music and dancing had gotten to be too much, and she was more than happy to find her way into the abandoned hallway. The main lights were turned off, but display lights hung over each painting, casting shadows on the floor and keeping the room a pleasant level of brightness.

The music faded away until the only thing she could hear was the sound of her heels echoing against the floor as the door closed behind them. June's lips parted in awe, staring down the line of art on display up and down the hall. She walked to the nearest one, an oil on canvas print of a Spanish city in a golden frame. "Are we . . . allowed back here?" Her voice sounded foreign in her ears, still tingling from such an abrupt change of atmosphere.

Diego shrugged, walking up to stand beside her, his eyes on the painting. "Definitely not, but my *mamá* donated most of these paintings, so they will get over it." June huffed out an amused breath, watching as Diego wiggled his brows at her in her peripherals. "If they catch us, that is."

June shook her head and rolled her eyes at him, stepping down the line of paintings, not bothering to wait for Diego. June had always loved museums. Loved art. To have it all to herself was intoxicating.

"Anything you like?" he asked, leaning casually against the wall. She could feel his eyes on her as he followed her from one painting to the next, paying more attention to her than the art on the walls. He must have been here dozens of times before, and still, he'd been eager to share it with her.

June chuckled to herself, reaching out to run her hand along the glass protecting a golden frame. "I'm afraid to answer that. You might end up buying it for me."

Diego laughed, and June turned to look at him—to see that charming smile on his face—only to find him with his phone raised and pointed at her. She stopped, brows furrowing at him. "What are you doing?"

He shrugged. "Collecting evidence." He raised his phone to take another picture and she stuck her tongue out at him, pulling faces until he lowered it again, glaring at her in feigned irritation.

"Evidence?" she asked, crossing her arms across her chest and eyeing him skeptically.

His face deadpanned. "Have you even heard of soft-launching?"

June snorted, rolling her eyes at him as she turned back to the painting, arms crossed over her chest. "You sound like Olivia now."

"Hm. Olivia seems like a very smart girl."

She shook her head, letting out a soft huff of laughter. Diego wasn't wrong. Olivia was extremely perceptive, to an annoying level. "More so when she isn't trying to force me on you," she pointed out.

Diego hummed thoughtfully. "Well, if that's the case then I owe her flowers and a goodie basket." June rolled her eyes at him and he immediately broke into a cheeky grin. "Don't lie. You like me a little, right?"

She watched him carefully for a long while, drawing steady breaths in the silence. Diego knew how to play the game, he was good at it. A top contestant. All fine and dandy until he met someone who refused to entertain it. "I like sponsors," she said softly. "Sponsors like attention. You get me attention. So, yes. I suppose I like you enough."

Diego's cheeky smile faded slowly into an unreadable look that June couldn't decipher for the life of her. Was he disappointed? Angry? Unbothered? She couldn't be sure. A tense silence stretched between them, as if a veil had been lifted, leaving them both painfully aware of what their arrangement really was.

He cleared his throat abruptly, looking away from her. "Alright, you like the attention? Here."

Diego shrugged off his suit jacket, leaving him in a white undershirt and a waistcoat. She allowed her eyes half a second to roam over him before he stepped forward and her gaze snapped up to meet his. "What are you—"

Before she could process what was happening, he had her by the arm. "Turn for me." Strange desire hit her like a kick to the stomach at his simple command, and without another word, she obliged. He stepped forward, draping his jacket around her shoulders. The scent of his cologne overwhelmed her senses, the dark scent of magnolia and sandalwood. It was several sizes too big, and she could still feel the lingering heat from his body seeping into her.

"I don't understand—"

"Come on, it adds to the intrigue." He positioned the jacket carefully on her shoulders. "There. Now it's obvious you are with someone."

He lingered a moment longer, his hand on her arm like he couldn't bring himself to pull away yet, and she cast a glance back at him over her shoulder.

The look in his eyes was almost predatory. The room felt smaller around them, the air thicker. For a moment, she was all too aware of how close they were standing. And for some inexplicable reason, she didn't want him to pull away. Everything was too hot—too close. Even the chill of the marble hallway wasn't enough to stamp it out. She tried to clear her head, to tell herself they were creating a narrative and this was all part of the act, but his hand still lingered on her shoulder and his eyes were boring into hers.

"This is ridiculous," she said, feigning a coolness she didn't feel. His proximity was setting her on fire.

Diego cocked his head to the side. "Nothing is ridiculous so long as they buy it."

Part of her knew he was right. His team, the sponsors, the fans . . . it all came down to them. She just hadn't anticipated how good he was at playing his part.

He stepped back finally, and June was torn between disappointment and relief. "Walk," he ordered. June obeyed.

She could hear his footsteps following her own, and it was impossible not to be aware of the fact that he was right behind her, just a few steps away.

She could still feel the ghost of his touch lingering on her skin.

"Stiff as a board. You are awful at candids."

"This isn't candid!" she exclaimed, and Diego laughed, a loud, intoxicating laugh that left her grinning too. She cast a look at him over her shoulder, only to meet Diego's raised camera. He captured the moment, lowering the phone, clearly pleased with his result. "There," he said softly. "Perfect."

Part of her wished she hadn't looked back. The sight of him smiling at a photo of her on his phone—his hair mussed, donning that easy, charming grin—sent a jolt through her. Something she didn't want to put a name to.

"Satisfied?" she asked, forcing her tone to be casual.

"Completely," he said softly. He moved forward, reaching to retrieve his jacket from her shoulders. "You want attention? That picture will get you it."

The moment Diego's hand landed on the jacket, June drew back. "It's cold. I'm keeping this."

Diego's brows shot up, taken aback by her refusal. "Oh, you think so? I'm afraid you don't get that option, *Princesa*." He stepped forward, the space between them narrowing until he loomed over her, fingertips grazing the fabric of the jacket.

She tried to not to be overly aware of just how close he was, boxing her against the wall of the hallway. She wasn't going to let him see that she was starting to lose her resolve.

"And why not?" Her voice came out far more steady than she felt.

He leaned in close enough that his breath ghosted across her face, his voice deep and gravelly. "You're fucking divine in that dress. It would be a crime to cover you up."

The moment his words hit her, tingles shot through her body. In the time she'd known Diego, he'd always come with witty jokes or cheeky comments, but nothing had ever sounded quite like that. His voice had dropped an octave, and that dark tone sent a shiver through her, leaving her frozen in place as he leaned in closer. There was a level of intimacy she hadn't expected. It was all just part of the act, but the way her skin tingled at his proximity said otherwise.

He reached forward, his hand sliding down the curve of her neck. His touch burned against her skin, seared like a brand. Her brain told her to shrink away, to create distance, but her body was frozen in place. He was so close now, his body just inches from hers. His finger hooked under her chin, tilting her head up to look at him.

The moment their eyes locked, the last bits of rationale crumbled around her. His eyes had darkened, the usual playful look replaced with something primal and raw. A heat that sent sparks straight to her core.

His hand trailed to the back of her neck, his touch feather-light, fingers splayed across the side of her throat. June shuddered as his fingers sunk into the curls at the back of her neck, his body grazing hers. This was bad. This was very, very bad. Because June couldn't tell him no.

In a single quick move, Diego pulled back and snagged his jacket, throwing it over his shoulder.

And just like that, it was over. All of the heat and tension cut so suddenly it left her reeling. Diego grinned, pleased with himself, and turned on his heel. "Come on," he called without looking back as he made his way up the line of paintings. "The others will wonder where we are."

A wave of frustration surged through her, cursing her own blindness to him blatantly toying with her. She had to take a moment to breathe, to collect herself, to will the heat that was surging through her body to die back down. *Bastard.*

It was payback for her earlier comment and they both knew it. For saying she didn't like him. A game. With one final breath, she gathered her skirts and followed him back into the party.

Chapter Twelve

"Can't believe you and Diego fucked in that hallway."

"Oh my God, Olivia." June buried her face in her hands. She sat in the center of the backseat, with the girls on either side of her, and Charlene riding passenger. No matter how many times June had told her contrary, Olivia was going to die on the hill that *something* had happened when the two of them disappeared.

"Oh, one hundred percent," Lola provided. "Did you see her face when she walked back in?"

"You should have seen his," came Olivia's voice from beside her. "Cat got the cream if you're picking up what I'm putting down." She barked out a laugh, smacking her hand across her knee.

Lola snorted. "Your poker face sucks, June. His mom probably knew you guys were getting freaky in her museum."

Olivia pushed herself forward. "Wait—how big? Say when." She held her hands up for size, slowly pulling them further apart. June didn't say when, watching as her hands went further and further apart. "Holy shit," she said after a minute, her hands far apart enough to fit a whole saddle. "Are you serious?"

Lola cackled and they erupted in a slew of arguments and contradictions, desperate for the juicy details of something that never even happened. She considered making something up just to get them to leave her alone.

Charlene piped up from the front seat, eyeing her in the rearview mirror. She raised a matter-of-fact lecture finger. "June, at the height of your career you have to know how important protection is."

Her face went beet red, and she wanted to scream. "Oh my God, Char! I'm not some horny teenager!"

"The healthier you are, the more fertile! With two athletes, a condom may not always be enough."

Olivia raised a finger in the air. "Uh, somebody needs to fact-check that—"

June buried her face in her hands. "Everybody shut up!—"

"Stop blushing and listen! If you need to get on birth control—"

June yanked her hat off and flung it at Charlene, then tossed her shoes, her bag, and anything else within reach. The car erupted into chaos, the girls screaming with laughter at June's expense. She was just as eager to dish it out.

June whirled on Olivia, "I'm sorry, who was on the arm of a *white boy* all night?"

Olivia's jaw dropped, clapping a hand over her mouth, followed by a muffled, "... Guilty."

In a matter of moments, their teasing turned to shared thirsting. Lola groaned, flopping dramatically across June and Olivia's laps. "I would chop my own hand off to take Catalina on a date."

"Put your seatbelt on," Charlene chastised.

She was promptly ignored.

"Okay, what is in those Cabrera genes because oh my *God*?" Olivia exclaimed.

The girls erupted in agreement, their car hurtling down the road.

Olivia sighed dreamily. "I would pay Oscar to take me home."

Charlene eyed her in the rearview mirror. "That's illegal, Olivia."

She groaned in protest, running her hands over her face.

June bit back a grin, shaking her head fondly at the girls. Despite it all, they'd actually enjoyed themselves. She supposed she had Diego to thank for that. She sighed heavily, picking up her phone as she let the girls explode around her.

She so rarely texted people outside of her team and it was embarrassingly easy to find his name.

> **JUNE: everyone is hounding me for details on how you are in bed. should i tell them how underwhelming it was?**
>
> **DIEGO: easy, Junebug. i'm always happy to refute false claims.**

June blushed, grinning down at her phone, butterflies swarming her stomach and the girls went suspiciously quiet around her. She jerked her head up from her phone to find them staring at her, donning bright, mischievous grins. "*Ooooooo*," Olivia cooed and June sank down into her seat as they exploded in laughter.

Even Charlene beamed from the front seat. "Oh, June's in *love*—"

June reached forward to pinch her, and Charlene yelped, the others howling with laughter. June groaned, sinking into her seat and burying her face in her hands as she readied for another round of merciless banter.

To Diego's credit, their plan worked. Any mention of June's piss-poor performance this year was swallowed up in the possible romance brewing between the two athletes. June's social media pages were entirely hijacked by it. The picture Diego had taken made it onto gossip pages the day it was posted, fans desperate for the pair to confirm their relationship—a confirmation that wouldn't come. The moment Diego was somewhere, Olivia and Lola were posting throwback photos to the same place, secretive posts that fans dissected as though their lives depended on it. It didn't matter that it was falsified. Fans were paying attention to anything other than her poor work in the ring.

But the distraction would only serve for so long.

June had work to do. Hades had to progress. Fast.

Every move June made was to become a better athlete. It consumed her entire life. From the horrific workouts she forced herself to endure, to the food she ate, the way she slept, and the content she consumed. All strength. All horses. All jumping. She hadn't imagined that being a professional rider would mean so little time in the saddle. Even less so was spent actually jumping.

They focused on flatwork. Focused on quick turns, on adaptability, being able to go from a flat-out sprint to nearly a stop to turn. They only jumped twice a week, and when they did, it was smaller than the heights they actually competed. But when they did jump, it was magic. So, June spent every second bettering herself out of the saddle to prepare for those few moments in.

It was May. She had three competitions this month alone. She *had* to work harder.

June stretched and put her headphones on, turning her music up until she knew Charlene would scold her for the volume. She hopped on the treadmill, starting at a casual walk, forcing herself to hold back, but every step she took fell quicker until she was damn near sprinting off the machine.

Movement was the only cure when she got like this. She'd always been a runner—from her family, her feelings, her problems.

She got it from her mother.

June turned her gaze out over the courtyard, her legs propelling her forward until her lungs ached and her mind finally cleared. The only trouble with being an athlete was that each time she pushed herself, it took more to exhaust her. She had to run faster for the right burn. Had to exert herself harder for the ache that soothed her.

June's phone buzzed from where it rested in a cup holder and she picked it up. A text from Diego. She slowed the treadmill to a walk, opening the message.

It was a selfie of Diego from the inside of an ice bath, his curls wet and pressed to his head. Even wet, his hair was perfect. It pissed her off. His bottom lip was pushed out in an overdramatic pout, the camera angled down to show off the perfect sculpting of his shoulders and pecs.

PUNCHING BAG: they're torturing me :((

The last thing June needed was a shirtless picture of Diego in her inbox while she was mid-workout.

JUNE: very subtle with the camera angle.

PUNCHING BAG: GASP are you checking me out? i sent you this so you can have proof that they murdered me, not so you could fantasize about me

June rolled her eyes. Two could play this game. She posed in front of the gym mirror, flexing her biceps and her abs, offering him a kissy face. She grinned, pleased with the photo.

JUNE: my abs are better anyway

Her phone was quiet for a long moment, and a strange anxiety settled in her gut. Not like she cared anyway, only that she felt strange and awkward and—her phone pinged.

**PUNCHING BAG: sorry had to teach myself
how to breathe again
PUNCHING BAG: if i would have known
all it would take to get
a sweaty mirror selfie
was a shirtless pic
i would have led with that.**

June laughed out loud, equally relieved and flattered when the next message arrived.

**PUNCHING BAG: also i've been told my
body is a professional work of art,
thank you very much
so if you need more pics to prove that
i'm more than happy to give you a better look.**

           JUNE: narcissist

PUNCHING BAG: just sharing the love.

The next weekend brought surprising quiet from Diego. She finished her flatwork sessions on Thursday, opening her phone to find no new messages, and again Friday. And again Saturday. It disappointed her and she hated it. She'd sent selfies with the horses. Pictures of Amelia's demented pug that Diego always laughed at. She finally changed his name to *Diego* in her phone, as if that would be enough to somehow summon him. She received nothing more than quick responses and absolute radio silence.

It was Sunday night when June's phone lit up and she went diving across the couch to it.

DIEGO: did you watch the race?

JUNE: what race?

DIEGO: i knew you hated me
DIEGO: MY race

And suddenly her worry felt utterly ridiculous. She'd gotten so caught up in her own worries she forgot Diego had a life outside of their deal.

JUNE: . . . am i in trouble

DIEGO: depends on why
you weren't watching

JUNE: i was saving a box full
of orphaned kittens

DIEGO: you are so full of shit

JUNE: fine. can i make
a tiny confession?

DIEGO: you're wildly in love
with me and
can't stop thinking
about me? that's nothing
we didn't already know. but okay.

JUNE: i hate racing

DIEGO: WHAT????

DIEGO: dammit i knew you were
too good to be true
DIEGO: you are confessing to a CRIME

                              JUNE: sorry!!! just the truth!!!!

DIEGO: :((((
DIEGO: i'm mostly teasing btw.
plenty of people don't
enjoy racing. it's not your thing, i get it.

                            JUNE: no it's not like that.
                                i actually hate racing

DIEGO: OMG!!! SHUT UP!!!!
i'm trying to justify your bullshit!!!!
DIEGO: what racer did you know?

                            JUNE: what do you mean?

DIEGO: nobody hates racing
unless they've known a driver.
DIEGO: fess up. was it
an ex-boyfriend?
DIEGO: tell him i want to race. i'll win

                                      JUNE: yeah it was

DIEGO: are you fr

                                            JUNE: no

DIEGO: so you're just saying
stuff to piss me off on purpose?

                            JUNE: it's cute when
                            you get all jealous :))

DIEGO: i'm not jealous!
i just don't understand!
how can you hate something
that's clearly the

best sport in the world?

                                  JUNE: excuse you!!!
                                 my sport is RIGHT there

DIEGO: is showjumping
even a sport?

                           JUNE: i'm going to pretend
                           you didn't say that purely
                             because i need you alive
                                  for this agreement

DIEGO: if i'm cute when i'm jealous,
you're adorable when you're pissed off :))))
DIEGO: you going to tell me
why you hate racing?

                                            JUNE: no.
                           JUNE: but it isn't personal.
                             JUNE: so don't hate me

DIEGO: I could never hate you

Chapter Thirteen

There was once a time when Mama Odie had asked June if she knew how to drive. She did, of course, despite being twelve and without a license. She was familiar with runs to the gas station, barn, and grocery store in her father's car when he was too drunk to drive. It was simple enough. Gas, brake, steering wheel. Of course she knew how to drive. It was that day June learned about a stick-shift. Manual versus automatic transmissions.

Stick, brake, clutch, gears, accelerator, all thrown together in a mess. The more she applied thought and reason, the more she killed the engine and came up short. If Midus was an automatic, Hades was a manual with a sticky clutch.

And Oviatt was an automatic with an F1 engine, spongy brakes, no power steering, and a death wish.

June didn't make it through a single grand prix clear the entire month of May. She rode Hades.

The month of June brought with it three more competitions. It would take Midus to bring her back from that. A Midus she no longer had.

Amelia hadn't said a thing all session, watching. Observing. Judging. Her job, but it still always felt personal.

After a particularly disastrous jumping session with Hades, June took him to untack. Isa went to take the horse from her, but she quickly declined. She needed a distraction from Amelia's ever-scrutinizing gaze. She untacked and hosed him down, applied ice boots on his legs, and placed him in front of an industrial fan to cool down. Hades leaned heavily on her shoulder as she scratched his wet neck. He knew when things didn't go to plan, and he always took it personally. She scratched where mane met neck and the gelding relaxed under her touch.

June heard the tell-tale sound of Amelia's boots clacking down the barn aisle. Amelia walked over, arms crossed over her chest as usual, watching the two curiously while keeping a good few feet between her and the towering gelding. "You're getting wet."

June blinked, her lighthearted grin dissolving into one of dread. How foolish to think she could escape Amelia in her own barn.

"I know," June said shortly.

Amelia shook her head solemnly, as though she had read her mind and found it falling short. "I never should have sold you that horse."

June's heart faltered, her stomach sinking, like the floor had been pulled out from under her. ". . . What?"

"He's not champion material. I knew this. I should have sold him to some little girl, not my student."

June blinked. Her words stung deep. *Some little girl.*

"You're too emotional, June. You make this sport about emotions when it is not. I used to think the same when I was younger. You think you have a special connection with every horse you ever ride, but the truth is, these horses . . . they can be your ticket to points, or the reason you lose. And that horse is the reason you are losing."

June wondered if getting shot would hurt less. Or stabbed. Or having her ribs broken one by one, or a finger ripped off and sewed back on.

Amelia didn't believe in her.

She tsked, shaking her head at June. "When you fail, it's on me for selling you that horse in the first place." *When you fail*. Not if.

"He's not what you need, June."

June had become quite accustomed to clenching her teeth in the barn. It was the only place she did so. Amelia the only person she allowed to speak so freely. Hades was exactly the horse she needed. The horse she loved to ride. The horse she felt safe on. The horse who would do anything to keep her safe.

June didn't say a word, rage building in her chest.

Amelia turned to walk away and June swore sharply, whirling to face her. "I'll ride Oviatt!"

It was the answer Amelia was looking for and she knew it. Amelia turned to face her, raising a brow. "Oh?"

June nodded. "I'll ride him. I'm ready. We can do it."

Amelia hummed thoughtfully, but she nodded in agreement before she turned to go. The moment she was out of sight, June let out a breath, relief and terror bundled into one. She shouted in frustration, slamming her hand down on the iron rail of the hitching post. Hades jumped. He wasn't like Midus. He wasn't used to her and her fits of rage.

This was a war June refused to lose. No matter the cost. June rode Oviatt. Amelia coached. That was all June needed.

Oviatt stood in the cross-ties, saddled and ready to go. That was the problem. He was always ready to go. June hated him. Each ride on Oviatt was a test of wit and will. The horse was as volatile as he was talented and June found herself clinging stubbornly to his back.

Every time she swung on that horse, she wondered if it would be the last, but if it came between keeping herself or her career alive, June knew which one she would choose.

In a week and a day, Valkenswaard was upon them. June was in no way, shape, or form ready. Still, the day was there, like a wave crashing down upon her. No amount of determination could make up for the time she had lost.

June didn't sleep, tossing and turning through the night.

The morning was even worse. Her mind was racing, her stomach tied in knots, and every nerve in her body was on high alert. She wandered the venue, her heart pounding so fiercely she figured she might as well put the adrenaline to use.

She found Lola, who wrapped her in a tight embrace, trying to comfort her through the nerves. June did her best to play it cool, but she was practically shaking with adrenaline, unable to remain still.

"You need to eat, June."

Even the thought of food made her sick.

Still, she found her way to the concessions and got her hands on a pretzel, choking it down. She wanted a drink. Desperately. A single shot. Just a little bit of something. She cast her eyes back towards the stand. She couldn't drink on the job. She couldn't. But her eyes still wandered toward the beer garden. They had to be selling something—*anything* to quell her nerves.

"Vaquera."

June froze like she'd been slapped, her eyes rocketing up, widening in horror. Sure enough, there was Diego, walking down the hallway toward her, wearing pleated trousers and a polo with another ridiculously expensive watch.

June abandoned her food on the nearest table, entirely disregarding anything except the idiot in front of her. She snagged him by the wrist, watching as his face contorted in confusion and then shock as she dragged him through the nearest door, slamming it behind them and flicking on the lights.

"What are you doing here?"

His brows raised in amusement, surveying their surroundings. "In the janitor's closet? I was hoping you'd tell me, *Vaquera*."

June blinked. And glanced. And then her face caught on fire. Of fucking course of all the places they could have wound up, it'd be the location of every cheesy romance's best make-out scenes. "Shut up. Why are you here?"

He beamed at that, clearly pleased with how riled she was. "I've come to watch you, obviously."

Her answer was immediate. "No." This could not be happening. Of all the times he could come to watch her ride, today was not the one. Oviatt was probably going to kill her and she did not need his trauma on her conscience. She stabbed her finger into his chest. "You are going to turn around, drive your happy ass back to the airport, and get on a plane. Got it?"

His shit-eating grin never faltered, his hand rising to flatten hers against his chest. "Lotus sent me, *Vaquera*. I'm here on business. We are each other's partners now, no?" He flashed her a charming smile.

Fuck.

She was nervous enough as it was. Adding Diego to the mix made everything so much worse. If Lotus was involved?

They'd want pictures and videos and interactions and questions and for him to meet the horses and her to explain the sport to him and—

June nearly bashed her head into the wall. Cameras on her and eyes on her. Her team, the public, and sponsors.

This was what you wanted, wasn't it?

If she was on Midus. If she was tearing through the season the way she had last year. If she wasn't having the shittiest luck of her entire life. Now? She wanted to shrink back into the wall and disappear.

She brought her fist up to her mouth, chewing nervously on her thumb. "You need to leave, Diego."

"I can't, *Vaquera*."

"You can," she insisted. "Tell them you're unwell—"

"I can't, June. I need this publicity as badly as you do. If it is your career or mine, I pick mine."

She grit her teeth, glowering up at him. Of course he picked his. The same way she picked hers. It was the nature of their sports. The nature of themselves. Nobody got this far without being a little selfish. June shook her head at him, but she could hardly be angry. They were two sides of the same coin. She fisted the front of his shirt, yanking him forward as she glowered up at him. He blinked down at her, brows shooting up in surprise. "Stay out of my way, or this deal is off."

Despite himself, the corners of his lips quirked up. *"Sí, Señora."*

June's rage dulled to a simmer at his acceptance, biting the inside of her bottom lip. She had too much on her plate to waste energy on Diego. "Wait five minutes before you come out of here."

He surged after her, catching her by the wrist before she could grab the door handle. "June—"

June ripped her hand out of his grasp, pointing a finger in his face instead. "Five minutes!"

Diego deflated, pouting at her, but he made no move to follow. She threw the door open and slammed it behind her, shaking off her nerves as she marched down the rest of the hallway. And then she paused, marching up to the bar trailer and ordering a glass of whiskey.

Chapter Fourteen

I *don't have to do this.*

The thought came every now and then, obliterating her focus and destroying the determination she relied on. As she sat on the back of the chestnut stallion, the thought rang through again and again. She didn't have to do this. She could pull out now. She could pack her bags, go back to Texas, turn Hades out in a field and let him live the rest of his life doing whatever he wanted. She could jump him in local shows for fun. Could take him out to ride the river. He wouldn't know the difference. He wouldn't care. He didn't know the stakes.

No more press junkets. No more stupid Lotus events. No more scandals. No more sponsors. No more blinding pain in her body from constantly pushing the limits.

No more ribbons. No more naps in Hades' stall. No more sneaking iced coffee around in a Lotus can. No more washing away the sweat of a Grand Prix showjumper. No more almosts. No more signing. No more chances. No more Diego. No more Charlene, Lola, and Olivia—

She thought briefly about Alessia. Not June—but Alessia Junior Walker. The little girl who begged her neighbors to get on a horse. The girl who fought for this. She imagined looking her in the eyes and telling her: *we made it. We jumped professionally. We had the chance to be champions—it was too hard.*

I quit.

She clenched her teeth, collecting Oviatt under her, focused down the line of his neck between his ears.

She couldn't quit. She could scream and cry and curse the whole time—but she couldn't quit.

"Don't come apart on me." It was half a plea, half a threat. They called for her. Everything went quiet. Immediately, Oviatt was chomping at the bit, hopping in place as if he understood the announcer. She grit her teeth, pulling him to back a few steps only for him to rear up on his back legs. June swore sharply, surging forward to keep her balance until he slammed back down and she righted herself. She grimaced. "Dick."

She could feel as the pressure of thousands of sets of eyes came bearing down on her, the announcer selling some sob story about her and Midus. But June was no sad story.

The bell sounded. All that was left was June, Oviatt, and the course ahead. Instantly, Oviatt surged forward at a dead sprint. They were up and over the first oxer in a matter of three strides, headed down the long stretch to the second at a full gallop when Oviatt spotted a different jump, veering hard to the left.

June sat down in the saddle, clinging to him with all her might as she yanked his head up the side and dug her outside leg into him. No fucking chance was he going off course with her as a willing participant.

She gathered his attention in the nick of time, pushing him toward the correct jump. He locked onto the target and was off like a rocket again, surging up a stride too early. June pushed herself into position, swearing sharply as they landed on the other side. His back leg clipped the bottom pole, but it didn't budge. He'd fucked with her time, but they hadn't gone off course.

They landed and June immediately pushed him into a gallop towards the next jump. The world descended into white noise in her head as they sprinted toward the next oxer.

Only a few more jumps. No more trouble. It had to be finished, not pretty.

She kept tight contact with the reins as she pushed him into a quick gallop again, his powerful long strides bringing them quickly toward the triple combination. He soared up and over the first one, clearing it with ease. Then the second. Just one more. They were almost at the base of the fence. One stride. Two—

Oviatt lurched forward too soon. They got halfway across the jump before gravity won, bringing them down directly on top of the fence. Oviatt scrambled for his footing, his legs wrapped up in the fallen rails. June clung to him for dear life, desperate not to be thrown off and trampled. The crowd around her gasped, but she barely heard a thing.

Oviatt caught himself miraculously, lurching out of the mess. June's terror quickly turned to rage.

They'd failed.

The last jump, and he'd taken it with him. Not just one pole—an entire fucking fence.

The reality of it slammed into her like a ton of bricks. She exhaled, her eyes closing for a moment before the familiar feeling of rage and frustration started to swell inside of her. She wanted to scream and cry and curse—but instead, she stayed silent, her eyes burning with angry tears.

They were out of the time allowed, and they hadn't jumped clear. It was over. The crowd clapped, but there was no enthusiasm in their cheering, only sympathy. Even the commentators seemed to struggle as they moved on to the next rider. She bit her tongue, pushing back the wave of emotions.

Don't come apart. Don't come apart. Don't come apart.

She repeated the phrase in her head over and over, desperately trying to hold back everything she felt inside. She was too frustrated to cry or get angry or even react. She just wanted to disappear.

The world around her quieted until it was only the steady thump of her heart. She sat, frozen for a long moment, the weight of her failure hanging heavy on her shoulders. It wasn't just frustration or disappointment, it ran deep, shame and self-doubt weaving it's way into her soul. Isa took Oviatt from her, offering her sympathies and support, but all June wanted was to disappear. She found her way to the stalls, June and Amelia's tack and equipment crowded into one unoccupied by a horse.

In the solitude, keeping it together became a losing battle. All the frustration and disappointment that had been building up inside her suddenly came crashing down. She let herself collapse to the ground in a quiet corner, the tears finally streaming down her face.

She curled her arms around her legs, pulling them tightly against her body as she let herself cry.

June didn't know how to fail. Not like this, in front of the entire world. She was out. Again. A bad ride. She couldn't remember the last time she'd had a good one. She felt pathetic. Small and weak. The entire world had rested on her shoulders light as a feather last season, and now, it crushed her.

Maybe June wasn't cut out for this. She didn't like competing, she liked winning.

She didn't even notice Diego walking into the stalls until she suddenly heard the sound of his boots next to her. He sighed heavily, looking down on her. "Oh, *Vaquera*. Charlene told me you might be here—"

In an instant, June shot to her feet. All the grief in the world could not hold back her rage. At the competition, at the world, at her situation, at *him*.

June caught him by the front of his shirt, dragging him into the stall. She squared her shoulders and readied for a fight. "How dare you," she spat. "Showing up to my competition without warning? Who the hell do you think you are?"

Diego held his hands up innocence. "I came to check on you," he said calmly, trying to keep his voice steady and reasonable as he stepped forward as if to comfort her. "I thought you could use—"

"I don't need you here," June fired back, cutting him off mid-sentence. She shoved him back as he stepped forward. "I don't want you here!" she shouted. She couldn't bear the thought of him seeing her like this—vulnerable and weak, and as far from a champion as she could be when his career was just fine. She hated that he'd seen her fail. Even worse that he'd come looking for her, like she was a child who needed consoling.

Diego didn't falter, standing his ground as June gripped the front of his shirt and pushed him back until he hit the wall. His steady gaze only infuriated her more—focused and unwavering like he saw straight through her anger and into her horrific inadequacy. "Lotus gave me a ticket. Go back to the hotel. Go for a run."

June's anger flared red hot at his suggestion. "A run? A run doesn't fix this!" Nothing could. Nothing would. Her knuckles turned white, clenched in his polo as she hung her head, hands braced on his chest. Her embarrassment was hotter than her anger, so she turned it into rage. She had failed, and he was here.

She was supposed to be good.

She wanted to be good.

Diego sighed as if he'd read the thoughts in her head, his hands landing gently on her shoulders. "You had a rough go. Run a mile. Go for a walk. But I'm not going to be your punching bag again." A weak attempt at humor lingered in his voice, as though he were attempting to diffuse the rage coiled tightly in her gut.

June wanted to scream. Wanted to break something, throw a punch, smash her hand through a window. She looked at him standing there, stoic and still, hands braced on her arms. He wasn't angry, not even frustrated. Just calm. Cool. She took a step back, putting space between the two of them as she let go of his shirt, wrinkled where she'd gripped it. He took that as an invitation, stepping forward to tuck a stray hair behind her ear. "Go blow off some steam. I'll cover for you. I've been doing this a lot longer than you."

She smacked his hand away, a sharp gaze cutting up to him. "And yet whose seat is up for grabs?"

She hadn't even realized what she'd said until Diego's face fell. His expression darkened, his easy, cool demeanor fading. She felt the shift instantly, the anger that bubbled behind her skin reaching the surface, boiling over and leaving her with nothing but an empty pot. Her lips parted in surprise. "Diego, I—"

Diego took a step back, his face hardening. "See you at the afterparty."

Her brow furrowed in confusion, taking a step forward as he tried to leave. "What?"

"Siegfried won. The other Lotus rider. You should be there." His voice was cool and detached, refusing to look at her, his hand on the stall door. "Smile and wave and put on a show." Without another word, Diego pushed through.

June watched as he left, a deep regret settling in her gut. She collapsed back against the wall and sunk to the floor, finally allowing herself to sob in peace.

Chapter Fifteen

It was Siegfried himself who finally found June. They'd formed an odd partnership after so many years being the only two Lotus-sponsored equestrians. June clung to any familiar face she could find in her early days of competition, and he'd taken a liking to her.

He was dressed for the afterparty. He so rarely attended them that June was surprised out of her sulking. He must have returned to his hotel, showered, changed, and returned. June choked on her embarrassment. How long had she been crying on the floor like a complete loser?

Siegfried didn't say a word, just crouched in front of where she sat on the ground in the stall and stared at her for a few moments with an unreadable gaze. June swallowed hard and sniffed, wiping at her eyes with the back of her wrist. "Don't look at me like that."

He raised a brow. "Like what?"

"With pity."

Siegfried shrugged. "Don't look so pitiful."

June glared up at him, irritated and amused at his audacity all at once.

He cracked a grin, reaching down to offer her a hand. "Took me four years to even be in the running for the title. You're right on track."

His words brought relief nothing else could have. Siegfried had three title wins to his name—one more than Amelia. If it took him that long, maybe she wasn't so awful after all. She took his hand and he pulled her to her feet.

"Serves you right," he said. "You wiped the floor with me last year on Midus. Your turn." A strange mix of emotions flared in her gut at his words—insult and flattery at the same time. June dusted herself off, swallowing hard.

Siegfried slung an arm around her, guiding her out of the stables. Siegfried's car—a black 1970's Ford Falcon—waited for them outside the venue. Siegfried was one of the only people June knew without a personal driver. He drove himself everywhere and worshipped his car almost as much as he did Frieda.

He took her to her hotel and June offered her thanks, turning to leave when Siegfried caught her arm. "You have thirty minutes. Charlene asked me to bring you to her ready for a party."

June groaned, whirling around to face him. "Tell her I'm sick."

He tutted. "Sick in the head, if you think I'm letting you get away with that. If I have to go, so do you."

She threw her arms up in protest. "Why do you have to go?"

He hated the parties. It wouldn't be the first time he had won, and then completely skipped out on his own celebration.

He shrugged. "Charlene will kill me otherwise. You, too."

"Save me a spot in the graveyard—"

He snapped his fingers at her, voice sharpening. "Thirty minutes."

June sulked all the way back to her hotel room. She stripped. Showered. Threw on a sparkly black dress. Readied herself for the party.

June loved her sharp wit. She loved her quick tongue and her sarcasm that she refused to reel in. Amelia scolded her for it, but her

PR team had turned it into her brand. The girl who refused to do what she was told. Her fans loved her ruthlessness the same way she did.

Until she bit the wrong hand. Until she hurt someone she cared about. Until she snapped at Diego. It was a blessing as much as a curse, always knowing just what to say to make it sting.

Siegfried waited for June, letting out a low whistle when he saw her. "You see? A shower and a pretty dress and you are all better."

Despite herself, June smiled. She had known the creepy comments from older men her entire life—Siegfried was not like that. They bonded like a pair of stray animals, no care for age or gender when their circumstances were largely the same.

Siegfried opened the door for her and she filed into the passenger seat, deflating into the leather. The car hummed to life, an address pulled up on his phone. June sighed, looking out the window. "Why do I have to be so mean?" The words were out before she could stop them.

Siegfried hummed. "You are not mean."

"Bullshit," she scoffed.

"I am assuming this is about the boy who I passed in the barn that like he had been slapped?" He eyed her suspiciously. "Did you slap him? You seem to have quite the reputation with your boy."

"He's not—" June drew a sharp breath. "He's not *'my boy'*."

Siegfried shrugged. "A handsome one, nonetheless."

June groaned into her hands. "*Not* you, too!"

He laughed and June shot a playful scowl in his direction. "You're not a mean person, June. I had the same fire when I was younger. And I know you're not the type to go for money, which means that boy must have somewhat of a personality. Talk to him. He will understand, and if he doesn't, he shouldn't be in your life anyway."

Siegfried had a way of soothing her that only Charlene had managed to master. He took her wild thoughts that spiraled out of control with what-ifs, and brought everything back to earth.

They parked and he opened her door, offering her an arm. They entered the event together where he clapped her on the back and they finally parted ways.

June made her way through the crowd, trying her best to keep from moping. She gathered another drink. If she couldn't bury herself in a fancy hotel bed, she could at least drown herself in free liquor. A hand landed on the small of her back. "How's it going, J?" June turned to her right, her jaw clenched and lip twitching in disgust. Coen Visser, a Dutch rider two years her senior. They'd spent the last year dancing around each other, chasing a title that could only be won with a combination of money and talent. Coen had the first; June had the latter.

She'd managed to avoid him thus far in the season, caught up with bad rides and escaping parties, but no such luck tonight. He seemed to determined to rile her every chance he got. Throw her off her game. June was safe tonight—she'd been off her game all season. She elbowed his hand off of her, taking her next drink from the bartender as it was slid to her.

"Don't call me that." She turned, moving to walk away when Coen's hand landed on her elbow.

"Come on, now, J. Since when do you run from a fight? It's kind of your thing isn't it? Ride like shit, get hammered in a bar, and then majorly fuck something up?"

June turned to face him, her glare hardening as he smirked at her. She didn't want to deal with him right now. Or ever. She fumbled for something to say, but what was her defense? Between the bar fight with Diego, her piss-poor performance all season, and her drinking record, it was a wonder she had sponsors at all.

How had she gone from almost having it all to begging for scraps?

"What do you want, Coen?" Her voice was sharp, bitter and venomous.

He grinned, a pleased glint in his eye at having so obviously gotten under her skin. "You know, if you actually deserved to be here, maybe you could score some points."

Anger flared hot beneath June's skin, her hand clenching the glass in her hand so tightly she swore it might shatter. She gritted her teeth, her jaw tightened in a way that made her look even more pissed than she already was. He had one of the most infuriating grins she'd ever seen. Her chest ached, the familiar feeling of inadequacy sinking its way through her bones.

Coen stepped forward, leaning down to speak close to her ear. His voice was low, almost patronizing. "You're a complete and total mess, and everyone here knows it. But hey, I won't tell if you don't."

His words were a punch to the gut, heat rising to her cheeks. Coen smirked down at her, his voice dripping with condescension. She opened her mouth to bite back, but a hand landed on her shoulder.

Coen's smug smile faded and June shot a look back to find Diego standing behind her. Even slamming him against the wall hadn't enraged him as much as Coen's presence seemed to.

He hadn't said a word, but his eyes said plenty. Coen shut up. He paused. Faltered. For a moment, he almost looked afraid. June hadn't even known Diego could look at someone like that. "Something to say, *cabrón*?"

He carried the weight of a storm-heavy sky, lightning poised to strike and ignite whole forests. June was all but pressed against him, his hand trailing down her arm to rest protectively at her hip, as if daring the boy to lay a finger on anything he had claimed as his own.

Coen's smirk faded as he took a step back, his cocky arrogance replaced with something a little more cautious. There was a challenge written all over Diego's face. Coen met his steel gaze and simmered. He may have been a prick, but he wasn't stupid. He could feel the tension rolling off of Diego in waves, and if the beginning of the season was any indication, Diego wasn't against taking a punch or two.

If the circumstances were any different, June would be downright giddy seeing Coen so nervous all of a sudden. His eyes widened as he took a glance from June to Diego. For once, he was at a loss for words. His jaw tensed as he found his voice, clearing his throat. "I was just saying hi."

Diego's voice dropped to a deadly octave, a low rumble carrying a sharp warning. "Say it in fewer words."

Coen swallowed hard, his face turning a little paler than it had been before. "S–sorry." Victorious satisfaction flooded June's senses. Watching someone like Coen be put in his place was almost worth the awful day she'd had. Diego's hand remained on her shoulder, a firm pressure. Possessive. Staking his claim.

Coen excused himself shortly, and in a matter of seconds, fled into the crowd. June let out a heavy breath, feeling just a bit lighter. Diego watched as Coen slinked away, his jaw still taut with anger. The tension in his shoulders slowly relaxed, but his hand remained where it was on June's hip. She could feel the heat from his palm through the thin fabric of her dress and shivered involuntarily, her skin prickling with warmth.

"Find a booth," he demanded. "I'll come to you."

June nodded, her heart skipping a beat at the order. She did as she was told, quietly slipping through the crowd and finding a deserted booth in the back, tucked away from the rest of the room. She settled into the leather cushions, folding her arms into her lap as she waited for him to come back.

It didn't take long for Diego to find her. Immediately, she shrunk back into her seat. She wasn't good at apologies or thank-yous, and she was well aware that one of each was in order. Diego supplied a glass of whiskey for each of them, and she quickly downed it, watching as a bottle girl immediately swept over to refill it.

He leaned forward on his elbows, eyeing her up and down. "I

don't think I even put on a show that well."

June swallowed hard. If there was one thing she could do, it was look good. That was the point of this arrangement, wasn't it? Selling her sex appeal in place of her talent that seemed to have gone missing. She just shrugged. "A pity party is still a party."

Diego smiled softly. Knowingly. Of course he knew. It was nice to talk to someone who got it. Someone who knew the sting of it without being her competition. "I . . . was wrong. Nothing is going right in this season but I had no right to take it out on you." She ran her finger along the rim of her glass, staring at it so she didn't have to look at him. "Anger is . . . well, it's all I've had most of my life."

He nodded shortly. "I understand—"

June's head snapped up shortly. "But you *don't*, though."

He couldn't possibly. Anger kept her alive. When her father's rage turned brutal, her choice was to flee or fight. Fleeing wasn't always an option. It was what had gotten them in this situation in the first place. When Diego grabbed her elbow that night in the bar, the instinct to survive took over all rational thought. She punched before she could even remember she hadn't seen her dad in years.

She'd learned to make herself ferocious. Make herself bigger and louder and scarier than she was, like a cat backed into a corner who'd do anything to get out.

And it worked. She got out. She survived the punches. She survived the terror. And this was all that was left. A scared girl who took everything too far and was then left with a gnawing pit of shame in her stomach. Because Diego didn't deserve it. He deserved kind and soft and loving.

Not whatever this was.

"No. I don't," he said honestly. "But it's not mine to get, is it?" He reached across the table carefully, taking her hand into his. Securely. Comfortably. Not like she would bolt off at any second.

Frustration welled in her, and she furrowed her brows at him.

"Stop. Don't make this worse."

Diego held onto her hand tighter, a challenge in his gaze. "Worse?"

"Stop being nice when I was awful to you."

Diego leaned in closer. "Stop acting like you're some big bad beast you need to explain away. I have done as bad or worse. Do not think I assumed you got this far as a meek-minded woman."

Her shame settled. It didn't disappear, but with each stroke of his hand, the defensive hair raised on her back was laid back in place. He understood. He was perhaps one of the only people who could. The stakes. The emotions. The intensity in a sport such as this.

Diego wasn't pretending to be unfazed—he truly was.

He dropped his grip on her hand, settling back into the seat across from hers. "It is all right, *Vaquera*. We are square."

June nodded, and he settled on that for an answer, quickly turning the tide of the conversation as though sensing how much she hated his understanding.

"Your friend's a real peach."

June huffed an amused breath out of her nose. "Well, he's right, so what difference does it make if he's an asshole?"

"Accidents happen, Junebug," Diego said softly. He was trying so hard to soothe her. To ease her worries. To comfort her. "I have driven into walls so many times. I've had to retire from races. I am familiar with this pain and it is painful, but it is not the end of the world."

She swallowed hard, nodding.

"You must bond with this horse, no?"

She didn't care about Oviatt. She cared that she was alone. "I'm okay, Diego. Really."

Diego didn't buy it for a second. He leaned forward in his seat, halfway across the table. "Don't do that," he said shortly. "Don't hide from me, June. It is unfair that you only share the good parts of your life."

June's throat tightened at his words. He saw right through her, and it was both refreshing and enraging. She'd always hidden herself away. She didn't know what to do about his intense focus on her. She didn't want to look at him, but his gaze was steady on hers, waiting for a response. "So, what? I bitch and moan about it and it all goes away?"

"No, but it does make it easier to carry," Diego argued, clearly growing frustrated with her dismissal when he was only trying to help. "Don't push me away when you're hurting."

Her lips parted, struggling to find a response. His eyes were hard, his tone firm. He was demanding a response, and she knew he'd wait all night for it. June was not weak. She did not need pity or help to get through . . . and yet, Diego's steady demeanor, the way he always seemed to know the right thing to say, was as soothing as it was infuriating. "Do you know what else makes it easier to carry?"

Diego paused, narrowing his eyes ever so slowly. "What, June?"

"Whiskey," she said decidedly. She took a long and deliberate sip from her glass, keeping her eyes on him over the rim as she took her time to swallow. It scorched on its way down, a fiery heat filling her chest and making her feel a little bit more like herself. She lowered the glass, her voice even, determined. "A fantastic listener, never criticizes, and is completely incapable of disagreeing."

Diego just sighed into his hands, rubbing them back against his face in exasperation. Then he stood, taking her hand into his and pulling her to her feet, the buzz in her head limiting her resistance. "Fine," Diego said. "Don't talk."

She blinked at him, at their hands as Diego intertwined them. "What are you doing?"

Diego rolled his eyes as if the answer was beyond obvious. "You lost."

She glowered up at him, half tempted to repeat the night they met. "Aw, shucks! I almost forgot! Thanks for that reminder!"

He cocked his head to the side. "You want sponsors?" The question didn't require an answer, so June didn't answer him. "You need eyes on you. Constantly. Bad ride? The attention drifts? Drag it back."

He led her out to the center of the dance floor before he guided her hands behind his neck, swaying to the music as if it were the most natural thing in the world.

June's mind was a little fuzzy from the alcohol. She wasn't expecting to get on the dance floor tonight. Diego's breath was warm against her skin, one hand splayed against her back, keeping her close, his glass still in the other. "Diego—" she began, her voice a mix of protest and surprise.

He just shook his head, smiling down at him "Shut up and dance, *Vaquera*."

Who was she to resist? Reluctantly, she let herself be pulled flush against him, her heart thudding in her chest at their proximity. The music swirled around them, a sultry beat that seemed to match the intensity of their movements. Diego's hand pressed firmly against the small of her back, keeping her close to him as he led them to the rhythm.

June tried to concentrate on the floor beneath her feet rather than the way his body felt against hers. The strong, hard lines of his torso pressed against her, his muscles taut and firm.

He leaned forward, his hand falling to her waist as he whispered in her ear. "Come on now," he crooned into her ear, guiding her body to roll into his. "You've had more than enough to drink to put on a show."

She glowered up at him, but she let out a breath, her resistance crumbling. He was a good dancer, his proximity intoxicating. Against her better judgment, she allowed herself to relax into his touch. She reached to his occupied hand, snagging his glass and

RACING HEARTS

downing the rest of his drink before she handed it off to a passing bottle girl. She guided his other hand to her waist before twining her fingers in his hair.

Diego's hands continued to guide her through the movements, his touch firm yet gentle as he led her through the steps. He was warm, the heat of his body seeping through his shirt and into hers, making her shiver involuntarily. The sensation, so unlike anything she was used to, was heady, almost dizzying. Her heart thumped wildly in her chest with each step, her mind a whirl of conflicting feelings.

"That's it, June." His breath was hot against her skin, the sound of her name on his lips sending a shiver down her spine. The music continued around them, thrumming in sync with the steady beat of their movements. "Just relax. Let go."

She knew she should push him away, knew it was dangerous to be this close, to let herself feel this way. The alcohol was getting to her now, her head spinning and her vision swimming. She was drunk, almost certainly too far gone to be making such risky decisions. But Diego's hands on her waist felt so right. His body against hers made her breathless. She couldn't stop the way she pressed closer to him, the way she curled her fingers into his hair and tugged just to see what he'd do.

He let out a soft hiss, followed by a velvet laugh against her ear as his hands pulled her even closer.

"Fuck," he hissed against her neck. "Don't do that." There was a hint of warning in his tone, the edge of a command.

"Why not?" June whispered, her mind muddled and her limbs heavy with a mix of drunkenness and desire.

His hands slid down to the curves of her hips, holding her against him with an iron grip. He leaned down, his lips brushing against the shell of her ear, voice husky and low. "Because you are even sexier than normal, and you aren't ready for what I'm going to do to you if you keep grinding on me like that."

Her heart skipped a beat, her breath catching in her throat as his words sent a shiver of desire through her.

"You chose whiskey, remember? I want you sober as a judge when I have you." He said it so casually, as though there was no question of if, but rather when, she would finally cave. He continued, leaning in closer. "I want you begging for me. I want you to remember every second of it. No regrets."

She pulled back a little to look up at him, her eyes wide in the dim, flickering light. She knew she should stop, should break away and regain control of herself, but she'd had far too much whiskey in hopes of drowning out her thoughts. It worked. Now, the alcohol and the intoxicating scent of his skin combined to overpower any remaining shred of sense left in her.

Diego's tongue flicked out to wet his lips, staring down at her like he wanted to devour her whole. The sight of his tongue against his lips made her heart skip a beat, her mind flashing to images of his tongue in a *very* different place. She swallowed hard, her eyes fixated on his mouth. Her hands remained fisted in his hair, her body drawn tightly against his. She felt lightheaded, his nearness overwhelming. She wanted to kiss him, to capture his mouth with hers, to see what he'd taste like.

Diego drew a sharp breath, and all at once, he pulled away. June nearly toppled over, but he kept a hand planted firmly on her waist. It was different now, something to keep her grounded rather than exploring every divot of her body.

The sudden absence of his touch was like a physical blow, leaving her feeling cold and unmoored. She stumbled forward a step, feeling the alcohol like a physical weight in her head. Her skin longed for his, her body aching for the feel of his touch. She looked up at him, her breath coming in ragged gasps as she tried to keep her balance. "Diego . . ." she protested, her voice thick and slurred from the alcohol in her system.

"Here," he said firmly, pushing her away, and a moment later, a different pair of hands was on her, holding her steady. "Get her home."

June turned and was met with the sight of Charlene, keeping her on her feet. A moment passed between Charlene and Diego, a conversation spoken only with their eyes before he spared her one last glance, and disappeared back into the crowd.

June woke up the next morning in Olivia and Lola's hotel room, laid out on the second queen bed while they were bundled up on the first. She groaned into the pillows, her head throbbing and desperate for water. She turned on her side, only to find Advil and a water bottle on the nightstand. Lola's doing, no doubt. June sighed her relief, whispering quiet praises as she sat up and downed the pills, immediately followed by the entirety of the water bottle. Her stomach was queasy and her throat burned in the way it always did after she threw up the night before. Sure, she'd had a shit round, but *yikes*.

"Ugh," June groaned, sinking back into the pillows and throwing an arm over her eyes to block out the light. "Never again."

Olivia's voice perked up from the other bed where she sat, scrolling on her phone. "You say that every time, babe."

Lola snorted, laying in Olivia's lap. "Good morning, Sunshine. How's the hangover?"

"You ever been hit by a truck? Like that," June grumbled in reply. "How bad did I embarrass myself last night?" She wasn't looking forward to hearing the answer, but she knew better than to assume she had any tact left in her inebriated state. She had a feeling she did something stupid, but she was trying her damndest to remember.

Olivia snickered. "Oh, just the usual. Drunk fighting, you kissed me and Lola both at one point, and pretty much fucked Diego on the dance floor."

Heat rushed to June's face, eyes widening. She let out another groan, pulling the pillow on her face to bury her embarrassment. "Please tell me you're making up at least half of that," she said from under the pillow.

Olivia just laughed. "Sorry babe," she said, amusement clear in her voice. "I couldn't make that up if I tried."

Lola grinned at her laptop, a hint of mischief in her tone. "I thought Diego was gonna throw you over his shoulder and pack you out of there."

A shiver ran through June at the image, heat pooling low in her belly as Lola filled the blanks her mind left out. She pushed the thought aside, her head still throbbing, a reminder of her poor decisions.

"Please get your ass in the shower," Olivia suggested, a smirk playing on her lips. "You stink of booze and desperation."

Lola barked out a laugh.

June flushed an even deeper shade of red. "Gee, thanks for sugarcoating it," she muttered, slowly sitting up and pulling herself out of bed. "Where's my phone?"

"Over by the door," Olivia replied, nodding at her phone, sitting on the dresser. "We had to take it away from you last night. You kept trying to drunk-dial him."

June's face flushed scarlet. She vaguely remembered the urge to call Diego last night, her alcohol-numbed brain completely lacking any sense of shame or impulse control. "Oh my God," she groaned, her head falling into her hands.

Olivia smirked. "You didn't get any through," she said, her tone annoyingly chipper.

June could've kissed them both on the mouth. Again, apparently.

She picked up her phone, a text notification from Diego occupying the screen. She opened it hurriedly, greeted with the sight of a picture of them crammed together on a dance floor and an article all about their budding romance.

DIEGO: holy shit. how much did we drink last night?

Attached was a laughing emoji. June let out a breath of relief, clutching her phone to her chest as she whispered prayers of thanks.

JUNE: enough. the whiskey went down like water and then i woke up.

DIEGO: imagine how drunk we're going to be when you win next month.

Despite herself, June cracked a smile. The publicity would be great, and Diego was fine. It was a win-win. Olivia and Lola perked up from their spot on the other bed. "What'd he say?" Olivia asked, propping herself up on her elbow.

June read the message out loud, the tension slowly leaving her body. "Looks like he was just as hammered as I was."

The girls' jaws dropped, looking at each other in absolute dismay.

Lola palmed her forehead. "Shut up, June. You do not actually believe that."

"Seriously, dude," Olivia agreed. "He's just brushing it off 'cuz he doesn't want to talk about it."

"Even better!" June exclaimed. "Because I don't want to talk about it!"

Olivia groaned, flopping back on the bed. "You're hopeless."

"Hey!" June protested. "I just don't . . ." Her voice trailed off, her brain still too fuzzy from her night to come up with a counterpoint.

"Yeah, hopeless," Lola chimed in. Olivia snorted in agreement.

"Thanks!" June replied, feigning chipperness as she blew her a kiss and then flipped her off. She grabbed clothes from her suitcase. "I'm taking a shower. Order some horrifically greasy food please."

"Greasy food coming right up," Olivia smirked in response. "See if that makes you any less delusional."

June made a face at them before grabbing her things, heading to the bathroom to shower off the previous night's shenanigans.

Chapter Sixteen

Time off seemed to be exactly what Hades needed. June had done as Amelia had requested, or rather ordered. She rode Oviatt in a Grand Prix. She was allowed to return to Hades, and she did. She couldn't do any worse than she'd done in Valkenswaard. For some reason, failing so tremendously did wonders for her confidence. If she could bomb that hard and still get back on, sooner or later, she was going to get it right.

Amelia was angry with her and she knew it. She stopped showing up to June's sessions, and June didn't even mind. June performed better without eyes on her—ironic, considering she was meant to perform in front of thousands.

The girls posted a photo of the three of them together at the afterparty, Diego's figure strategically placed in the background. Between implications of him being at her competition, the photo in the club, and the post, Lola could hardly keep up with the sponsorship packages. June's apartment was constantly filled with boxes from brand deals, her social media alight.

Her season was fucked, and yet she'd never been more popular.

July and August went by slightly better than the beginning of the season. She made it to the second round of competition in London and Rome.

June found herself watching the Formula One races more and more. Despite herself, it was actually quite entertaining, and not just because Diego looked gorgeous in his race suit. He took second in Hungary—third in Belgium. She adored watching him. Adored the way he ran to his team and jumped over the barricade into the throng when he did well. His team loved him, and she was relieved to see that people had his back. That he was not alone. She was only a tiny bit jealous to see him doing so well.

She loved seeing this side of him. Happy, successful. It was no wonder he had such a fanbase. Diego Cabrera was the sun. Wherever he went, he lit up the world around him.

She felt like a groupie, watching snippets on her phone of the afterparty from inside the club, Diego dancing as his team lifted them up on his shoulders. His joy was contagious.

The next weekend's race took place in Austria. June dived into the sport, just to further their agreement of course. It had nothing to do with the fact Diego was incredibly fun to watch.

Each Formula One season consisted of a battle for two championships—one team oriented, the Constructor's Championship; one individual oriented, the World Driver's Championship. It was the first year Diego and Lotus Bugatti Racing were contenders for both.

June watched the screen intently, cheap bottle of wine in hand with her feet propped up on the chair she had dragged over from the office. As much as she enjoyed watching his cheerfulness with his team, her favorite was watching him on the track.

Fast hardly suited the man—he was otherworldly. The fun, easygoing man June had come to know was nowhere to be found the second the lights went out. He was an aggressive driver, making risky maneuvers, shooting through barely-there gaps, playing mind games with his opponents. The man inspired awe and terror in equal amounts.

They were on lap fifty-three, and Diego was leading.

Until a Mercedes clipped his back tyre, sending him straight into the wall. June shot to her feet, stumbling in her drunken haze before she caught herself.

Panic surged through her, dragging her back to memories of a dirt oval track from a lifetime ago. The one where she watched someone lose their life.

She hated racing for a reason. The danger had once been why she loved it, taking Ava every weekend in the summers. Now, the danger was why she hated it.

But Diego was swearing on his radio and throwing his hands up. Alive, fine, and *pissed*.

Once she knew he was alright, June sank back down onto the couch.

Formula One drivers had top-of-the-line safety precautions. Fireproof race suits, helmets, neck braces, a protective barrier around the cockpit. They were far from as vulnerable as equestrians. And yet, it still terrified her.

June sat forward. Diego got out of the car, clearly trying his best to remain composed, but she could see in the line of his shoulders and the way he ripped his helmet off that he was anything but. He made his way to the media pen and the interviewers desperate for the first word on what had happened as though everyone hadn't been watching.

Diego had the heart of a fighter. For all the familial help and money in the world, he still knew how to fend for himself. It was late that evening when she finally caved and texted him. She went back and forth on what to say. On whether she should console him, tell him she'd been concerned. That she was glad he was okay.

JUNE: hey there's a wall there

DIEGO: thanks, i hadn't noticed
until you pointed it out.

>JUNE: what was it you said?
>'it's not the end of the world?'

DIEGO: you're not going to let me
live that down, are you?

>JUNE: oh definitely not.
>you're okay?

DIEGO: my ego is bruised but my head is
still attached so i guess i can't complain

>JUNE: well that's always good.
>attached heads are a beautiful thing

DIEGO: i'm going to punch Leo in the face

>JUNE: the Mercedes driver?

DIEGO: did you hear what he said to the press?

June was familiar with it. Leo made a comment to the press afterwards saying that '*Diego clearly can't handle the kind of pressure that comes with being the championship leader*'. He blamed the accident on Diego. It wasn't anything new by Formula One standards, but she knew it got under his skin.

JUNE: a semi-wise man once told me 'people like to talk out of their ass. don't listen to them.'

DIEGO: you're really enjoying throwing my own words in my face, aren't you?

JUNE: oh it's the highlight of my week. maybe even month.

DIEGO: you're a nightmare

JUNE: you have yet to mention once that i was watching your race

DIEGO: believe me, i noticed. i just wish you were watching when i was actually doing well.
DIEGO: what made you change your mind?
DIEGO: i thought you hated racing

> JUNE: i do.
> JUNE: but i don't hate you

DIEGO: damn, that actually
made me feel better

> JUNE: lol. you're very
> easily flattered.

DIEGO: only by you, querida

> JUNE: i'm glad you're okay.

DIEGO: just a scratch, i promise,
but your concern is very charming

> JUNE: what can i say?
> my charm is my best quality

DIEGO: i can think
of a few others

JUNE: shut up
JUNE: you drove beautifully
until the accident.
JUNE: i watched the whole time.
JUNE: and i'll be watching next race
when you're on the podium too.

DIEGO: oh my god don't say stuff like that
DIEGO: i just fully had to look
around my hotel room for cameras

Constantly texting Diego slowly morphed into calls. It started as an extension of messaging at first, when the banter got too fast and too outrageous, he'd call her, and she got to bully him over the phone. Slowly, it delved into actual conversations. As a world-class insomniac, she could always count on him to answer. The differing time zones often meant what was night for her was still day for him. And even if it wasn't, Diego never seemed to sleep, and they never seemed to run out of conversation. Diego convinced her to share her location with him, amused by the fact they were never in the same place for long. It was stupid, but June enjoyed watching their dots move across the globe.

June sat outside on the fire escape of her apartment, looking up at the stars with her phone to her ear. Their conversation morphed from teasing into a more solemn tone.

"Do you ever miss home?"

June settled on honesty. "Not like I probably should."

"Really? I miss my *mamá's* cooking. Miss living down the hall from my sister."

She sat back and kicked her feet up, crossing at the ankles. It was one of his tactics, she was coming to understand. Lowering her defenses by first lowering his own. She hated that it worked. "I mean . . . I came from Texas. Florence is much prettier."

He hummed, prompting her to continue and June sighed. "I miss . . . *things* about it. The cafe I worked at. My neighbor and her apricot tree. We made jam together every year. I miss the barn cat at my old stable." She chuckled fondly at the memory. "His name was Bear. Followed me around like a dog."

Diego chuckled, and she could hear the smile in his voice over the phone. "Did you really work in a cafe?"

June huffed an amused breath out of her nose. "Yes, Diego. Some people work real jobs."

"Hey, racing *is* a real job!"

She laughed, crossing an arm over her chest as she leaned back against the brick of her apartment building. Her voice grew quieter, amusement turning to nostalgia. "I guess . . . I guess I miss the people. We were all neighbors, and family, and friends. Didn't have to second guess everyone's intentions. Lot different from things out here."

He was quiet for a minute, processing her words, before he spoke again. "Sounds like you actually liked it a lot."

June bit her lower lip, turning her gaze out over the city lights. How could she ever prefer that to this? A place of her own. No more threats of her father's anger. Chasing her dreams. "Nostalgia likes to make things better than they were."

"You're always nostalgic, whether you admit it or not. All your country music and your cowboy boots."

June sighed. Maybe he was right. "Shut up."

"Make me." The playful challenge in his voice was undeniable.

June remained unperturbed. "You know what I really miss?" He waited for her to continue. "My sister." The softness of her own voice surprised her.

A small silence passed before he spoke.

"I never knew you had one." There was a hint of curiosity in his tone.

"Yeah," June whispered. She couldn't believe she was telling him this. Not even the girls knew. "Ava. About three years younger."

"Ava and June," he mused fondly. "That's cute. You two must be very close."

"Ava and Alessia." She wasn't sure why she said it. Only that *'Ava and June'* felt impossibly wrong. She may be able to change her own name, but that didn't change the way it sounded when placed next to her sister's.

Diego couldn't keep the shock from his voice. "You have two sisters?"

June huffed a breath of amusement through her nose, leaning back against the wall. "Uh, no. No . . . my name is Alessia." Her voice lowered without her permission, like she couldn't repeat the name at a respectable volume. "Alessia Junior. June."

There was a moment of pure silence, as though he was attempting to fit the pieces of this new puzzle into place, to understand the parts of her she'd so rarely put on display.

"Alessia." His voice was a whisper, like the simple utterance of her name was sacred. Like he was suddenly speaking in a holy place. When he spoke, his voice held no judgement, only quiet understanding. "It's a beautiful name. You don't like it?"

She swallowed hard, as though the words were hard for her to force out of her throat. "The name isn't the problem."

"Then what is?" he prompted.

Being named after the mom that left me with that man. She didn't know much about her mother. Where she was. What she did. Who she'd become. June didn't blame her for leaving.

What she couldn't understand was why she'd left her daughters behind.

She cleared her throat. "June just . . . suits me better."

"It does," he agreed simply. "Summer girl. Free-spirited and untamable. You should've always been a June."

Something in her chest twisted at his words, something small and sharp and uncomfortable. For a reason she didn't care to analyze, the thought of Diego being privy to the parts of herself she kept tucked away, where no one could see, made her skin burn.

". . . Ava just moved to New York to dance on Broadway, actually, which is insane because I paid for her dance lessons. It's just . . . odd. We were inseparable, and now we're thousands of miles away from each other. I thought we'd always be close." It was a confession that broke her heart to say, but it was as though she were rewarding him. Allowing him another slice of vulnerability with every one he devoured up. With every chance he had to leave her out in the cold, he left her feeling warmer instead. "I moved to Tuscany like . . . a month after she moved to Austin for dance school. She never really . . . forgave me for it. Thought I just sent her off to get rid of her, which is total fuckin' bullshit. I lived for that girl. I was so lost without her. So when the opportunity to move to Italy and do something with my life fell into my lap I—I took it."

When he spoke, his voice was impossibly soft, like he would break her further if spoke too loudly. "How could anyone hold something so . . . understandable against you?"

"Understandable?" June challenged. "No one ever sees it as anything other than selfish. She moved because I told her to. Because she got an offer from a dance school. Because I didn't want her to have to live in that house anymore."

Diego was silent for a long moment, as if racking his brain for answers. Some way to comfort her. "That's the opposite of selfish, June." His voice was soft, gentle.

June nodded slowly, swallowing hard. She wanted to believe it.

Wanted to believe she'd done right by Ava. Maybe that was why she so desperately needed to win.

She needed to prove she'd left for a valid reason.

She'd thought it a million times: that she had done the right thing. But to hear it from someone else? From Diego?

". . . Thank you," June said softly.

June stared at the contact on her phone. *'Best Sister Ever <3'.*

Ava had stolen her phone and did it herself years ago when June was driving her back from dance class, and June didn't have it in her to change it.

There had once been a time when June didn't go more than a few hours without a text from Ava. When she moved to Austin, those texts lessened. She was busy chasing her dreams. When June moved to Tuscany, Ava stopped responding almost completely.

June texted her on holidays. Sometimes, she got a text back. The last time they'd called was eight months ago. Ava had been offered a job to dance on Broadway. She was moving to New York. It was the night of her going-away party and Ava had been drunk with her friends in Austin.

June was in Riesenbeck.

She answered the call to Ava sobbing, begging June to come home. Asking why she'd left her all alone. Sorrow dissolved into anger until Ava was shouting at June and someone took the phone away from her.

It was the same call June had imagined giving her mother if she'd only had a way to get in contact.

Eight months later, June still couldn't shake the guilt. She stalked Ava's socials religiously. She knew she'd made it to New York. Knew she'd settled in. Knew she loved it.

June missed her. And Diego was right. June pressed call before she could back out. She started to think Ava wasn't going to answer when endless ringing gave way to a voice. "Hello?" There was worry in her voice, as though she automatically assumed if June was calling her, something must be wrong.

"Hi," June said softly, unable to force her words out any louder. "Uh . . . hey. How are you? I just wanted to catch up."

Ava sighed in relief, and June could imagine her clutching her chest the way she did. She'd always been the more extroverted of the two. The more expressive. The more lively. "Jesus, I thought one of those horses finally crushed you."

June choked back a laugh. "Nah, can't get rid of me that easily." She leaned back against the wall of her apartment. ". . . How's New York?"

"Oh my God, Al."

June's heart did a flip at the old familiar nickname.

"It's unreal. It's everything I ever dreamed of. Minus the rats. They seriously do not overexaggerate about the rats, they're insane. But there are so many people, and they're all so interesting, and there's so much to do. I thought Austin was crazy, but New York is just . . . *wow*."

This was the way it had been with them growing up. Ava rattled on, June listening enthusiastically. They fell back into their old routine so easily it was almost scary. Like no time had passed at all. It was fifteen minutes of Ava ranting about New York before she cut herself off abruptly. "Okay, but can we please talk about your boyfriend because *what*?"

June laughed out loud, caught off guard. She didn't correct her. "I thought you'd never go to a race again after that accident." June tried not to grimace at the casual mention of the memory. Once upon a time, June loved racing. She'd grown up in rural Texas. Motorsport was the only thing to do outside of horses or farming. From dirt bike racing to off-roading in shitboxes and trying not to die.

She'd spent more weekends at The Valley Speedway with Ava than she could count. A dirt oval track, but racing was racing. June grew up sneaking into the pits. She adored the cars—sprint cars and hobby stocks. She lived for the thrill of it. The sound of the engines drowning out everything, spitting dirt and rubber as they flew past the stands. The smell of racing fuel burning in the air.

At least, until she and Ava watched someone go screeching off the track and into a cement barrier. The man didn't survive. The headlines all said how rare it was. How he must have had preexisting conditions for the crash to have killed him. June never went back. It was the first time she'd realized just how dangerous it all could be.

She wasn't sure why she didn't just tell Ava the truth, only that pretending with Diego was fun. "Have you *seen* him?" June asked. "Can't exactly say no to that."

Ava faked a gag, laughing out loud. "Ew, that pretty much makes him my new brother. I will *not* think about him like that."

June laughed out loud. She thought vaguely that Ava and Diego would get along, and then quickly shut that thought down. They were barely even friends. It didn't matter if they got along. This attachment with Diego would not be a long one.

Ava and June didn't talk about that night from eight months ago or that fateful phone call, but they threw a Band-Aid over it and promised to text and call more often. She supposed she owed Diego for that.

Chapter Seventeen

Charlene very rarely found her way to June's apartment, so when she did, June knew she was in deep shit.

Olivia and Lola lounged across the couch in June's living room, limbs tangled together, some trashy reality show droning on the TV. They opted to ignore it in favor of scrolling through videos on their phones and showing them to each other.

The moment Charlene entered, they all exchanged looks, ready for some kind of beatdown.

It never came. Charlene was eerily quiet. Perfectly composed. June blinked. She wasn't sure what she'd done wrong, but it had to have been something.

Charlene cleared her throat. "Thoughts on Suzuka in two weeks?"

"Bless you," Lola said immediately.

"Oh my God!" Olivia exclaimed. "Like one of those guns that shoots bombs?"

Lola didn't even look up from her phone. "That's a bazooka, Liv."

"Oh."

"It's an F1 track," June specified, plopping down on the couch beside Olivia. When Charlene raised a brow at June, she threw her hands up in innocence. "What? I've been paying attention."

"Can you blame her?" Olivia asked. "Have you seen Diego in that racing suit because *awooga*—"

Lola elbowed her in the ribs and Olivia shut up with a pointed glare in her direction.

"I have no need to go to Japan, Char," June said. She was baiting her. The implication was clear, but June needed her to say it.

Charlene just sighed. "Look, you're dating Diego Cabrera—"

"*Not* dating!" June argued, and Charlene narrowed her eyes at her, shutting her up.

"As your friend, no shit. As your manager? Yes, you are. You've never been more popular and so long as you're relevant, we all have jobs."

June sighed. She supposed she couldn't argue with that. That was the point of this arrangement anyway, wasn't it? To make those around them think June and Diego were in this for real. If even her manager was picking at it, they had to be doing something right.

Charlene crossed her arms over her chest, brows raised as though she were scolding June. "Diego goes to two of your competitions and you don't go to one of his races? It makes you look like a bad girlfriend, June."

The girls choked on their laughter, Olivia bumping June with her foot. "Yeah, June. Step it up girl."

"Seriously," Lola prodded. "You need to make him a scrapbook or get sweaters with your anniversary date on it or something."

"Not dating!" June huffed, discarding her tea on the side table before crossing her arms over her chest. "Diego has only been to one of my competitions . . . so, it's fine."

Charlene nodded, swallowing hard. "Technically true. However, after this weekend, it will be two competitions. So."

June's jaw dropped, the girls whirling to face each other with excitement. Diego meant content. And teasing. Lots of teasing.

"Diego's coming to Riesenbeck?"

Charlene shrugged, glancing away from June. "Formula One has a two week break before the next race. So, I—*Lotus* invited him. At no suggestion of mine."

June groaned into her hands, melting into the couch. Having Diego there messed with her head. Like when Amelia watched her. It threw her off her game. She peeked up at Charlene through her fingers. "But he's just going to be in the stands again, right?"

Charlene nodded, and June could have cried in relief. "And he'll be with the girls the entire time to gather content."

The relief vanished in an instant. Of course he'd be with the girls, offering the real behind-the-scenes look at life on the Global Champions Tour. Lola and Olivia spun toward each other, practically buzzing with excitement. They disregarded their social media scrolling in favor of jotting down ideas.

June glared at Charlene, and she shrugged, offering June a semi-apologetic look. "Suzuka is in line. Come to terms with it." And without another word, Charlene turned and left. June groaned, melting back into the couch as the girls chattered about content ideas for the weekend.

At least she'd be on Hades this time. Maybe she and Diego could dance again. June's cheeks flamed, and she beat that thought down immediately. *You aren't supposed to remember that*, she reminded herself. Still, despite her best efforts, she couldn't seem to forget.

June's nerves were on fire for the next week. Diego was going to be there.

There was more riding on this weekend than just points. Eyes and cameras would be on her as Diego's *something*, even if nobody could quite put a name to it. She had to be worthy of the attention. Hades seemed to understand the importance. Things were finally, finally coming together. Sure, the season was already coming to a close, but any points were good points. If they could hone in for the next season, June would take what she could get.

Riesenbeck was one of her favorite venues on the entire Global Champions calendar. She adored Germany. It was also Siegfried's favorite location, the closest to home. He got to speak German. Got to drink German beer and eat German food. Nothing could have made him happier.

She focused on that instead. On her love of the city and the venue and her horse rather than the nerves the thought of Diego brought. She hadn't seen him since Valkenswaard, nearly three months ago. Maybe he'd remembered that night in the club, her hands fisted in his hair, pulling him closer. Maybe he'd be angry. Irritated. Frustrated. Maybe he'd want to call their agreement off—*Shut up*, she scolded her brain. Things were fine. Things would be fine. She'd only been doing her part in the agreement. It wasn't her fault that he was gorgeous and they'd gotten a bit carried away. Plus, she'd been drunk. She could always blame it on that.

They checked into the hotel the day before, horses settled in at the barn. It was early morning the day of the competition, but June couldn't sleep. She found herself at the stables. She spent more time than necessary pruning Hades' stall, spreading shavings like her life depended on it, cleaning buckets and polishing tack. Anything to keep her mind occupied.

The hours passed quickly as June busied herself with all the pre-competition preparations. The routine was familiar, comforting, and it gave her something to focus on, keeping her mind at least partially occupied. The thought of Diego was still there, a constant, nagging presence in the back of her mind. She pushed it aside, immersing herself deeper and deeper into the tasks at hand.

The longer the day waned on, the worse her anxiety grew. Diego had to be there by now. She didn't stay in any one place for too long, too afraid of being spotted by him.

She'd have to see him eventually. It was inevitable. She wandered through the booths selling everything from merch, to food, to raffle tickets for cars, hoping she could get lost enough in the crowd to make sure he couldn't find her.

She heard Olivia before she saw her, Lola following behind as they rounded the corner, talking to someone behind them. June didn't think twice, bailing through a door and into a boutique, slamming the door shut behind her. June turned around, glancing at the scene before her. A Global Champions Tour merch booth. Of course it was. Why couldn't it be a damned food truck?

The moment she was spotted, she was swarmed by people asking for autographs and bombarding her with questions. She leaned into it. Anything to avoid him.

An hour later, she found her way back into the stables, scratching Hades through the stall. She was being childish. She should call him. Tell him to come say hi. But the moment she heard the girls coming, she pulled the door open and ducked into Hades' stall, hiding behind him.

What is this, high school? she scolded herself, but she didn't come out, perfectly content to busy herself with picking hay and shavings from Hades' water.

They walked right past her, and June let out a sigh of relief, slipping out of the stall and hustling off in the opposite direction.

When Isa came to saddle, June took over. So long as she was busy, she didn't have to think about Diego. She found her way to the warm-up arena, forcing her nerves back down when they threatened to swallow her whole.

June spotted Diego with the girls and instantly rushed off to warm up on the opposite side of the ring. She knew she wouldn't be able to avoid him anymore after the competition, but as of right now, June had to focus—a task nearly impossible if Diego was near.

The girls turned to head back towards the stands and June nearly collapsed. She'd gotten away with it.

And then, Diego stopped, the girls continuing their pursuit without noticing they'd lost him. He turned on his heel, abandoning the girls and making a beeline for her. June spurred Hades into motion, but even that wasn't enough to deter him. There was no avoiding him, marching right toward her. She pulled Hades to a stop, flashing him a false smile as though it were the first time she'd seen him. He didn't return it.

"Diego!" she exclaimed. "Hi!"

"Have I done something to upset you?" he asked, crossing his arms over his chest. His voice was so genuine, refusing to give in to her little game, but that wouldn't stop June from playing it.

"I don't know what you mean—"

"You've been avoiding me like the plague all day. Hiding in a booth? And your horse's stall? I'm not blind."

She swallowed hard, her face falling. "Do you really think confronting me now is the best time?"

"I'm not confronting you," he argued.

"Google confrontation and *this*—" she gestured between them, "—will be the first picture that shows up. I need to focus, D."

"D?" he repeated, his brows raising with a grin. "You've given me a nickname, now?"

She grit her teeth, her cheeks flaming, stomach flipping at the sight of his teasing smirk. "Diego," she scolded. "I need to focus."

He turned, clearly smug as he faced forward. "Right, right. Focus." She waited for him to say his goodbyes. To turn and leave. To head to the stands. But he just stood beside her, facing forward.

"Diego!" she hissed.

He turned to face her, flashing her a charming grin. *"Sí, amor?"*

She grit her teeth, refusing to give him a reaction despite the way he was taunting her. "Go with the girls!"

"No," he said sternly, looking forward again. "I can watch from the gate."

June swallowed hard, dizzy with stress. "Diego, *go*—"

"No," he said again, turning to face her. "You see, I've figured out your problem."

A flush crept up her neck at his remark, her heart quickening as he stepped beside her, that infuriatingly smug smile tugging at his lips. He seemed to relish in her discomfort, his eyes alight with mischief.

June threw up a hand in disbelief. "Well, since you know everything, please, do tell."

"You don't handle your adrenaline well," he said simply, and June's face went red. She'd spent her entire life in the saddle hiding that fact from people.

It was the truth. One she pushed down again and again. Her nerves got the best of her. Destroyed her where they should have strengthened her. She thought she hid it well, but here was Diego, reading her like a book. "In the car, we have someone in our ear the whole time to keep us levelheaded. Telling us how to proceed. How to win. Keeping us calm. That's what you need."

June grit her teeth, swallowing her. "Okay well, that's racing. This is a sport you do alone."

"Hm," Diego hummed. "No wonder you're losing."

June's head snapped to the side, shooting daggers down at him. "The fuck did you just say to me?"

"It makes sense," he said simply. "If you think you are alone, then you are, June. Loneliness doesn't make you brave, it makes you weak."

June could have jumped off her horse and beat him into the dirt. "What would you know about it? You think I need someone else for this? I can ride!"

Immediately, Diego broke into a grin. "I know," he said. His eyes were alight like he was seeing something truly glorious unfolding right before him. "So, go ride."

His hand fell to her thigh, giving it a reassuring squeeze. "Come on, June. You have the skill. Deep breaths, and it's all yours."

June blinked at him, swallowing hard. The deep anxiety in her gut morphed. It no longer cared for the full crowd awaiting her and Hades in the arena, but caring what Diego thought. Because Diego saw. The glaze she had painted over herself made no difference to him. He saw right through it. Right through her. And it terrified her. She'd thrown up wall after wall and to no avail when it came to him. He walked straight through each attempt to hold him at bay as easy as breathing.

She'd expected relief at finally being seen. Instead, she felt awfully naked in front of him.

She bit her bottom lip, her body riddled with tension. The urge to run, to escape him and his seeing eyes, quadrupled. ". . . We need to keep warming up—"

"You're perfectly warmed up, and you're up next. Just wait with me a while won't you?" He didn't move his hand. Didn't budge, a steady anchor in the storm of her own anxiety.

He didn't look at her, but his presence was there, his thumb rubbing soothing circles against her leg. He drew slow, steady breaths and June found herself matching them subconsciously. Until Diego glanced at her and June understood all at once.

"I'm sorry, are you trying to trick me into taking deep breaths?"

He flashed her a handsome smile, caught red-handed. "Is it working?"

June blinked, her lips quivering up into a semblance of a smile. ". . . Maybe."

He gave up the pretense of ignoring her, turning fully to face her. The sight of her smile left him beaming victoriously. He kept one hand firmly planted on her, the other stroking Hades' neck. June could do nothing but stare at him, eyes wide and lips parted. They called for her next, and June hurried forward to the gate. She had been so focused on Diego, she didn't have time to let the nerves of the competition pierce her heart.

June had never walked into an arena feeling . . . calm before. Even on Midus, her nerves were a live wire that commanded her every move. Everything felt different. The crowd was merely that—a group of people in seats rather than a godly creature that controlled her fate. The judges were merely that—observers. June was the one in control.

They entered the arena with purpose, Hades eager to please.

She'd never been so aware of the atmosphere before. Had never been so in tune with the way the sun filtered through the building, the sound of hoofbeats, the smell of horse and sweat, dust and leather.

The bell sounded. They were off like a bullet, Hades launching into motion. They flew across the arena, Hades' strides long and light.

They passed by the first jump clean as a whistle, June's body moving on instinct, every muscle working in sync with her horse's every movement.

It didn't feel like a competition. It felt like practice. Like she was in Amelia's barn rather than in Riesenbeck. Perfect.

They took the turn hard and fast, Hades setting back on his haunches to whirl around before they were off again, sailing to the next jump.

June didn't allow her mind to think, only feel. They cleared jump after jump after jump, June's body moving effortlessly through the course, Hades a living extension of her, knowing what she wanted before she did.

They were approaching the last jump, the final moment to prove themselves.

The familiar anxiety that ravaged her before an arena had not been allowed to let loose with Diego at her side.

They soared over the final oxer with ease. Not a single pole down. Not one penalty. She pumped her fist in the air, engulfed by the sound of cheers and collapsed in the saddle from relief. It was the best course of the season. Slower than she wanted, and nothing like she'd done with Midus, but the applause had never sounded so sweet.

They exited the arena, and June slumped in her saddle, arms wrapped around Hades' neck. He was clearly proud of himself, ears perked forward, an extra pep in his step. June laughed, unable to stop her smile. She wouldn't be on the podium and she knew it. It wasn't fast enough for that. But she was clear. And she was on Hades.

A set of hands landed on her hip, and June whirled to find Diego. His face was alight with triumph, cheering loudly as he caught her and dragged her off her horse. June yelped as he tugged her into his arms, holding her tight enough to suffocate her as he jumped up and down victoriously. "That's what I'm fucking talking about!"

June laughed out loud, her cheeks aching from smiling, her heart aching from the buzzing cocktail of adrenaline and joy.

Isa, Charlene, and the girls came swarming down an instant later, enveloping her in a hug, offering Hades all the praise in the world. "Fifth!" Charlene cried, holding her by the shoulders and shaking her. "Fifth, June! And on Hades! Fifth!"

The rush of satisfaction hit harder than the buzz of any drink, her head falling back as she looked up at the ceiling. Fifth.

She sighed in utter relief. Not the podium. Not where she wanted to be. But it was points. It was better.

June laughed, hugging back, her heart soaring.

Her eyes flicked back and forth between the girls, to Isa, to Hades, back to Diego's arms around her. Her mind felt like a fireworks display, a cacophony of color. She could feel her chest swelling a fraction for each person she laid eyes on and the moment seemed to glow. "Come on!" Diego exclaimed, pressing a kiss to her temple as he slung one arm around her, and one around one of the girls as they all grabbed each other and Hades. "This calls for a celebration."

Celebration.

The word hit with a pang she didn't expect. She hadn't celebrated anything in a long while, let alone a mediocre showing. This time, she'd earned it. She may not have podiumed, or won, but she wasn't disqualified, and she wasn't last.

June laughed out loud, beaming at him. She'd never seen anything like the utter pride and affection in his gaze. She leaned into his side and allowed him to hold her close.

Amelia often decided on a club for the afterparty, but Diego disregarded it entirely, taking them to one he deemed better quality. Of course he knew the best clubs all over the world. She didn't even care to argue with him. She'd never seen him so happy. Making him smile like this was all the encouragement she needed to pull better scores.

The club was every bit what June would have expected of Diego's taste. The line was out the door to get in. The music could be heard from nearly a block down, heavy bass seeping into her bones. The lights flashed through the open door, a kaleidoscope of color lighting the night.

The girls exchanged thrilled glances when Diego nodded toward the bouncer, and he immediately let them through, not even glancing at the line. The bass nearly knocked June off her feet, and in an instant, they were skittering off to the bar. Diego passed a card off to open a tab, and when the girls reached for their own wallets, he laughed and swatted their hands away. "My treat."

He turned back to the bartender to order a round of shots for everyone and Lola leaned over to June, whisper-shouting in her ear over the music. "If you don't marry him, I'm going to."

"Oh?" June challenged. "And Catalina?"

Lola pinched her.

If Diego partied this hard when she did decent, she'd hate to see what he looked like when she did well.

Everything was loud. The booming music, the shouting and the squealing from the girls, the laughter as Diego ordered shots left and right for her and her crew. June had never felt so weightless before. So alive. When June asked Diego to dance, he chuckled and shook his head, leaning in close. "No cameras here, *Vaquera*. Enjoy yourself."

June's heart dropped to her stomach, alcohol doing nothing to dampen her disappointment.

Cameras. Of course.

Why should they need to dance together if not publicity? June offered him a tight-lipped smile hoping the betrayal didn't show on her face as she disappeared into the crowd and slipped off with Olivia and Lola.

How could she have been so foolish?

His refusal was a scratch on her pride, a reminder of her own vulnerability that made her feel desperate and pathetic.

There was a difference between being friendly, and being friends. And they were not friends.

She didn't know how to tell him that the last thing on her mind when she found him was cameras.

The longer the night went on, the more she was certain something was off with Diego. The moment eyes turned away from him, his shoulders slumped, his eyes slid half-shut, his easy confidence wavered.

When he slipped out onto the terrace to get some air, June threw back the rest of her drink and followed.

Outside was immediately cooler and quieter, and June's ears were ringing from the newfound freedom from the volume. "What's wrong?"

Immediately, Diego tensed. He didn't look at her, elbows braced on the balcony. "Nothing—"

"Don't lie to me."

Diego sighed like it was all he could do, staring at the drink in his hand, refusing to meet her gaze. "It's . . . Lotus. They extended my contract. Three more years with the option to extend."

A wave of equal parts dread and anxiety washed over her. It worked. Diego's seat was secure. Their deal was up.

"Oh," she said softly, followed by a droning silence.

He gripped at his own arms until his fingers were white. "*'Oh'*? That's it?"

She worried at her bottom lip. This wasn't how this was supposed to go. It was October. Their seasons were winding down. "Congrats."

Her mind was a million miles away. It had been possibly the worst season she could have managed. She didn't stand a fucking chance. Her career was as good as dead. She might as well delegate the will now.

"We should do a clothing line in the off-season."

June blinked, letting the words settle in her mind. "You . . . what?"

He raised a brow. "You don't want to? I was going to offer to buy you another horse outright, but I knew you wouldn't accept it. Figured you might be easier persuaded by this."

June blinked. And blinked. Entirely unsure of what to say. "Are they cutting your salary?"

"Mine?" he actually laughed. "*Chica testaruda*, I had the best season Lotus has had since they bought the team two decades ago. My paycheck is perfectly intact."

Her confusion tripled. "You have your seat."

He quirked a brow at her. "Yes?"

"I don't expect you to stick around."

This time, Diego was the one rendered speechless. "Stick around?" He turned around then, finally facing her in his entirety. His brows were drawn together in a mix of hurt and disbelief. "You

. . . We aren't square."

"Yes, we are," she argued. "I promised you your seat, and you promised me sponsors—"

His voice hardened, punctuating each word. "We are not square."

June opened her mouth to argue, and he held up his hand, cutting her off immediately. "June, I would sponsor every cent of your career if you would only let me."

The words hit her like a ton of bricks. The idea that he would take her on. Be responsible for her. That he wouldn't let her fail. She'd never had that before.

The surprise must have shown on her face, because he sighed and ran his fingers through his hair, rolling his eyes at himself like he'd never meant to tell her that. That only served to stun her more. That he meant it. "I'm not stupid enough to think you'd actually let me. I know you better. But at least let me help."

June fumbled for something to say, dumbed and cowed by his confession. "I . . . I hardly did anything to help you get your seat. You don't owe me—"

"Not everything in life is debts, Junebug."

She promptly closed her mouth to keep a choked noise of raw emotion from escaping. Every time she tried to argue, he shut it down. He had a talent for shutting her up.

He shrugged simply. "It is good for my reputation, being seen with you so often. People paint these romantic fantasies of us." He lowered his voice, gentle and soft against the quiet of the night, the thrumming bass from the club raging on behind them his only accompaniment. "It's like magic watching you on those horses. Jumping in those arenas. You come to life. Maybe it's selfish of me, but I want to see this through. Will you let me?"

June's immediate response? *No.* Things were simple before. Using each other for attention. For opportunities.

Diego chuckled in disbelief, shaking his head. "I've never had to beg someone to let me help them before."

She grit her teeth at the jab, feeling a pang of shame at her own stubborn pride. Was her ego worth more than her career? This was different. June couldn't anchor him to stay. That meant risk. Meant trouble. What happened when watching her ride wasn't enough anymore? ". . . Fine."

"Louder," he demanded immediately.

June grit her teeth, glowering up at him. "*Fine*. We'll do the merch line. But it's fifty-fifty. I'm not your charity case."

He shook his head, a smile on his lips. "You're impossible."

She bit the inside of her cheek, fighting a smile of her own. "I know."

His eyes softened toward her, blinking as he simply watched her. "That's alright," he said. "I'm patient."

PART TWO

WINNING ISN'T EVERYTHING, IT'S THE ONLY THING

Chapter Eighteen

In the end, June didn't go to Suzuka. With flights and paddock passes ready to go, June got blissfully sick. She'd never been so happy to contract strep in her entire life. She laid in her bed with an aching throat and cough drops tucked into her cheek, watching her TV as Diego had to retire the car due to a punctured tyre from an earlier collision. She sighed in relief. A part of her had been terrified he was going to win it and she wouldn't be there.

June made it through October and November without a race due to conflicting schedules. She didn't even come close to winning a Grand Prix. She didn't qualify for the Super Grand Prix. She'd been the commentators' main talking point all season. She knew they all reveled in her failure. The Sensational Rookie's fall from grace.

As for Diego, with three races remaining, he was pushed out of the running for the Driver's Championship. Her team came to the conclusion he had no interest in June attending a race for the rest of the season. She was free. He took fourth overall. June took thirty-fourth.

And just like that, the season came to an abrupt halt. The holidays were upon them. Lola and Olivia went back to their respective homes to see family, the chaos of their hallway reduced to stagnant silence. June absolutely dreaded the end-of-season break. At least last year she'd had Midus. At least she had a monumentally terrific season. This time, June had only the work load to distract her from her failure. Now, in the middle of a break, it threatened to ravage her whole. Everyone left, and suddenly, June was alone in Italy.

Four years ago, baby-June probably would have shit herself at that fact. She wished her Italian was better.

The days passed in a prolonged blur. The sun rose, she ate, she filled her hours with horses and devouring books by the dozen. She trained. She taught Hades how to 'smile' for a photo.

She trained.

June slept. A lot. She went to cafes—to practice her Italian, of course. It had nothing to do with the gnawing ache of loneliness deep in her bones. Even the horses didn't dampen the hurt now. She rode. She trained.

June had been alone her whole life. She'd come to rather enjoy her own company. But she'd always had Ava. Now, all she had were horses that only wanted fed. She was lonesome. The ache was familiar. Had she been lonely the whole time? Her whole life? The reply came sharp—*of course, you have.* She'd never really had the time to think about it before.

She trained.

She stared at the ceiling and let the hours pass. She contemplated redecorating her apartment, but she didn't have much talent for interior design.

She trained.

Her phone buzzed.

BEST SISTER EVER <3: merry christmas al!!!

She wondered if it ever got easier.

All the busy hours in the world could not fill the everlasting cavern of loneliness in her heart.

The break passed as all breaks did—slowly. January passed. February showed its face, and June tried not to collapse with relief. Just like that, they were thrown back into the havoc of competition.

The season kicked off in Qatar—this time without June ending up in jail. Time off had been good for Hades. He started the season strong. Eleventh place. Not impressive by any means, but they made it through each round clear, and they earned points. Oviatt only seemed to get worse. June had searched high and low for another horse, but Amelia's opinions remained the same. Against her better judgement, Hades and Oviatt were this season's horses yet again.

Despite June's best wishes, she couldn't hide from Formula One forever. The call from Charlene came at the beginning of March. With track renovations scheduled for later in the year, the Monza Grand Prix had been moved to mid-March. June couldn't very well turn down an invite to her fake-boyfriend's Grand Prix in her own country. Monza was considered Lotus's home race, being an Italian company, and June could never say no to them either.

June arrived in Monza Friday morning. June wasn't sure she could stomach the four full days a race weekend entailed, so she settled for three. Friday: a practice session. Saturday: a practice session and the qualifying race. Sunday: race day.

Diego insisted on driving her to the paddock, mainly because he wanted journalists to see them arriving together. He picked her up from her hotel the way he'd promised. The crowd seemed to have followed him, and the moment he arrived, the grounds around them erupted in chaos. He gathered her from the lobby, ushering her out.

June nearly passed out at the sight of his car. A Bugatti Chiron, as he had told her, so black it swallowed all light around it. It was low to the ground and the engine growled in a way that made June's heart pound with excitement.

He opened the door for her, ushering her in, and the growing crowd went wild. Diego turned to offer them a wave before he made his way into the driver's side. June sat tucked into the corner of her seat, eyes wide as she took in the interior. Pristine black leather with white stitching. There wasn't a speck of dust or a single scratch. A touch different from the SUV she and the girls were toted around in.

"You can relax, you know," Diego laughed as he threw the car into drive. "It won't bite."

June huffed, caught red-handed. The purr of the engine was addictive. "Do you relax while driving this?" she challenged, but Diego merely shrugged. Of course he did. Perhaps this was what she looked like to him on her horses. "This thing is more expensive than anything I've ever owned."

Even his laugh sounded more luxurious driving this car. "What do you drive?"

June scoffed. "I don't have a license." She never got one back in Texas, unable to afford the mandatory driver's education classes and Ava's dance classes. She drove all the time. But she served the local cops their morning coffee, and they all knew it was June. They'd just pretend they hadn't seen anything.

He almost looked offended. "Well, we'll have to fix that."

June eyed the car, a smirk growing on her face. "Can I drive it?"

Diego's head whipped to the side. "You just told me you don't have a license!"

She threw her hands up in innocence. "I don't have a license! That doesn't mean I don't know how to drive!"

Diego snorted, eyes fixed on the road. "No, you cannot drive it. Nobody drives my cars except for me and the valet."

June's jaw dropped, laughing in disbelief. "That is the *douchiest* sentence you have ever said."

His head swiveled to look at her, fumbling to defend himself. "N—No! Not like that, I just mean—"

June laughed out loud and Diego huffed, but he was smiling. "Ugh, *June*."

Diego shut up, as though humbled but he had sparked June's curiosity. She leaned in closer, pinning him under peering eyes. "How many cars do you have?"

His answer was automatic. "Nope. I'm not telling you now."

June swatted at his arm. "You have to!"

Diego shot a sheepish look in her direction. ". . . Seven. But this is my nicest one! Most of the others are vintage collectibles."

June laughed at his attempted mix of showing off and humility. "The nicest one to drive me around in? I'm honored."

Diego merely chuckled, casting a glance in her direction. "Everything for this weekend is the nicest. I want everything perfect for you."

June blinked, taken off guard. *Perfect for you*. Everything he said held weight, and yet he said it as if it were weightless. It was a strange mix June never knew how to take.

He cleared his throat abruptly. "That's how PR relationships work. People won't talk if I'm not going above and beyond."

Of course. How silly of her to forget. June offered him a tight-lipped smile and watched out the window.

Diego turned up the music, singing along as they coasted along the highway. It felt odd to go such a normal speed in a supercar, minivans packed full of kids passing them with ease. Diego wasn't in a hurry, windows down, enjoying the beautiful scenery.

Until a white car pulled up beside them. Another Bugatti, identical to his car in everything except color. It was his teammate Oscar, windows down, blasting music. He revved his engine at Diego, grinning at the proposed challenge.

Diego tutted, waving his hand dismissively. "I have my lady with me, *cabrón*. Get lost."

June's heart leapt—half at his words and half at the promise of going full speed in a supercar. Her reply came automatically. "Race him."

Diego's head whipped to the side, his mouth half open as though he were about to ask if she was certain. Clearly, he found his answer in her gaze. He whipped around to meet Oscar's gaze as he reached to adjust a dial on the steering wheel and turn a key in the side door. It felt like the split second in the arena before the bell sounded, energy and power palpable in every breath, waiting to be cut loose.

Diego gripped the wheel with both hands.

The car roared to life under his touch and they shot off into a gap between vehicles on the highway. June yelped as the force of it slammed her back against the seat, the world dissolving into a blur beside her. Air whooshed through the windows, her hair whipping across the empty space.

June hollered into the rushing wind and Diego joined her, both of them shouting their delight until they were dissolving into laughter. Diego stole glances at her in utter delight as they darted between cars on the highway.

"Watch the road!" June screamed.

Diego had to shout to be heard across the rushing wind. "This isn't even fast, *Vaquera!*"

"This is so illegal!"

"Only if they catch you!"

He reached for the volume dial, cranking it up. Oscar had gotten caught behind a stack of cars on the highway and he was diving between them, gaining on them in the distance. There was nothing but clear stretch of road before the pair. Diego rolled the windows up before he gunned it, shooting off across the highway. She watched in the rearview as Oscar's car shrunk to the size of an ant in the distance. All the turbulence and rollercoasters in the world could not have prepared her for the sheer force of gravity diving between lanes at nearly two hundred miles an hour. She had a death grip on the *ohshit* handle, torn between terror and utter thrill.

She'd never known this kind of speed. Even on the back of a horse, where there was no such thing as a seatbelt or safety restraints, she could never have imagined a thrill that could equal it.

They reeled it back in as they got closer to the track, and Oscar finally caught up, cruising alongside them with a scowl.
Diego held onto the wheel with one hand, leaning out the window to shout at him. "Hey *cabrón*—"

Oscar just shook his head, clearly irritated at having been bested. "Shut up!"

Oscar coasted behind them as they rolled into the Monza track location together. It was nothing like June had ever seen. She hadn't expected the most prestigious in motorsport to be the same as her hometown oval dirt track, but she'd at least been hoping for a comfortable resemblance. The moment fans spotted Diego's car, they swarmed, dying for a peek at Diego Cabrera in the flesh. June being in the passenger's seat didn't help, and she fought the urge to sink down onto the floor and away from the prying eyes. She vaguely wished she'd simply gone to the garage later with Charlene, who Antonia had invited along, but it was far too late now. The security guards ushered the group away from the road, allowing Diego into the gated parking lot.

They parked, and Diego hustled to open the door for her. Fans strained over the fence, peering to get a look at the girl on Diego's arm. She forced a smile and waved as they screamed a mix of her and Diego's names, cameras going off all around them. June swallowed hard. This was the plan. It was what they wanted. Attention. June looking like a good girlfriend.

Diego placed a hand at the small of her back, guiding her forward. "Alright?" Diego asked.

She forced a smile at him. "Great."

"Liar." He offered her an arm that she gladly accepted. "Don't worry, it overwhelms me too. We get to the garage and everything is calmer. Swear it."

Somehow, the fact that it affected Diego too made it easier.

The raceway was packed with fans. Most wore team merch—a surprising amount in Lotus gold and white. It was only the second practice session of the weekend. The crowds around the fence were loud, and June flinched away from the noise, but Diego navigated them through it with ease.

He flashed a card at a scanner and they were through security, heading for the Lotus garage. It was blissfully quieter, though the mechanics and crew members looked over to them, some pausing to take note of the woman on his arm.

Diego passed her off on Antonia who automatically swept her under her arm, rushing to find a team shirt for June as Diego was dragged away for preparations. June let Antonia take charge, the older woman's familiarity a calming presence, and her no-nonsense attitude kept June's nerves at bay. June hadn't been on a track in a long, long time.

She was given a pair of headphones, allowing her to listen in on the team's chatter as Diego took to the track. The Monza track was different from the other tracks June had seen—filled with far more straights and far less turns. The speed was nearly guaranteed to hit unprecedented highs. Diego took third in the practice and was clearly pleased about it. He jumped out of the car, brimming with energy. It was something she'd always admired. Every practice, qualifying, and race he treated the stakes the same. Treated the reward the same.

It was the thrill of the race that fueled him, the adrenaline that came from pushing the car to its limits, to find the balance of speed and performance. There was no second of complacency for him, no room for mistakes. The determination was nearly infectious.

He handled the chaos of the pit lane with practiced ease. Cameras surrounded him, mechanics and crew members rushing about. He pulled his helmet off, sticking it under his arm as he unzipped the top half of his race down to his waist. He wore a set of black fireproofs, his hair mussed and sweaty. If she thought Diego was sexy before, the man was otherworldly in a race suit now.

Diego found her easily, abandoning his helmet on a stray chair before he slung an arm around her and June feigned a grimace, trying to push him off. The cameras were on them, and they needed to give the fans a show. Diego pressed his sweaty face to June's and she faked a gag, pulling him into a hug nonetheless.

He tightened his grip like he was afraid she'd pull away for real.

The fans in the stands went wild enough to hear in the garage.

She pulled back to smile up at him, hands cupping his face. "You were incredible."

Diego's hand fell to her wrist automatically, his smile genuine and infectious. "Only because you were watching."

She rolled her eyes at him. "You're always incredible."

And then, the unthinkable—Diego *blushed*. He tried to hide it, glancing at the ground, and then the wall beside her—anywhere other than at her. But June had seen the redness creep up his neck, just beneath the collar of his fireproofs. A single genuine compliment had been enough to get the smooth-talking Diego Cabrera blushing. It was ridiculous and impossible and so endearing that all June could do was laugh.

"Are you *blushing*?"

He laughed and shoved at her hands, regaining some of his smooth swagger. "Shut up. It gets hot in the car." An excuse. He was absolutely blushing. He slung his arm around her, pulling her close to him. "Come on. Let's go get something to eat. I'm starving."

Diego treated her to a tour of the city. Ironic, considering it was the country she'd lived in for the last five years, but she hadn't seen it all yet.

He took her to a charming local restaurant where they all knew him by name. Diego was well-liked anywhere he went, treated more like family than a customer. She understood why too. His manners that first luncheon weren't just to impress Charlene, it was just his nature. He was kind and friendly to everyone he ever met. June adored it.

Diego dropped her off at her hotel, insisting on walking her to her room.

Despite herself, June actually enjoyed her day. She showered, changed, sat on her bed watching a shitty rom-com on the TV. It was late when a knock sounded at the door. Immediately, June retrieved a boot to use as a weapon. She snuck forward, peeking through the eye hole, and was met with a pacing Spaniard on the other side. It had been several hours since he had dropped her off.

June dropped the boot, kicked the deadbolt, and slid the door open. "Diego?"

He whirled to face her, as though he were the one caught off guard.

"What's happened?" she asked.

Diego cleared his throat, shrugging casually despite the fact he looked like he'd seen a ghost. "Nothing."

"It's almost midnight."

Diego blinked. "Is it that late? I'm so sorry, I—" He cut himself off, looking down.

June reached forward, placing a hand on his shoulder. "Are you alright? Do you want to come in?"

Diego back peddled, blanching at the suggestion. "Oh—Oh no. I shouldn't. It's . . ." He reached into his pocket to retrieve something which he held out to return to her. It was her bracelet. One she'd removed and left in the cupholder of his car after it had pinched her one too many times.

"Oh." She reached forward and took it from his outstretched hand, twisting it in her fingers. "Thank you." She didn't tell him that it was entirely unnecessary to bring it to her. She was riding to the track with him tomorrow as well.

"Okay." He took a step backward with a shy smile. "Goodnight, then." Without another word, he turned and made his way down the hall. June stared after him in bewilderment. He hadn't made it two doors down before he whirled around and marched to her, resolve painted across his face.

He stopped before her, letting out a breath. "It means a lot that you're here."

June's heart stuttered at his words. For all his cocky arrogance and self-assuredness, it sure took a lot of nerve to tell her that.

"I didn't think you ever would, and I—" He cut himself off, swallowing hard. "Thank you."

June's grin was immediate, overwhelming and genuine. She reached forward, placing her hand on his forearm. "I wouldn't miss it for the world," she said. "I'm sorry it took me so long."

Diego's eyes were so full of hope, she could have drowned in them. He beamed like the world was his, and she'd placed it in his hands. He took a deep breath, stepping back. "*Buenas noches,* Junebug." With a final nod, he turned and disappeared down the hall, leaving June staring after him.

Chapter Nineteen

The next morning brought the final practice session and the qualifying round. The garage was electric with the buzz of the impending race, and June found herself surprisingly excited.

Diego stepped into the car, ready for the final practice. His weekend had been strong thus far, consistently pulling good results. It only took a single lap to understand this practice was not following the rest of the weekend's lead. The car was slow, turning radius was awful, brakes were spongy. He landed in eleventh. He stepped out of the car, irritation plain on his face as he was whisked away to the media pen. They were met with a three-hour break for the team to analyze the driver and car data before qualifying. June hid away in the garage. She was used to rigorous schedules, but in a different sport, it all felt so much more overwhelming.

Diego emerged from the data room, no less irritable than when he had walked in. He watched the rewinds on the TV, tsking as he set down his water bottle before he came to find her.

June offered him a smile, reaching to give his shoulder a reassuring squeeze. "It's alright. Qualifying and the race is where it counts."

Diego offered her a quick tight-lipped smile before he swiftly changed the subject. "Come on, the other drivers want to meet you properly."

He was eager to forget about his performance, and so she let him guide her through the garage. His hand rested on the small of her back, the firm pressure of his palm warm against her. The rumor mill had been circulating through the paddock as much as it did through the rest of the world. The moment they emerged she heard the coos and laughter amongst the drivers. She wondered how much teasing Diego had been subjected to for bringing her along.

The other drivers were eager to greet her, and Diego seemed to take great pride in showing her off.

Oscar, who she had already met at the charity auction so many months ago, and again racing to the track, immediately pulled her into a friendly hug.

Diego moved his hand from the small of her back to her arm, keeping her close to him while the other drivers teased. It was so natural that June almost let herself forget that they were just pretending. The other drivers seemed relaxed around her, and they all laughed as they traded friendly jabs with Diego. But he kept her close, as if the moment he released her into the paddock, the other drivers might swoop in and steal her away.

The top Mercedes driver emerged from the garage and she recognized him immediately from the race graphics and the podiums—Leo Lemieux, the current reigning world champion. Three races in, he was in the lead for the World Drivers' Championship. He was good-looking, tall and easygoing with platinum blond hair and long lashes. "June Walker." He acknowledged her with a handsome smile as he extended his hand for her to shake. "It's a pleasure to finally meet you. I'm quite the fan."

Diego clutched June's arm in a vise grip, all lightheartedness fleeing as the man neared to introduce himself. June pulled out of Diego's grasp as it neared to the point of pain, extending her hand to meet Leo's. "It's nice to meet you as well. Congrats on the recent drives."

Diego drew a sharp breath behind her, and Leo seemed very pleased with this response. He thanked her, and then reached forward and clapped Diego on the back. For a split second, June wondered if Diego was going to punch him. Leo excused himself and headed back towards his own garage. The other drivers, sensing the change in Diego's demeanor, said their goodbyes and followed suit.

The moment the drivers dispersed, Diego turned to June with a look that demanded an explanation. "'*Congrats on the recent drives*?" he repeated.

June's brows furrowed at him. "I'm sorry, was that not sportsmanlike?"

He drew a sharp breath, rubbing his hands over his face, shaking his head in disbelief. He turned back to the Lotus garage. "I have to get ready for quali. Find Antonia again."

Her lips parted in shock, watching as he turned and marched back to the garage, his body wrought with irritation. June tried to keep from scowling as she grit her teeth and sought out Antonia. She found her in the garage where she took a seat beside her and shrugged her headphones on, crossing her arms and waiting.

The time for the qualifying laps soon came, and June found herself sitting on a rolling tool chest in the garage, headphones on to keep informed as she watched from afar. Anger had been bubbling in her chest ever since Diego had dismissed her, but the moment he stepped into the car, the anxiety returned. Qualifying consisted of three sessions, starting with all twenty drivers and eliminating them five at a time until only the ten fastest remained. Diego was determined to be among them. Determined to be at the top.

As the laps progressed, the tension in the garage increased. The engineers chattered off a million things until even June was irritable, and Diego finally shouted over the radio. "Shut up and let me drive!"

That shouldn't have been as hot as it was. She was still mad at him, but it was hot.

The mechanics and crew members watched closely, tracking the radio reports from the track, the car's speed, fuel and tyre temperatures, and the number of laps left in the session. Whatever tweaks the mechanics had managed between sessions had worked. The car was back at its previous race pace, and Diego was flying through the laps. Everyone waited anxiously, and June found herself clenching the edge of her seat as the minutes passed. Diego's lap times were good, but the end of qualifying still left him in second place. Behind Leo.

The drivers made their ways out of their cars and into their garages. Despite an incredible qualifying and a competitive starting spot on the grid tomorrow, Diego was agitated. His team offered congratulations and encouragement, and June stepped up to the pool. "Good work," she smiled. Diego merely nodded at her before he brushed past. Her lips parted in surprise. The cameras were on them. She was at her first race. This *had* to go well, and yet, Diego was acting like a child.

He didn't say a word to her, barging off to his driver's room. A single sharp knock was the only warning he got before she marched in, closing the door behind her. "What's your problem?" she snapped.

If Diego hadn't been irritated before, he sure as hell was now. Barging into his room to find him in the middle of undressing. "My problem?" he spat, shedding his fireproofs and pulling on a shirt. "Aren't you supposed to be buddied up with Leo?"

June's heart stopped in her chest, a moment of inconsolable betrayal ravaging her. Was that what he thought of her? Every moment she had spent trying to get along with his fellow drivers—to prove to him that she was likable, that she was someone he should keep around—all he saw was a friend whoring herself out. And then, the disbelief turned to rage. *"Excuse me?"* she spat, taking a step forward. "Are you seriously *jealous* right now?"

Diego drew a frustrated breath, running his hands through his hair before he turned back to her. "There were cameras around," he said sharply.

"Cameras!" June laughed in disbelief. It all came back to the damn cameras. "Cameras a hundred yards away who can't hear what we're saying! But they can see you stomp off after I spoke to your rival. You're the one making us look bad!"

Diego rubbed his hands across his face in frustration. For a moment, she almost thought he was shaking. "I need you with me on this. Not trying to shack up with another driver!"

June wanted to slap him. Wanted to punch him again. Wanted to shove him against the wall and make him shut up. "Oh, *I'm* the player now?" If he was going to bite, she was going to bite back harder. "How many girls have you taken back to your hotel this season?"

For what it was worth, Diego almost looked offended. "So that's what you think of me."

"Clearly it's what you think of me!"

He was so close to her now that she could feel the heat coursing through his body. "Oh, I don't think you're a player, I think you're just desperate."

June's jaw dropped. Any sympathy or attempt at understanding died in her throat. "Desperate," she spat back at him. "You're right. Maybe I'll go see if Leo agrees. Thanks for the idea, Diego." June shoved away from him, opening the door partway when he reached above her and slammed it shut, effectively trapping her inside with him. He had her cornered.

"Oh no, you don't get to walk away after that," he hissed.

He pushed her out of the way, leaning back against the door as he crossed his arms over his chest. She wasn't sure whether to be angry or pleased that he'd stopped her. That he hadn't let her leave to be angry. She'd gotten the reaction she wanted—any reaction at all. "Oh," she said shortly. "Must not be too desperate."

Diego's jaw was clenched tight enough to break. He was breathing hard, his fingers dug into the flesh of his palm. She was getting under his skin, and she was grateful for it.

She shoved at his chest. "I'm not you, Diego. I don't just fall into bed with anyone who acts interested. I'm focused on my career."

He cocked his head to the side, his lips twitching up in amusement. "Oh, we're bringing careers into this, are we?"

June froze like she'd been slapped. "What's that supposed to mean?"

HIs expression changed all at once. His eyes widened as he realized what he'd said, backing down. ". . . Forget it."

"No," she surged forward, shoving him back as she raised her voice to a shout. "You made your bed, you fucking lie in it! What's that supposed to mean?"

Every time he opened his mouth, he only made it worse. His back was flush against the door, and she was now standing mere centimeters away.

"I just . . . it's just . . . you . . ." He huffed, completely at a loss for words as he tried to come up with a way to dig himself out of this hole.

"Fucking *say it*, Diego!"

Her scream was the final straw.

Diego swung at her.

June gasped, whirling to shield her head with her hands as she braced for the blow.

It didn't come.

Her entire body shook with adrenaline, her hands quivering as she lowered them from her head. June spared a glance at him.

No.

No, Diego hadn't swung at her. He'd thrown his hands up. Frustration. Not the white-hot rage June had known her whole life. And now? Horror. His lips parted in surprise, his eyes wide like they were trying to say everything he couldn't, conveying a language neither of them knew but both understood.

I would never.

There was no stopping the tears. They spilled without permission, streaming down her cheeks until they hit the floor.

He took a step forward, his voice soft and hands out in front of him like he was approaching a cowered stray, starving and digging through trash cans. Ready to bolt. And she was.

"June—"

She held her hands out defensively in front of her, stepping back. "Don't."

"Mi amor—"

June turned and darted around him and out the door, desperate to get away. From him. From herself. From the past.

Sometimes, it was like she'd never left that house. Things had settled since qualifying. Fans had funneled out of the stadium, the paddock and track vacating until all that was left were mechanics tinkering in garages, and June sitting on the Lotus roof.

It was the only place she'd ever found refuge in Texas. The only place her father was too drunk to follow. Not Diego though. Of course he would follow. Of course he *could*. Just another reminder that she was no longer in the life she had left behind.

Of course, he never would have struck her. Still, knowing it all, she had flinched.

The sun was sinking behind the stadium when Diego finally found her—her all cried out, him settled from any anger. Now, there was only the bitter ache of what had happened. The guilt of having flinched away. Of having thought, even if for only a split second, that Diego was capable of such a thing.

She kept her legs tucked up to her chest, arms wrapped around her, jaw clenched tightly as she stared out over the track, sun setting over it and casting an orange glow over the blacktop.

"It's cold," Diego remarked softly, drawing his jacket off and pulling it around her shoulders.

She knew it was, but the chattering of her jaw and the stiffness in her fingers were comforting. Still, she was grateful for the warmth. It smelled like him. Felt like him.

He said nothing else for a long moment, sitting beside her in silence until it seemed he could no longer take it. "I would never—"

"I know."

"Do you want to talk—"

"No." Her answer was immediate.

"No. No you never do talk about things that hurt, do you? That's why they never heal."

June drew a deep, shaky breath, staring down at her own shoes. "I'm not—I'm not some kind of victim. I'm fine. I got out."

"No," he agreed, letting his feet dangle off the edge of the roof. "No, you are far too stubborn to be anyone's victim. That doesn't mean that you deserved what happened."

It was the first time she had heard it in her life. Not pity, but sympathy. *You didn't deserve it.* She bit her lip to stop it from quivering, letting her head fall on his shoulder. His arm fell around her, pulling her securely against his side. He leaned over to press a kiss to the top of her head before he rested his chin on her. "You will tell me someday, hm?"

June swallowed hard, and she nodded, a silent vow. *I'll let you in one day. Not today. But someday.*

It was a challenge.

Stick around. Stay. Prove to me someone can.

"I'm sorry I yelled at you," he said softly. "You didn't deserve that. Leo just has a way of making me feel like a failure in a way nobody else does, and seeing you with him . . ."

She leaned into him. "You're better than him."

"The driver rankings say differently. Quali said differently." She'd never heard him like that before, his voice stripped of its usual boisterous confidence.

She nodded knowingly. She was more than familiar with feeling inadequate. "Well, I say that you're better. And I'm always right, so . . ."

Diego let an amused breath out of his nose, his lips quirked up in a smile.

"Just means he's got a hell of a fight coming his way tomorrow. I can't wait to watch you pass him"

He chuckled softly, shaking his head softly as he stared down at his feet. "You have so much faith in me."

June huffed a breath, bumping his shoulder. "Uh, I'm a WAG now. That's my job."

He laughed out loud, leaning his head onto hers. There was a quiet intimacy in it. Referring to herself as part of the wives-and-girlfriends club. It was fake. They both knew that. But it was still a secret just for them. They watched the sky until the orange turned to black, stars peeking out from behind clouds.

Diego jumped to his feet, offering her a hand. "Come on. Let's get you down before we both freeze together."

June could only smile and take his hand, letting him pull her to feet and back to the safety of the paddock.

Chapter Twenty

As much as June loved racing, something about watching Diego take the track still intimidated her. She'd been seated in the Lotus garage with Antonia and the rest of his team. Charlene reached across her seat to put a hand on June's shaking leg to steady her. Reassure her that this was okay. That she should be consumed with the thrill of the race rather than the terror of what-ifs. But the what-ifs lingered.

It was the speed, she figured. Watching a camera tracking the cars for TV was nothing like watching them rip past so quickly the colors were the only tell as to which car belonged to which team.

It was the fact that this was dangerous. It was the fact he had four wheels under him instead of four legs.

But he had been there for her. It was her turn. Diego was one of the most talented drivers of his generation with a promising future, and she desperately wanted to be there to see it.

Diego looked at home on a track, like he belonged amongst the pavement and the smell of burning rubber and race fuel. If she thought Diego was beautiful at her competitions and in nightclubs, the man on the track was an entirely different beast. His white-and-gold race suit was zipped down to his hips, his helmet braced under one arm. He was ready for the fight.

The Italian national anthem was sung, and immediately after the drivers were pulling on their helmets, jumping in their cars, and slamming down their visors.

He knew where the finish line was and he'd be damned if he let anyone cross it before him.

The safety car led out the formation lap, drivers warming their breaks and tyres for better grip before they lined up on the grid before the lights.

Each of the five lights lit up red one by one.

The lights went out, and Diego was off like a bat out of hell. She knew he was competitive. Knew he was good at what he did. But to see it in person was entirely different.

He stayed at the front of the pack, refusing to allow another driver through the gaps as the rest of the cars lurched forward into turn one. He held his place firmly and aggressively. With the two most competitive cars, Leo and Diego surged forward ahead of the others, their teammates following a few places behind. They may have had the same cars, but everyone understood the real fight was between Leo and Diego.

The speed of the race was astonishing. It was a blur—a literal, physical blur. Each time the drivers whirled past the pit she was left reeling, her head whipping around in attempts to follow.

The Diego she knew was so light-hearted. It was easy to forget this was who he was. A thrill-seeking, trouble-making fighter. A racer.

He stayed locked in a fight with Leo for first. Each move he made was calculated, playing mind games with the Swedish driver as if he was made for it. He was fearless, unbridled confidence in his movements. It was like watching a chess match at two hundred miles an hour. Each curve and straight brought different opportunities to pass. Diego didn't lessen, hunting down Leo like his life depended on it.

June leaned forward in her seat, her heart lodged in her throat, her hands gripped together so tight her knuckles were turning white.

It was an endless loop of moves and countermoves, both drivers fighting to push the other off-kilter and onto the defense.

Diego shot into an opening, squeezing just far enough up on the track to pull ahead. The garage exploded in excitement, just in time for Leo to overtake Diego again on the next corner. If it put a damper on Diego's determination, he didn't show it.

June wanted nothing more than to close her eyes. To cover her ears. To stop watching. But she couldn't look away. Not while Diego was out there. He took the outside line again, and again, and again.

Each time Diego was able to regain his lead, Leo was hot on his tail, shoving him out of the way.

The race moved into its final laps. Leo was in the lead, keeping the younger driver at bay. Diego was nipping at his heels, but every attempt to regain the lead was blocked.

The Swede was playing a game of cat-and-mouse, keeping himself in front of Diego. But then, Leo lost his grip.

It was an instant of him braking too soon, turning a tad too wide, and Diego shot through the opening and cut inside. Then, Diego was in the lead, shooting out of the corner before Leo was even halfway through.

Diego zipped ahead, putting space between him and Leo. The garage erupted in screams, grabbing one another, cheering and shouting. Giddiness consumed her, pride welling in her chest. He was leading. Diego was winning. He added a second to the gap between them, and then another.

Even Charlene, with her professionalism and usual poise, was cheering, her hands balled into fists, pressed against her lips as she watched the race unfold.

Diego was still in the lead in the final laps.

June's eyes were locked on the screen as he came around the corner, her smile electric and all-consuming.

Everything happened at once.

He had no time to see the debris from another crash come hurtling across the track. Like he had a target painted on him, it aimed and fired.

It ricocheted off the halo of the car in a pieces, a piece of debris flying through the barrier and striking him directly in the head.

Diego went limp in the cockpit. The car went hurtling down the track with no driver to guide it. The car slammed into the wall, the force of impact hard enough to send shudders through the stands.

A horrified noise escaped June's throat, a hand clapping over her mouth.

The silence was deafening. A red flag waved vehemently to stop the race. Tension ran thick through the crowd.

Diego wasn't moving.

Vaguely, June could hear the terror around her.

She froze in place, her eyes wide, breath caught in her lungs as she stared in shock at the scene reflected on the screen.

There was movement on the track, paramedics rushing to the car. They scrambled to get him out of the car. Diego fell into their arms like a ragdoll. Not a single muscle contracting. No reaction at all.

They laid him on the ground, medics crawling around him. They were checking his airway. Trying to get him breathing.

June couldn't hear a thing. Everything sounded like it was coming to her underwater.

June was running before she knew it, rushing for the track. No. *No.*

No, he couldn't be.

The moment June started for the gate, someone grabbed her around the waist, hauling her back. *Charlene.*

"Let me go!" she cried, struggling against the arms wrapped around her. "No! Let me go! I have to go to him, let me go!"

She couldn't think. She couldn't breathe. She needed to get to him. She needed him to be alive.

She collapsed into Charlene's arms, sobs wracking through her body. "No—No."

Antonia was at her side, grabbing her by the face. "Look at me—Look at me, June! We'll go to the hospital. We'll meet him there."

But somewhere deep within, June knew the truth. "He's dead."

"You don't know that!" Antonia screamed, as desperate for it to be true as she was. It was then June realized she was crying too. The world seemed to be spiraling out of control. Everything fuzzy and off-kilter. The noise in the grandstands was a roar, but it was all a buzz in her ears. The only thing she could focus on with perfect clarity was the fact he was dead.

She was vaguely aware through the fog her brain was drowning in that Charlene and Antonia were pulling her toward the exit, forcing her to follow on legs that didn't want to hold her weight. With every step away from him, June's heart ached more, panic ravaging her.

She could hear the screaming from the radios, demanding to know if he was alive. June was ushered into a car, hardly able to think or see over the image replaying in her mind of the debris hitting his helmet. Of the force of him slamming into the wall.

June's body hummed, the world disappearing around her. She wanted to crawl out of her skin. She couldn't think. She couldn't talk. She couldn't breathe.

She hadn't told him. She hadn't told him any of it. She'd spent so long hiding herself from him and now she would never get the chance to do anything differently.

Antonia cried out in relief, a hand clapped over her mouth. "He has a pulse."

The words slammed into June like a freight train.

He has a pulse. He's not dead.

The world came into sharp focus. June's breath left her in a whoosh, her heart pounding in her chest so hard she wondered briefly if it would explode. Abruptly, June sobered, like ice had been poured down her back. She had to get to him. Had to see him. To see that he was alive and that it was true.

She stumbled into the car, wide-eyed and stunned. Charlene pulled her close, and June buried her face against her, as if Charlene's embrace alone could make all of this disappear.

The streets of Italy rushed by in a flurry, minutes passing like hours.

The moment the car stopped at the hospital, June flung the door open, greeted with dozens of cameras and microphones.

The journalists had gotten there first. She was surrounded by bright flashes, cameras pointed in her face, mics stuck out in front of her. She flinched away, overwhelmed by the camera flashes and the questions flying at her from all sides.

"Miss Walker, tell us—"

"How do you feel—"

"Is he going to live?"

They pressed in around her, shouting and grabbing, trying to get to be the first ones with the story.

All at once, she broke away from Charlene and Antonia, pushing into a dead sprint. She shoved through the sea of journalists. She had to get to him. Had to find Diego. Her feet hit the cement, propelling her forward through the doors of the hospital and to the front desk.

"Diego Cabrera," she demanded.

She saw the staff flip the switch into de-escalation mode, abandoning any work on their computers. "We can't share private information of patients."

June slammed her hand down on the desk. "Where is he? Is he okay? Take me to him!"

Charlene was at her side in a second, grabbing June by the wrists and dragging her back. She offered her apologies to the woman before she ushered June back into the waiting room. "Enough," Charlene spat, her voice sharp enough to cut through June's hysteria. "We can't do anything but wait."

A choked sob escaped June, and Charlene's arms fell around her, dragging her to sit. That was all they could do. Sit and wait.

The nurses informed Antonia when Diego arrived in the emergency room. As his manager, she was the closest thing to family he had there. They kept her updated, and Antonia in turn kept June and Charlene on the same page. His vitals were steady, but he was in rough shape. The force of the debris hitting his head coupled with the impact had snapped his neck brace and He had shattered a vertebrae in his neck, and he was rushed into surgery.

June was sick to her stomach. They sat together in the waiting, the hours droning on with no updates. Charlene disappeared to find a restroom, and June turned to her phone for comfort. The girls had been texting her from home constantly, attempting to reassure her he would be okay.

The worst thing June could have done was Google *'F1 crashes'*.

She had expected bad. She hadn't expected to see a marshal brutally torn apart to the point of being unrecognizable, or to watch them remove a decapitated driver's lifeless body. She had expected collisions—she hadn't expected the debris, tyres, or entire cars hurtling through the air.

Her mind ran rampant, imagining Diego in place of the others. Imagining her friend torn to pieces in a second. Her friend destroyed by a stray tyre. Her friend's life ended brutally from a fire, from a malfunction, from a failed piece of equipment.

From exactly what had happened today.

She hadn't even realized tears were streaming down her face until somebody pulled her phone out of her hands. "No," Antonia said. "Don't. It's better not to even think about it."

But June had already thought about it. She had already seen it. Had already tainted her mind with the horrific stories from the past. Her entire body was shaking, uncontrollable tears streaming down her shock-ridden face. "Why? Why would anyone want to be a part of that—"

"Why do you get on that horse?"

June grasped for an answer. "But—but—"

Antonia just shook her head. "Sometimes there's a very specific urge that only one thing can fulfill. It's horses for you. For Diego? It's racing. He knows the risks."

She whirled on Antonia, tears streamed down her face. "It could *kill* him! It nearly did!"

"He's tougher than he looks."

June choked on her sob, clutching at her aching heart in her chest. "Not tougher than this!"

Antonia sighed, sitting down beside her. "It's why we love him," she reminded June. "Diego is a racer. It's in his blood."

June couldn't handle it. Her breaths came in hurried gasps, her hands shaking as she clutched at the seat of her chair.

June's entire world blurred except for the panic consuming her at Diego's state.

The blurred images were not enough to save her from the prowess of her mind, the horror of Diego's accident combining with the brutal reality of drivers and stewards less fortunate than him.

The panic had June in a vise grip, no touch or sound getting through to her. Her breaths came in short, quick gasps, a sharp pang in her chest. Moments passed in a blur before Charlene returned, and her arms wrapped around her, holding her with a protective fierceness. "Breathe, June. You have to be there when he wakes up."

When he woke up. Not *if*. Because he was okay. Because everything was going to be okay.

The suggestion was enough to bring her clarity. She had to be there when Diego woke up.

She needed to be there when he woke up.

The words echoed in her mind, cutting through the pain and the pounding in her chest as she clung to them. She needed to be there for him. She burrowed her head into Charlene's side and forced herself to breathe.

June pulled herself together. At least, enough to resort to pacing and picking at her fingers until they bled.

It was a long time before the surgeon finally made her way to the waiting room to announce things had gone well.

June collapsed in her relief, clutching at her chest as though the consolation were too much to handle.

The woman spoke heavily-accented English in a soft cadence, as though they may all fall apart if she spoke too loudly or too quickly. "He's in rough condition. His vision is impaired from the concussion, but he'll get it back. He's in a lot of pain. He's very heavily sedated, but he is awake for now. He's in room 215, if you'd like to see him—"

June was out of her chair before the doctor finished, pushing past her and through the door. Antonia and Charlene didn't follow, taking the time to speak with the surgeon. They let her go. She had to see him. June sprinted down the hall, numbers whirling by until she stood at the entrance to his room, hand braced on the wall.

June steadied herself, drawing a deep breath and letting it out slow. His vision wasn't right. She had to be calm. Not panic him more. She pushed the door open softly, taking a few steps into the room.

June nearly collapsed at the sight of him on the hospital bed. She had never seen him look so small. His face was covered in dark purple bruises, his breathing slow and labored. There was an IV in his arm, a nasal oxygen tube resting low on his face. She knew it was bad. To see it in person made it all that much more real. She opened her mouth to speak, but he beat her to it. "June?" Anxiety and hope blended together as he called out for her, his head staying carefully centered, staring forward with a blank, terror-ridden expression.

"It's me."

Immediately, he began to shake. His hand reached toward her as much as he could lift it, and June rushed forward to take it.

"June." He whispered her name like a mantra, desperate to keep hold of her. "June."

There was a chair in the corner, and she dragged it over to sit at his bedside. She brought his hand up to her lips, pressing kiss after kiss to his knuckles, tears streaming onto his hands. "I'm here," she whispered over and over, kissing his hand, his fingers, the inside of his wrist. He held her hand with an iron grip, like he was afraid she'd disappear the moment he let go. "I'm right here, Diego. I'm not going anywhere. I'm right here."

His words came out panicked, more fearful than she'd ever heard him. "I can't see—"

"I know, D. Doc said it won't stay long. It'll be okay."

He clung to her like she was his only anchor in a storm-bound sea. "I—I can't stay awake—"

"He's on a lot of sedatives," the nurse supplied from the corner where she was tidying up items on a tray, doing her best to pretend she wasn't there. "It's normal to be drowsy."

June squeezed his hand, nodding towards the nurse and mouthing a quick *'thank-you'*.

"You hear that?" June asked, and Diego squeezed her hand tighter in confirmation. "They're going to take care of you—"

"Stay." His eyes fluttered with the effort it took to keep them open, fighting the sleep that threatened to pull him under.

"I'm here. I'm not going anywhere. You're okay," she breathed. "Just rest."

Diego sighed as though he'd needed her permission. A moment later, his eyes shut, slipping into a deep sleep as the sedatives hit him at full force. June raised his hand to her mouth, pressed a gentle kiss to it, and held it to her face as she sobbed.

Diego's brief moments awake after the surgery seemed to leave everyone in much higher spirits. Antonia took one look at Diego and excused herself from the room, wiping tears from her eyes. It was as though him being stable had given her the permission she needed to finally cry.

Charlene booked them into a hotel close to the hospital, trying to persuade her to join them to get some rest. But June had told Diego she would stay. So, she did.

Hours passed. The sun rose, climbed to its peak and then slowly began to descend. Doctors checked on him hourly. Nurses brought food and drinks for her, trying to coax her into at least attempting to sleep, but their words and efforts went in one ear and out the other. Diego had broken his neck, he had several broken ribs and a bad concussion. He would be asleep for a long time, they explained. He was on enough medication to keep him docile for days at a time. But that didn't stop her from waiting.

She dozed in the chair when she could, but her grip never went lax. The thought of leaving Diego alone in this sterile, white room only made her anxiety and guilt rise. She didn't let go of his hand.

June's reaction to the crash had posted again, and again, and again, dissected on blog posts and podcasts. The replay video of Diego's crash had spread across the internet like wildfire, brought to slow motion to analyze the exact areas the debris had hit and the trajectory of the crash. June watched it once. The force of the impact in slow motion coupled with the onboard camera going dark made June so nauseous she put her phone away for the rest of the night.

June stayed at his bedside, gently stroking her thumb over his knuckles. The silence pressed in around her, covering the room in a thick blanket. The sounds of beeping machines and nurses shuffling about faded into the background.

Her head nodded, and her eyelids drooped, but she refused to close her eyes. Her body was exhausted and begging for rest that she stubbornly fought off, hanging on to consciousness and Diego's hand.

It was the sound of the heart monitor beeping faster that brought her to.

June lurched upwards, panic setting in immediately only to find those big brown eyes wide open and looking at her. "June?"

Her heart leaped into her throat at the sound of his voice. It was scratchy and raspy and hoarse, but it was his voice. She had missed it.

"Diego," she managed. She squeezed his hand as tears began to well in her eyes.

He was alive. He was awake.

Diego let out a sigh, squeezing her hand gently. "I promise I normally drive better than that."

His attempt at humor was weak, his usual energy lacking. He was exhausted and in pain and drugged to the nines... but he was alive.

"Why are you so far away?" he whispered. "Come here."

It didn't take June much convincing to comply with his request. She perched on the edge of the bed, mindful of all of the tubes and wires connected to him, as she gently took his hand into hers.

"You can see okay?" she asked.

He hummed in confirmation, his chest rising and falling in weary, shaky breaths. "I admit, I am seeing a couple of you." He squeezed her hand. "Lucky me."

She let out a surprised laugh. Her anxiety and adrenaline were fading with every word he said. She was left with a mixture of relief and exhaustion that made her feel like liquid. She swiped at her eyes with the back of her wrist, forcing away the stubborn tears that refused to yield. "Casanova." She reached forward to sink a hand into his brown curls, ragged and dirty. "I think this is the worst I've ever seen your hair."

Diego managed a huff of laughter, his voice gravelly from disuse. "Don't rub it in."

Chapter Twenty-One

Diego insisted she sleep beside him, and June obliged. June was certain it would take a full week of sleep to recover from the previous days. What she got was six hours before she was woken by a set of nurses gently pulling her off of the bed. Off Diego. She sprung into a panic, but Diego was awake, and alive, and in enough pain there was sweat pouring down his face, every muscle tensed as he gritted his teeth against it and let out a low groan. The nurses administered another round of painkillers through his IV, but the pain was inadmissible.

For all her teasing about Diego being a soft, pretty boy, he was tough as nails.

Diego's mom and sister arrived at the hospital that night. June had met them each before—his sister at a club and then a holding cell, and his mother at the art auction gala in Valencia. But it was an entirely different thing to see them in a hospital in Italy, their faces puffy from crying.

June had never seen Diego as relieved as he was when he saw them. *"Mamá,"* he whispered, holding his hands out to each of them. "B."

The moment they touched him, they dissolved in a fit of sobs, tears pricking at Diego's lash line as they showered him in kisses and offered up prayers of thanks, clinging tightly to him.

June had to leave before her own tears overwhelmed her. It was hard enough to look at Diego in such a state. Hard enough to know he'd nearly died. He was so well loved, but all the engineers and managers and friends in the world could not replicate a mother and sister's love, nor their grief.

Reyes found June in the waiting room hours later, curled up in an armchair, exhausted, and brimming with anxiety the moment Diego was out of her sight. The moment June saw her, she stood, lacing her fingers together as she waited for the woman to speak. Diego had her eyes, and looking into them brought her to tears all over again.

Reyes' arms were around her instantly, clinging to her as if she were holding the entire world in her hands. "Thank you, *mija*," Reyes whispered, pressing a kiss to June's head. "For staying with my son. For being with him."

June took a deep, shuddering breath. *Mija*. My daughter. My girl. A choked sob escaped her throat, collapsing against Reyes, and she enveloped her in a hug..

It had been two days since the accident when Diego was finally able to sit up. He seemed to gather strength with every hour, and with it, stupidity. The better he felt, the harder it was for him to take things easy.

June had never been so grateful for a long break between competitions. She had nearly two weeks until Miami. The last thing she wanted was to think about horses—or anything other than Diego. Days passed in a blur. Charlene attempted to persuade June to leave the hospital, but she couldn't be away from him without suffocating panic. Nightmares had found their way into June's sleep, the crash playing again and again the moment she closed her eyes. So, she stayed with him. She took turns with Bianca and Reyes sleeping in a cot beside his bed.

Within a week, Diego had enough strength to stand on his own. The worst of his concussion symptoms had receded. His ribs would only heal with time. His neck was the worst of it. A shattered vertebrae. They'd had to remove fragments of bone, fusing the rest of it. It would take a minimum of eight weeks to heal, and nothing could have upset Diego more. Even knowing it all, even nearly dying from it, he couldn't wait to get back in the car.

June, on the other hand, was so grateful she could cry. Eight weeks of reassurance. Of knowing Diego couldn't race. Eight weeks of knowing Diego wouldn't die. June overheard a doctor tell a nurse that the force of the debris hitting Diego should have decapitated him. It would have if it hadn't hit the ring around the cockpit first.

June's appetite had been nonexistent for the past week, but her hunger remained. Forcing herself to eat only got harder and harder. So she ate with Diego every chance she got. June returned from the cafeteria with two box lunches in hand. They ate in silence, some Spanish show on the TV that Diego had become enamored with. June's mind was in a very different place. She hadn't touched her horses in nearly two weeks. She had a competition that weekend, which gave her all of two days.

June swallowed hard, forcing her voice into a casual tone. "I'm going to pull out of Miami."

Immediately, Diego snagged the remote and paused the show, a horrified look on his face like she'd slapped him. "No. No, you are not. June, you *can't*."

She shook her head vehemently, tears threatening to overwhelm her again. "How do I leave you?—"

"Am I more important to you than a season title?" The question was a genuine one. One meant to slap some sense into her. But June's answer wasn't immediate, and that only made everything that much worse, a tear slipping down her cheek.

He abandoned his food and took her face into his hands, forcing her to meet her eyes as he wiped away the tears. "You have to. For the love of the sport. For the love of the horse. Never, ever let anything come between you and that. Especially not me. Not this." He pulled her into a hug, whispering a string of curses in Spanish. He rubbed his hands up and down her back. "You have to, June."

She knew he was right and she hated it. She couldn't afford to miss out on points, even if it was only one competition.

Everything about Miami felt tainted. Last time she'd been here, she'd lost her career. Lost her chances of a Global Champions Tour title. Lost Midus.

Now, without Diego, she spent every moment waiting on a call, wondering when the bad news would come knocking. When something would go wrong.

The anxiety threatened to swallow her, panic swarming her chest at the thought of Diego. If anything were to go wrong, she was entirely powerless. Miles and miles, hours and hours away, she could do nothing.

Could you do anything if you were there?

Riding Oviatt was almost calming. At least on him, she knew where the threat would come from. At least on him, all she could think about was staying alive.

The round was quick and easy. Oviatt channeled her energy from buzzing nerves to something she could use. They flew through the course in perfect harmony. Fourth place. It was the best she'd done since stepping off of Midus. Congratulations came from every direction all around her—even the commentators who had been ragging on her for over a year offered praise. She should be ecstatic.

Instead, all she could think of was Diego in that hospital bed.

June paced in the stalls, clutching at her chest in attempts to soothe herself. She swallowed over the bile rising in her throat, holding fingers to her neck as she tried to force her heartbeat to slow. Force the panic to dwindle.

Bianca and Reyes were with him. He was with some of the best doctors in all of Italy. He was in good hands. Still, she was sick to her stomach. With the most points she'd scored in a full year, all June wanted was Diego.

June had never been so grateful to be back in Italy. The moment the plane touched down, Antonia was waiting at the terminal. The girls piled into the car, but there was none of the usual banter. They sat in dead silence, listening as Antonia updated them all. "He's doing well. Really well, actually. The nurses are afraid he's going to eat enough to put them out of business."

June couldn't help but chuckle. The sight of the hospital rising in the distance brought about equal feelings of relief and dread. Last time she'd arrived here, she'd been convinced the only thing the doctors could do was pronounce Diego dead.

Now, he was on the mend.

Diego wasn't in his bed when they finally made it to the room, but rather lounged across the armchair in the corner of the room. He flicked through the stack of *'get-well-soon'* cards from friends, family, and fans alike. He'd been bombarded by them the moment people discovered where he was staying. There was a surprisingly small amount of bouquets, and June commented on that fact.

Diego shrugged. "That's because I sent some to every room."

A smile tugged at her lips, her heart warming as she pulled up a chair to sit in front of him. He looked well. Exhaustion weighed on his face, but there was life returned to it that had been missing the past couple weeks. He had a new neck brace, one meant to be able to take on and off.

It was big and bulky, and Diego flicked at it disapprovingly. "Makes me feel like a neutered dog."

June laughed out loud. "You look it, too."

"Gee. Thanks." He scoffed, brows raising as he rolled his eyes at her.

She chuckled, reaching forward to take his hand, rubbing her thumb across the back of his hand in soothing circles. He'd healed an exponential amount. The doctors were talking about releasing him the next day, which still left the question of the rest of his recovery. "Where will you go?"

He looked to their hands, flipping them over so her palm was face-up on his own, tracing the lines of her skin with his fingers. The change in routine seemed to have shocked his entire nervous system, from being an athlete to being bedridden for two weeks. It was a new habit. Something to soothe the restlessness. "Back to Monaco, I think."

June blinked, letting the words settle. Of everything he could have said, that was the last thing she'd been expecting. "By yourself?"

He shrugged. "The other drivers are close, and Antonia will keep an eye on me. I mean, *Mamá* offered to take time off, but she has a big art show coming up she can't miss out on. Bianca invited me to stay, but New York City is so loud—"

"Come to Florence." The words were out before she could stop them.

Diego blinked, taken aback. "What?"

She swallowed hard, meeting his eyes once before she looked down to their hands. "It . . . it looks better for us if you do. If you go to your girlfriend's." The words steamrolled out, spewing her logic as though this decision was based on rationale and she wasn't coming up with it on the spot. "You'll need good publicity now more than ever, and it gives us lots of chances for content. If you don't come it'll make it look like I don't care and that isn't good for my image either. My place is pretty small, but I have a spare room and—"

He grabbed her hand again, squeezing it tightly as he met her eyes. "I don't want to burden you, June."

He looked so genuine all June could say was the truth.

"I can't sleep," she whispered. "I . . . I have these nightmares. Of the crash. Of you dying. I can't settle until I see that you're okay. It's . . . please, Diego."

She wasn't sure what made him agree. If it was pity, or the promise of not burdening his family, or even just the shortened travel time of remaining in Italy, but the next morning when Diego was officially released, he told his family he'd be going with June.

Part of June had been afraid of offending Reyes and Bianca, but she saw the weight lifted off their shoulders. Saw the relief that he would be with her. June was oddly touched. Diego was their light, and there they were, entrusting her hands to hold it.

Diego slept most of the day away in a hotel as June and Charlene bristled about to iron out details of the travel to Tuscany. Charlene opted to fly ahead of them, June and Diego following the next day. Antonia returned to Monaco where she would gather Diego's things for the impromptu stay in Italy and ship them to him. Diego woke only once to scarf down a plate of food from room service before he immediately fell back asleep.

Lola and Olivia had spent the last two weeks hounding June for constant updates on Diego's condition. Having him so close seemed to relieve them. They didn't even tease June for bringing him back with her. The girls readied June's apartment for June and Diego's arrival that night.

The train ride was a short one, just under four hours to travel the expanse from Monza to Florence. Their seats were first class in an attempt to keep him comfortable and allow him to sleep, but June was certain with his level of exhaustion, he could have slept anywhere. He cursed his brace until he realized it doubled as a neck pillow. He slept the majority of the trip, his body still exhausted from the sheer energy it took to heal from his injuries. June handled their bags, threatening to beat him the moment he reached for them. Carrying anything over five pounds was extremely off limits.

It was dark when they finally arrived at the train station in Florence, and Charlene was waiting to pick them up. They parked in front of June's apartment, where Charlene carried their bags inside, insisting the two of them get settled. June happily obliged.

The girls had rearranged June's office as requested, the small room converted into a guest room. The desk had been pushed off to one side, a queen-size bed taking up the other with a single nightstand and blackout curtains hung over the window.

She owed those girls her life.

Diego didn't even bother to change, just stripped to his boxers and fell asleep.

The first three days in Tuscany, Diego hardly left his makeshift bedroom. June made sure to supply him with plenty of food, water, and pain medication, but he barely touched it. She tried not to worry, but the panic gnawed incessantly at her chest, followed by acute guilt. He'd been doing good in the hospital. He'd been eating, walking, awake and alert.

Was her tiny apartment driving him crazy? Had the reality of his situation finally set in?

June rode horse after horse—anything to keep Diego off her mind. The doctors had said he'd need rest, and lots of it, but June wanted him awake. Wanted him alert. Wanted him to be Diego. It took every ounce of restraint in her not to rip the curtains open and force him to have breakfast with her.

The third night back, June couldn't take it anymore. She finally barged into the room with a plate of food, flicking a lamplight on. It was seven o'clock and Diego had hardly eaten anything in days. She marched over, placing a hand on his shoulder. "Wake up."

Diego's eyes fluttered open, taking in the sight of her above him in the small office that had become his cave, before his gaze settled on the light in the corner of the room and he huffed in discontent. He threw his arm over his eyes.

June snagged his limp arm, lifting it up. "Sit up."

Diego groaned, rolling over on his side, and she grabbed him by the shoulder, forcing him to roll onto his back. "I mean it. Sit up. You haven't eaten a damn thing."

"Not hungry," he grumbled.

"You will be after a couple bites. It's oatmeal and toast. It'll settle easy."

Diego grumbled again, shoving his head into the pillows and June set the plate on the nightstand before she grabbed him by the shoulder, pulling him enough to make him understand she was not to be argued with about this. "Diego. Get up."

"What's the point?" he grumbled, head still half-smothered in the pillows. June's heart dropped. She'd known him for over a year, and she'd never heard him sound so defeated in his life. "I can't race."

Ah. How foolish of her. Of course that was what this was all about. "It's going to take even longer if you don't take care of yourself."

Diego didn't budge. June sighed, running her fingers through his hair gently. "Come on," she urged. "I could sure use your help at the barn tomorrow."

He peered up at her through one eye, a suspecting smirk on his lips. "*My* help?"

June hummed in agreeance, nodding. "I have so many horses to ride tomorrow—" True, but nothing she wasn't used to, "—I could use help catching and grooming them." It was bullshit and they both knew it, but Diego was the kind of man who had to make himself useful. If that meant teaching him how to halter and groom a horse, June could manage that.

He groaned, finally pushing himself up to sit, as if the promise of being helpful to her was enough reason to at least try.

June pushed a glass of water into his hand, and he drank. One sip, and then he was chugging the entire thing down. When he finished it, June pushed the plate into his lap. "Eat it and I'll leave you alone."

It took all of three cautious bites before Diego was devouring it. June sat beside him on the bed, drawing her legs up under her. He scraped the plate clean before June finally cracked a self-satisfied smile. "You want some real food now?"

Diego nodded shortly. "Yes, please."

The simple sight of the empty plate and Diego's confirmation left June feeling much better. She hopped to her feet, gathering his dishes. "Good. I'm making chicken marsala. Go shower, it'll be ready in fifteen minutes."

Begrudgingly, Diego got up and stumbled off to the bathroom.

June returned to the kitchen, finishing up the chicken and vegetables simmering in a pan. Everything felt a bit lighter with Diego awake. A bit easier.

It was about ten minutes before Diego exited the bathroom with nothing more than a towel wrapped around his waist, his neck bare. Any lingering comfort June felt turned to despair.

She'd never seen him look so awful. His skin clung to the bone from dehydration, stitches visible on the back of his neck from the surgery, bruises covering the front and back of his torso from his broken ribs. He slipped into his room to change, and June had to take a few deep breaths, staring down into the pasta to fight back the growing guilt.

She should have woken him sooner. Should have taken better care of him. But then he was in a t-shirt and a pair of sweats, stepping out into the kitchen, and June was left with no choice but to shake it off. He needed her to be strong for him, not throw a pity party. She nodded towards his bare neck. "You're supposed to keep that on, you know."

He shrugged, taking a seat at the table. "It probably won't kill me."

June shot a glare at him, marching off to the bathroom to procure the brace. He returned the glower, but he didn't protest as she helped get it settled back in its rightful place. She had promised to take good care of him. She planned to make good on that promise. She snapped the final restraints into place, bending to press a kiss to his head before she retrieved dinner.

Chapter Twenty-Two

June wasn't used to cooking for more than just herself, and in her panic, had made enough to feed a small village. But Diego was hungry, and only half of it went in the fridge.

The next day, Diego woke up starving. He ate her out of house and home before he ordered enough groceries to drown them both. June was a shit cook, but with nothing else to do, Diego had taken quite a liking to it. As it turned out, he was rather good. Lola and Olivia came over for dinner on several occasions. The sight of the three of them together made June's heart swell with affection. Unable to tease June for how her handsome fake-boyfriend was in front of him, the three of them became far more like siblings.

Diego began accompanying her to the barn daily. She showed him how to halter a horse and groom for tacking. He still wasn't cleared to lift over five pounds, and therefore wasn't allowed to saddle, which irritated him beyond belief, but the small tasks she could assign to him he attended to diligently.

Oviatt only seemed to get worse with time. The more she rode him, the more anxious he got. From the second June swung a leg over him, he was hunting for the first jump, nearly rattling out of his own skin. There was no room for nerves—no room for anything other than sheer confidence and control. Oviatt could jump. June had to hang on. Point him in the right direction. Pray.

In private, Diego scolded June for working so hard. She was so used to the intensity of her life that having Diego with her made her feel guilty. He wasn't from this world. He didn't understand it. He chastised her for sleeping too little, scolded her for doing too much. He was a driver in a car made for him. June was a rider on a set of horses she had to make. "You know," she told him finally. "You don't have to come if it bothers you."

Diego had laughed at her. Like clockwork, he was at the barn with her the next morning. He helped with more the more his condition improved.

Three weeks after his accident, Diego was at her side for the Mexico City Grand Prix. The moment it was announced Diego was out for the first half of the season, the world assumed his career was over. To see him healthy and in such high spirits left his fans and the F1 community feeling much relief. News spread fast, but rumors spread faster. Online speculation exploded, fans taking his presence in Florence with her as confirmation of their relationship.

Diego frowned at his neck brace, flicking it disapprovingly. "It ruins my outfit."

June teased him mercilessly for it, only because it made her feel better to look at it as silly rather than to allow the tears that the sight of it threatened to produce. He didn't wear it as consistently as he should have, but June didn't argue. She may have hated it even worse than he did.

He was healing more every day. Still, his breath caught when he moved too quickly, his hand still strayed to his neck, attempting to rub the soreness away.

Amelia came occasionally to coach or ride a horse, but she was so rarely around these days, opting instead to spend most of her time in the city or at her penthouse. June didn't blame her. Watching June ride used to be fun. Now, it was like a trainwreck in slow motion.

Hades was still unpredictable, but he was consolable. He was at least progressing. June and Hades were a match, at least. Oviatt only seemed to get worse with time. Diego may have hated him even more than June did. She could hardly swing a leg over him before he exploded. Oviatt needed to move. June had gotten very good at holding on for dear life.

The second June landed on his back, he surged up. His head cracked her in the face. June tumbled off and into the dirt, stunned as pain shot through her face. June landed far from gracefully, directly on her back, wrenching the air out of her lungs. In an instant, she was up on her knees—instinct fueling her rather than determination. She fell down on her hands, bracing herself against the dirt as she begged her lungs to work again.

No matter how many times June hit the dirt, it still surprised her. Like she'd thought the last one would be the last of her career. Like she thought she'd progressed enough for it to never happen again. The unfortunate truth was that it was always going to happen again. At least, until one finally killed her.

In a matter of seconds, someone was at her side, drawing her into steady arms and a solid chest. Diego. "Are you alright?"

June nodded, still trying to catch her breath. Blood poured from her nose, and she brought the side of her hand up to staunch it. "I'll do better," she promised. But it wasn't a real promise. She felt sick, and the thought of getting back up in the saddle left a burning sensation in the pit of her stomach. "I'll get it together," she lied.

"What the hell are you talking about?" Diego scolded. "That horse is mad."

June shook her head. "It's my fault. I was distracted. It's my fault." Her eyes were fixed on the ground in front of her, and the more she looked at the dirt, the more bile filled her throat. She didn't belong here. She wasn't good enough for this sport.

Amelia's voice rose up from across the barn, and June could see her without having to lay eyes on her—arms crossed across her chest, irritated. Disappointed. Annoyed. "There's nothing wrong with that horse." Coming off in front of Amelia always made everything worse. Her words sent a new wave of embarrassment and panic through her chest. Not good enough. *Not good enough.*

"What the hell are you talking about?" Diego shouted. Louder this time. Angry. Downright rageful, like he could turn and murder that woman any second. "Fuck's sake! She's hurt and you're worried about arguing over that fucking horse!"

"Why don't you stick to cars and leave this to the professionals?" Diego puffed up like a porcupine ready to shoot quills in every direction. June's hand shot to grip Diego's arm, halting him in place.

She didn't want a yelling match. This was not Formula One. He had no place in this world or this sport. He had a tendency to forget himself, and Amelia was beyond spiteful when provoked.

"I'm not hurt," she lied. Of course she was hurt. The ground always hurt. Her face hurt. "Just startled. He jumped, and I wasn't ready. It's fine." Diego ground his teeth together, squeezed his eyes shut, resigned himself to shut his mouth and stay at her side.

Amelia lingered a moment longer, like a taunting sibling waiting for another chance to bite before she finally sighed in disappointment and resigned. "Isa, put Oviatt away. June?"

June looked up at Amelia expectantly, knowing full well what she wanted. An acknowledgment of defeat. An apology. June did not have either of those things to offer. Her eyes were fixed on the ground again as she took a step away from Diego. "I'm fine."

Because that was the only option. Be alright, or die, and dying wasn't an option until she held a season title.

Amelia offered her a single, sharp nod. "Good. Don't let it happen again."

June nodded in response. Her stomach turned again. She felt the weight of Diego's frustration behind her, the weight of Amelia's judgment, and the weight of her own failures in her chest. "I'm going to get some air," June murmured.

June found her way outside with a limp. Her hands shook with adrenaline and pain, hobbling to lean against the barn.

The air outside was clean and crisp, becoming more breathable with every step she took away from the arena. She knew Diego was following her, but that didn't slow her retreat.

Diego grabbed her arm, pulling her back just to face him and June sighed deeply, halting in her tracks. She couldn't run from him forever.

He took a deep breath, trying to steady himself for a moment. She knew he didn't want to sound mad, but the rage was prevalent in his every move. "How do you let her speak to you that way?"

June didn't flinch, offering him a deadpan stare. "She's my coach."

Diego huffed in disbelief, running his hands through his hair. "That's not an answer, June. That woman is as mad as her horse."

She grit her teeth, turning away from him and resuming her walk. "That's probably why she's won two season titles."

Diego hustled to keep up with her. "She's crazy, June. She's going to kill you."

"Shut up, Diego." It was the only reply she could offer him other than punching him in the face.

Diego caught her by the hand again, pulling her back, and June whirled on him. "I have to win."

He blinked, his brows furrowing and lips turning into a frown. "No, you don't."

She grit her teeth, and wondered if he knew how hypocritical it seemed. "Yes, I do."

He could never understand it. What did she have if she couldn't prove herself? If she couldn't rub it in her father's face—in everyone's faces? Amelia, every commentator, every competitor. Everyone who had ever doubted her. *You were wrong. I am worth something.*

Spite, then. Was that why she was doing this? "Amelia thinks that Oviatt is the answer."

"He's not."

June whirled on her. "You'd tell your Team Principal no?"

"If he asked me to kill myself, yes!" Diego raised his voice, frustrated and tired of her reasons that were never adequate to him. "You don't think you can win on Hades?"

She sighed, covering her face with her hands. That was all she wanted. But Amelia was dead set on Oviatt. She didn't trust June's judgment. But Amelia had given her everything. Who was she to deny her? "Amelia doesn't."

The two sat in silence for a while, accompanied only by the sounds of birds and the occasional exhale from June as the pain in her face lessened.

She knew he was trying not to be angry at her, but his frustration and helplessness seemed to grow by the moment.

The silence stretched between them, and all she could do was sigh. "I would be nothing if it weren't for her, Diego."

"That's not—" His tone was sharp and he cut himself off. He was done arguing now. His voice softened. "That's not true."

He sounded so sure of it. June was less so. "She's all I have."

"You have me . . ." he whispered, a pained look on his face.

June nodded absently, staring down into her hands as she picked at the skin of her fingers. "Right," she whispered.

He blinked. "You don't believe me."

June met his gaze, unable to do anything more. She hated it, but he was right. No matter how hard she wished, having Diego was not enough. Sooner or later, he was going to find something else. June would take the back burner, and once again, she would be nothing to him.

She hated sounding like a scorned child—but when you peeled back the layers bit by bit, that was all that was left. A girl who had been left again and again. A woman who would make people leave again and again just so she'd never be the one begging someone to stay. "I believe that you think that."

"You are so infuriating," he grumbled, shaking his head. He wasn't angry anymore. He was just tired. "I'm going to help you win." he said, his hand landing firmly on her arm.

She so badly wanted to trust him. Almost as much as he wanted her to trust him.

"Promise me you won't ride that horse again." There was no hint of play in his voice, just a strictness that said he expected her to listen to him for once.

"You know I can't, D."

His lips pulled into a frown at her refusal. "If you keep riding that thing, it's going to kill you, June. And I won't be able to do anything."

"And?" she challenged. "You zip around a track at 200 miles an hour. You think I'm not terrified of that?"

He lurched back, gesturing to all of him in his own desperation. "Look where it got me!"

June swallowed hard, gritting her teeth, but the fight hadn't gone out of her yet.

"At least a car has a steering wheel and brakes, June." He was getting frustrated again. "You hit the ground, and I was the one who came running. I have a team full of support. You are alone."

"That's how it's always been," she said shortly, clearly frustrated. "You think I don't want to win on Hades? Of course, I do. But Amelia sees something that I don't in Oviatt. I'm trusting her."

Diego sat up, frustration apparent in his hardened eyes. "You're putting your faith in the wrong people."

She scoffed. "You mean instead of people like you? People who have never been on a horse?"

He was clenching his teeth as he stared at her, anger swirling in his eyes. He reached out and grabbed her shoulder, pulling her to look at him. "I'm not your enemy," he hissed, his voice tight. "I just don't want to see that horse kill you." His brows were knitted together, concern pulling through his anger.

She blinked at him. Once, then twice. *I'm not your enemy.* Of course he wasn't. He was concerned for her. She shook her head softly, his hand moving with it. "I have nothing if I don't have jumping."

"You have me," he repeated, the words pouring out of him softly, without any sign of hesitation. He sounded more desperate now than ever. "You have me." With a hand on her shoulder, he pulled her toward him, letting his forehead rest on hers. "You're not alone."

June swallowed back the uncomfortable guilt swelling in her chest. She pulled back and away from him. "Thank you," she said softly. "I need to get back to training."

He stared up at her, his eyes filled with a pained look like he wanted to follow her. To shake some reason into her. But he didn't. What more could he say?

Instead, he gave a nod.

As she stalked off towards the stables, she could feel his eyes on her back.

June was sore that night. She always was after hitting the ground, but this time, her pride stung too. Diego had a way of making her feel crazy, turning a fierce fight to be the best in the world into something as simple as riding a horse for a medal. But it was more than that. All of this was more than that.

She stood in Hades' stall, brushing his already clean coat. Hades enjoyed being groomed, and June liked having a repetitive motion to soothe her mind. Especially knowing Diego was waiting for her at home, probably ready to scold her again.

June heard the tell-tale sign of somebody coming down the aisle, and peeked around Hades to find the culprit.

It was Amelia, stopping to lean against the wall outside of the stall with her arms crossed. She said absolutely nothing. June's eyes widened, not acknowledging her coach as she went about her normal routine.

It was only when June's back was turned that Amelia finally spoke. "That boy of yours . . . he worries me."

June froze with the brush to Hades' coat as she let the words settle. Because they had to make sense. Everything Amelia said made sense. But this didn't.

". . . Diego?"

Amelia didn't budge. "Is that his name?"

June's lips parted, partially in surprise, and the other in hurt. Ninety percent of the articles written about June in the last year included Diego's name. He'd been living here for two weeks. Either she was purposely trying to rile June by pretending not to know, or she genuinely didn't know. Because she wasn't paying attention. "He works for Lotus, and I made him sign NDA—"

Amelia let out an amused breath, kicking off the wall and making her way towards June. "Oh, please. He's no threat to me. He's a threat to *you*."

June blinked. Frozen. Unsure of what to say. There was always the right thing to say to appease Amelia, and June could not find it. "Diego's done nothing but help me—"

"Has he?"

June was a deer in headlights, the truck of her inevitable destruction hurtling toward her, and yet she found herself unable to move. Unable to say anything to save herself from this disaster. Her question sounded so genuine. All June could do was think. Of course he had. He'd supported her, helped her rediscover her love for the sport, and offered a steady hand to hold.

"Seems to me like he has a lot more on his mind than your career."

June tensed, and then let out a heavy breath. Of course. The deal. Why wouldn't it look odd from the outside? Especially to someone who knew how rarely June entertained boys. Why wouldn't Amelia think Diego was trying to take advantage?

"It's not . . . he's not like that. We're not—it's just publicity—"

Amelia didn't even flinch. "Oh, I'm not talking about your little PR romance."

Every ounce of relief June had acquired went spiraling back into hopeless anxiety. She stumbled for something to say, but Amelia cut her off. "Honestly, June, I'm not blind. You don't even have time for friends, but all of a sudden you're traveling the world for a boy? Of course I knew there was something more. I'm talking about him being a distraction."

June's stomach twisted with a mix of anxiety and dread, her heart clenching. Every word out of Amelia's mouth left June feeling impossibly stupid.

Amelia coughed up a laugh. "Are you really so naive?"

There had been several times that June hated Amelia, but none quite so much as right now.

"You want to make a name for yourself in this sport? You are," Amelia said, but it was far more of a warning than reassurance. "June Walker: the girl who sleeps her way to the top."

June wished Amelia would just punch her. Just stab and gut her. Just rip her heart out and leave her in the cold.

"You want your accomplishments overshadowed by some boy?" The question answered itself. June kept her mouth shut. Amelia threw up her hands in frustration. "I can't protect you from this, June."

June was beginning to wonder if Amelia could protect her from anything. Not losing her career. Not losing her horse. Not the rumors. What did she do for June these days? What more did June owe her?

"Who's going to be by your side when you take home your title?" Ah. Yes. June supposed there was always that. The lingering promise of success. The idea of being a champion.

"*Who*, June?" Amelia demanded.

June coughed up the answer. "You are."

Amelia settled—her fire doused, her ruffled feathers smoothed. June's loyalty reassured. "Correct," she spat. "Reevaluate your priorities, June." She didn't say another word. Just turned and left.

June dropped back against the stall door, sliding down to sit as the numbness settled in. She had to win. She *had* to win. She had not fought this hard just to fail now. Just for someone else to receive her credit. She let her head fall back against the stall.

June Walker had to win.

Chapter Twenty-Three

The Madrid Grand Prix held a special significance now that Diego was in her life. Being in Spain with her Spanish fake-boyfriend drew plenty of public attention, and Diego seemed more at ease to be back in his home country. June adored the Madrid venue—a lush, green, outdoor arena with a heat that reminded June of Texas. It brought her no comfort now. They'd already walked the course on foot in preparation to ride it, and June recited it like a mantra. Each jump, arc, and turn. Study it. Memorize it. Eat, sleep, and breathe it. June bounced back and forth on the balls of her feet, forcing herself to draw deep breaths. *Make it happen.*

Amelia's words didn't leave her. As much as she'd like to say it was bullshit—that June hadn't been distracted, that Diego had only had positive effects on June's career—Amelia was right. Their deal had been to create a joint reputation. Trouble was, that reputation had different implications for the two of them.

She shook her hands, as if she could fling the nerves off her fingertips like water. They'd already warmed up, but Oviatt got too high-strung to sit on him until they entered the arena. So, she waited on the ground until it was her turn. At some point, Oviatt had stopped looking like a horse and started to look like a winged beast with red eyes and horns, blowing smoke out his ears. June let out a final breath. "Someone give me a leg up?"

Diego was at her side in an instant, a protective hand on her arm as he stared the horse down, like he'd kill the animal with his bare hands if it meant protecting her from it. And yet, there he was, taking her weight in his hands and hoisting her onto Oviatt's back. The moment she touched him, Oviatt was crumbling to pieces beneath her. He popped up, the girls scrambling to get out of the way. Diego reached for her. Before he could lay a finger on her, June was shouting at him. *"Don't!—"*

Oviatt swung his head to the side, nearly clipping Diego before Isa wrenched on his lead, dragging him back.

"Charlene!" June called. The anxiety must have been prevalent in her voice, because in a matter of seconds her manager snapped into action.

"Come on." She ushered the others toward the crowd. Diego paused, lingering like it pained him to leave her. He sighed in defeat, shaking his head as he turned for the stands.

The moment she was without them, dread swarmed June with a devilish fervor and she beat it down.

Amelia stood beside her on her own horse. "Don't touch him," she warned. "Hold on. Stay out of his way. And breathe for fuck's sake."

Breathe.

June clenched her fists, staring down his neck as she forced herself to fill and empty her lungs manually. Breathe. That was all she had to do. And yet, the terror remained. June managed to get Oviatt through the gate, even as he began to hop in place, popping up and down like a seesaw that wanted her dead. The gate closed. They circled once. The bell chimed. June held on for dear life and Oviatt lurched into motion hard enough to pop her out of the saddle. She sat back in the saddle, desperately trying to slow him down, but Oviatt had a mission.

Breathe.

June forced her vision straight ahead despite the way her mind begged her to refuse. To hold him back. Holding him back never meant anything but trouble. Oviatt landed, clearing the five stride distance in three before he leapt. June surged up and over with him.

Clear thus far. Fast.

Too fast.

June could hardly keep him in check. She felt more like a passenger on a runaway train. June pulled him back, desperate to slow him down as they headed into a triple combination.

Oviatt ripped his head forward and up, focused on fighting her more than the impending combination ahead. June sat back, trying to redirect his focus, but it was too late. The jump was already there. And then, at the last possible second, Oviatt leapt.

He crashed into the top line of the jump, every ounce of momentum caught in his front end. His feet scrambled for purchase in the air, catching in the tangle of fallen rails. He was too far forward, the angle was off. There was a single moment of clarity as they sped toward the ground: they were going head over heels. Oviatt was going down too.

June scrambled to bail, but it was too late. She hit the ground hard, Oviatt's body landing partially on top of her. Her entire body exploded in agony, the air knocked from her lungs. The pain in her head was instant, screaming at her through the blurred vision and the fog clouding her mind. Her fingers dug in the dirt, grunting with the effort it took to push herself up. *Up.* She had to get up.

Oviatt stomped over her as he got back to his feet, tearing over her and loose in the arena. Had he stepped on her? June wasn't sure. Everything hurt.

She ended up on her back, staring up at the blue sky on a perfect, clear, sunny day.

Stand up, her mind demanded, vaguely aware of Oviatt tearing around the arena. She couldn't be laid out in the dirt, but she couldn't fathom the idea of using her legs right now. Blood trickled down her right forearm, breeches torn from her inner thigh down to where her tall boots joined up at the knee, swollen and purpling.

"June . . . June . . . Can you stand? Are you alright?"

She looked up.

Paramedics.

This was real, then. She stared at them wide-eyed as they hustled around her fast enough to make her dizzy. All she could do was shake her head.

"No," the woman said shortly. "Use words. Don't move. Just—Just stay as still as you can, okay?"

June tried to nod again, but pain shot through her head and she cried out, squeezing her eyes tightly shut. "O–Okay! Okay."

A hard board was slid underneath her. In the next instant, she was being loaded into an ambulance. She was vaguely aware of the warm, wet feeling across the side of her head. The paramedics rushed about, providing oxygen and IVs and all the stabilizers in the world. They ordered her about—told to follow a finger or to say something or to keep her eyes open—but June's head ached too badly to listen.

Everything hurt. June closed her eyes and listened to the whirring of tires on pavement.

Tires.

Cars.

Diego.

She thought of Diego, allowing the image of him in her mind to comfort her, until she remembered his warnings. Until she remembered that he was right. Somehow, he always was.

By the time the doctors were done with her, June was beginning to believe in divine intervention. All of the luck in the world could not have let her out of that wreck alive. She had separated her shoulder landing directly on her arm, and she was covered in bruises. Oviatt had stepped on her thigh in his panic to get away, but he'd mainly hit the outside of her leg. What could have been broken was just bruised and battered to high heaven. The worst of it was the concussion. She hadn't even realized she'd lost consciousness in the arena. Despite it all, she was okay. She was going to be okay.

There was no brain bleed, no indication of permanent damage. She was okay.

It wasn't until the second doctor came in that she realized she could have been very not okay.

Charlene stayed with her the whole time. She was crying. June didn't think she'd ever seen someone cry over her before.

The girls made their way to her sometime after the second doctor, June finally deemed well enough they could see her, at least for a moment.

Lola and Olivia entered softly. Quietly. She'd never seen them do anything but explode into a room in a flurry of light and energy. Lola kept an arm around Olivia. Their eyes were puffy, and Olivia was still frantically wiping away tears as they both stepped forward.

June's left arm was bound in a sling, but she reached out to them with her right. They rushed forward to take it, Olivia intertwining their fingers as Lola gripped her by the wrist. They didn't speak, too much to say to ever wrap it into words, but she saw it in their eyes. The terror. The grief that the prospect of losing June brought out. The knowledge that these kinds of accidents killed. That June should've been another number in the statistic of riders killed by rotational falls.

They weren't allowed to stay long before Charlene was ushering them back out into the waiting room, insisting that June needed rest.

Everything felt fuzzy. The exhaustion was prevalent, but the pain outweighed it. The lights had been dim the entire time, but they still felt too bright, pain perforating through her skull. Her shoulder ached. Her leg stung where Oviatt's shoe had torn through the skin and it had to be glued back together.

They'd given her as much Tylenol as they could, but the pain was persistent. June dozed as much as she could without being able to relax.

By the time the third doctor finally made his way through, she realized she should have died. That she was not immortal.

Diego looked at her like she was already a ghost.

He stood in the doorway, wide-eyed and pale at the sight of her. Charlene excused herself, wiping her eyes as she went.

June didn't know what to say. All she could do was stare. "I'm sorry," she whispered. Oviatt was going to kill her. They both knew it. But June still had a trophy waiting for her. "I'm sorry," she whispered again.

Diego clenched his jaw, his fists clenched tight enough they were shaking. He was mad. Why was he mad? Because she could have died? Because she put herself in danger for the sake of a title? But what was she without a win? She *had* to win.

Diego took a step forward, forcing himself closer to the bed like he was watching the accident all over again in slow motion. "You could have died," he bit out, voice catching.

She knew it was the truth. "I didn't," she said immediately. Defensive. She knew it was stupid. Part of her was still terrified, but she had been so close. It was a fast round, and a clear round. She would have had it. She almost did have it—a true and genuine win under her belt. Until her horse had gone down and nearly crushed her under him.

"You didn't *this* time." He stood beside her, letting out a shaky breath as his eyes roamed over her battered body. "But every time you do this, you know damn well it could be the last time." He was shaking.

She bit her bottom lip, squeezing her eyes tightly shut to ward off equal parts exhaustion and despair. Tears threatened to overwhelm her, and all she could was lean into the pain, praying it was enough to drain the cavern of fear settling itself deep into her chest. Was this what she wanted? How was this better than riding her neighbor's horses? When she was thrilled for the next chance to step up onto their backs?

But she had to win. Win or die trying. "I'm sorry," she said again. Sorry that he cared for her. Sorry that she couldn't brunt the pain of what caring for her did to a person. All she wanted to do was reach out, to let him hold her. To be held. She couldn't remember the last time she had been held.

"Please, June" he begged, voice low. "Please."

"I won't ride him again," she said automatically. "I won't."

Diego's entire body tensed, like if he moved too quickly, the illusion would shatter. "You . . . you won't?" He said it like he could hardly believe her words. He had asked her before, and the answer was always no.

All she could do was nod. "I won't. I'll ride Hades. I'll take out a loan if I have to. I'll get a different horse."

As if on instinct, he moved closer to her, taking her hand into his. ". . . Swear it," he whispered like a prayer.

She nodded softly and immediately regretted it. Her head throbbed, and she wished she could burrow into herself and hide from the world. "I swear."

He let out a low breath, his entire body sagging in relief as his hand settled on her shoulder. June could have cried at the warmth of his touch.

"I'm okay." She squeezed his hand where it rested on her uninjured shoulder, ignoring the pain.

A single tear streaked down his cheek. He wiped it stubbornly with the back of his wrist, swallowing hard. "I know. You just . . . scared me. That's all."

"Stop," she scolded, her eyes welling with hot tears. Her body was throbbing. She had known pain before, but the pain in her back and in her head was unfathomable. He brought his other hand up to brush it away, the pad of his thumb brushing over her cheek tenderly. She caught his hand, closing her eyes. "I'm serious. If you cry, I cry, and it hurts too bad to cry right now."

"June," he breathed, eyes never leaving her face. And then, she couldn't hold back the tears. They fell freely, exhaustion and pain and fear completely overtaking every instinct to build up her walls and disappear from him. She bit her bottom lip hard enough to break skin, trying desperately to focus in on the pain rather than the welling tears.

He gently pulled her bottom lip from her teeth, rubbing his thumb over the broken skin. "Don't do that," he scolded gently.

She winced, gritting her teeth and gripping Diego's forearm hard enough to paint bruises across his skin. She willed the sudden wave of pain to dissipate, fighting back a whimper threatening to rise in the back of her throat. Everything hurt, from her torn up leg, to her shoulder, to the unrelenting pain in her head.

Her grip on his forearm seemed to send another wave of fresh concern crashing over him. He let out a shaky exhale and lifted his free hand to gently cup the side of her face. "I'm getting a nurse. Whatever medicine you are on is not working—"

"I'm not—I'm on Tylenol," she whispered. She grit her teeth and closed her eyes, burying her face into the crook of his arm as if he could save her from the pain.

"*Tylenol?*" he mumbled, shaking his head. "*Cariño*, why didn't you say anything?" Diego stood. "You need something stronger, I'll be back—"

"No," she whispered. "No, please don't."

"Why?" he asked, almost pleading with her for an explanation. "It's not working, June. You need something stronger."

She shook her head, and regretted it immediately, throbbing from her concussion rendering her entirely useless. She let herself ease back against the pillows, squeezing her eyes shut. Somehow, it was easier this way. Easier to speak to him. To admit something so intimate to him when her eyes were closed. "It runs in my family," she admitted. There. There it was, out in the open. "My dad's a raging alcoholic, my mom left when she found out pain pills were *way* better than raising kids. How much I drink is bad enough, but I—" her lip quivered and she cut herself off immediately. Even squeezing her eyes shut wasn't enough to stop the new influx of tears from escaping. She wasn't sure anything ever would be. She choked down her emotion as she finally opened her eyes. "I can't. I can't become them."

"*Cariño*," he said softly, and when she opened her eyes, he was staring at her in disbelief, as though everything had slotted into place at once. His hand coming up to carefully brush away the tear track on her cheek. "You won't be like them. You won't. I won't let you."

His words were a punch to the heart. Diego's hands cupped either side of her face, forcing her to look him directly in those big brown eyes, so full of sincerity she could drown in them.

"Stay," the word came out a strangled plea, desperate and familiar on her tongue. "Please. Please stay." She wondered if this was where she was always going to end up. A broken-down little girl begging someone not to leave.

He nodded, his thumb carting across her cheek to brush away the tears as they fell. "I'm not going anywhere, *Cariño*. Except to get you some better medication, okay?"

June choked on a strangled sob, nodding in resignation. *You won't be like them. I won't let you.* The words echoed in her head over and over again. Despite herself, she trusted them. Trusted him. That he would hold her while she shook. That he wouldn't let her lose herself, even if he had to chain her to him to do it.

He let out a shaky exhale. "I'll go find a nurse."

She nodded again, and in an instant, Diego rushed out of her room and into the hallway. She clenched her sheets in her hand until her fingers went numb. The urge to run settled in the moment she was alone. To tell him to leave. That she could fight this fight on her own, but before she could build up her resignation, Diego returned with a nurse, rubbing at his forehead as though he could feel the stress wrinkles marring his perfect skin already. He took June's hand as the nurse rushed to her IV, medications laid out on a cart she toted in.

June could feel the exact moment the medication hit her, the tension slipping away from her. She sighed in relief, relaxing back into the pillows. Her fingers closed tighter around Diego's, and then squeezed, encouraging him to come closer. He dragged a chair up to her bedside, holding her hand to his face. Tight. Close. Enough to prove to himself that she was still alive.

It reminded her very much of a moment not so many weeks ago, their roles reversed. Her breathing slowed, eyes fluttering shut. With the pain ebbing, June was left with a comfortable lull and her own exhaustion, the tension leaving her face as her pain melted away. The instant relief made her feel a bit drunk—or rather, high, she supposed. "Is this how it's always going to be?" June murmured. "Us taking turns in a hospital bed until it kills one of us?"

She'd meant it as a joke, but Diego's face contorted in pain, his eyes instantly welling with tears. He dragged his hand across his body in a cross motion, whispering something in Spanish that sounded like a prayer before he brought her hand up and buried his face in their tangled fingers.

In the darkness of the hospital room, the first sob escaped. A choked, muffled cry from Diego. The tears slipped down his face and onto her hand. She reached out to smooth them away, but before she could, her body went comfortably numb and June welcomed the darkness of sleep.

June was released the next evening with strict orders to rest and take it easy until her concussion symptoms lessened, anytime within the next one to six weeks. The pain was worse the next day, a deeper, duller ache in her head and bones that June hadn't been prepared to deal with. She could handle sharp, acute pain. It was the lingering nausea and dizziness she couldn't quite bear.

"You shouldn't be flying," Charlene concluded. "We'll have to put you up in a hotel—"

"Absolutely not." Diego's voice rang out firm, persistent, and downright offended.

Charlene raised a brow at his sudden sharp tone, crossing her arms over her chest. "She can't go back to Italy—"

"She'll come with me."

The entirety of the room turned to face him, June included. "With *you*?" Lola snapped. She sounded firm, disgruntled, as protective as June had ever heard her.

"No chance," Olivia spat. "She's ours. She's hurt. She'll stay with us. We'll get an Airbnb—"

"And completely neglect everything back home for weeks while June is recovering?" Charlene reminded them, always the voice of reason. "Lola, you have a slew of sponsors to meet with. Olivia, you're going to need to do a million interviews to smooth things over." The girls deflated at the news. Of course, it was impossible, but June was so flattered her heart was pounding. She felt warm. Loved. Uncomfortable tears pricked behind her eyes and she quickly blinked them away, swallowing hard.

"My family has a vacation home four hours away. We can stay there. I'll drive. Take care of her." Diego's eyes met hers over the distance, filled with an earnest pleading. To go with him. To let him help her. June bristled at the idea of Diego caring for her, simply because he could. Because he *did* care for her.

At least she paid the girls.

Diego? Perhaps he needed something to occupy him. To save him from his own boredom without racing. "Please," Diego pleaded, more to her than the others. "For my own peace of mind."

The others attempted to argue, but June beat them to it. "I . . . think that's a good idea. Yes. Thank you, Diego. I can pay for the rental car and—"

"Hush," Diego said firmly, making his way to her side as he pulled out his phone. "It's done. I'll call my *abuela*. We'll get you settled in a hotel tonight and we can drive there tomorrow."

June sighed in relief. Another thing off her plate. Diego would nurse her back to health the same way she had for him. The girls would handle her career. Things were going to be okay. The only thing she had to worry about was sleeping off this headache. Begrudgingly, the girls agreed. Charlene had already turned manager mode, bristling to arrange the details of their transportation and meetings.

June turned her gaze on Diego, whispering her thanks.

Diego said nothing, only bent down and kissed the top of her head, his hand planted firmly on the small of her back.

That night, she slept in a hotel with the girls, all of them cuddled up on the same bed. The idea of leaving her seemed to irk them all, but they respected June's wishes. There were more important things than holding June's hand right now. They ate breakfast together before they said their goodbyes, Charlene threatening Diego's life if anything happened to June, but his perfect confidence seemed to soothe their anxieties.

Diego rented a car. A nice one, but nothing like one of his own. She was grateful for the comfort it brought, the sense of normalcy. "Try to rest," Diego encouraged, but she could hardly relax from the motion sickness crawling at the back of her throat—let alone entertain the idea of sleep.

They stopped often—far more than she would have liked. She could only bear thirty minutes at a time before she had to get out until she could breathe without feeling like she was going to puke. Diego's driving was impossibly smooth, but even it couldn't save her from the suffocating pressure in her head at every change in direction. It took eight hours to get through what should have taken four.

She tried to push through the final hour, only to feel the bile rising in her throat as they descended into Zaragoza. "I'm gonna to be sick."

Diego understood the urgency, immediately pulling off the road. The moment the car ground to a halt, June bailed out, bracing against the car as she tried to quell her nausea.

The driver's door slammed shut, and a moment later, a hand landed on her back. She shook her head, pushing Diego away. "No. Go stand over there. I don't want you to see thi—" The nausea overtook her and she doubled over, vomiting away from the car.

Diego seized the opportunity to be kind without getting yelled at while she barfed. He reassumed his spot at her side, drawing her hair out of the way in one hand and rubbing circles on her back with the other.

She wanted to punch him. Tell him to get lost. But it was comforting and she couldn't bring herself to care. She remained hunched over for several long moments, her throat burning. Swallowing hurt. Blinking hurt. Eyes being open hurt as much as eyes being closed. Diego's hands braced gently on either after a long while, helping her to stand upright before he led her over to a cement barrier. She sat, clearing her throat as though that would help, but everything stung.

"Sit tight." His hand slipped away from her back, leaving her cold and uncomfortable. A strange weight settled in her chest at how much she craved his contact. He didn't give her long to ponder on it, returning with a water bottle in hand. He pushed it to her, encouraging her to drink and she did: a tiny sip, and then when it stayed down, another.

"I'm sorry," June finally said when she could speak again. "This wasn't supposed to be such a pain in the ass."

Diego's arm fell around her, both comforting her and discouraging her from her apologies. He held her tight, his thumb rubbing gentle circles on her arm that helped quell the nausea. "No sorrys. We'll just sit here for a while, no?" He pulled back just enough to smile down at her, and June returned it—weak, but genuine. He jutted his head toward where the sun had just begun to set over the mountains. "Look. Zaragoza says hello to you."

Chapter Twenty-Four

Everything was dark when they arrived, streetlights illuminating a steel gate leading down a winding rode. Diego had to punch in a code before the gate swung open and they were rolling up to the garage. He took her bag for her, leading her into the house with a hand on her back. He had become more possessive since the accident, always touching her in one way or another. To steady her or to remind himself she was still alive, she wasn't sure which.

The interior was gorgeous, a mix of ultra-modernity and traditional Spanish architecture that wowed June. Or at least, it would've if she wasn't so exhausted. "Come on," Diego nodded towards his right, "let's get you settled." He led her through the living room past the kitchen and down a long hallway, helping her to the end where she found her bedroom for the next several weeks. He set her suitcase in front of the wardrobe. "Here, I'll help you unpack."

June's hand shot out to catch him, stopping him mid-action. "I'm going to bed."

He must have seen the exhaustion on her face, because he didn't argue, only fetched her toiletries bag and set it in the bathroom attached to her room before he returned. "My room is across the hall if you need anything. Get some rest." He leaned down and kissed her on the forehead. Her heart skipped a beat, but her exhaustion didn't allow her to dwell on it.

She managed to brush her teeth and change into a set of pajamas before she collapsed in bed and fell asleep.

It was well into the next day when she finally woke. The trip had taken more out of her than she cared to admit. Diego wasn't in the house, but the door was open, letting in the warmth of the Spanish sun from early-summer morning. She stepped out onto the covered terrace and was met with a massive garden, landscaped to perfection. Flowers and trees covered the vast expanse of the yard, a pool large enough to do laps in rested just off the side.

The outside was as tastefully decorated as the inside, a mix of neutrals with pops of bright red and deep blue in the patio furniture. Diego lounged in a hammock strung beneath a tree, one leg on the ground rocking it, an orange cat perched in his lap. His head perked up at the sound of steps on the wooden terrace, spotting her making her way out to him. *"Oi,"* he scolded. "You're supposed to be resting."

June shrugged as she made her way to him. He grumbled his protests, but he sat up and turned, scooting over to make room for her on the hammock.

She took a seat beside him, unsteady with only one hand and he grabbed her gently by the sides, helping her to lay back beside him. The brightness of the vast expanse of blue sky and fluffy clouds made her head ache, and she turned to the side just to be met with Diego already looking at her. The intensity of his gaze on her made June's heart stop, her lips parting in surprise.

Diego held a cigarette between his fingers. Unlit.

Her eyes remained glued to his as she spoke. "I didn't know you smoked."

"I don't," he admitted, and at her raised brow, he corrected himself. "At least, I don't anymore. Haven't for a while."

She nodded toward the cigarette in his hand. "Why you hanging on to that?"

He sighed and rolled onto his back as he tucked it into his shirt pocket. "Nostalgia."

"Nostalgia isn't a reason to hold on to something that serves you no purpose."

He shook his head up at the sky, tucking his arms underneath his head. The silence was strung out between them, like each were waiting for the other to say something first. June couldn't stand it.

She cleared her throat, turning away from him. "This place is gorgeous. It's no wonder you didn't want to go back to Italy with me to my shitty apartment—"

Diego shot a glare in her direction, swatting her uninjured arm. "That is not what happened."

She giggled, pleased at having riled him.

He rolled his eyes at her, relaxing back into the hammock. "We'll have to come visit again when you're better."

He said it so simply, as if it made all the sense in the world for the two of them to travel together just for the hell of it. June tried not to let it get to her. It was all of ten minutes in the sunshine before June's head began to ache worse than it had when she woke up and Diego rushed her back in.

The house had been set up by Diego the night before, but it was still largely devoid of food. He ordered her some takeout and went grocery shopping, insisting she stay to rest. Charlene called while June was on the couch, listening to an audiobook, bored out of her mind without Diego. She was grateful for the distraction.

"The drive was fine." She omitted the part where she puked her guts out into some bushes. "I had a few bad episodes yesterday, but I think that was just from traveling—"

Charlene cut her off, her voice riddled with concern. "Bad how?"

"Just nausea. Headaches."

"June..." Charlene drew out, the warning in her voice loud and clear. *Don't push too fast. Be careful. Take care of yourself.* She didn't have to say any of it for June to know what she meant.

"I know. I know, okay? Diego's taking care of me. Wouldn't even let me go grocery shopping with him. I'm fine." June could practically see Charlene's skeptical frown through the phone, but she didn't argue, wishing her well and threatening her to take care of herself before she ended the call.

Diego finally returned as she was ending the call with Charlene, a paper brown bag full of groceries braced on his side with one arm around it, iced coffees in a drink carrier in the other hand. He dropped the grocery bag on the counter, and when June moved to stand up to come help, Diego balled up a straw wrapper and flicked it at her. He made his way to her with a coffee in hand, placing it in front of her. June groaned longingly. "I can't have caffeine—"

"Oh please, *Vaquera*. It's decaf."

June could have kissed him. She thanked him prolifically, and he made his way out to haul the rest of the groceries in.

Moments later, her phone lit up with a picture of Olivia, taken from above that made her look like an ugly little ant. It was a tradition— something to curb their boredom, taking turns snapping ridiculously stupid pictures of each other from the worst angles they could manage. The sight of it made June smile. The second call was a much louder, much more enthusiastic affair, Lola and Olivia shouting over each other. Charlene must have made them wait until she'd called to gauge the situation. "How's playing house with the pretty boy?" Lola asked.

June snorted. "I've been too busy puking on everything he owns to play much house."

Olivia scoffed. "Yeah, and he's definitely thinking about how much cuter it would be if you were puking 'cuz you were pregnant with his sexy little Cabrera babies."

Lola howled with laughter and June could only sigh. "You guys are weirdo freaks."

That only egged them on. "I'm just saying, a baby is like the ultimate publicity stunt—"

"Oh my God, Olivia. You can't have a *baby* as a publicity stunt." A sentence she never thought she'd say. Diego was outside, grabbing groceries from the car and she'd never been so grateful to be out of earshot in her life.

"I can't, but *you* can!" Olivia exclaimed. "I think we really need to a have a communal baby that we can dress up and—"

June groaned, and Lola interrupted, talking over Olivia's ridiculous babbling. "But how are you?"

"I hurt, but I'm better than expected," she concluded.

"And he's taking care of you?" Lola questioned.

She chuckled fondly, shaking her head. "He's . . . He's Diego. Of course he is." A chorus of *aww* and cooing on the other end made her wish she could punch her girls through the phone.

Diego stepped back into the house, carrying a bag under each arm and June quickly turned to the phone. "I gotta go but you guys take care, okay?"

"Yes!" Olivia exclaimed. "Go get me that Walker-Cabrera baby I ordered—"

There was rustling on the line and a shout that indicated Olivia had been rightfully smacked, and then a chorus of shouting and goodbyes before the line ran silent. She blinked, dropping her phone on the couch. Diego grinned silently to himself. "What?" June asked.

He smiled wider. "You make ridiculous faces on the phone."

Diego refused to let June help with putting away groceries or making dinner, insisting that she rest. She lay on the couch and stared at the ceiling. A dull headache was pressing at her temples and making her a bit nauseous. She dozed for an hour, and then Diego was waking her to eat.

Diego was a wonderful cook—she'd learned that in Florence. Dinner was a Spanish-style chorizo pasta on the patio with a non-alcoholic red wine. Because *'you can't have dinner in Spain and not drink wine'*, according to Diego, but alcohol was off the menu until June's head was in a better spot. She fell asleep easily that night, pleasantly full and surprisingly relaxed.

She woke in the middle of the night to the vaguest feeling of something being off, wiping at her nose, only for hot liquid to come pouring from it moments later. She ran out of bed, catching the blood in her hand as she stumbled into the kitchen. Now, the only accompaniment to June's silence was the sound of blood dripping into the sink, staining the quartz a bright red. The constant drip had gone from uncomfortable, to irritating, to downright terrifying as she watched blood coat the sink, refusing to clot.

She tried tissues, but each one was soaked through instantly. She tried a rag, but it was just as ineffective. So, here she stood, hand braced on one side of the kitchen sink as bright red blood dripped from her nose. Ten minutes later, June found herself stumbling into Diego's room, a wad of rags pressed to her nose. She didn't bother turning on a light, shaking him gently. Sleepy brown eyes met her own, and he hummed in discontent, rousing slightly. Her own voice came out gruff, sticky with a mixture of disuse and the blood that had managed to make it down her throat. "Is a forty-minute nosebleed enough to go to the hospital?"

Diego shot out of bed before the words were even fully out of her mouth, abruptly and entirely awake as though someone had dumped ice-cold water over his head. He grabbed her gruffly by her uninjured arm, dragging her with as he crossed the room in two quick strides to flick on the light. "Yes, that's—*what*? Yes." He paused, a hand braced on either side of her face as he assessed the situation. He braced his fingers against her jaw, turning her head back and forth before he reached up to draw the rag away from her face. The moment he did, blood dripped down her chin and onto the plush white rug. She rushed to catch it but it was too late. She swore sharply, pressing the rag back to her nose. "Shit, sorry. Do you have stain remover or—"

His hand landed at her hip and he turned her sharply, marching her forward. "Get in the car."

June glanced at the blood on the carpet, and then back at him. "But—"

"*Now*. We're going to the hospital." He all but stuffed her into the passenger seat. In a matter of moments, they were driving, nothing but the whirring of the tires on pavement to drone out the silence.

June leaned back against the seat as she pressed the wad of rags against her nose, breathing labored and a bit panicked as she focused on the street before them. She glanced at him once, then again. His eyes remained carefully on the road, his jaw set and riddled with tension. "Are you angry with me?" The words were out before she could stop them, blood sliding down the back of her throat and she grimaced.

Diego didn't so much as look at her, his answer automatic. Too automatic. "No."

A beat of silence. She studied him: the sharp line of his clenched jaw, the way his gaze didn't drift from the road, his tight grip on either side of the steering wheel. "Yes, you are."

"No, I—" He bit his tongue, a muscle in his jaw jumping as he gripped the wheel tighter. "I'm not." He said finally, though his voice was tense. He took a deep breath, shaking his head, and said nothing else.

"Why are you mad?"

"I'm not—"

"Don't lie!"

"Why didn't you wake me up?!" His voice rose to match her own, angry and irritated and a touch afraid. June bristled, a sharp retort on the tip of her tongue, but she swallowed it back down. She hesitated. Turned to look out the windshield.

She knew he had a point, even if she didn't want to admit it. "I didn't think it was that big a deal."

He snapped his head to glare at her. "Not that big a—Jesus Christ, look at you. You look like something out of a horror movie," he hissed. "You'll bleed out in the damn kitchen before you come to me." The air grew hot and tense, the AC doing nothing to cut the heat between them.

June turned to glare out the window, refusing to look at him and instead watched the buildings fly by. "I hurt," she whispered. She hated how small her voice came out. How broken. "Everything hurts. If I woke you up every time something was wrong, you wouldn't get a second of sleep."

And maybe Diego saw it, the exhaustion and the pain and the pure misery that was bubbling within her. Or maybe he just didn't have any response to her admission. He was silent for a long while before he reached out, taking her hand softly into his own. The anger seemed to have gone away from him, rubbing his thumb across the back of her hand. When he spoke, his voice was barely above a whisper. "Wake me up anyway."

June's eyes flickered down to their hands, his thumb rubbing slow circles on the back of her own. She could feel the ridges of his knuckles, the rough bumps on his palms from old calluses and scars. It was grounding, and she felt some of the tension drain from her body.

Diego handled the visit to the ER. The nurses spoke Spanish, so Diego translated. They ran a million tests, and it was light out before June was finally cleared and they were exiting the hospital. The force of the accident had caused several blood vessels in June's nose to burst. The doctors were certain she'd merely scratched her nose and aggravated them again. Her body was already exhausted trying to patch up a concussion, blood clotting became difficult.

Diego made them run a CT scan and an MRI. Even then, he had three separate doctors look at the reports. No brain bleed. No long-term damage. Just a girl with a concussion and a bloody nose.

They gave her a powder to help it clot and finally sent them both home. June practically collapsed on the couch the moment they got home and Diego scowled down at her disapprovingly as she drew the throw blanket over herself. "Your back will be sore if you sleep on the couch. Come to bed."

She promptly ignored how the insinuation made her stomach flip. She pressed her head against the throw pillow. "Tired."

Diego made his way to her and grabbed her by the hand, tugging her up to her feet. June grumbled, but she made her way to the hallway. When she turned for her room, Diego laughed. He shook his head. "You're sleeping in my room until I can trust you'll actually wake me up when you need me."

June swallowed hard, torn between irritation at being treated like a child, and affection for the way he cared for her. Her head hurt, and she was too exhausted to argue. He pushed the door to his room open, waiting for her to enter first before he followed. She crawled into the less-marred half of the bed, deeming the other as his side.

June's nose didn't bleed again. She slept in Diego's bed every night after.

Diego took June's care as his personal responsibility. He handled each doctor's appointment and therapy for her shoulder, set timers for ice packs, and brought her medication. Her shoulder was healing quick, and she rarely had to wear the sling anymore. Diego's doctors' appointments were less frequent than her own. There was nothing to aid his healing except time. So, they were forced to wait.

With each of them out of commission, they had nothing to do but entertain each other. June insisted she didn't mind him watching TV, but he refused. "We're in this together," he said, and he meant it. They played countless card games. Diego bought them coloring and puzzle books. They baked very, *very* shittily. For being such a good cook, he sure couldn't bake. They sat on the floor one night, checking their brownies religiously. They had been in the oven at the highest temperature for an hour and a half and still refused to set. The outsides wound up completely burnt while the insides were still raw. They spent the better half of an hour laughing until it gave June such a horrendous headache she had to go lie down.

They played audiobooks on a speaker. Turns out, they both had an affinity for classics. Spanish classics were better, he determined, but due to her limited knowledge of the language, they stuck to the one they both understood. However, that didn't stop Diego from his daily Spanish lessons.

Diego had always been beautiful. June wasn't blind. But at some point, the attraction she felt towards him had morphed. In the early days of their agreement, it had all been for the cameras. Even the banter between just the two of them—texting and bickering—felt like it was a performance. She wasn't sure when she'd stopped performing. She got greedy with him, unwilling to share him with the rest of the world. She updated the girls when they asked for it, but she didn't give them more than a few words. She stopped seeing him as Diego Cabrera, and started seeing him as her Diego. She'd never been cared for the way he cared for her.

She lay on his lap, listening to *A Picture of Dorian Gray* as Diego alternated between attempting to solve a Rubik's cube and teaching himself how to braid her hair. "This is . . . kind of nice, isn't it?" June mused. Diego's hands stilled in her hair, and June shifted to look up at his concerned face.

"Nice? June, you're hurt."

She huffed. As if she didn't know that. She was the one waking in tears from the pain, migraines causing distortion, and violent spells of terror and confusion. Diego often had to hold her during them, soothe her worries and the violent fear that she was alone. Back in her childhood home, her father around the corner. She wasn't sure where the fear came from, only that it was debilitating. But Diego soothed her. Brought her back from it every time. Held her tightly and whispered soft words in Spanish until she calmed.

June blinked up at him from her spot in his lap.

Diego didn't have a bad angle. She despised it.

"I just . . . can't remember the last time I took a break like this."

Diego blinked down at her. "It's concerning that it took a concussion and a separated shoulder to get you to take a break."

June sighed, flopping back down into his lap. "Ugh, whatever—"

Diego chuckled, pleased at having riled her. He took her face into both his hands. "But, it is nice. Spending time with you like this." His head was crooked to the side, his expression soft and genuine as he grinned down at her. An uncomfortable warmness settled through her, tingling from her heart into her flushed face, clear down into her toes. A million thoughts swarmed her head all at the same time, but only one rang through loud and clear.

Kiss me.

Oh.

Oh.

The sudden moment of clarity left her mouth dry, a stampede of butterflies set loose in her stomach.

She was getting too bored in this house all alone with him. Her mind had been supplying extremely unhelpful ways of keeping them both occupied. She cleared her throat. "Shut up. I'm listening to this book."

Chapter Twenty-Five

June's headaches were becoming less and less frequent, but every now and then, there came one so brutal that all she could do was lie in a dark room with an ice pack over her eyes until it faded. It was one such day Diego had a doctor's appointment. He sat with her in the dark for several moments, holding her hand. ". . . I'll cancel my—"

"Shut up and go."

Diego sighed, leaning back in his chair, and she could imagine him running his fingers through his hair the way he so often did. "I don't like leaving you alone."

"Go," June scolded. "I'm fine."

Still, it took some convincing. Begrudgingly, he surrendered and did as she requested, but not without supplying everything she could possibly need within arm's reach and plugging in her phone.

It took several hours for June's headache to finally fade. The headaches weren't as persistent anymore, coming less often and fading more quickly. She'd be back to normal in no time. She had to be. It had been three weeks since her accident; nearly eleven since Diego's.

She sat on the couch in the living room drinking tea with an ice pack held to her head— more for comfort than pain— when Diego came bursting through the door. He wore a bright grin, practically skipping, his enthusiasm bouncing off the wall. It tripled at the sight of her. "*Vaquera!* How is your head?"

"It's fine," she chuckled, setting down her ice pack. Diego hurried to take her tea, discarding it on the coffee table before he knelt in front of her. She chuckled, poking him in the cheek. "You're in a good mood."

He laughed—loud, joyous, and victorious. She couldn't even be angry for the pang it sent through her head. He drew her hand into his own, meeting her eyes. "They cleared me."

In an instant, June's heart plummeted to her stomach. She felt the blood drain from her face, her mouth going dry. "Oh." It escaped her before she could stop herself, trying to hide the overwhelming dread. "That's—That's great, Diego. That's—"

If he saw her terror, he did not mention it, too wrapped up in his own relief and bliss to see anything else. He stood, dropping her hand as he turned around and ran his fingers through his hair, sighing as though a massive weight had been dropped from him. "They want me in Austria tomorrow night. I mean—*Dios mío,* I never thought this day would come." He rattled off in a mix of English and Spanish, talking more to himself than to her.

She was grateful for it.

June's entire world had just been ripped out from under her. She'd been so relieved at the idea of not having him in the car, she forgot it wasn't permanent. She stood tentatively, her heart hammering hard enough to make her head ache again. " . . . Austria?"

"I know! Isn't it great—" He whirled, and the moment he saw her face, his smile slipped. "I . . . June, I know the timing is less than perfect, but Catalina said she would come stay and—"

June shook her head. "Why Austria, Diego?" But she knew the

answer. The Austrian Grand Prix. It was Tuesday. If they could get him there tomorrow, he could race. He could do the practices. Do qualifying. Be in the car.

Diego sighed, looking to the floor before he met her gaze, shaking his head solemnly. He opened his mouth to speak, but June beat him to it. "It's too soon. You were just cleared. You can't get back in the car again already—"

He scoffed, as if that were the most ridiculous notion in the world. "Of course I can. I'm a racer."

A racer who had broken his neck in an accident. A racer who had nearly been killed. A racer who wouldn't stop until the wreck that *did* kill him. She choked back her panic, trying to keep herself steady as she attempted to reason with him. "You—You can't get back in that car, Diego. Tell me you aren't getting back in that car."

Diego got half a sentence of argument out before her words truly landed and his face scrunched in confusion. "June. I'm a driver. Of course, I am. I can't just be your little house nurse forever."

In that single moment, June's terror dissolved into grief. Into betrayal. Into embarrassment. Her lips parted in surprise. It was like he'd taken her heart, ripped it out of her chest, and then shoved it into a blender. Her pride was wounded, as though she were some little girl who needed to be taken care of.

The moment the words were out, Diego's face sunk in regret. "No, June, that wasn't what I meant—"

"No? I think it was exactly what you meant." She shoved past him and he caught her by the elbow.

"*Vaquera*, please. I misspoke—"

June ripped out of his grasp, gritting her teeth against the pain from the sudden movement. "I'm going to lie down. I have a headache."

Diego immediately reached for the ice pack. "Here, let me—"

June snatched it off the couch before he could. "Oh, no. I can take care of myself."

He winced, turning to face her. "But you don't have to—"

June whirled in the doorway, facing him down the hall, grateful for the distance. She'd allowed herself to get too comfortable. Too relaxed. "Have fun in Austria," June spat. "Let's hope that broken neck holds up in a car." She slammed the door shut. Instantly, she heard the crash and thud of something being thrown on the other side. She didn't open the door, only kicked the lock, curled up in bed, and buried her pounding head amongst the pillows.

The knock didn't come until several hours later, gently rousing June from her sleep. The sun had set and the pounding in her head had lessened. "June?"

She blinked blearily, sitting up to rub the sleep from her eyes. Diego's voice came from outside her door. "Can I come in?"

June didn't answer, staring down into her hands while she fiddled with the blanket in her lap. The door creaked under his weight as he leaned against it. "Come on, June. I know you're listening. I'm sorry. These last few weeks have been some of the best of my life. I don't want my own stupidity to ruin that."

She bit her bottom lip, fighting the tears welling in her eyes again. She didn't know what to say, words lodged in her throat. She fumbled with the door, pulling it open just for Diego to stumble and catch himself on the doorframe.

He didn't say anything for a long while, watching her carefully. She frowned up at him. "I thought you were out for the rest of the season."

Diego's gaze went from relief to sorrow. To apologies. His brows knitted together, reaching out to set his hand on her shoulder. "I thought so, too," he reassured her. "But I healed quick, and the reserve driver isn't performing the way they need him to. So, I'm back in." He let his hand trail up the back of her neck, grounding itself at the base of her head and urging her to look up at him.

She shook her head, looking down to his shirt. Focusing on the dark grey fabric. Distracting herself with something real. "You won't be in the running for the Driver's Championship, or the Constructor's. What's the point?"

Diego drew a deep breath, like the words stung him, a sharp reminder. But his voice was steady when he spoke. "Racing is about more than championships. I love it. And maybe not everyone understands that, but that's okay."

June's heart ached. It burned with terror. With the knowledge that one day he wouldn't get so lucky. That he would be back in that damned car. Back on that damned track. His life was resuming, and there was nothing June could do to stop it.

"I leave in the morning."

June offered him a single, sharp nod, gritting her teeth to keep from crying as she looked up to him. "Good luck."

He blinked down at her, big brown eyes wide with apology. "*Mamá* said she'll come stay with you. Or Antonia. Catalina offered too—"

"I'm okay, Diego," she said firmly. "I'll be okay for a few days."

He seemed pained by the idea, brows furrowed with concern as he stepped closer, making him look at her as he spoke. "You're certain?"

June forced a tight-lipped smile. "I'm certain." And she was.

That night, when Diego said his goodbye and slipped away to bed, June booked her ticket back to Florence.

Back home.

Chapter Twenty-Six

June wasn't technically cleared to fly yet, but her symptoms had lessened significantly, and nobody could legally stop her. So, June got on the plane. Her head ached from the pressure, but she made it to Florence safe and sound.

When the girls picked her up from the airport, there was no boisterous banter that so often followed them. Their voices were quiet, they offered tight hugs, they held her close. June's heart warmed. She was so grateful to be home. So grateful to be back with the people she loved.

June found her way to the barn and went straight to Hades. He nickered to her softly, and June tried not to tear up, but ultimately failed. She wrapped her hands around his head, holding him tightly to her.

She hoped he hadn't missed her nearly as bad as she'd missed him.

"Isa?" June called.

Isa popped around the corner from the wash bay where she'd been bathing another horse, smiling softly at her. "Yes?"

"Will you saddle Hades for me?"

Isa's smile fell. She said nothing for a long moment, her hesitation plain.

June only offered her a reassuring smile. "I'll take it easy. Swear it."

Begrudgingly, Isa obliged. June had never been so grateful to step back into the saddle. Hades seemed to notice her own fragility, and he was extra careful. Extra gentle.

Riding again was good for June. If nothing else, it lifted her spirits, walking around the arena, and then around the facility.

June hadn't told Diego she was leaving. She hadn't called him or sent him a text, she just left him a note. As she watched the Sprint Race Friday morning, she knew it was the right choice. Diego was completely and entirely in the zone. It was as though he'd never left the track at all.

June turned the TV off. She hoped she'd never have to watch a race ever again.

June stepped back into her routine without hesitation. She had to take it easier than she liked, but she did it all nonetheless. A gym session that really just consisted of walking on a treadmill and lifting a few small free weights. A flat session on Hades where they only walked or cantered. The jarring nature of a trot was still too painful for her head.

Diego texted her relentlessly to check up on her. June answered with short reassurance that she was fine. She didn't tell him she'd gone home, but it was Monday, and he'd return to an empty house that night.

Isa had taken over schooling a few of Amelia's young horses while June was out, and a few small jumps were set up in the arena. They should have been easy, but June carefully steered clear of them. The sight of rails strung across a jump stand brought a pang of terror to her chest. She wondered if that fear would ever fade.

She slept in her own bed.

She didn't know when her small apartment had begun to feel so big. So empty.

The next morning, the cycle began again. June woke while it was still dark, stumbling into her kitchen, starving and fiending for a cup of coffee. Her caffeine intake had been limited by the concussion, but she hardly cared now. Her symptoms had lessened enough she was going to drink a gallon. She went through the motions, reaching to fill the pot.

The voice sounded from behind her. "What the fuck?"

June dropped the coffee pot in the sink, scrambling for the nearest defensive item as she whirled to face the perpetrator.

Diego.

Diego was in her living room. He had a single duffle bag dropped at his feet, wearing a simple pair of jeans and a crewneck. He must have traveled all night.

Realizing her weapon of choice had been a roll of paper towels, she chucked it at his head. "What is wrong with you!" she shouted, clutching at her sputtering heart.

He dodged the projectile easily, but he didn't waiver in his pursuit. There was a paper in his hands, and he thrust it at her. She recognized it immediately. Her note.

The ink was smudged, and the paper warped as though he hadn't let go of it from the moment he found it. "You promised me you would be fine alone."

June took a step back, gesturing to the expanse of her apartment around her. "Aren't I?"

A noise of disbelief escaped Diego's throat, throwing his hands up in the air. He sat on the couch, and then immediately stood again like he couldn't decide what to do between one minute and the next. "Charlene told me you're riding again?"

There was nothing to refute, so she didn't. She drew a sharp breath, turning back to her original task as she put on a pot of coffee.

"*Vaquera*, you can't—"

She whirled on him, disgusted with his audacity. "If you can get back in the car, I can get back in the saddle."

Diego groaned in frustration. "You are not cleared!"

"I don't care."

"June–"

"I don't care!"

Diego stared for a long while, lips parted in surprise as the cogs turned in his mind. "What are you saying?"

June set her jaw, staring at him across the room. "I'm saying that after a year of absolute misery, things were finally starting to go my way! I'm not giving that up now."

He shook his head, a tiny movement, so small it almost seemed involuntary. He looked afraid. As afraid as she was watching him climb back into that car.

"If you get to drive again, then I get to ride."

His hands went up in surrender. "Okay." His voice came out small. Resigned. He had lost this battle, and he was taking it with grace. "Okay," he surrendered.

He took a tentative step towards her, and then another when she didn't retreat, wrapping her up in a hug. The fight went out of her the moment his arms were around her, and she fell against him easily, a shuddering breath escaping her. She pulled him tighter against her, like allowing herself relief that he had come back to her. "Promise me you'll be careful." June offered him a single, sharp nod.

He sighed into her hair, relaxing like a great weight had been lifted from him. "You should have called me, you asshole. A note? Really?"

That surprised a laugh out of June, and she snorted, burying her face into his chest. "I guess that was pretty asshole-ish, huh?"

"Careful, Junebug. That almost sounds like an apology."

She huffed. "I don't do those."

He smiled softly, pulling back to tuck her hair behind her ears. His eyes held so much affection it nearly made her sick. "I know, June. I know."

"Are you staying?"

His lips pressed into a thin line. "For a couple of days."

She understood it. They were thrown back into the havoc of racing and riding. They had more to focus on than simply spending time together. Their weeks of bliss were over. June nodded firmly. "I'm glad you're here."

Diego smiled softly, pulling her back into his arms, holding her like he was afraid she would disappear if he so much as looked away. "Me too."

They fell back into their old routine easily. Diego made them eggs and toast for breakfast. They shared a pot of coffee. Things were easy. They always were with him. June insisted they watch a movie in her room, and when they both fell asleep halfway through, neither complained. Sharing a bed had become natural, and she would be lying to say that she didn't enjoy it. Something had shifted in June's heart, a strange variance that left her lingering in the *what-if?*

They weren't friends, not quite. She wasn't sure if they could ever go back to friends. Maybe if they'd ever been *'just friends'* in the first place. Her hand drifted towards his on the bed. Not touching. At least, not quite. Too close to call it nothing, but just far enough to keep pretending like it was.

Diego looked pale seeing her climb back on a horse, but at least it was Hades this time. A simple flat session. June didn't have it in her to look at a jump quite yet. She decided she should be officially cleared for that, at least.

Diego still insisted on taking care of her. His attentiveness seemed to have doubled since he'd been cleared. He insisted on untacking for her, on putting Hades away and feeding per her instructions.

He kept a steadying hand on her everywhere she went, as though he were terrified she was still unsteady. June couldn't admit that it was comforting. That she wished she could face the entirety of life with his hand in the small of her back or in the crook of her elbow.

"I never told you thank you," she said from the dining table, watching as he cooked dinner.

He raised an eyebrow at her from the stove. "You've told me thank you a million times. It's no trouble making sure you're alright—"

"I mean for the deal."

That made him pause, watching her carefully, and June continued. "I mean it. I never would have done any of this without you. As much as I hate to say it, you were right. I did need you." There was a heavy weight to her words that had not been there the first time he said them—grabbing her elbow at a Petal event as she went to walk away.

Diego smiled softly to himself, offering her a single sharp nod in acknowledgement. They slept in the same bed again that night, and when she woke with his arms around her, neither of them said a word about it.

Chapter Twenty-Seven

June arrived at the barn early, Diego in tow. June heart stopped at the sight of Amelia's Bentley pulled up beside the barn. She hadn't seen her since the accident. Amelia hadn't called or text her once.

June arrived to find Oviatt saddled, Amelia standing at his side.

Any lightheartedness fled the pair immediately. "What's this?" Diego said shortly.

A part of her had thought after the accident, Amelia would finally concede. Oviatt was dangerous. He had nearly killed her. And here he was saddled. June gulped, anxiety flooding her. Diego's hand landed at the small of her back, the pressure soothing and warm against the building terror in her gut.

Amelia scoffed, arms folded over her chest. "Have you never seen a horse before?"

Diego and Amelia had had very limited interactions, but each of them went about like that. It was a matter of ten seconds before they were at each other's throats.

Diego grit his teeth, seething rage. "June is done riding that thing," he spat. For a single moment, June allowed herself to hope. To imagine a world in which Amelia's brows furrowed in understanding. A world in which she hugged June and whispered apologies.

But June lived in the real world. The world in which Amelia laughed and turned her gaze on June. "Is that true?"

June had spent the last five years of her life as Amelia's whipping girl. She didn't ask questions. She did what she had to. Amelia owned her. Every breath she took was hers. Every move she made, every round in the ring, every second she was alive belonged to Amelia. Diego couldn't understand that. He didn't know what it was like.

Amelia craned her head to the side. "Is that true, June?"

June swallowed over the lump in her throat, choking back the raw fear building in her. June had never told Amelia no before. Even for the things that were impossible, she found a way. She always did. She couldn't look at Diego as she shook her head. "I'll ride him."

Diego whirled, his eyes wide and lips parted in absolute terror. "June." His voice came out a plea, shaking his head.

Amelia scoffed, eyeing the pair with utter disdain. "I warned you." And she had, hadn't she? Warned her that Diego would insert himself into her career. Would distract her from what was necessary. How could she gauge her own thoughts when Diego was in her ear spewing about a horse he had never ridden?

But he's right, isn't he?

June shook that thought away. She could not afford to think like that. Not with Diego and Amelia pulling her in two separate directions.

"Sort it out, or I will." Amelia's order was firm, and she turned her back on the pair, leaving Oviatt tied where he was.

Amelia left, and June whirled on Diego, livid. "Get on him," she challenged. "You want to be my coach? Be my coach, Diego! Get on him!"

Diego's eyes darkened, his rage melting into desperation. "June," he begged. "Don't do this."

Her chest heaved. Rage burned in her eyes as tears welled up. She jabbed a finger into his chest. "Don't get back in the car."

"June—"

"Don't get back in the car!"

Diego's face furrowed in utter desperation. And he said nothing. What was there to say? He had to race again. He *would* race. Again, and again, and again. Her eyes burned with the effort to fight back her tears, burrowing her sorrow in rage as she shoved him backwards. "What, Diego? It's not so fun when you're the one watching?"

He caught himself, surging forward to grab her by the arm. "He nearly killed you!"

June's voice raised to a scream. "I would rather die than go back to having nothing!"

Diego took a step back, like he was finally seeing her for the first time. His rage turned into a horrific pity that she could not stomach, the anger in his voice dissolving into something so quiet she could hardly hear him. "Do you think they'll finally love you when you make yourself a martyr?"

Her body shook with rage. Her eyes welled with tears. Her mouth opened and closed, unable to find the words to respond. She felt pathetic. Broken. "The doctor said the force of the impact should have decapitated you."

The fight went out of Diego the moment the words were off her tongue. June grit her teeth, refusing to cry, but the tears welled anyway, and her voice still shook. "I dream of it almost every night. Your body in the car, and your head on the track." She choked on her words, unable to fight the tears freely flowing down her cheeks now. "I thought the next time I saw you would be in a casket. For fifteen minutes of my life you were *dead*. If you get to race again, I get to ride again."

Diego reached out for her and June flinched away from his comfort.

He winced, drawing a sharp breath. ". . . I'm sorry."

It wasn't a real apology. No promise to change. No lying that things would be different. They both knew neither of them could walk away from the lives they had chosen. Quiet resignation was all she got. But at least it was honest. "We're square."

Diego twitched, his mouth falling open in surprise. "What?"

"I said we're square! You got your seat, and I got my sponsors. We're square."

His face contorted in pain, staring at her in shock for a few long moments before he finally spoke. "Is that all this was to you?"

June grit her teeth hard enough she was certain they'd crack. She didn't answer him. Couldn't answer him.

Diego nodded, swallowing hard. "Fine," he said. "Kill yourself for people who wouldn't love you if you had ten titles. I won't stop you. But I care about you far too much to watch."

The grief hit her all at once. A goodbye. A permanent one. They let it linger in the air a moment longer than they should, eyes glued to each other over the expanse of the barn. Neither of them budged, like they couldn't bear to leave this. But eventually, someone had to move.

Diego looked down, shaking his head at the floor. She watched him turn and stride from the barn, each step he took leaving her with an ache in her chest. She wanted to race after him, throw her arms around him and beg him to understand. She planted her feet. He didn't look back.

When he was finally gone, a sob heaved from her chest. She dropped to her knees in the dirt, clutching at her broken heart.

With the world dangled on a string in front of her, she gritted her teeth and turned back to Amelia.

Amelia didn't make her ride Oviatt that day. When she returned, June was shaken, and Amelia could tell. She granted her some sliver of mercy, as though rewarding her for her loyalty like some guard dog. She told Isa to untack and put Oviatt on the walker.

June stood in the tack room, methodically cleaning her saddle. If she could just focus. If she could just shut it all off. Not think about Diego—*don't*. A pang of horror shot through her, and she wiped at her eyes. *Don't*, she scolded. But she thought of his betrayal-filled eyes and his words. *Kill yourself for people who wouldn't love you if you had ten titles*. The tears welled without her permission. She sniffled, wiping at eyes. *Turn it off*, but a sob escaped and she was done for. June stumbled back until she hit the wall. She sunk down to the floor, clapping a hand over her face to muffle the sobs.

The only people June relied on were the ones she paid. She wasn't sure why she had forgotten that. Perhaps it was because she and Diego were in a trade of sorts. Her publicity for his sponsors. She could hardly believe she'd been so foolish as to give someone power over her. She was smarter than that. Tougher.

One doctor's appointment later, and June was cleared to jump again.

June didn't know if she'd ever swing on a horse again without utter terror. She couldn't step in the saddle without the fear flashing through her mind. Oviatt had nearly killed her. She hadn't come off—he had flipped over on her. That was entirely out of her control. And when she hit the ground, he had stepped on her.

June rode Oviatt again. Amelia was at her side, the way she'd promised she'd be. Her words echoed in June's mind repeatedly. *Who's going to be there when you take home a title?*

Amelia. It was always going to be Amelia. Diego was a distraction. He always had been.

Part of her had thought that Diego would call. He would get

home and settle and text her.

It was two weeks later when she finally realized he wasn't going to.

It was going to get easier. One day, she would stop staring at her phone, desperate for something from him, but the ache had to devour her whole first.

With each ride, her terror of Oviatt abated, turning into something more like understanding. A partnership was formed. They both agreed to get through the day. June let him jump. She stayed out of his way. It was the only way to survive. They found an understanding.

Even Amelia was becoming more and more pleased with every ride. Oviatt and June found a rhythm. A terrifying, sickening rhythm where June was entirely out of control, praying he would gauge each jump right, but a rhythm nonetheless.

The Saint-Tropez Grand Prix was fast approaching. June's first competition back.

Her phone was silent.

She wasn't sure when the attachment had formed. When she had started counting on him at her side in the warm-up ring. But now when she looked, all she saw was his absence. She was alone. Of all the things in the world, that was the one she could rely on. The way she was when she was six. And again at seventeen. And again, now.

By some miracle, they'd gotten through the first round clear. Oviatt entered the arena like a time-bomb, and June sat each hop and buck, keeping her hands as light as she could manage without being ripped out of the saddle. She couldn't fight him. Couldn't fight anyone. Didn't she know that? Fighting got her nowhere.

The bell sounded, and June held on for dear life. Her hands clenched in the reins until they went white. She guided him through the course, giving him enough leniency to get over the jumps however he pleased. That was the only way to keep him from killing her.

But the fear was there. Every time he went up, she wondered if he was going to land on his feet, or on her again.

A jump loomed before her, a massive triple combination that she had walked earlier. She guided him with her seat, and as little as possible with her hands. She let him gauge when and where he was going to get over it. They soared through it, leaving the course standing behind them. She wanted to say she was relieved, but her hands still shook. A good round. Good time.

June was swaying as she exited the arena.

The moment she saw Isa coming to collect Oviatt, she scrambled off the horse and passed him to Isa's care. She dropped to sit in the dirt, resting her head against her knees as she sucked in breaths, but they seemed to come in shorter and shorter gasps every time. Her mind raced with thoughts, replaying every moment she had sat on that animal. Every moment he could have tripped. Every moment he could have flipped over on her, every moment she could have died—

A pair of hands grabbed June by the arm, dragging her to her feet and June's head swiveled side to side, trying to gather her bearings. It was Charlene. She beamed with utter pride. June barely managed to get her feet underneath herself, the world spinning around her and every muscle of her body aching.

"Get on," Charlene demanded. "You have to get back on, June. You won."

Charlene's tight grip was the only thing keeping her standing. "What?"

Her mind was still racing and spinning, trying to find some sense in the world. Her hands were shaking, but Charlene led her like one would a toddler, guiding her back toward Oviatt.

They came to a stop in front of Oviatt, who gave an impatient flick of his tail. He wore a blue blanket over his saddle, her stirrups pulled through slits in the side—*'Longines Global Champions Tour'* engraved across the side of it. June wasn't given time to argue or even think. Charlene gave her a leg up, and June fumbled into the saddle, her hands shaking as she grabbed for reins, fighting the urge to immediately drop to the ground again. The lap of honor was nearly painful. She'd let herself catch her breath out of the saddle. Now, she was back on him, a sash around her shoulders.

The lap was over quickly, and she'd never been so grateful to be on solid ground again in her life. June passed Oviatt back to Isa—and then June was swarmed. Charlene, Lola and Olivia screamed and wrapped her up in a hug.

They were babbling on and on about her win, slapping her on the back and congratulating her, but June's mind wasn't working. She'd always thought she'd feel better, relieved, ecstatic. Instead, her body ached. She was sore all over, and her heart was still beating so fast she was certain it was going to burst from her chest. The girls ushered her off to the podium.

To the top step.

She had done it.

She'd won. It didn't smother her anxiety, but it soothed it.

June took a deep breath, her first in weeks. She looked up to the sky. From the top step. All alone, just as Amelia had promised.

This was how it had always been. June did her best alone. People complicated things. Her only friends were on her payroll. The champagne fell like rain all around her, hiding the tears seeping down her cheeks.

The gold medal hung like a chain around her neck.

Saint-Tropez was just the beginning. June's confidence took a massive boost. She'd won. Finally, for the first time in over a year, June had won a Grand Prix. Oviatt may kill her, but at least she'd die at the top.

June learned to do as Amelia said. She stayed out of Oviatt's way. He did have the scope. Oviatt could jump.

She just had to control her own anxiety.

June took third in Paris, stood on a podium in front of the Eiffel Tower the way she'd always dreamed. Gained another medal. Took home more points. Stockholm brought fifth. Not the podium, but good points.

June was almost more grateful to be off the podium. No lap of honor.

The sight of Oviatt brought a sweltering heat to her veins that left her feeling shaky and weak. The moment his feet left the ground, her mind helpfully supplied her with images of the fall. Of hitting the dirt. Of Oviatt coming down next to her. Of a concussion that could have easily been a brain bleed. Of nearly dying. The Monaco jump-off went swimmingly, a 68.3 second course. Clean. June was swaying when the course ended, exiting the gate. The moment she saw Isa coming to collect Oviatt, she bailed off. Isa caught the reins as June fell to her knees, her vision clouded over with panic. Her entire body was trembling with the force of the terror ravaging her.

The crowd's applause roared through the Grand Prix course. The cheers shook the ground beneath her shuddering form, or at least it felt like it. The sound brought back images of a different arena, different screams, different faces. The faces that had been there in Cannes. Those faces that she'd almost died in front of. The world was spinning. She was going to throw up.

They were in Monaco. Diego lived in Monaco. Was he there? Was he in the crowd? Of course, he wasn't. He wouldn't be again. Diego had stepped back and seen something in her that made him run. Was it the same thing her mom had seen all those years ago? June clutched at her heart, digging her fingers into the dirt with her other hand.

Isa caught her by the shoulder, eyes wide in concern. She was saying something but June's ears rang too loudly for the sound to penetrate the fog in her mind.

She tried to speak, but it was a strangled sound, somewhere between a cry and a groan. Her fingers continued to dig into the dirt, as if she was trying to use it to ground herself. The applause roared again. A few of the other riders had turned to look at her, and June could feel their judgment from a mile away. The scared, weak little girl who couldn't handle a few jumps. She gasped for breath, squeezing her eyes tightly shut.

The pain in her stomach refused to lessen, and June finally doubled over, vomiting into the dirt beneath her. The bitter taste of bile filled her throat along with the stinging burn of acid.

Isa squeezed her shoulder, but it did little to make her feel any better. The world was still spinning, and June's head was full of fog. "June," she said softly, urgency in her voice. "June, you took second. You have to get back on."

A sob escaped June's throat, tears streaming down her face. "I can't."

"You can," Isa's voice was light and encouraging, but all June could feel was the panic.

The thought of getting back on Oviatt, of riding the horse she'd almost killed herself on, brought a new wave of nausea. Her stomach churned, and bile rose in her throat again. The world was a hazy blur of colors.

She shook her head, her entire body trembling. "I can't," she repeated, her voice wavering. "I can't." She staggered to her feet, and she turned and ran.

Chapter Twenty-Eight

When the knock came at the stall door, June immediately knew it was Charlene. She said nothing, hunkered down on the floor between the toilet and the wall. *Go away*, she prayed. *Please go away.*

"June, I know you're in there." The sound of Charlene's voice sent a fresh wave of guilt through her. She'd rather Charlene see her drunk and breaking chairs than like this.

She squeezed her eyes shut, leaning her head against the cool brick of the bathroom wall. "I think I ate something." The lie was weak, and she knew Charlene wouldn't buy it.

The silence that dragged on confirmed that Charlene had seen through her deception. Then, finally, "Let me in."

June sucked in a sharp breath, the tears immediately welling. She tucked herself against the wall, shaking her head even though Charlene could not see it. The silence in the room grew even louder, filled only by the sound of her harsh breathing. In. Out. Her chest ached. Her throat hurt. Her eyes stung. And then the knocking came again, this time louder.

"June," Charlene called out, her voice torn between an order and a plea. "Let me in."

A weak sob escaped her throat, staring down into her hands. She'd peeled at her fingers until they bled. "I thought it would feel so different."

Charlene sighed across the door. And then, rustling as she crawled onto the bathroom floor. June's breath caught in her throat at the sight of perfect, pristine Charlene on her hands and knees crawling under the stall door of a dirty bathroom. "Char—"

Charlene righted herself, huffing a piece of hair out of her face as she turned to June, her face as unreadable and calculating as always. Immediately, June's hands went to her face, trying to hide her tears. "I'm sorry," she choked. "I'm sorry."

Charlene eyed June as though she were assessing an injury. She sat beside her on the bathroom floor as if it were the most natural thing in the world, grabbing June by the shoulders and pulling her into her arms. "Come here, Kid."

And just like that, the dam broke. June fell into Charlene's arms, sobbing into her chest. She kept a vise grip on Char's arms, her lighthouse in a storm. And it was a storm. The panic, the fear, the shame and guilt, all crashing down on her with a vengeance.

"It wasn't supposed to be like this," she cried, her voice sounding pathetic even in her own ears.

Charlene, for her part, didn't comment on June's pathetic state. She simply let the kid cry on her chest, rubbing her back in wide, soothing circles. "That's the thing about dreams. You spend your whole life chasing an idea just to realize the things you actually loved and wanted are long gone."

June buried her face in her chest, a sob wracking through her. "Did I leave everything behind for *this*?"

Charlene was quiet for a long while, searching for the right words to say. "It's okay, Kid," she said softly. "It's okay."

Even she didn't sound like she believed it.

June got away with being absent from the victory lap under the guise of being ill. Technically, not a lie. Still, not the full truth. The excuse extended to her getting out of the afterparty. She went back to her hotel early, took a hot shower and curled up in a ball in her bed. She watched *Spirit* and remembered the time Diego had joked about watching it with her.

Part of her had hoped he'd been watching that night. That he'd see her mysterious disappearance and finally call her. That he'd be in Monaco. That he'd invite her over to talk, or offer to take her to dinner to make her feel better, or even just call.

He never did.

When the knock came at her hotel room, she let herself feel a bit of hope, like all her longing had finally willed him into existence. But when she opened the door, there was Olivia. And that made sense. In a way, that was better. She held up a bag of Chinese takeout food and June grinned weakly, letting her in.

They sat together on the couch, watching some home renovation show. June allowed the comfort to wash over her—to sit close, rubbing shoulders with Olivia and stealing bites of beef from her plate.

Olivia's phone dropped, and June reached down to pick it up absentmindedly. Her eyes landed on the lock screen, and June blinked down at it. She remembered taking the picture vividly, even though she'd never actually seen it. It was one Diego had taken, Olivia and Lola with arms wrapped around June, all of them laughing, and tangled up with each other. June's heart stopped for a moment. It was the night June had taken fifth on Hades last season.

Olivia caught sight of her staring at it and immediately snatched the phone out of June's hands, a blush coating her cheeks. "I . . . What?" Olivia said, suddenly defensive.

June shook her head. "I just hadn't seen it before."

Olivia blinked, allowing her gaze to wander back to the photo. She was quiet for a moment, but she chewed on the inside of her cheek the way she always did when she actually thought before she said something. "It was . . . like, probably the best night of my entire life? I was just . . . so happy for you. So happy for all of us. When I graduated with my PR degree, I thought, *'great, I suffered through four years of college just to make stupid, trending videos for some evil plastic surgeon in LA'*. I was so scared of ending up with some Plain Jane, or someone who wasn't good at their job. And then there was you. I just—" Her thumb swiped over the photo fondly, as if she could reach back in time and touch the memory. Hold it close. Let it console her. "That night was really special. You really had to fight for those points, and there were so many people cheering you on. I just thought, *'Yes. Exactly. This is the June I get to share with the whole world'*."

June had never really considered the way Olivia thought of her. She was a wildcard. Easy to make content for when she was constantly in some predicament or another, but she didn't exactly think of herself the way Olivia did. Good at her job. Interesting. Someone Olivia wanted to be around.

June discarded her takeout container on the coffee table, taking Liv by the arm and leaning her head against her. She smiled involuntarily. "That was a pretty good night, huh?"

Olivia reached up and played with June's hair, running her fingers through the short locks. June could count on one hand the number of people that cared for her. Liv was definitely at the top.

June let her eyes flutter shut, savoring the feeling of being cared for. She'd missed it.

Olivia buried her face in June's hair, twined around her as she sighed and finally spoke. "Are you . . . going to keep doing this?"

June pulled back just enough to look up at her. "Of course I am, Liv."

But that wasn't the answer she'd been looking for and it was written all over her face. "I mean . . . you should start looking for another horse."

The thought was like ice water being poured down her back, and

June shivered. She had picked her path: Oviatt and Amelia.

She sat up, pulling away from Olivia and instead opted to stare at the TV, refusing to meet Liv's eyes.

She swallowed, her stomach twisted into a tight knot. "Why would I do that?" she managed, though her voice felt weaker than normal.

"June, you're fucking terrified."

"No, I'm not," June protested, her voice a bit too defensive to convince either of them. Tonight had belied her. She pulled her knees up to her chest, wrapping her arms around them like a shield. ". . . I'm finally winning." It was a weak protest. Even she knew it wasn't enough. "What kind of person does that make me if I'm afraid to win?"

Olivia shook her head sadly. "You were never afraid on Midus."

Even the thought of Midus made tears spring to her eyes. The thought of how different it could have been. How different it *should* have been. Where would she be now? A title win under her belt? Fighting for another? Maybe Hades would be where he was supposed to be, not forced to pick up so much slack. It was all going to be so different.

"You haven't been the same since your accident, June." Olivia's voice was strained as if it hurt her to even say it. To suggest that June had changed. That Oviatt was still stomping her into the dirt the same way he had the day they fell.

The words hit like a punch to the gut. They were hard truths, and June tried to push them away, but Olivia was right. She had been different since her accident. That fall had left more than just physical scars. But how to admit that? How to admit that she was too cowardly to do the one thing she was supposed to adore?

She was afraid of falling again.

She was terrified Oviatt was going to kill her.

"Yes, I am."

"I know you, June!" Olivia shouted, desperate and close to tears. "I know you. I've known you all along."

A tear slid down her cheek, unchecked, and she hastily wiped it away. "You don't know shit."

"Really?" Olivia challenged. "I know you never feel good enough even when your talent scares the shit out of everyone else. I know you never admit you care for anything or anyone because you're as emotionally available as a fence post, so you lean on your horses, and now you don't even have that! Midus was your everything! Hades was your everything! And now you ride a horse you hate because you're so obsessed with winning. This isn't *you*, June!"

June jumped to her feet, squeezing her fists tight enough her nails dug into her palms, leaving crescent-moon indents behind. "This is me!" Her voice came out louder than she'd intended, the volume surprising both her and Liv. "This is me. I'm finally winning!" The tears were flowing now, and she angrily brushed them from her cheeks. Her cheeks burned with shame, and her heart was hammering at a breakneck pace. "I'm winning."

"Is it enough?" Her voice was soft, her question genuine, but her words hung in the air like the axe of an executioner, waiting to fall given the right command.

She'd sacrificed everything for this. Everything. This was the path she'd chosen. June grit her teeth. "Yes," she lied. It left a bitter taste on her tongue, and she had to swallow several times before it went down. It sat like a rock in her stomach, heavy and unpleasant. June was never a good liar. Olivia saw right through her and she knew it.

She watched June silently for a few long moments. "Good," she said finally, "because you're the one who has to live with it." Without another word, Olivia snagged her jacket and left June staring at the door after her.

June wished she could have said that panic attack was the last. If anything, it was only the beginning. June didn't sleep anymore. So often she was plagued by unbearable thoughts. Night, after night, after night. Falling asleep was no longer a possibility for her. Hades and Midus remained untouched and unridden. Oviatt was June's mount now.

She lunged him for nearly an hour before even stepping on, desperate to at least somewhat tire him, but all it did was frustrate them both. June got quite good at stepping on and staying out of his way. Each competition brought a rise in their standings and a rise in the points, and yet, Amelia wasn't satisfied. She never seemed to be. June spent a lot of time on the internet, most of it looking at new horses. If she could push through this year, she could find a new horse. Ride again. Be free again.

. . . If she could convince Amelia.

But why would she? She was winning, wasn't she? Could she really ask for anything more?

She'd typed up half a million sale ads for Hades, a few for Midus for the right home, but she never could make herself hit post. Oviatt was the one she wanted gone. Even winning, she still wished she was on Hades. On Midus.

June stood in Midus's stall, leaning back against the door as she stroked his face. It should have been him. None of this would have happened if she were riding him.

Amelia came storming down the barn aisle, and June's throat immediately closed with fear. Each footfall was one of pure rage, and the anxiety rose in her gut with every second as Amelia closed in. June stepped out of Midus's stall to greet her, opening her mouth to speak, but Amelia merely thrust a paper into her hand.

"What the fuck is this?"

June blinked, caught off guard as she took the paper and looked down. It was an email. Her email. One she'd sent to Siegfried Vaun asking if he knew of anyone willing to provide her with a new horse. She blinked. And blinked. Her lips parted, staring down at it as she swallowed hard. "How . . . ? This is my personal email—"

"What. The. Fuck." She punctuated each word, sheer venom dripping from her words as she ripped the paper from June's hands and threw it on the ground. June had never heard her so angry.

June stared, absolutely dismayed. "How did you get that?"

Her eyes blazed with fire, rage tucked in her voice that made June want to shrink down.

Or hand her a beer.

"Have you learned nothing?" Amelia spat. "I have eyes and ears everywhere. This is *my* barn!"

June flinched back, hot tears pricking at her lash line as a deep feeling of betrayal settled in. Her mind immediately flashed to Siegfried, but he would never betray her like that. He hated Amelia.

Amelia's lips curled back with venom. "You left your email signed in on my laptop." June could have died then and there. Everything she'd fought for, and it was her own stupidity that shot her in the foot.

"Everything I've done for you, and this is the payment I get? Trying to sign a different horse behind my back? Drugging Oviatt?"

June's mind sputtered to keep up, trying to follow the web she weaved. "What are you talking about? I would never—"

"No?" Amelia taunted. "That's not what Oviatt's blood test said."

". . . What?"

Amelia stepped forward, lips curled back in a mix between bared teeth and a smile. "That's not what I'm going to tell the FEI."

The federation of equestrian sports. She could be banned from all competitions for life, depending on what was found—and all at once, June understood.

Amelia had drugged her own horse. She had hurt Oviatt just to frame June. Just to take out the competition. No one would ever believe June over Amelia.

"You're done."

June felt like she'd been kicked in the gut. Her vision blurred, tears welling in her eyes.

"Leave," she spat. "I'll ship your horses to you."

June surged forward, protectiveness flaring in her veins. "I'm not leaving them with you, you fucking psycho!"

Amelia's palm cracked across June's face, and she reeled back, her hand going to her stinging cheek.

"You really think it was talent that got you here?" Amelia snapped. "You think that if it had been any other kid in that arena in Texas things would have been different? You were desperate, June. That's something you can't teach. You were willing to do anything, and that's what I needed. Someone compliant and that was what you were. But you have no loyalty. No idea what it takes to be a champion. Get the fuck out of my barn."

This couldn't be real. It just couldn't be. June had given herself to Amelia and this barn for as long as she could comprehend. This was her life.

Her voice quivered. "And go where?"

Amelia's face contorted in a mix of disgust and pity. "I don't care."

She'd already driven the knife into June's back, but her words were the final twist of the blade.

Amelia scoffed in disgust, shook her head, and jutted her head toward the exit.

Slowly, June stumbled back to her apartment. *Hers?* No. Amelia's. Everything was Amelia's. Her *life* was Amelia's.

And now, Amelia didn't want it.

A horrified noise escaped June's throat, staring at the expanse of the home she'd resided in over the last five years. She had tried so desperately to force herself into the boxes provided for her, reshaping and rebuilding herself until she finally fit.

She never did.

June stared at the walls of her apartment, allowing her eyes to roam over the small space she had called her own. Why had she ever called it her own? She had allowed herself to become complacent. To become comfortable here. She forgot what happened when she became comfortable.

A burst of rage propelled her forward, down the hall and into her room where she grabbed a duffle bag and haphazardly began stuffing items into it. She scrounged through the apartment, grabbing the most important things she could think of—clothes, toiletries. She rattled off the list she was used to—*show gear, formal wear, makeup bag*—but not anymore. Never again.

June threw her bag on the floor, her fingers locked around a painting in her living room, ripping it off the wall and chucking it. A scream tore through her throat, and then the next painting, and the next. Her photos ripped from the wall, the trinkets she'd gathered over the years thrown from her shelves. How stupid of her to collect trinkets. To think she finally had a place to call her own. None of it was hers. None of it mattered. From the collection of clothes, to the blankets she'd gathered just because she enjoyed them. None of it mattered.

None of it ever had.

She tore everything from the walls and hurled it out into the hallway with a feverish sense of obligation, desperate to be rid of it all—pillows and chairs and curtains and decor.

"June!" a voice called from out from down the hall. She didn't so much as stall. Olivia came tearing inside, dodging flying projectiles from June's bookshelves. "June! What the fuck?"

"What's going on?—" Lola stumbled after her, over the mess June had created. June didn't say a word, and when she marched into her room and grabbed her suitcase to fill, Olivia grabbed her by the arm. "What are you doing?—"

"Leaving!" She ripped from her grasp, and Olivia stepped back like she'd been slapped.

June didn't have it in her to care, chucking items into her bag. "Lotus will find you a new client."

Lola stepped forward, placing a hand on Olivia's arm protectively. "What are you talking about?"

June whirled on them sharp enough that Olivia flinched. "Amelia said I'm done. That I'm not worth it. Can you fucking blame her? All I've done since I showed up is cause problems—"

Olivia shook her head feverishly. "That isn't true!"

"Yes it fucking is!" Her scream echoed off the room, and the girls went silent, staring at her in horror.

June couldn't explain it. Couldn't fight it. Couldn't change it. All she could do was what she'd always done.

Leave.

June slammed her suitcase promptly closed, refusing to look at the girls even though she knew they were both crying, holding onto each other and staring after June.

She should do something. Say something—*anything*—but there was a taxi waiting for her out front

June pushed past them, and without another word, she left for the last time.

PART THREE

THE LIGHT ISN'T ON YOU, IT'S IN YOU

Chapter Twenty-Nine

Everything was foggy. June knew vaguely that she'd gotten a flight from Florence to Austin. She knew she'd booked bus tickets. She knew she arranged for her horses to be transported to the nearest boarding facility—a place to leave them for a while until she could get them on a flight to Texas.

Traveling had once been a comfort to June. After five years of a new country every month, flights, shuttles, taxis, and security checkpoints had become muscle memory. She was grateful for it. The routine dragged her forward, propelling one foot in front of the other. Florence to Austin, Texas. A Greyhound from Austin to Waco. A taxi from Waco to Odie's front porch.

Home. Well, not exactly. But she had nowhere else to go.

The path to Odie's home was easily trod, up the winding lane to where her house sat on the hill. Across her flower garden, up the stone steps, across the porch. Single suitcase in tow. Backpack slung over her shoulder. Three raps across the mahogany door. Eleven at night.

Odie answered the door with her shotgun. Her fierce manner dissolved into recognition, then affection, then confusion in rapid succession. "Alessia-baby?"

It had been years since they'd found themselves like this—June knocking on her door in the middle of the night with nowhere else to go, Odie torn between asking endless questions and simply ushering her inside. The moment Odie's voice hit her ears—strong but kind, thick-accented Louisiana—it was real. She was in Texas. Showjumping was a thing of the past. She'd lost it all. Amelia had betrayed her.

June would never win the Tour.

A choked sob escaped her throat, and in that single moment, Odie's arms opened. June collapsed in her grief, allowing Odie to catch her. She tried to explain—but it came out a garbled mess of unintelligible hysteria. "Hush, baby. Come to bed." Odie scooped her up under her arm, ushering her inside. Muscle memory led her in and up the stairs to her old room. She'd half expected to find it in a state of disarray, but when Mama pushed the door open, it was exactly as it had been every day she had lived there. Waiting for her.

Odie ushered her into bed, and June collapsed, dragging Odie down beside her. She went willingly, scooping June up into her arms. "Who do I need to kill?"

A choked mixture of a sob and a laugh escaped June's throat, and she buried her face into Odie's side. Odie held her tighter, kissing the top of her head. "Get some rest, baby."

June couldn't sleep. So, when she was sure Odie was asleep, she snuck down to the kitchen and found a bottle of whiskey.

She drank until the pain faded.

June woke well into the day to find Odie gone. *At the cafe*, the note on the fridge said. She found her way to the liquor store. It wasn't like she had anything else to rely on, to look forward to, to care about.

Odie was largely the same—a few more wrinkles on her dark skin, a few more pounds on what she deemed her 'gumbo-hips', a few more streaks of white in her curly hair—but she was still her. Kind, never questioning, opening her house to June the same way she did when June was seventeen and Ava went to Austin, leaving June with only an empty, dark house and a drunk father to go home to.

It was all of three days before June was able to choke out the truth of what had happened. Amelia had betrayed her. June's career had been snipped at the roots by the same person she had trusted to foster and nurture it.

Her phone buzzed as she laid in bed, sick off of cheap whiskey. With blurry vision she glanced at it, seeing Charlene was calling again. She let it ring.

Another buzz. A text this time.

CHAR: Please pick up, June.

She felt sick. Sick of herself for being this person. She picked up her phone and chucked it across the room. It clattered to the ground. June burrowed back in bed, her head buzzing and eyes filled with tears. She willed herself to sleep.

It seemed all June ever did since returning to Texas was think of Diego.

She should call him. She supposed she could now. Tell him that she wasn't riding Oviatt anymore—that she wasn't riding at all. That Amelia hated her guts almost as much as she hated herself.

But then it would be real.

She knew what would happen. Diego would celebrate. He would offer to drag her along to his races. His friend who no longer was much of anything to him without their deal.

Or maybe he'd hate her. She couldn't bear it either way

So, she didn't call him. In fact, she didn't call much of anyone. Not even Charlene who had begged her to stay in touch, or the girls whose calls she'd been ignoring for a week. She lay in bed. She drank herself sick. She thought about everything she'd lost.

That is, until a knock came at the door. She groaned, unwilling to get up. She lay there, hoping Odie would just go away.

The door opened without a reply. She entered softly, with none of her usual grief at the sight of June in bed so late or in such a disheveled state. Odie nodded to the cans on the ground. "How many'a those ya' had?"

June didn't even look at her. "Enough to catch up with Dad."

She was a failure just like him now. She supposed she only ever really had two options in life—run, or drink herself to death. The first one hadn't worked. Now, she had the latter.

Odie closed the door behind her, crossing her arms slowly. June knew Odie was looking at her, but she couldn't bring herself to meet her gaze. Odie took a deep breath as she moved to sit on the bed next to her, resting a hand on her shoulder.

Tears immediately pricked June's eyes. She brought her knees up to her chest, hiding her face as she fought the sobs. She was too drunk to be able to lie to Mama. "Why wasn't I good enough?" she whispered. She hadn't sounded so Texan since she'd left. "I don't get it, Mama. I did everything. I worked so damn hard I made myself sick. And it wasn't enough."

Odie pulled June into her chest. "It ain't your fault, June. You've always given everything you had." Her hand moved to the back of June's head as her other arm wrapped around her middle, holding her tight against her. "Ya' know, you can always come back to the cafe, baby."

June let out a bitter, broken laugh. "I don't wanna be some waitress, Mama." She'd been so close. Touring the world with her horses, fighting for a place with Midus, and then Hades. And now it was all ruined. She was ruined. Her career was done. And she'd lost the only things that had ever meant shit to her. Her home, her girls, her career, Charlene, and Diego. God, how she missed her Diego.

Odie held her closer. "We gotta get you somethin', Alessia-Bear. I didn't raise ya' to give up." They sat silently for a moment as Odie looked around at the state of June's room. It was a mess, empty beer cans and liquor bottles scattered across the floor.

June grit her teeth and let her head fall against Odie's shoulder, silent tears streaming down her face. "I don't want to do this anymore," she whispered.

Odie's breath caught in her throat slightly at June's words. She took a breath to compose herself, not losing the tight grip she had on her, holding her close to her chest. "What do you mean, baby?" she said softly, though June was certain she knew what she meant.

"All I ever do is fight, Mama," she whispered. Her voice broke, silent tears streaming down her face. "I don't wanna fight anymore."

Odie let out a shuddering breath, resting her chin on the top of June's head. She held her like that, in silence for several moments, unsure of what to say, unsure of how to pull her back from the edge. "My daughter didn't die in a car crash, baby," she finally said, rubbing June's back gently.

June paused, blinking slowly as the shock pulled her from her grief. "I . . . what do you mean?" As long as June had known her, that had been the story. It was how she'd wound up with her first horse. Her owner, Odie's daughter, was killed in a car accident.

Odie nodded in resignation, speaking slowly. "There was no car crash," she said quietly, holding her close, as if she'd flee from her at any second. "That mare killed her. It was a freak accident. A wet arena and a barrel pattern. Mare lost her footing and my baby hit her head on a metal barrel. Killed her 'fore she could blink."

All June could do was stare, swallowing hard. June had grown up on that little paint mare. She'd spent her childhood on her back and at her feet. June called her Lightning. She was the most gentle soul June had ever known. Perhaps that was why. She knew what loss really looked like. "Why . . . Why did you never tell me?"

Odie looked down at the top of her head, continuing to caress her back and head gently. "'Cuz you wouldn'a listened, baby," she said quietly. "You saw that horse and you lit up. Your life was rough enough. Who was I to tell a little girl she couldn't love her horse? I didn't have the words. By the time I did, it was too late. You were in too deep. But look at me, Alessia."

June obliged, turning to face the woman who had done her best to shelter her. To save her. The first kind hand she'd ever known. "My baby died with a smile on her face. She wouldn'a traded a single minute, even knowing how it ended. That's all that matters. It's not about how you die, baby, it's about how you live. So live well."

June's bottom lip quivered, and she bit it to keep herself steady.

"If you don't love being in the saddle anymore, sell it. Get away from it. It's dangerous."

Even the thought of letting go made her sick to her stomach. June couldn't imagine. No more Midus or Hades. No more tack to clean, or stalls to muck, or moments in the saddle to keep her sane. She could sell them. She could let them go. She could be free.

"I can't," she whispered. "I can't let go."

Odie's hands came to rest on either side of June's face as she looked at her. She placed a gentle kiss on her forehead, still holding her face between her hands as if to make sure June didn't run. "Then you get back in the saddle." There was no room for argument in her voice. Just strict orders. She ran her thumbs across her cheeks to wipe away the tears. "I don't care if you never jump again. I don't care if you never enter a damn show for the rest of your life. But you get your ass back on those horses and I promise you—I *promise* you everything is going to turn out just fine."

All June could do was cry and hold her. She had to ride. She had to get back in the saddle. Had to be with her horses again. "Look at me, Alessia." Alessia did as she was told. "I'm here to hold your hand while you get on your feet, but I'm not letting this happen—" she gestured to the mess of cans on the floor. "Love it again, ya' hear?"

She nodded, wiping tears from her cheeks as she sat there in her arms. "I hear ya', Mama." she said quietly. She tried not to let the shame swallow her whole as she glanced at the state of her room. The bottle had sucked her in. Deeper than she'd ever allowed before. But as she sat there, Mama Odie's arms around her, she began to believe again.

Mama Odie gently stroked her head. It was a comforting motion, a soothing one that was full of motherly love. Finally, she pulled her arms away just slightly, keeping her hands on either side of June's face. "I want ya' to take a shower, baby. Wash all this sadness off ya'. We can clean this mess up later."

June chuckled through her tears. "You tryna' tell me I stink?"

Odie laughed too, her laugh warm and bright, as she placed a soft kiss on June's forehead. "You smell like cheap liquor, baby," she said, unable to keep from smiling. "So, yeah, ya' do stink."

June did as she was told.

Chapter Thirty

June went back to waitressing. It came easy, like she had never left. She was much too lonesome without it. If her social life needed to consist of serving the elderly their morning coffee, that she could do.

June went back to Blackjack Stables. An empty paddock waited for Hades and Midus to fill. She had them shipped in from Italy along with all her tack. She didn't ride.

Once, this place with its simple wooden stalls, tack lockers, and a wash bay, had been the grandest thing June could have ever imagined. Now, it was riddled with bitter nostalgia and the dreams of someone June no longer recognized. She didn't work other people's horses. She could barely find it in her to look at her own. But the boys seemed content, free in a paddock with neighbors to pester.

Little ranch-bred quarter horses. They were a far cry from the warmbloods she worked with for Amelia. Not the flashiest. Just good, sturdy, honest horses who could do the job. They were the exact opposite of everything she was trained on in the show circuit. In a barn full of ribbons, points, and awards, she'd let Amelia mold her into something she wasn't.

Maybe she never was meant to be a showjumper. Maybe being a cowgirl was all she really knew.

Hades and Midus jumped out of their paddock more than once, just to find their way back into it. It was as though they were trying to tell her they missed it.

June added a hot-wire border over the top.

She waitressed from five to two, came home to mess with horses, fell asleep early. Stuck to her routine. She didn't touch a drink.

It was a slow day at the cafe when one of the younger waitresses perked up from where she sat on her phone. "Holy shit, June. Your boy won."

June froze where she'd been wiping down the counter, eyes widening. "... What?"

She turned the phone. It was an article. *Diego Cabrera Wins the Singapore Grand Prix.*

Her heart dropped to her stomach, blinking at it. At the image of Diego on a podium. And she wasn't there.

She didn't scold the girl for calling Diego her boy, only nodded sharply and went back to work.

The next time Charlene called, June picked up.

Charlene spoke hesitantly, like she couldn't believe June had actually answered. "... You alive?" Charlene said, that same light snark in her voice she always had.

She smiled sadly. "Barely," she admitted. "I'm sorry I worried ya'."

Charlene's tone immediately softened some, hearing the sadness in June's voice. "Can't say I was surprised when you didn't answer. Thought about coming to Texas to beat your ass."

June couldn't help but chuckle, wandering up and down the aisles of horses in the barn. "I know. I'm sorry."

"That's a start," Charlene said with a sigh. "How are you, June?" she asked, her tone becoming slightly more serious now. It was always like this. She would start easy with sarcasm and snark, but underneath, June knew she was worried about her.

June said nothing for a long moment, half tempted to act like her service was shitty before she finally spoke. "Part of me never thought I'd leave."

"We all thought you'd die here." There was a mix of truth and humor in Charlene's voice. Then, it melded into sorrow. "Never in a million years did I think I'd have to see you go."

June wanted to scream. To slam her fist into the wall. To get on Oviatt just so he could off her like he'd always planned.

There was another long pause, one that felt like ages, though it was likely only be a few moments before Charlene spoke again. "We miss you, June. *I* miss you." Charlene's words came out just above a whisper, devastatingly genuine.

June closed her eyes tightly to ward of the pain. She said nothing. What was there to say? "I, uh— my service isn't good through here, I should probably let ya' go."

Charlene knew it was bullshit and June knew that she knew. But it was also code for *'you're breaking my heart, and I can't take it.'*

"Yeah. Uh . . ." She paused for a second before finally just saying it, "I love you, idiot."

"I love you, more. Hug the girls for me?"

Charlene chuckled at that, but it sounded sad more than humorous. "Yeah. I will. Come home soon, you hear?"

Come home. She hated to remind Charlene that they didn't share a home anymore. Where was home now? "Bye, Char."

"Bye, June." Charlene's voice was melancholic, like she didn't want to hang up the phone. But she had to. There was too much to say.

Mama was headed to Louisiana to visit her son and grandbabies. She'd asked June to go with her, but June reasoned that someone had to watch the cafe. June liked the responsibility. It made sense. She spent her hours in the cafe or lying in the pasture with Midus and Hades. She couldn't bring herself to call the girls. She would. Just not yet.

She didn't even know where she was driving until her car ground to a halt in front of the house, her body instinctively following each intersection and road until it landed here. It always landed here. The single-wide trailer she'd raised herself and her sister in. The house that no longer belonged to a Walker.

She didn't know where her dad was. They hadn't spoke in five years. Odie mentioned at one point he'd put the house up for sale. June couldn't bring herself to check the obituaries.

June watched a pair of sisters sprinting across the lawn, their father chasing after them, catching them both up into his arms with a theatrical yell. She smiled softly, thinking about the painting somewhere in a women's shelter in Valencia. It brought her comfort now. Now, it was real. Not her home, filled with screams and sobs and shattered hearts, but theirs. Filled with laughter, and bedtime stories, and chicken nuggets for lunch.

It comforted her that the walls June had spent so long cursing had gotten a real chance. Had been allowed to rear and raise a real family. The Earth was not forever tainted by the stain of the poor excuse of a family that had been hers, the yard was not so beyond disrepair from years of hard dirt that nothing could grow. The paint was not forever chipped and peeling yellowish white, but a soft, gentle baby blue. The yard was full of lush green grass and flowers. She almost didn't recognize it.

She wondered if it recognized her.

She threw the car in drive, and for the first time in her life, she left that house without running away.

The week passed slowly and in routine. Rise early. Feed horses. Cafe. Waitress. Home. Rinse and repeat.

The knock didn't come until two in the morning. Groggily she got to her feet and made her way to the front door, rubbing the sleep from her eyes. June answered the door with Odie's shotgun tucked under her arm. "This better be g—" She cut herself off, stuck in her tracks, her voice caught in her throat as the breeze caught her hair and left her feeling entirely swept away. "Diego."

Diego stood on the porch, one hand wrapped around the neck of a bottle. He looked just as she remembered him—dark eyes holding worlds of emotion in them, hair messily brushed back from his face. It had been two months since he'd left her standing in that arena.

She said nothing for a long while, their eyes trained on one another, saying the words she couldn't. *I missed you. You're here. You came back. I didn't think you'd ever come back. Will you stay?*

Stay.

Stay.

Please stay.

"I knew we weren't on the best terms, but—" Diego nodded to the gun under her arm.

An attempt at a joke.

June blinked, leaning the shotgun against the interior wall. She was dreaming, surely. She glanced at the whiskey bottle in his hands—hardly a swig gone—then at him. "Since when do you drink whiskey?"

He huffed a laugh, shaking his head. "I don't," he admitted. His gaze remained fixed on her as though he were terrified if he so much as blinked she'd disappear. "Call it a Hail Mary. Thought the taste of you might stop me. Might help."

June's stomach flipped at the implication. That he was here despite himself. That he couldn't stay away. "Did it? Help?"

He huffed an amused breath, but it was drenched in barely contained emotion as he shook his head. "It made everything so much worse."

June swallowed hard, gripping at her bicep with her off-hand. "You shouldn't be here."

Diego's eyes searched hers as she spoke, like he physically needed to hear her say something else. His face remained forcibly neutral, and she hated that she knew him well enough to know that the furrowed lines between his brow meant he was looking for something in her, too.

"I know," he said quietly before he offered a slight smile, "but I am here."

". . . Why?"

For a long moment, Diego said nothing. He looked at her, his dark eyes searching her face, before he spoke. "Because I miss you," he said softly. "Because I haven't been able to stop thinking of you for months."

June had been craving those words since the second he left Amelia's barn. Craving a text. Or a call. And now it was 2 a.m. and here he was.

And June couldn't stand it.

She'd rebuilt her life. She didn't need curveballs. Didn't need Diego in her ear telling her she needed more even though she *knew* she did. When he was gone, she could convince herself she was happy. But Diego saw right through her. She couldn't stand to love him just to watch him leave again. "You should . . . you should go."

Diego sighed, peering into her soul with those ebony eyes the way he always did. "Is that what you want?"

No. The thought came immediately and it terrified her. "Yes."

Diego's head cocked to the side, messy brown curls falling into his face and June had to bite back the urge to smooth them away, a dangerous challenge in his gaze. "You can't even convince yourself. How do you expect to convince me?"

June's lips remained parted in surprise, drawing a painful breath as she blinked back emotion and begged herself not to cry. Not to cave. Not to throw herself into his arms despite how desperately she'd missed him.

He watched her, his dark eyes tracing the way her lips parted. She took in breath after labored breath trying to hold herself together. She hated how easily he affected her. How strong a power he held over her. And yet, she knew she couldn't turn away.

"I won." He said it like he was reporting the weather. It's cloudy. It rained. *I won.*

"I heard," she returned, cow-tongued and wide-eyed. She drew her arms around herself, hugging her own figure as she tried to remain levelheaded.

His voice lowered, as though he had seen her discomfort and he was trying to soothe her. "You said we were square."

June clenched her jaw. "We are—"

"We aren't."

"We *are*."

"No," he spat, his hand flexing at his side as though he was going to wrench her forward to him. "No, you took so much more from me than I ever bargained for."

She shut her mouth at that, biting back the words that were on the tip of her tongue. She knew he was right, damn him. He saw through her once more with frightening precision. This bargain had taken more than its fair share from both of them.

June's hand lingered on the door. She waited for the moment when he would walk away from her away, leaving her as shattered as it the first time. "You should leave, Diego."

He didn't flinch. "No."

She grit her teeth, fingers tightening on the door. "Leave!"

"No!"

She was shouting at him, and he was shouting back—falling back into their old routine as easy as breathing.

She dropped her hold on the door, anger flaring in her chest. Each exchange sent a new pang of desperation through her heart. She couldn't admit to herself how desperately she missed him. She couldn't admit that she had opened his contact again and again and again just to stare at it and cry. She couldn't admit that each breath she took knowing he despised her was one she didn't want to take.

She surged forward, planting her hands on his chest as she pushed him back and away from her. "You aren't listening to me—"

"No, *you* are not listening to *me!* I'm not going anywhere!" Diego pressed forward against her hand, her arm straightening to keep him away. He leaned down, close enough to smell the alcohol on his breath. "I won. And you weren't there. And I would rather die than ever experience that again. I was on the top step of that podium and all I could think about was you."

June blinked, shaking her head as her heart sped in her chest. "What are you—"

"I love you."

Her heart dropped to her stomach, swallowing hard. She blinked, the earth tilting beneath her, her ears tingling from the confession. *I love you.* She stepped back, dropping her hand from his chest as she drew her arms back against herself. "I'll get you a motel—"

His answer was immediate. "No."

June stepped back, swallowing back the emotion bubbling up in her throat. "You're not thinking straight—"

He took a step forward, clutching at his chest like his heart pained him. "I love you."

She shook her head, her breath caught in her throat. "You don't know what you're saying—"

"I love you."

"No!" she cried. "No! I'm not who you have painted in your head, you don't—"

"I love you."

She dropped her head in shame, tears stinging at her eyes. "I wasn't good enough."

"I love you."

She surged forward to shove him again, but he caught her by

the wrists, refusing to let go. "You aren't listening to me! I wasn't enough. They saw something, and it's only a matter of time before you see it too!"

Diego shook his head, the light of a thousand stars in his eyes when he looked at her. "I love you, June."

June choked on a sob. "Stop saying that! Stop!" But he refused. Every time she tried to protest, every way she tried to counter his statement, he cut her off and repeated the same thing: *I love you.*

"I love you. It took me a year to muster up the courage to finally say it, so no I will not stop." He held her wrists tight as he stepped in closer, his face soft with affection. His voice grew quieter, more gentle now. "Even if you hate me—"

"I don't!" June cried, smacking her fists against his chest. "That's the problem! I hate that you left!"

Diego squeezed his eyes shut and drew a sharp breath between his teeth. "I had to—"

"I *know*—" she whimpered, pathetic and desperate and heartbroken, "—but you still left."

He wrapped his hands around her wrists to hold them still. She couldn't push him away. Even if she wanted to, he wouldn't make it easy. This wasn't how it was supposed to be. She was supposed to be able to run away, push him away, keep herself safe from getting her heart shattered.

"I left because I could not stand to watch you get yourself killed. I thought it would work. I thought you loved me more than those horses. More than your love of the sport. I was stupid. And even now, even scorned, even aching, I love you. I love you, *Vaquera*!"

The use of the old nickname hit her like a punch to the gut. The dam that held tears at bay broke. A strangled sound forced it way through her chest as her throat closed. She was falling apart at the seams.

He hadn't gone because he didn't love her. He'd gone because he *did*. Because he couldn't stomach the thought of losing her. She fought against him again, wanting to shove him away, to put up every wall against him. But she couldn't. "You—" She cut herself off, her voice strangled with tears. "You're a fool."

"I know," he laughed through the tears, wiping her own with a swipe of his thumb. "And I love you as you are. Stubborn, and unmoving, and so full of passion. You are everything."

He was tearing down all the defenses she'd built against him. Every shield she'd put herself behind was falling with his words. His declaration. He was killing her, breaking her heart and mending it at once.

She felt the tears falling down her cheeks, her hands trembling in his grasp. This was not a fight she was equipped to win.

"Tell me you don't love me." There was a plea in his voice, a desperation that begged for the truth, no matter the cost.

June choked on a breath, her voice wavering as she looked up at him. Her heart was hammering in her chest so loudly that she was sure he could hear it. The words wouldn't come. They stuck in her throat, refusing to be spoken into existence. She tried again as a tear rolled down her cheek, "Diego—"

"Te amo, mi cielo."

A strangled sound escaped her, followed by an uneven sob as the words finally left her. "Of course, I love you."

She felt weak. All her defenses, all the reasons that she had used to justify pushing him away faded into the background. The only thing she felt was the overwhelming need to be close to him. To let herself feel what she had been trying to suppress for months.

June caught him by the neck, dragging him forward. He met her halfway, dropping his bottle without hesitation. It shattered on the porch as he buried his hands in her hair and closed distance between them, slamming her lips to his.

The kiss was fire, months of heartache melting away into the background as her senses were flooded with Diego. She felt the breath leave her, replaced by the taste of dark whiskey and Diego's lips on her own. His body covered her, pressing her into the siding of the house. Her mind went fuzzy, all coherent thoughts fading to instinct as she fisted her hands in his shirt, gripping it like a lifeline. Diego took control of the kiss, claiming her against the porch.

"Diego," she whined, pulling him closer.

The sound of his name on her lips fueled him, his tongue pressing to her lips, begging for access and she granted it easily. His hands found the divot of her back, pressing her into him like she would suddenly disappear if his grip went lax, her hands clawing at his hair for purchase.

"Inside," June gasped out between kisses.

He hooked his hands under her thighs without a second thought, hoisting her up onto his hips and her legs locked around him automatically. He didn't break the kiss as he moved inside, kicking the door closed behind them.

"Up the stairs," she demanded against his lips.

He grinned as he moved down the hall with her perched on his hips. "Bossy," he mumbled, nipping at her lips.

He managed to navigate them toward her bedroom door, his eyes fluttering closed as they reached the top of the stairs and she tugged at his hair, smothering his neck in kisses. He shoved the door open and they stumbled inside together, still tangled in each other's arms. He didn't bother flicking on the light, instead crossing the room and setting her down against the bed. Her fingers fisted in his shirt before he could get too far, pulling him back on top of her. He went willingly, his hands coming to rest on either side of her. He took a moment to just look at her, the dark eyes she'd been craving for months taking in the sight of her spread out on the bed before her with a greedy reverence. His thumb carted across her bottom lip. "God. You're stunning."

She felt his breath against her face, his eyes tracing her body as he hovered over her, taking in her every detail. Her breath caught at his words, her heart beating hard in her chest. He looked at her like she was his muse. Like he wanted to make art out of her. Her hands came to rest on his chest, the thin material of his shirt the only barrier between them. "Kiss me, Diego."

His reaction was immediate and overwhelming. One of his hands caught her hip, pressing her down against the bed while the other found the bottom of her jaw, holding her firmly in place as his tongue pressed into her mouth, stealing her breath with a desperate hum. She whined again, her fingers finding their way into his hair and pulling, the way she had so many months ago on a dance floor in Valkenswaard.

It seemed to drive him as wild as it had the first time. He groaned against her, nipping at her bottom lip before kissing her jaw, then down her neck, as though he had to have all of her all at once. He drew back sharply, breathing heavily. His hand trailed from her jaw, down her neck, over her shoulder and down to her hip where his fingers knotted in the hem of her shirt. He met her eyes. "May I?"

She shuddered in anticipation, nodding softly.

His eyes roamed over her form as he tsked. "Use your words, *Querida*."

She bit back a whine at his command, desperate for his touch. It was downright unfair for him to be so infuriating and so attractive at the same time. He knew exactly the kind of influence he had on her. She took a shaky breath, looking at the way his hand was grasping the hem of her shirt. "Yes. Yes, please."

Every drop of her headstrong stubbornness melted away when it came to him—when it came to something she'd been desperate for since the moment she first saw him in that bar, an Armani suit drenched in liquor.

His hands caught the hem of her shirt, peeling it up inch by tantalizing inch, like he wished to savor each piece of her as it was revealed to him.

Her face was burning, her heart hammering in her chest. His eyes were drinking her in like he was dying of thirst, and yet he was so patient. He let his fingers trail over her stomach, his gaze flickering up to hers to watch her reaction. She shivered at the feeling of his calloused fingers gently grazing the soft skin of her torso— across her neck and collarbone, back up to her jaw, down the center of her neck clear down to her naval before he traced a path up the side of her ribs and across both breasts and then down her other side.

Every part of her that he touched left a trail of fire. Every caress had her shivering, her mind racing. She was used to passion and heat, not this adoration that he displayed, taking his time to memorize each dip and curve of her body.

His hand cupped and massaged one of her breasts as his lips found hers again. She melted against him, the combination of his touch and his kiss driving her crazy. Her hands came up to his chest again, desperately wanting to get him out of his shirt. Wanting to give him the same treatment. "Diego," she gasped between kisses, clawing at the bottom of his shirt and lifting up, Diego pulled back just fast enough to rip the clothing up over his head before his lips were back against hers.

As soon as it was off, her hands were on him. Pressing against his chest, his shoulders, anywhere she could reach. Her nails scraped down his abs and he let out a low groan. June's hands fell to his jeans, undoing them in record speed and he grinned down at her, clearly pleased with her own rush to have him.

The moment his jeans were over his hips, Diego's hands closed around her ankles, dragging her to the end of the bed, and then out of her pajamas.

June had known lovers before, but none so perfectly made for her. None whose touch set her aflame quite the same as Diego's.

He could never confine himself to just one movement—it was his hips, and his lips against hers, and his hands tangled in her hair and exploring each dip and swell of her body all at once. A mix of pleasure and desire and affection and love. Gentle and rough. Sweet and demanding, all in the same moment.

Diego was as kind a lover as he was intense.

He was perfect. All-consuming. The noises he pulled from her were downright animalistic as he pressed his hips into her, dragging her leg up over his shoulder to change the angle. The pleasure was overwhelming and she knew Diego could feel it, meeting her eyes. "So close already, hm?"

A strange mix of irritation and lust filled her. God, his cockiness was such a turn-on.

Time dissolved until June was entirely lost. Diego's arms around her was all that remained.

Chapter Thirty-One

When June woke, Diego was gone. A wave of panic fled through her, and she sat up sharply. "Diego?" She called. No answer. She tossed her covers to the side, throwing the door open as she exited the room. "Diego?" A little louder this time, staving off the growing panic.

"In here!" The sound of his voice mixed with the sound of clanking dishes reached her ears. "You're awake, q*uerida*?"

June nearly cried out in relief as she moved down the stairs. He was here. Of course he was. Why wouldn't he be? He was in the middle of whipping eggs when June made her way downstairs, the smile he flashed her bright enough to make her heart stutter. "Whatcha' makin', baby?"

"Omelets," he said, frowning at the pan. "I'm afraid they're not very pretty."

She forced out a chuckle over her uneasiness as she made her way to the stovetop, reaching forward to wrap her arms around him and bury her face in his back.

He hummed, as though he could feel the anxiety rolling off of her in waves. His hand covered hers where it rested on his stomach, squeezing it tightly. "I'm not going anywhere."

She let out a shaky breath, her body pressed against his back. "I know," she said, her voice a whisper. She shook it off, refusing to let her own anxieties ruin such a perfect morning. Diego was here. Diego loved her. Diego was making her breakfast.

Diego abandoned his spatula on the counter, turning around to draw her face into his hands. "I'm not going anywhere."

She nodded firmly, but the doubt was still imbedded deep into her soul.

Diego studied her expression and seemed to find it lacking. He held her face in his hands as he leaned down and kissed her. June met him halfway, clutching him at the wrist as she melted into his kiss. It was a though if she couldn't believe his words, he was determined to make her believe his actions. His fingers sunk into her hair, drawing her head back to deepen the kiss. He pulled back, just enough to whisper against her lips. "There's no one else in this world for me. No one so perfect as you."

Her stomach flipped with desire at his words, and she melted into his embrace, fisting her hands into his shirt. He backed her up until she bumped into the counter, his intention to have her perched on the edge completely clear.

"Naughty," she whispered, but she didn't stop kissing him, didn't take her hands off of him. "It's too early."

"It's never too early," he growled softly, a sly grin on his face. "Especially for you, *querida*." He pressed himself against her, trapping her between his body and the counter. "You don't know how hungry you make me." Her breath caught in her throat and he hummed in approval.

"You're going to burn your omelets."

In a single motion, he reached over and flicked the burner off, moving the pan to a cool spot on the stovetop. "I changed my mind," he mumbled, his lips moving down to her neck. "I'd rather have you for breakfast."

June's breath hitched in her throat as his lips claimed hers again. His tongue flicked against her lower lip as he sought entrance into her mouth, and she granted him immediate access. A whine escaped her throat, spurring him on. It was as though now he'd had her, he never wanted anything else ever again.

His lips trailed from hers to her jaw, down her throat, whispering praises as he went. He caught the bottom of her shirt and tugged it off in one quick movement. June gasped, and immediately, his eyes flicked to hers, seeking permission. She nodded hurriedly, and he didn't slow down. His hands kneaded her thighs, gripping tight enough to bruise as his mouth trailed down her torso. June's head fell back, fingers burying in his hair as he worked lower.

His fingers caught in the waistband of her shorts, meeting her gaze as he tugged them down over her hips, leaving her completely bare to him. Her breath caught, eyes locked with him as he lifted her up and onto the counter. He didn't look away from her as he sunk to his knees, pressing open-mouthed kisses to the inside of her thighs as he drew her legs over his shoulders.

June shook in anticipation, unable to look away as he buried his head between her thighs. Her fingers closed around the edge of the counter, her knuckles turning white with the effort to keep from falling apart. She inhaled sharply, a low moan escaping her.

He smirked against her skin, unrelenting in his pursuit. June wasn't sure which way was up or down—all she knew was Diego.

He held her in place as he brought her spiraling out of control, both anchoring and teasing her with his tongue. He didn't pull back, doubling his efforts.

"Diego," she cried. "I—I can't."

He chuckled against her sensitive skin, the vibrations making her cry out. "You can," he murmured. "I know you can, *Vaquera*. Just one more for me."

She whined at his words, her body shaking with the effort to stay upright. "Please," she begged, her voice broken and desperate. "Please, I can't—"

He ignored her pleas, his tongue dancing over her sensitive flesh once more. "Take it," he ordered, his grip on her hips firm. "You can take one more. Let go for me, *querida*. Let me hear those pretty sounds you make."

She couldn't help but obey him, her body arching off the counter as her climax crashed over her like a tidal wave. She cried out his name, her hands grasping at his hair as he held her through it. When she came back to earth, she was slumped against the counter, utterly boneless.

He kissed his way up her body to her lips, clearly pleased with himself and the job he'd done at wrecking her to pieces. He pressed kiss after kiss to her lips, letting her taste herself. "Mm," he hummed, keeping eye contact as he pulled back to lick his fingers clean. "Breakfast then?"

She panted, her chest heaving with every breath. She could only muster a nod. She was so utterly wrecked, and they hadn't even made it out of the kitchen. "Breakfast."

With Mama gone and Diego in the middle of autumn break, they spent two full weeks playing house. She went early to work at the restaurant, Diego coming to visit during her breaks and to kiss her senseless in the beer closet and tip the girls outrageous amounts for the food June refused to charge him for. They slept in her bed—*their* bed, Diego insisted, and she obliged, even if it would always be her bed to her. She didn't lament having him in it.

So many months of yearning gave way to the best sex June had ever had in her life. June was torn between being nauseous at the thought of Diego ever having been with another girl, and appreciation at the fact that he could make her finish four times in twenty minutes. And yes, four. He set a timer and made her count. Their past sex lives were very different and they both knew it. June had a handful of hookups to her name—Diego had a reputation. She didn't like being a jealous girl, but she couldn't help it sometimes.

Finally, she asked. "When was the last time you were with someone else?"

Diego lay next to her in bed, his fingertips tracing soft circles against the skin of her shoulder. He paused his movement and drew a short breath. "Honest answer?"

June grimaced. "Never mind, I'm good—"

"Ten months ago."

"What?" June sat up, propping her head on her arm. He had to have been sparing her feelings. She'd assumed he'd been with someone, or *many* someones the entire time. "You have a very different reputation."

"A true one," he admitted. He never tried to hide it from her. Diego had been a part of his fair share of escapades. "... Until I took someone home and said your name. I sort of ... drew back after that one."

June's jaw dropped, a sharp possessiveness flaring in her gut. "You're kidding. Ten months ago?"

Diego let out a short laugh, his fingers trailing down her neck and over her shoulder. "Oh, June. You've owned me from the second you punched me in that bar. I thought if I took home enough redheads it would dull the ache. It just made it worse. I needed *you*."

She bit her lip, listening intently, her grin growing. Good. She'd driven him crazy, just as she'd wanted. June caught him by the neck and dragged him into a bruising kiss.

Their clothes found their way into the same hamper. Diego cooked them dinner nightly, the way he had nearly every time they'd been together. June was immensely grateful for it, and to her delight, he only got better and better. He woke with her alarm, insisting on having the same schedule as her. They fell asleep together every night, talking and laughing to the point of exhaustion.

June told him everything. She'd never done that before. Any questions he asked, she gave an honest answer to. Her family. Texas. Her life before. "I don't really blame my mom for leaving," June said. "My father was awful. A drunk and a wife beater. But I do blame her for leaving us with him."

Diego lay on his side, propped up on one elbow and listening intently. He was shirtless, hair mussed with disheveled sheets draped over the rest of his body. "You *should* blame her," he said, brows furrowed in annoyance on her behalf.

"Don't look so offended for me," she replied in a soft tone, one hand coming up to brush his cheek. She was laying on her back, head propped up by the pillow under her. "I guess . . . she really relied on Ava and I looking out for each other."

"She relied on you looking out for Ava. If you were six, she was . . . three? She relied on *you*."

She went quiet for several beats, nodding weakly. She'd come to terms with a lot of things that she knew to be true. And many polar opposite things could be true at once. Her mom was right to leave their father; to leave June and Ava was nothing short of evil. Her dad tried to love them; he was always going to love the bottle more. He was always going to resort to his anger. June did her best; June came up short time and time again in raising Ava. June loved Ava more than anything in her life; June never should have been expected to raise a child.

She'd come to terms with some things. But to say it out loud? To say it to Diego? It terrified her. But it was him, and it was dark, in comfortable privacy. "Yeah," she said, voice hushed and quiet. "I was six, and she was three."

Diego's reaction was swift. He scooted closer to her on the bed, slinging an arm around her and using it to pull her into him, flush against his chest. He buried his face into the crook of her neck, pressing a kiss to her throat as though to ease the hurt that came with saying it out loud. "That's too much for a child," he murmured, against her pulse point. "Too much for anyone."

June swallowed over the growing lump in her throat, nodding slowly in resignation as the tears welled.

"Oh, *mi vida*," he said finally, running his fingers through her hair. He looked like he wanted to turn the time back. To find her sooner. To ice the bruises of her past. Like he would have protected her from the very worst life had thrown at her. Like he would for the rest of their lives. All he said was, "Your heart is so big it is a wonder you can carry it all on your own."

"I don't," she admitted softly, smiling as she leaned into his touch. "You've been lugging around the dumb thing since I punched you in that bar."

Diego smiled softly, his eyes roaming her face before he kissed her gently, resting his forehead against hers.

The way he touched her was different every time, like he'd wanted her in so many ways, he could never have her in just one. His hands were light and soft, taking their time memorizing the map of her body as though it were the only place he ever wanted to be again.

When she whimpered, he shushed her softly, pressing gentle kisses across her skin. "Beautiful, beautiful girl."

It was utter bliss having him the way she'd wanted him so desperately for so long. Late that night, they lay in bed facing one another, June's hands tracing the curve of his neck and shoulders, up into his hair. He hummed appreciatively whenever she played with his hair, and she had no problem with it, twisting his perfect curls between her fingers and pressing kisses across his face. But tonight, he wasn't relaxing. He tapped his foot, bouncing his leg the way he always did when his mind wouldn't quiet. Restless and agitated despite his closed eyes and head pressed into June's hands. "You think so loudly," she teased.

Diego's eyes sprang open, a light blush covering his cheeks at having been caught red-handed. "Shut up."

She laughed, drawing his head forward to press kisses across his hairline. "What is it?"

He shook his head, burying his face into June's chest, letting her wrap her arms around him and hold him tight.

"Tell me or I'm going to let go," she threatened playfully.

He huffed his disapproval. "You're no fair."

"Never claimed to be."

Diego sighed, sliding back just enough to look up to her. "You don't jump anymore."

June froze, her lips parting in surprise. Of all the things that could have been bothering him, that wasn't what she'd been expecting. She'd practiced the excuses a million times in her head, but they got caught in her throat. "Diego . . . I'm done jumping."

In the darkness, his confusion and disappointment looked like devastation. ". . . Done?" he repeated softly. The word felt poisonous on his tongue. Dangerous. Final. Real.

June didn't trust herself to speak, so she simply nodded. Diego just shook his head. "No, you're not."

She opened her mouth to protest, but Diego beat her to it. "You're not finished jumping. You're not." He sounded so sure. So genuine. She wished she could tell him otherwise.

"There's no point in jumping lower divisions—"

"You don't need the lower divisions. You've jumped at the highest level—"

June huffed in frustration. "Diego, I bombed it. I ate shit. Amelia ruined my life. She framed me for drugging a horse. The odds I'll ever get jump in the Tour again are nonexistent—"

"Because Amelia told you so?"

June's fight died on her tongue. Everything she knew—about showjumping, about this world, about herself—it was all secondhand, poison fed down from Amelia.

"You're not done, June."

All she could do was sigh. "We'll see."

"You aren't finished. You still have at least three titles to win. Then you can quit."

Quit.

Oh, how June hated that word.

Chapter Thirty-Two

It was odd not to be constantly pushing herself to the limit. Between waitressing and coming home to Diego, she got more than her fair share of cardio in. But all the physical exhaustion in the world couldn't make her sleep well at night. She still brimmed with energy. The moment her head hit the pillows it was bombarded by thoughts. She tossed and turned until she finally drove herself mad enough to climb out of bed and out to busy herself. Cleaning the house, prepping food, watching TV. At least, until Diego woke up and found her gone. He'd stumble downstairs, smother her in kisses, and drag her back to bed.

His arms around her helped to soothe her, but even his steady presence couldn't persuade her to sleep.

So, she resorted to studying jump courses. She made them up, memorized them, jumped them again and again until she simply couldn't get it wrong. At least, so long as the course stayed in her mind.

June took fewer shifts at the cafe, determined to soak up every minute of Diego's attention while it was devoted only to her rather than to his races. Part of her was convinced she could stay like this forever, playing house, enjoying domestic bliss with her boyfriend as though this had been their life for years. But things couldn't stay the same forever. The end of autumn break was fast approaching, and Odie was due home at the end of the week.

Lotus expected Diego back in their garages soon, and June was once again met with her cruel reality.

"You should come," Diego insisted, lounging against the table as June cleaned up their dinner mess. It was their ritual; he cooked, she cleaned. The next Grand Prix was in Austin. She *should* go. She had no real excuse not to. Austin wasn't far. Diego wanted her there.

She had nearly watched him die last time. She never wanted to be in the public eye ever again.

June didn't look up from where she scrubbed their dishes. "And be bombarded by the other WAGs just for them to say *'Oh my gosh! I'm so glad you finally quit that silly horse game!'*" There was a bitter edge to her voice, scrubbing the dishes more aggressively than necessary.

Diego narrowed his eyes at her. "The girls are nice. You'd like them if you got to know them."

She shot a look of betrayal at him over her shoulder before she returned to scrubbing her already clean dishes. "Or, no, how about the journalists who will eat me alive the second I step into the paddock? *'Failed Showjumper Turned Mediocre Girlfriend'*."

His head cocked to the side, gaze filled with a suffocating sympathy. "You're a great girlfriend. And you didn't fail." He stood, making his way over to lean against the counter beside her. "If you aren't ready to go public with us, I understand, June."

June paused, bracing on the countertop as she stared down into the sink. They'd been public for a year and a half. What difference did it make now that it was real? Even if a part of her still begged to keep him for herself. "It's not—it's not that, D. I . . ." she sighed heavily, unable to look at him as she spoke. "I want to be worthy of you," she whispered. "I don't just want to be your failure."

Diego stepped forward, wrapping his arms around her from behind. He kissed her shoulder, burying his head in the crook of her neck. "You are everything, *Vaquera*."

June drew a sharp breath, letting her head fall back against him. It ached. God, why did it still ache?

"June?" He picked his head up.

"Hm."

"You wouldn't feel this way if you were done jumping."

June didn't answer him.

"Your horses here, managing a cafe, surrounded by friends and neighbors, and it isn't enough."

June huffed, turning around in his arms to face him. "It *is* enough."

He raised a disbelieving brow at her. "No, it isn't. You think I don't know that? Think I don't know you? You've settled June, but your heart won't." He drew a deep breath, as though he were steeling his nerves as he met her gaze again. "I'm going to propose an idea, and you're not going to say no until you've thought of it, deal?"

"We aren't getting married, yet," June said automatically, though she wasn't honestly sure she could tell him no if he were to get down on one knee.

His eyes opened, raising a challenging brow at her and June tried not to cave and tell him the truth. "We'll circle back to that," he said and she laughed. "Your mom will be home next week?"

June's heart swelled at the casual mention of Mama Odie. Of her being June's mother. She nodded.

Diego opened his eyes fully then, settling back. ". . . So?"

"So?" June returned.

He nodded softly, a moment passing as though he were attempting to gather courage. "You are going to stay with her?"

June blinked. She mulled over his question, turning it over and over in her mind as though it was a clue, a piece of paper detailing an answer if she could just hold it in the right way. "I guess . . . I guess,

I don't know."

Diego nodded. And then nodded again and again, not looking at her as he took her hands into his, rubbing them soothingly. ". . . Come with me."

". . . Diego—"

Brown eyes shot to hers automatically, interrupting her before she could finish. "I know. I know it is not what you want, but it will only be for a bit. Finish this season out with me, *mi amor*. Then we get you set up with me in Monaco, or here, even! Just . . . come with me. Please."

June had heard Diego desperate before—begging her to stay away from Oviatt, or to let him in—but this begging was different. It was clouded with affection rather than fear, and June didn't know what to do with it.

"Junebug, you have no idea how long I've only dared to dream of this." He rubbed his thumb across her hand, his sights carefully trained on it as he refused to look at her. She could almost see the glint of glassy emotion behind his eyes. "Of you in my arms, feeling even a fraction of the way I do for you. Forgive me, but I am not man enough to say goodbye again quite yet. Not while I know you are unhappy."

June swallowed back her emotion. "I am happy."

"You are not." He lifted her hand in his and pressed a kiss to the knuckle of her thumb, squeezing his eyes tightly shut like it pained him to say it. To burst her bubble. To remind her that he was right. She wasn't happy. She could busy her day, complete her tasks and find some minuscule joy in her productivity, but it wasn't the same as what she'd known.

It wasn't what she wanted to chase. June wasn't all that sure she even cared about being title winner. But she wanted to fight for it again.

June drew a shaky breath, gritting her teeth and closing her eyes. ". .

. I know."

Diego nodded softly, almost in relief that she'd finally admitted it. "So, what are you going to do about it?"

She squeezed her eyes closed to ward off the tears. "I don't know."

He sat up, pushing a lock of her hair behind her ear. "Come with me, *mi vida*."

June choked out a noise of frustration, turning away from him as she busied herself with the dishes once again. "I won't be any happier as some groupie—"

"I was." His answer was quick. Concise. Honest. Genuine enough that June paused, sparing a glance in his direction. He took that as an invitation, continuing. "Watching you when I couldn't race. Seeing you in your element with your team. It set me on fire again, Junebug. Your passion. Sharing your passion with me." He leaned forward, pressing his forehead to hers softly. "Let me share mine with you, *mi vida*. We see where it goes. But I don't want you wallowing anymore."

Maybe that was what finally got her to say her tearful goodbyes to Odie and let Diego close the door to the rental behind her.

June hated pity. She didn't need it from anyone. Not him, and especially not herself. So, to Austin they went.

June showed up in the paddock, dressed to the Texas nines. She stuck out like a sore thumb in the paddock in fringe dress and boots, but Diego loved it, so she didn't really care.

She watched him take to the track with minimal anxiety and a blazing love in her heart for the man determined to get her on her feet. He took third.

June watched from the garage as he was covered in champagne before he went tearing to his team—to her. He tackled her in a sticky champagne-soaked hug and June screamed her laughter as he pressed a million kisses to her face before the Lotus team swarmed him. He forgot his trophy on the podium. A steward had to bring it to him.

They went to a country bar to celebrate, Diego dragging half of the F1 grid with him. June thought the sight of Diego in Wranglers, a black pearl snap, and a set of square-toed boots might kill her. He was always handsome, but dressed like a cowboy was enough to do her in. She taught his crew the line dance to *Boot Scootin' Boogie*, showed them the basics of swing dancing. She'd never felt so much like herself in her entire life as she did at the intersection of her past and future. Diego caught on to the Footloose dance in record time and she wanted to punch him. She'd spent hours in her room trying to figure that one out.

She put on a show raunchy enough to make Diego blush at *Save a Horse, Ride a Cowboy*.

She taught him to swing dance, and in all of three passes he was a pro, slinging her across the dance floor in her fringe dress.

Diego sang along to a surprising amount, familiar with song after song as they came on. He was in the middle of belting out *Callin' Baton Rouge* when June whirled on him. "Why do you know these?"

Diego laughed, slinging her around him. "I missed my cowgirl!"

She blinked at him in amazement as they were brought back together to two-step. "You listened to country because you missed me?"

If she didn't know any better, she'd think Diego was blushing at the confession. "So what if I did?"

Of all the parties June had been to, this was her favorite by a mile.

June had never woken up hungover and happy at the same time, but she reached across the hotel bed to find Diego, she realized anything was possible.

The next three weeks brought a triple-header as they sped into the end of the season. They traveled to the Netherlands the next day in anticipation for the Zandvoort GP. Diego insisted on going earlier than the other drivers. Travel was good for the soul after all, or so he insisted. Dinner the following evening was a grand ordeal, a rooftop terrace at some Michelin-starred restaurant Diego was fond of. He ordered a bottle of top-shelf wine and a spread of traditional Dutch food for her to try. June nursed a glass of wine. She only drank when Diego did. It was her new set of rules. He didn't struggle with it the way she did, so she adopted his routine.

They enjoyed dinner and talked about all of the places he couldn't wait to show her. He was more talkative than usual, suspiciously so. He rambled about the dinner rolls, the menu, and the weather. June narrowed her eyes at him. She was just about to say something when a hand landed on her shoulder.

June whirled, irritation plain on her face until she saw him. A face she'd grown mighty familiar with, though typically with a helmet on rather than with gray hair gelled to the side. June's jaw dropped in surprise, blinking through her shock, her thoughts of the race and Diego completely discarded. ". . . Siegfried?" She stood unceremoniously, fumbling to pull him into a hug.

"June." Siegfried says, returning her embrace. "You look well."

"So do you." June pulled back, looking him up and down as though to cement the fact that he was truly there. "What are you doing here?"

Siegfried merely shrugged. "I was in the neighborhood. Thought I would just pop by and say hello."

June couldn't stop the sting of disappointment in her chest. "Really?"

"No, for fuck's sake!" He unbuttoned his suit coat, grabbing a chair from a nearby table and pulling it up to theirs. A few of the other patrons turned to shoot sidelong looks at them, but they made no move to stop him. June turned to shoot an apologetic glance at Diego for their date-crasher, but Diego merely sat back and crossed his arms, looking mighty pleased with himself. June understood all at once.

He'd been unsuccessful in convincing her to jump again. He'd called in the reinforcements. He smirked, raising a hand to call for an extra glass as Siegfried joined their table.

"I can see your wheels turning," Siegfried said, folding his hands and resting his chin on them as Diego poured him a glass of wine. He took a small sip, raising an eyebrow in appreciation, looking at June with a smile. "Let me save you the trouble. I retired."

June's jaw dropped, staring at him in utter horror. Siegfried had been her only hope that Amelia wouldn't take the title again this year. "Retired?" Siegfried was always threatening to retire when he didn't like something. To actually step down . . . ? "But . . . why?"

He held up three fingers. "Three titles wins. Three. I'm done, June. I have done all I wanted to in the show ring. I don't care about winning anymore. I care about beating that heinous bitch Amelia into the dirt."

June's stomach turned sour at the sound of Amelia's name. She downed the rest of her wine glass. Diego shot her a warning look, but he said nothing. "How are you going to beat her if you aren't competing anymore? You just lost the one thing to stop her."

"You are so stupid," he said simply—a joke. At least, June hoped. He laced his hands together, leaning forward on them. "You."

June blinked, staring at him wide-eyed. She shot a glare at Diego. He raised his hands innocently, smiling with amusement and taking a drink from his own wine glass.

Siegfried took a measured sip of wine, smacking his lips together in approval at the taste before holding it up to the light. "You and I are going to beat Amelia. She's done."

"I don't see why you need me for that."

He set his glass down on the table. "Stupid, stupid girl. They are terrified of you. Amelia is terrified of you."

June blinked. She hated how familiar his light insults were, something she missed deeply. She tried to deny to herself the relief that came at his words—he never stopped being who he always was. "Yeah, right." She reached for the bottle of wine, refilling her own glass.

"I'm serious." And he was. Dead serious. Not even the faintest hint of a smile. "June, Amelia only gave you a chance in the show ring because she expected you'd bomb and stop asking. We all did. When you were decent in the lower divisions, she thought she could turn you into some little prodigy. And then you almost took a championship on a horse that was her leftovers in your rookie year? When Midus came up lame, it was like her prayers had been answered."

June grit her teeth and watched as Siegfried raved on, her stomach tightening with dread and disbelief.

"Her stallion is mad. He's tried to kill every person who's ever ridden him. She stuck you on him to fuck you over. And then you start winning on him? Fuck's sake, June. You're like a living legend in the Tour."

June sat there for a moment, absorbing his words quietly. It made her stomach turn—the things Amelia had done for her own gain. She wanted to deny them, to try and make excuses for her the way she had for the last five years, but she couldn't. She wanted to believe Amelia had only wanted the best for her, but as she looked at Siegfried's face, she knew that was foolish. She clenched her jaw. "She made it very clear exactly where I stand in her world. She'll make damn well sure I'm never invited to another competition again. She destroyed my career. There's nothing I can do about it now."

Siegfried unbuttoned the jacket of his suit coat, reaching inside to procure an envelope before he slid it across the table to her. June's brow furrowed, staring at the white paper with distrust. "Open it."

June's eyes flicked up to his, reaching out tentatively before she retrieved it and opened the envelope. Inside were several papers, stapled together, a full vet report. June recognized it well enough. The same one Amelia had used to destroy her. But this one was slightly different. Different numbers. Different findings. *Different.*

"A copy of Oviatt's lab reports. The real ones."

She swallowed back the bile threatening to rise in her throat. It couldn't be that simple. It couldn't. "No, she drugged him—"

"Did she." There was no question in his voice, only challenge. "Amelia only does what she has to. You think she'd go to the trouble when she's got a vet to type up a fake report?"

June blinked. Looked at him. Looked at it. "And this is the real report?"

"I have a vet tech willing to vouch for it."

June eyed it, trying to wrap her head around the truth. She'd thrown away her career for this. She'd been framed, and she ran. She hadn't even entertained the idea of fighting back. She met Diego's gaze. "How did you know about this?"

Diego shrugged sheepishly. "I didn't. But I knew there had to be a way. I asked Charlene how to fix this and she pointed me to your friend."

"Not friend," Siegfried corrected, holding a finger in the air. "Her coach."

June shot Siegfried a look, desperately trying to understand what she was hearing. ". . . Are you serious?"

"Dead. You will come to my barn in Riesenbeck. I will coach you. You won't be training any horses but your own. It will be your career, no one else's."

She thought of the arena. The spotlight. The victory laps. Of what it was like soaring through the ring with Midus. With Hades. A chance to return to the top. Could she really refuse?

A dangerous hum of anticipation was growing in June's chest. The idea that this was real. That this could happen. They could beat Amelia at her own game.

"So what do I do?" June asked. "Turn her in to the FEI?"

Siegfried snorted, leaning back in his chair. He picked up the paper, waving it in hand. "This isn't the answer, June. It's insurance. Amelia never submitted anything, and you won a Grand Prix," he reminded her, and June's heart dropped to her stomach.

Any athlete who won a Grand Prix during the season was automatically invited to the Super Grand Prix.

"I don't have my horses."

Siegfried's eyes turned to Diego at the other end of the table, and Diego's gaze shot to the table, brows raising as he pursed his lips together. June narrowed in on him instantly. "What did you do?"

Diego picked up his wine glass with a shrug, speaking into it hurriedly, the words running into each other in his rush to get the confession out. "Just... arranged transportation for them behind your back. They'll be in Riesenbeck in two days."

Her jaw dropped, anger swarming through her. "You did *what?*—"

"You see!" Siegfried gestured his hands toward Diego. "It is already taken care of. We will meet them there. That woman's reign is over."

June glared daggers at Diego sharp enough to make sure he knew they were definitely fighting about this later. But a part of her knew Diego was right. June wasn't finished. She hadn't given it her all. She hadn't won yet. She'd never be done until she had a championship in her hands. Just when she thought she'd slipped away, here was the one person who could drag her back, sinking his claws in.

"You don't need them for the Super Grand Prix, anyway." Siegfried smirked. "You will ride Frieda."

June's jaw dropped. Frieda. Siegfried's gray mare. She couldn't have imagined a more perfect horse. He never let *anyone* ride her. "Are you—"

"Serious? Yes. You will ride her until Hades is ready. Amelia may have been a shit trainer, but I am not."

June's heart clenched, staring at the man. He had been the one championing her career from the very beginning—she'd just been blind. From the Lotus contract, to Charlene's card in her hand, and now this. Bringing her back to the Tour. It was all him.

Never again would Amelia own her. Never again would June have to be afraid.

Siegfried met her gaze with steady eyes, as if reading her mind, he nodded. They were a team now. With Siegfried in her corner, they were unstoppable.

The moment they were out of the restaurant and had parted ways with Siegfried, Diego went rushing for the car like his life depended on it. Probably because it did. He caught the driver's side door handle, pulled it open an inch before June got to it and slammed the door promptly shut, leaning back on the car with arms crossed over her chest. "'*Let me share my passion with you*,'" June mocked, throwing his earlier words at him as she cocked her head to the side. "Why didn't you tell me?"

Diego huffed in surrender, clearly understanding he had pulled one over on her, and he wasn't getting out of it unscathed. "Because it would have been a fight."

She righted herself, standing to her full height. "As opposed to this fight?" she challenged, gesturing between them. "What if I would've said no?"

"Did you?"

"That's not the point—"

Diego stepped forward, pinning her in place with his eyes as he leaned down over her. "Sooner or later, you're going to have to accept the fact that I know you." A strange feeling settled in her chest at his words, blinking up at him. Diego frowned, shrugging as he moved to turn away from her. "You weren't happy in Texas."

"I was perfectly content—"

"And that's how you want to live your life?" He whirled back on her, eyes ablaze with a fierce passion. "*'Content'*, until said *'contentment'* turns out to actually be squashed resentment and regret. I know you, June. All it took was a genuine chance, and you're back in the fight. I'm sorry I went behind your back, but I won't apologize for this."

June huffed out a breath, staring at him for a long while. She reached forward and Diego tensed automatically, like he wasn't quite sure if she was still keen on knifing him, but the moment her arms closed around him, he enveloped her in a hug, pulling her tight against him. He murmured into her hair. "She cheated you, and we all know it. You are terrifying, *mi amor*. So terrify her."

A familiar anxiety settled in her gut. The fear of not being enough. Not being capable. Not being able to in the way he was so certain. "I wish I had half the faith you do in me."

Diego chuckled, pulling back just enough to be able to look at her, tucking a stray hair behind her ear. "Well, I'm your WAG. It's my job."

June laughed out loud, burying her face into his shoulder and he wrapped her up in his arms like he could protect her from the world if he could only hold her close enough. "You are the world, *Cariño*. So, give that bitch a run for her money."

She nodded firmly, a stubborn smile on her lips. In that moment, she made a silent vow. Diego could not have this much faith in her for her to merely give up. He had fought for this on her behalf. Had gotten her back in the game. Would continue to fight for her in a way no one ever had. June had a job to do, and it would take Heaven and Earth to stop her.

Chapter Thirty-Three

June stared down at Charlene's contact on her phone. She'd called her hundreds of thousands of times, but this time was different, and it terrified her. June needed her team. She needed them beside her again. She needed Charlene. She pressed call. It rang twice before Charlene picked up.

"What's wrong?" Habit from so many incoming calls with June in trouble one way or another.

June laughed. "Nothing's wrong, Char."

"Oh." Silence. Excitement crept into Charlene's voice. " Did you . . . did he—"

"Yes," June chuckled. "I talked to Siegfried."

"And? You're coming back?" Shock. Shock and joy and a thousand questions all trying to fight their way past Charlene's mouth.

"That's . . . the plan. Which means—"

"Yes." Charlene cut her off without June needing to finish. They'd spent years together, and their understanding of one another was close to telepathy. "I'll be your manager again. A million times, yes."

June smiled in relief. She'd never doubted that Charlene would help her, still, it was a breath of fresh air to have the words spoken. She was getting her team back. "It's a big ask. Moving to Germany—"

Charlene snorted. "*'Big ask'*. Oh, as if. We're never home anyway."

June giggled, relieved and giddy. Diego wasn't the only one rooting for her. Charlene had been in her corner for years. Nothing she'd accomplished thus far would have been possible without her. "Thank you. For pointing Diego in the right direction. You made this happen."

Charlene took in a deep breath, and June could just envision her standing somewhere. Arms on her hips, head tilted in disbelief. Then Charlene laughed. "You are so welcome for making you do that red carpet with him. Per usual, I was right."

"Alright, we get it, Charlene; you're the best manager in the entire world."

"Damn straight, I am. It only took four years for you to finally realize it."

June snorted. "I knew all along."

Charlene's voice settled into manager mode. June never thought she'd have missed that tone of voice so much. "We'll figure everything out, June. That bitch won't control us ever again."

June nodded despite knowing Charlene couldn't see it. The weight was lifted off her shoulders in a way it hadn't been in a long time. Charlene would take care of it the way she always did. "Char?"

"Yeah?"

"Do . . . Do you think the girls will come with?" She couldn't hide the fear in her voice. Charlene had been her anchor, but the girls were the life jackets keeping her afloat. She couldn't stand the idea of having one without the other.

Charlene was quiet for a beat as June spoke. Then she laughed gently. "Like hell they're not following you. We're a team, and a damn good one, too."

June sighed in absolute relief, trying to fight back the tears. Her team. Together again. "Yeah. Yeah, we are, aren't we?"

"The best. Now, shut up and call the girls."

June laughed and wiped her eyes. "Talk to you soon, yeah?"

"Very soon."

The line disconnected, and June relaxed slightly, leaning back against the chair.

She'd expected calling the girls to be easier, but it was so much worse. She hadn't talked to them in months. Not a single word since she disappeared those many months ago. She'd hurt them. That was what had stopped her all along from finally calling her closest friends in the world.

She had screamed at them. Left them the way she was so terrified they were going to leave her. And now, she had to ask them to join up with her again. To follow her to Germany. She resolved to call Lola first, finding her contact on her phone and staring at it for a long while. Finally, she slammed her finger down on the video call button before she could back out, propping her phone up. She figured it would be easier if she could see her face. Within four rings, Lola answered, and by the grace of God, Olivia was at her side.

"June!" Olivia cried, throwing her arms around Lola as if by proxy. "There you are, you sorry bastard! Where have you been?"

An amused breath escaped her, shaking her head. It wasn't exactly easy to sum up. "Texas," she said honestly. "Been trying to recuperate, and then Diego convinced me to go to the Netherlands with him, and now—" She definitely was not doing this right.

"Diego?" Olivia practically screamed. "Diego? You two are talking again? What did we miss?"

June laughed out loud, clapping a hand over her mouth. The last weeks had been some of the happiest of her life, and even with the uncertainty looming overhead, for the first time, she was excited. She brought them up to speed, including many of the details she'd left out to Charlene, like Diego on her porch at two in the morning—which elicited screams as Lola and Olivia grabbed each other—ending with a certain trip to the Netherlands, where Siegfried showed up at their table.

That was met with much less squealing and far more confusion. "Amelia blackmailed me," June explained. "She framed me for drugging Oviatt and threatened to ruin me if I didn't leave. So I left. But Siegfried has proof she framed me. He's taking me on. I'm moving to Riesenbeck."

The girls exchanged an expectant glance with one another, and June nodded, steeling herself against her request. "I'm not finished. I can't be. I have to see this to the end." She could feel the tears welling up in her eyes, swallowing hard over the growing lump of emotion caught in her throat. "When I lost my chance to do this with Midus, I thought the title was the only thing that mattered. But the entire time, it was you guys. You're the glue of this. There's no point in crossing the finish line without you. I know I fucked up. I disappeared, I didn't explain. I left you hanging, and nothing eats me up more, but I can't do this without you two. And even if I could, I wouldn't want to." June bit her bottom lip, a pit of despair opening in her gut, threatening to swallow her up.

Part of her had expected an immediate answer. That the words being out would be enough to soothe her, but the girls stared back at her as though trying to comprehend all that she was asking. To work for her again. To be part of her team. To move countries.

And then, the girls broke into beaming smiles. Olivia was the first to speak. "Fuck. Yes."

Lola squealed, wrapping her arms around Olivia. "Fuck! Yes!"

June's hand fell to her chest, as though she could hold her bursting heart and keep it from exploding in her chest. "Oh, thank God." The girls laughed, clinging to each other and beaming in pure joy. Her head fell back against the back of her chair, grinning like a fool.

She didn't know what she'd done to deserve this. A second chance. Hands to guide her, and hands to hoist her up, and hands to hold. But she wasn't going to squander it now. June had a Super Grand Prix to win. No matter what it took.

Chapter Thirty-Four

There came a moment where June realized the life she'd been trying to outrun since she was seventeen had finally caught up to her. When Amelia left her high and dry, June had lost everything she'd been chasing. She'd gone back to Texas, to waitressing, to Odie's. She'd left horses and the showjumping world behind. She'd lost her team, her coach, her life. She'd be damned if anyone ever took it from her again.

That was what Amelia had failed to realize—a starved dog bit harder and didn't let go.

What wouldn't she do to hold on now?

The threat of greatness no longer crushed her, it emboldened her.

June had only four weeks to get back into the groove of riding and competing. She had to focus. She couldn't stay in Zandvoort for Diego's race weekend, and in the middle of a triple header, Diego couldn't follow her. She would fly ahead with Siegfried where Lola, Olivia, and Charlene would follow later in the week.

Diego would race in Zandvoort, returning to Monaco for the week until the Brazilian Grand Prix, and then the week break until the Las Vegas Grand Prix. That left them apart for over three weeks.

With a free weekend in the middle of it all, he could have followed her sooner—she knew he wanted to, and June wanted him with her always—but they both understood it wasn't wise. June needed to summon the kind of fierce determination that had led to her becoming The Sensational Rookie.

Diego, the man who had broken down her walls and made her feel the happiest and safest she'd ever felt with another person put a damper on that stubbornness that she couldn't afford. Diego never mentioned anything about it in his plans, but June appreciated his willingness to give her space.

Still, her gratitude couldn't hide her anxiety or sorrow at the idea of not having him for nearly three weeks. She had just got him back, and part of her was still afraid he was going to walk out that door and never return. It was Diego, she reminded herself. That was never going to happen. At least, not again.

They spent the night before wrapped up in each other's arms. Diego drove them all to the train station, the only time June had ever actually seen Siegfried accept a ride from someone.

Diego walked them in, and Siegfried excused himself at the entrance, leaving the two alone at the check-in.

It was only going to be three weeks. They'd done months apart before. This was nothing. Still, a lump had lodged itself in June's throat and she attempted to clear it away. "We totally have enough time to sneak into the bathroom for a quickie."

Diego choked on a laugh, shaking his head at her as he drew her into a tight hug, hands rubbing soothing circles in attempts to lessen her dread. He knew her too well—she always resorted to jokes when things got too real. She buried her head against his chest, and he placed a kiss among her hair. "June?"

"Hm?"

He drew back, taking her face into his hands and pinning her in place with his gaze. Since the moment they'd met in that bar, he'd been very talented at making her shut up with just a look. "You didn't get here by accident. You'll say it was fate, or luck, or whatever other bullshit you think. It wasn't any of that. It was *you*. A light that shines as bright as you can't help but draw others to it."

The tears sprung to her eyes, and Diego wiped them away, kissing the crest of each of her brow bones before he pressed a kiss to her lips. "I love you." The words hit as sharply as they had the first time he'd said them to her, on her porch at two in the morning.

"I love you, too." And she meant it in a way she'd never dared to dream being able to mean it before.

With one final kiss, June gathered her bags and disappeared through the crowd She allowed the busyness of the train station and finding her seat to distract her from the physical pain the distance between her and Diego brought.

Siegfried was waiting for her just inside their coach, grinning cheekily to himself. *"'He's not my boy,'"* he quoted at her in a painful imitation of an American accent, her words from over a year ago. June shoved him playfully and he slung an arm around her as they made their way to their seats. "Told you he was a good one."

June couldn't argue. It was a six hour journey before June found herself standing on Siegfried's estate.

Siegfried owned more acres than June could fathom. His house was tucked back into a grove of trees nearly a mile away from the barn. June's new residence was much smaller, and much closer to the barn. He was a very particular man and preferred to do things by himself. As such, he hadn't had a groom in several years, but he still had fully furnished groom's quarters. The nicest June had ever seen. It was a quaint white farmhouse—just like she'd always dreamed of. A yard. Lots of windows. A porch with a rocking chair. She fell in love the second she saw it.

She slept alone. Woke up alone. But for the first time in a long time, June didn't feel lonely. As she stepped into the sunlight in a new set of riding breeches, helmet under her arm, June felt the best she had in months.

She made her way to the barn with an extra pep in her step. Diego had been right, she wasn't done jumping. The smell of the horses and hay welcomed her home as though the months away had never happened.

Stepping onto a horse again felt like springtime, the ice and desolation of a frigid winter giving way to green grass and sprouting flowers. Part of her had been afraid the few months without an English saddle and jumps set before her would render her useless. Now, sat in the saddle, her body responding automatically to the animal beneath her, she realized that was ridiculous. The knowledge was sewn deep into her soul, as much a part of her as her Texas accent and Mama Odie's biscuits. She could forget it existed for years, and still, the slightest reminder pushed it to the forefront of her mind. It was not something she could ever truly be rid of.

Frieda was a powerhouse of a horse, a 17.3 hand gray mare who cared only that she was the winner. She knew what a good round looked like. June knew that much just from watching Siegfried ride. He lent her tack and a helmet until hers arrived.

Training with Siegfried was an entirely different beast than Amelia. His comments were short and precise. He focused on riding effectively per the horse, rather than riding pretty. He shouted aggressive praise at her from the judge's chair. It was odd not to be outright bullied for every small mistake. June was slowly realizing that this was how it should have been all along.

Sessions never went the way they did with Amelia. A bad stride? Siegfried didn't even comment on it, immediately focused on the next jump. Fix it. Go again. An ugly jump? He didn't care so long as it was clear. Pretty didn't win. Fast and clear did.

June walked Frieda around the arena after yet another incredible session. They were getting more in sync with each passing round. "Amelia targeted your confidence," Siegfried said. "She knew she couldn't beat you in skill alone."

June winced, staring down Frieda's mane. "She *did* beat me."

Siegfried scoffed. "A round like that—" he gestured between her and the expanse of the arena, "—she cannot beat. You are The Sensational Rookie. You will succeed, June."

She had never experienced anything like his unrelenting confidence in her.

Riding Frieda felt like riding Midus again. Every jump, every combination, every step was better than the last. Her fall with Oviatt back in the spring had rattled her confidence, but with each ride, the fear lessened. Frieda was solid. She didn't falter. It was like she had springboards built into her legs.

It was the end of October, with the Super Grand Prix set for only a month away. June had four weeks to be back in shape well enough for the end of the season. For her first competition back. Pressure weighed heavily on her, but it didn't crush her beneath it the way it used to. She'd lived without it, and she never wanted to again. It pushed her now. To be better. To prove she deserved a spot in this sport.

Training resumed. June had only three horses under her care. Frieda, Midus, and Hades. The boys arrived two days after her. Diego had her things shipped in on the flight alongside the horses—an English saddle she hadn't uncovered in months, her tack all packed neatly into her tack trunk the way it had been since she'd left Italy.

She hustled to unload the horses, choking back emotion at the sight of them. Her boys who had both given her their all. Midus, who would spend the rest of his days in a grassy field with friends, retrieved for walkabouts and bareback rides whenever they felt like it. Hades, who was just getting started. A proper start this time, no longer forced to pick up so much slack. They had the whole world in front of them. June let the tears fall.

She rode Frieda daily. She didn't jump Hades. At least, not for now. They strictly did flatwork. She mostly walked Midus from the ground just to spend time with him. She rode him bareback some days in the pasture and across the estate simply because he'd been cleared for it and they both enjoyed it. It was the first time in a very long time that she rode just because she enjoyed it. She didn't have eight or ten horses to ride in a single day.

Everything felt okay again. Everything felt *good*. But the sight of the girls sprinting towards her across the estate took the cake. June bailed off Midus, leaving him where he was to gather the girls up in a hug the way they had so many times before.

Lola and Olivia crashed into June, squeezing her tight enough to hurt, but she didn't mind. She felt lighter than she had in months as she held them close. "I've missed you," she whispered quietly.

"You were the one who ran out on us, ya' shithead," Olivia pointed out, but there was no malice in her words, and she didn't loosen her grip.

A pang of guilt shot through June, but she snuffed it out, squeezing them both. "Biggest mistake of my life." And it was honest. She wished she'd handled things better, but she was here now. Things were different. Things were right.

Midus had followed June to the girls, nudging the trio with his massive head and nearly pushing them all over. The girls squealed, abandoning June in favor of throwing their arms around the bay. He buried his head in Lola's chest, Olivia's arms flung around his neck as she scratched him. It was a sight that filled her with a wave of relief to watch. She gave his neck a soft pat, taking a moment just to watch the girls shower Midus with affection.

They chattered relentlessly as they led Midus back to his paddock. Olivia had moved to cover a hockey team in Canada. Lola, on the other hand, had been in New York working for Catalina Cabrera, creating content for her fashion brand. June had exploded at the news. "You left working for *Catalina?*"

Lola giggled and shrugged, holding up her phone to display a lock screen of Catalina and Lola wrapped around each other on a couch, each holding a glass of wine. "It's complicated for your girlfriend to be your boss anyway."

June's jaw dropped, and she immediately scooped Lola up into a hug, lifting her off the ground as she offered her congratulations.

Olivia and Lola had stayed in close contact the entire time June had been in Texas, and while she was clearly unsurprised by this news, she was just as happy for Lola.

At the paddock, Hades came running immediately, seemingly as pleased to see the girls as Midus had been. They showered him with love, cooing over how good he looked and how happy he seemed. June's heart nearly burst from their words, leaning against the fence and grinning at her friends. Olivia and Lola exchanged a mischievous grin with each other, and June's eyes widened in suspicion. "We have waited *long* enough to hear about Diego." June laughed, and they joined in, grabbing her by the hands and hauling her off toward the house.

They spent the majority of that night curled up on June's couch catching up with a plethora of snacks in hand. They treated themselves to a house tour first, noting some of Diego's clothes in her suitcase, clearly pleased with having been so painfully right about the two of them.

Months had passed, and yet, it was as though they hadn't lost a second. The girls fit back into her life as easily as they had the first time, and it gave her a sense of purpose to be able to hear the sounds of her girls in her home. Their laughter and cheers. The way their faces lit up when they saw Siegfried. Training was no less rigorous with the girls there, but it had certainly become more enjoyable. They blasted Taylor Swift and attempted to get Siegfried to dance with them, which more often than not led to them being chased out of the arena with a lunge whip, screams and laughter echoing from outside of the barn. Her life had become more than just training, it held companionship. Something she'd never truly had.

Her reunion with Charlene was a much quieter affair, exchanging knowing looks, soft smiles, and tight hugs.

June had gotten into the habit of expecting the worst, but with Frieda, everything was fine. June had to attend a competition with Frieda in order to be eligible to ride her in the Super Grand Prix. She steered away from anything LGCT related, instead opting for a competition right in Riesenbeck. A 1.50 class. June jumped clear. Siegfried insisted that was all she needed to focus on. Frieda would bring the speed. She took second, so, she guessed he was right.

She tried to keep everything hush, but she knew there were already articles circulating detailing her return to the showjumping world, speculating the future of her career. June kept her head down and prayed Amelia wouldn't see it.

June's phone buzzed and a pang of terror shot through her. She fumbled for it with shaky fingers, expecting the worst. Maybe Amelia had found out. Maybe Amelia had followed through on her threat and framed her. Maybe her invitation to the Super Grand Prix was revoked. Maybe—

It was a screenshot of an article. "*The Sensational Rookie Makes a Sensational Comeback*".

DIEGO <3: THATS MY FUCKING GIRLFRIEND BITCHES!!!!!!!!

June laughed out loud, nearly in tears from her relief.

DIEGO <3: magic as always mi vida

And then, she was in tears, overwhelmed with her own gratitude and love for Diego Cabrera.

She trained harder. Second was good, but June was going up against the sixteen best riders in the entire world. She could do better than that.

And yet, she could only train so hard. For once in her life, she didn't have the capacity to burn herself out. She had limited horses. She had Frieda and Frieda alone. She could only jump two or three times a week. The rest had to be flatwork.

June focused on refining her mental toughness. She went for walks. She let the terror—of the impending fight, of the arena, of facing Amelia—wash over her in full intensity, breathing deep and walking until it finally faded. Slowly, the panic stopped coming so quickly. Stopped staying for so long.

Despite herself, Siegfried's tactics were working. With every day, June was feeling more and more like the girl from BlackJack Stables. The world was full of possibility again. Competing held the promise of winning. Jumping held more than falls and being stomped into the ground.

The weeks wore away terrifyingly quick. In no time at all, the competition was a mere week away. June was torn between holding to the time for all it was worth, and wishing it would just pass already.

"Are you ready for this?" Siegfried asked finally.

"No," she admitted. "But I wasn't ready for anything the last two years of my life have thrown at me, and I think I'm making it through pretty alright."

Siegfried nodded in approval, clapping her on the back. It was never over the top, these moments between them, but it was more than June had ever had. Everything she'd ever needed.

The sun was setting, and June had only a few days left until the Super Grand Prix. She sat on the couch in her big bay window, one she had dreamed about since she was a kid, flipping through a book when the door opened and shut. June sat up, torn between immediate defense and wishful thinking—

Diego. He kicked the door closed, toting a suitcase behind him, a duffle bag slung over his shoulder. He was so handsome he took her breath away, in a dark blue polo and tan trousers. He dropped his bags, rushing forward and June flung her book, meeting him halfway, wrapping him up in a hug. He laughed, swinging her around in a circle.

He set her back on the ground, and June beamed up at him. "I thought your flight was tomorrow—"

He smothered her words in a bruising kiss, his grip on her waist tight as he dragged her forward against him. "Changed flights," he murmured between kisses, grinning against her lips. "Was going crazy—" Another kiss, backing her up until he had her pressed into the wall. "Had to see you."

June giggled against his lips. "So needy," she teased and he growled low in his throat.

"Always, for you." He reached over her to the curtains, flicking them closed before he was all over her again. His lips found her jaw, open-mouthed kisses trailing down to her neck. Her hands slid under his shirt, fingernails dragging across the muscle of his torso and he groaned his approval, pressing a final kiss to her collarbone before he dropped to his knees. Her breath caught in her throat, desire coursing through her in rolling waves of heat as he planted a hand on her hip and pressed her back against the wall, drawing her leg over his shoulder. Diego was greedy with her body, like he'd spent so much time abstaining from her, now he couldn't get enough.

It didn't take long until he had her spread out on the daybed beneath him, already ruined from his tongue and fingers alone. June met him with feverish urgency, her hands alternating between twining in his hair and scratching down his back. He groaned into her mouth, and June drew back, gasping with pleasure. She bit down on her fist.

Diego stopped abruptly, brown eyes flicking to meet hers in a challenge and June's heart stuttered.

"Oh *Vaquera*," he scolded, his hand closing around her wrist, dragging her fist away from her mouth. "It's just us for miles. I want to hear you scream for me."

Well, who was she to deny such a sweet request?

Diego captured her lips again and June sent up a prayer of thanks for a variety of flight options.

Chapter Thirty-Five

The Super Grand Prix was set in Prague, the Capital of the Czech Republic. The last time June had been here, it had been under very different circumstances during her first season. Her best season. *Yet,* Siegfried's voice in her head reminded automatically. Her best season, yet. She never thought she'd be here again. Certainly not like this.

She fell back into the routine as easy as breathing—packing, loading her gear, a drive in a horsebox. She savored it in a way she never had before. Checking in, finding stalls, getting settled.

June stayed on high alert, as though Amelia would appear around every corner.

Diego stood steadfast at her side. He'd reassured her a million times that he'd stay out of her way. This was her fight. He had helped her every step of the way, but it needed to be June at the other end of the gun pointed at Amelia's head. She made him promise not to punch Amelia on sight. Begrudgingly, he agreed. Still, she knew he wouldn't hesitate when it came down to it. June had never known that kind of safety in her life. The kind where she could lean on someone. The kind where she could allow herself some slack and trust that if she were unable to pick it up, Diego wouldn't let her fall.

June got her own horse ready, something she loved. She'd gotten so caught up in the prestige and luxury of having a groom, she'd forgotten how much it calmed her nerves. Methodically picking hooves and brushing from head to toe, placing her own saddle pad and saddle, securing her own breast collar and doing her own bridling. Frieda reminded June so much of Midus. It was as heartbreaking as it was comforting.

June and Diego sat in front of her stall on her tack trunk. He was desperately trying to distract her. He was explaining racing to her in depth, the data, the tyre management, the strategies. June loved listening to him and he knew that. He took her hand in his and placed it palm down on his knee, tracing from wrist to fingertip on each finger again and again and again to dispel her nerves. He was good at that, keeping her from losing her head.

Charlene and the girls flew in later rather than driving with Frieda. They bombarded her the moment the moment they saw her, scooping her up in a hug like they hadn't seen her in a year. They stood in a circle around her, chatting, distracting her from the impending threat of the competition. It actually worked. They talked about everything until it was time to warm up; their flights, the guy in the airport with six pretzels in one hand, the little girl next to Olivia on the plane who made her watch Bluey with her. June half listened, too caught up in her own gratitude for people in her life who cared this much. Who knew her so well.

June passed Frieda off to Siegfried, headed for the restroom. One last chance for a moment of privacy to gather herself before she went to the warm-up ring. She pushed the door open, drawing a deep breath. And then, she stopped in her tracks, her heart halting with dread.

Amelia. She was drying her hands, directly across from June.

This was not how June had planned it. And yet, here she was.

Disbelief tore across Amelia's face and then rage. Amelia lunged forward, catching June by the arm. "What are you doing here?"

June wrenched out of her grasp, Amelia's nails leaving indents in her skin. June took a firm step back, raising her chin in defiance. "I won a Grand Prix. I was invited."

Every muscle in Amelia's body tensed, as if she were seconds away from slapping June the way she had that final day in Amelia's barn. Dark eyes hardened, taking in every detail of June's appearance. She was largely the same—short red hair, though longer now, and lightened by the Texas sun. She'd lost a few pounds and plenty of muscle mass, but that was gained back easily enough. The confidence she held now was the difference. Amelia had tried to wrench it from her, but June clung to it with fierce determination.

June had spent so long admiring this woman, and now, she couldn't see why, like a tugboat strung along in the dark, until the line was cut and she was left stranded in an ocean. She wasn't sure why she'd ever followed her now. Not when June always knew Amelia would leave her to drown. "You made enemies, Amelia," June took a step forward, cocking her head to the side. "See, there's this thing they teach you in Texas. Maybe not every snake is poisonous, but the one you treat as harmless will be the one to put you in your grave."

Amelia's jaw clenched as she looked the other woman up and down. She stepped closer, her hand reaching out to touch the other equestrian's arm, placing her hand on June's shoulder. It was a gesture she'd done a thousand times before, but this time, it felt more possessive than it did intimate.

"I've made enemies?" She questioned, taking another step forward. "You're the one who abandoned me. Drugging the horse I allowed you to use. It's only affection for you that kept me from turning you in."

June stepped out of Amelia's grasp, unwavering. "Oviatt was never drugged."

Amelia let out a scoff, her eyes narrowing slightly as she stepped forward again. "I know what I saw. You drugged that horse. You sabotaged me." She spoke firmly, as if trying to convince the other woman that what she saw was irrefutable.

"Don't be stupid, Amelia. I have copies of the real vet report and people willing to vouch that you framed me."

Amelia paused like she'd been slapped, glancing around the bathroom to make sure they were alone before she set her jaw. "And what exactly do you think you're going to do with this information? Throw me in jail? I have the best lawyers—"

June's answer came automatically. "I want a fight."

Amelia's eyebrows shot into her hairline. "Excuse me?" For a moment, she almost looked impressed.

June didn't flinch, keeping herself level with her former coach. "I want a fair, honest fight for the season title. Because I can win, and we both know it."

Amelia almost looked taken aback by the request. The idea of there even being a threat to her reign seemed completely unfathomable. "You want to challenge me for the title? Are you serious?" Her voice was incredulous, not wanting to believe such a thing was possible. June Walker, a girl that had appeared out of nowhere with almost no accomplishments, a rider from a barn in Texas, of all places. The thought was ridiculous.

"Be honest with yourself," she said firmly. "You'd never win."

But her tone sang a different tune. Four weeks ago, those words would have sent June skittering right back to Texas, but Siegfried's voice overpowered it now. June shrugged. "Then you have nothing to lose."

Amelia's fingers curled into a tight ball. She was cornered, and she knew it. All of her plotting had been destroyed in one swift moment and there was nothing she could do about it.

Amelia let out a scoff, a sharp and harsh little sound that echoed off the bathroom walls. Her face twisted into a grimace. "Fine," she spat, venom spewing from every part of her as though the word was painful to utter. "You want a fight? It's your funeral."

In a single motion, Amelia turned on her heel and stormed from the bathroom. June stared after her with a clenched jaw until the door closed behind her, then collapsed back against the wall in relief.

Chapter Thirty-Six

Her conversation with Amelia left her feeling emboldened. She'd faced her old coach. For once, Amelia had been the one to flinch. June had walked out on top. She'd allowed herself to dare to hope that Siegfried was right. Now, she was beginning to believe it. She readied for sneers and jabs from her competitors in the warm-up ring, but they never came. Instead, any who looked her way merely offered her smiles and *'welcome back'*, or *'good to see you'*. Most were too focused on their own warm up to pay her any mind at all. How ridiculous, she thought, that she'd ever placed such importance on herself to think everyone was out to get her. That was where her weakness lay. She focused so much on what people thought of her that she second-guessed everything she knew to be true.

After riding Oviatt and Hades for a season and a half, Frieda was a damn unicorn. For the first time in nearly two years, June was excited for a competition. Lola and Olivia waited in the crowd, Diego, Siegfried, and Charlene at her side waiting to enter the arena. The girls had fought tooth and nail to wait with her, but Diego wouldn't even entertain the idea of not being with her. June waited for the onslaught of nerves she'd become so accustomed to with bated breath, but they didn't come.

Instead, all she felt was adrenaline and excitement. June was up next.

She leaned down to kiss Diego and he met her halfway with a beaming smile. "You're magic, *Vaquera*. Give 'em hell."

A phrase he'd learned from his time in Texas. June's heart nearly imploded.

Siegfried clasped her hand and gave her a single nod of encouragement before he let go. It was more than enough. Diego and Siegfried slipped off, and June entered the arena.

June had fallen in love with showjumping from the first crossrail. She'd forgotten that was why she did this. She loved horses. She loved competing. No one could ever take her love of the fight from her ever again.

The bell sounded, and June and Frieda rocketed forward. Jump clear. That was all June had to do. Frieda would handle the rest. The jumps were meant to be next to impossible. The highest fences and most difficult combinations. June had been terrified she would step into the arena and choke. Terrified that in the moment she would think only of her failures. Think only of her fall with Oviatt. But with a wall jump as tall as Frieda hurtling at them, June had no time to think anything at all except for over and up.

She heard the crowd hold their breath as she counted the strides—two, three, four, five—up and over. Before they'd even landed, they were hunting down the next jump. Up and over. Then, a triple combination. Up and over. One stride, two. Up and over. One, two. *Up.*

And over. Clear.

They soared over the final jump.

The crowd's applause was instantaneous the moment Frieda's feet hit the ground. It was a clear round. It was fast enough to qualify her for the next class.

June's relief practically melted her into the saddle, beaming as she praised Frieda.

She sat at fifth place.

Amelia was in fourth. The sight of Amelia's name above hers made her sick to her stomach. She had not come this far just to fail now. *There's another round*, she reminded herself. The fight wasn't over.

The moment June left the arena, her crew was at her side, celebrating her success. She'd made it through to the second round. Other's couldn't say the same. She had a chance. They were good at reminding her when to get out of her head.

Amelia sat on her horse in the cooldown ring, sneering in June's direction.

June wished she could afford to shoot her right off her horse. Round two. She focused everything on round two.

The time wore on between rounds one and two. June held her spot as the final riders made their way through. Two had been disqualified in round one. That left fourteen riders. Amelia was one of them. June had to beat her.

June promised God that if Amelia somehow took out an entire fence or two she'd start going to church again.

June sat at the gate, waiting for her turn. She was terrified, and it was hard to stave off that kind of panic. Amelia was ahead of her in the ranking. She'd had an entire season of competition leading up to this. June had a month back in the saddle.

Had June come this far just to lose again? Was that all she would ever do? June was up next.

Siegfried's hand landed on her calf, abruptly drawing her from her thoughts. There was an urgency to his gaze as he spoke. "Ask Frieda for everything she's got."

"What?" They'd spent the last month just having June stay out of her way.

"She'll give you the world, June. Ask for it. Ride hard and ride fast."

June blinked. "Are you sure—"

"June." His voice was sharp, but kind. "You know what you're doing. You know you can do this. Leave it all in the ring."

June let the words settle. She let them embolden her. Let them give her a boost of confidence in her final moments before the ring. She thought of Charlene's words, her familiar voice soothing her nerves. *Make it happen.* She thought of Siegfried's words. *Leave it all in the ring.*

It was up to speed now. June was up. She steeled herself against her nerves and urged Frieda into the arena. She seemed to be attuned to the newfound energy, bristling with excitement. Not in the way Hades or Oviatt had been—ready to explode without a moment's notice. Frieda carried herself with all the weight of a gun before the trigger was pulled, her mind set on the fight.

Fastest and the least amount of faults. The bell sounded. They flew into action, Frieda's long stride carried them to the first fence. Speed was the name of the game, and Frieda brought it with every step. They soared of the second fence. The moment Frieda's feet touched the ground, June asked for more. They needed speed. Faster. They covered the ground quickly, Frieda stretched out, cutting out a stride as they rode up to the triple combination. June held her breath, but they were over it clear. They flew through the combination, June barely landing before the soared over the next.

They were through the course in just over a minute. The crowd erupted in cheers.

With seven riders set to follow, June was in the lead. She scarce dared to hope, and yet, she was shaking from the thrill. It was a good round. Even she couldn't deny that.

The praise swarmed her the second she exited the arena. She spotted Charlene first, who pumped her fist in the air. "That's my girl."

June's heart swelled with affection. She knew that somewhere in the crowd, Lola and Olivia were going wild. Diego and Siegfried met her. Siegfried was visibly pleased, eyes crinkling with something akin to pride. Diego on the other hand could hardly contain his excitement.

The arena lit up with the sounds of a crowd going wild as a new leader took their spot at the front.

June's heart sunk. She'd immediately been pushed out.

Diego's hand landed on her leg, squeezing in a consoling grip. "You're fine, *Vaquera*. You're still on the podium."

For now, at least.

June nodded in thanks, offering him a tight-lipped smile. "Okay. I'm going to the cooldown arena before I throw up."

The trio stepped back in understanding as she slipped away. The hard part was over. Now came the worst past. The waiting.

June didn't watch Amelia's round. She couldn't. Had she given it her all just to still not be enough?

She walked Frieda out, praising her every step of the way. So, maybe June hadn't kept her spot. Maybe every single rider had outdone her the second she left the arena. June was still here. She was competing on a horse she loved and trusted. She had a coach who believed in her. She had an entire season of this waiting for her.

She had her manager, who had been more of a mom to her the last four years than anything else. She had a pair of girls who were her closest friends in the world. She had Diego. Her Diego who had come back to her, and always would.

A gaggle of screaming people brought her attention to the gate. She shot a glare in their direction until she realized they were *her* people. They were sprinting at her, Olivia and Diego leading the pack. June turned Frieda toward them, meeting them halfway.

They were shouting something about a third jump, or a third round, or—Diego caught her by the leg and dragged her off Frieda as the others caught up. He grabbed her face in both hands. There were tears in his eyes. "Third place!" he shouted, smiling so wide it was like his heart could hardly contain his happiness. "You did it, June! You did it!"

June opened her mouth to ask, but Olivia beat her to it. "Amelia's in fifth! You beat her!"

The others had surrounded her, screaming and hollering as they enveloped her in a hug. She couldn't take her eyes off Diego, her ears still tingling as she tried to digest his words. And then, a bubbling laugh of disbelief escaped her. The tears were instant, and Diego wiped them with the pad of his thumb. "I did it," she whispered.

I did it.

Diego laughed again, pulling her into a hug. "You fucking did it!"

June couldn't stop the sobs as she collapsed into the hug, enveloped in the arms of those she loved. Charlene, Lola, Olivia, and Diego. They hollered and cried, even Charlene. June could hardly take it.

And then, there was Siegfried holding Frieda, who looked even more proud of herself than June.

Siegfried—horribly grumpy and gruff Siegfried—was *smiling*.

June choked on her emotion as she met his eyes. She reached her hand out to him and he took it, holding steadfast. Her coach. The reason she got a second chance. She choked over the words. "Thank you."

Siegfried smiled, and then, he laughed out loud, shaking his head in disbelief. A single word. "Sensational."

The single word made her heart clench, tears pouring down her face with renewed fervor.

"The lap of honor!" Charlene called, pulling back from the hug abruptly before she pried the others off to her. "Go June! You have to go!"

June laughed out loud, unable to contain her joy, spurred into motion by Charlene's urgency. Siegfried held Frieda as Diego boosted her on. Tears still ran down June's face, smiling so wide her cheeks hurt.

No lap of honor had ever tasted quite so sweet.

The cheers of the thousands in the stands could not hold a candle to her own crew, screaming from the sidelines. For the first time in her life, nothing could have mattered more. Not a trophy, not the money, not even besting Amelia.

Who's going to be by your side when you take home your title? Those had been Amelia's words. June had panicked at them, because without Amelia, she would be alone.

But of course, that wasn't the truth. It was always going to be them. Through thick and thin.

She was tackled into another hug the moment she was out of the arena before she was pushed off to the podium.

Every moment of June's life had led to this moment. She hadn't won the season title. She hadn't won at all. But she was standing on a podium in Prague. She was competing. She was with her family. The spray of champagne coated her, and never had it tasted so sweet.

Chapter Thirty-Seven

The morning after a competition always brought an odd shift. The combined nerves of dozens of competitors, their teams, and their horses washed away into a quiet calm in the aftermath. June stood in the stall, scratching Frieda's neck and supplying her with as many treats as June could have possibly stuffed into her pockets. June was exhausted and slightly hungover, and the happiest she had ever been in her life.

Siegfried came storming into the barn, drawing June's attention abruptly. "Did you hear?" There was a tension in his voice that carried over to his frown, stirring a deep dread in June's chest. It must have shown on her face because he didn't make her wait. "The bitch retired."

Of all the news June had been expecting off his lips, that was perhaps the last. He didn't have to specify who. *Amelia*. "She . . . what?"

Siegfried made a dissatisfied grunt in the back of his throat, hands braced against his hips. "Announced it this morning."

June shook her head in disbelief. "Is she—"

She hadn't even got the question out before Siegfried was pointing her in the right direction and shooing her along. June sprinted down the line of stalls, before she caught sight of Amelia across the lawn. People June had never seen before were packing her things and horses into a trailer, Amelia standing off to the side. It was a sight June was familiar with, though the one doing the work before had always been June.

Amelia turned as she heard June coming, grinding to a halt in front of her. "What—What is this?" She huffed breathlessly, shaking her head in desperation to understand. "I wanted a fair, honest fight for the title."

Amelia turned, hands clasped behind her back as she turned and walked across the lawn. "Walk with me."

June, baffled and so used to following her command, did as she was told. She knew Amelia would never cough up answers where others could hear. At least, not the truth. Not that Amelia was keen on truth in the first place. "I'm selling my horses," she said simply once they were out of earshot from the others, as casually as if they were talking about hotel reservations or schedules. "Retiring. I'm done."

June stopped dead in her tracks, a childish anger flaring in her gut. "That isn't fair—"

Amelia whirled on her, a barely contained rage in her own features. "I already had to lose to you once. I won't do it again."

Her words left June reeling, staring after her in bewilderment. Amelia was going down and she knew it. Her last act was to rip the rug out from under June's feet. She grit her teeth, refusing to give Amelia the satisfaction of once again having bested her. She'd had her cornered. Flanked from all sides. She didn't realize Amelia could dig down. "Your pride is worth more to you than your career? Everything you built here?"

Amelia took a step back like she'd slapped her, eyeing her up and down like vermin digging through her trash. "My career died the moment you decided to tear me apart."

For a long moment, June could do nothing but stare, dumbfounded and confused. And then, a cruel sense of satisfaction settled in her gut. "You're afraid."

For once in her life, Amelia stared at June utterly stunned. No smart remarks. No chance to make her feel small. She'd never make her feel small again. Because June was more than she could ever be.

"I thought the world of you." June leaned back, peering down Amelia from head to toe as she shook her head in disgust. "Now, I just wonder how I was that fucking stupid."

Amelia barked out a laugh. "Naive child," she mused, but the words didn't sting like they used to. "I gave you everything here. You don't have what it takes."

June held her head high, taking a firm step forward. "You're the one running."

For a long moment, neither of them said anything, watching each other in a silent standoff.

June's face softened slightly. ". . . What will happen to Oviatt?"

That startled her more than anything else June had said. As if the idea that June could give a shit about the horse was unfathomable. "Excuse me?"

"What will happen? You've publicly condemned the horse, and he's had half a million blowups on international TV."

Her lips curled back into an evil grin, a smugness about her that June wanted to smack right off her face. "I'll shoot him in the fucking head." Even in defeat, she still clung to every drop of poison she could dangle over June's lips.

June didn't flinch, just shook her head sadly at the woman standing before her. "I want his papers in my name and a contract by the end of tonight, or I'll release every bit of information against you to the public and let them deal with it."

Her hands landed on her hips, cocking her head to the side. "And what are you willing to pay for him?"

"My silence." June stepped forward into her space, and it was the first time June had realized how much smaller than her Amelia really was. No longer was she the otherworldly force that June had spent so many years cowering under, but rather a woman who had slammed the final nail into her coffin.

"Is that a deal, Amelia? Any horse you cannot sell because your subpar training has made them mad comes to me, or I swear to God I will ruin you. You won't fight me? Fine. I'll win on the horse you couldn't train."

Amelia stepped back and shrugged. "Pay for the shipping and he's all yours."

June shook her head. "No. I'll come pick him up myself. Along with Isa."

Amelia's eyes flared with rage, opening her mouth to argue, but June beat her to it. "Along with Isa," she demanded. June wouldn't allow another soul to be manipulated into being Amelia's perfect soldier.

Amelia was cornered and she knew it. Her voice dropped to a venomous hiss, her lips still trained in a perfectly civil smile. "Let's hope this time when he lands on you, he kills you."

June blinked, startled, yet somehow still unsurprised. "When I win," she started, taking a step forward into her space with a viciousness she had never turned on Amelia before. "I'll do it remembering exactly how pathetic you looked in this exact moment."

June extended her hand for Amelia to shake. Her eyes jetted to June's hand, recoiling with utter disgust. She turned away, and headed for the van. June crossed her arms over her chest, watching as Amelia's crew packed the rest of her things in the van. Amelia stepped into her car, and in the next instant, she tore out of the yard, spitting gravel as she went.

A gentle numbness settled in as Amelia drove away for the last time, leaving June entirely on her own. She thought it would terrify her. The woman had been her rock. Or, at least, she had told June that she was. The last years of her life had been plagued with the need to be better. To belong. How long had she spent fighting for this?

She hadn't realized that it was inevitable. She couldn't fail. Because June didn't quit. She was going to get knocked off her feet again. And again. But she would get up. It was who she was.

"June," a voice said behind her, breathless and familiar. June whirled to face him. Diego, panting and staring at her wide-eyed. He gave her a once-over, then glanced at the empty spot where Amelia had been, and back to her. "Siegfried told me . . ."

June said nothing, only walked forward and pulled him into a tight hug. Diego's arms wrapped around her automatically, cradling her head against his chest as he held her close. "Are you alright?" Diego asked. June relaxed into his touch, a breath escaping her lungs that felt as though it had spent her entire life encased and waiting to break free. She nodded. It was the only answer she could give. Hopeful and true.

"I think . . . yeah. I just bought Oviatt."

Diego stepped back, a horrified look on his expression. "You *what*?"

June laughed of disbelief, nodding. But she was excited. Things hadn't been the way they were supposed to, but they were in June's hands now. He was in June's hands. And things were going to be very, very different. Oviatt was hers. She thought of Amelia's words. *Let's hope this time when he lands on you, he kills you.*

June met Diego's eyes. "Are you mad at me?"

All Diego could do was shake his head and sigh, pulling her back into his embrace. "I knew full well when I showed up on your doorstep I was giving up any hope for peace in my life ever again."

June laughed out loud, tears of relief pricking in her eyes as she borrowed her face against his chest.

"She's gone," Diego whispered. "You did it."

A strange mix of anxiety and relief flooded June's senses at the mere idea. Amelia had owned June for so long. Now, she was free. Whether she failed or succeeded was up to her now. Well, and Diego. Siegfried. Lola and Olivia. Charlene.

She grinned, leaning into Diego's embrace with a flush of excitement. "Oh please, we're just getting started."

June didn't think there would ever be a moment when Diego climbed in the car that she wouldn't panic. But, with every chance to see it, the fear was abating, if only slightly.

He took third in Abu Dhabi. Despite being out for half the season, Diego brought home significant points. Talks of the fastest car Lotus had seen in years, coupled with Diego's impressive performance, brought him to the front of commentators potential list of contenders for the next year's championship.

Diego drove with her to pick up Oviatt. Isa had jumped at the chance when June offered her a spot—as a rider, not a groom. With Siegfried's retirement, Lotus was looking for a new showjumper to sponsor.

Lotus jumped at the chance to sponsor June again, especially after Diego and June had made their relationship public. Diego had asked her to marry him half a dozen times, *"For publicity, of course"*, he reasoned sarcastically.

June wouldn't let him put a ring on her finger just yet, but he insisted on getting her a gift for their *'two year fake-dating anniversary'*, as he had deemed it. June got him a custom bottle of the same tequila he'd spilled on her their first night, and Diego laughed, and then nearly cried.

Diego got her a weanling filly—a beautiful seal brown color with a blaze down her face. She was from the same lines as Midus. June sobbed so hard she could barely breathe.

The girls got an apartment in the city, close to Charlene and the barn. Diego had all but moved in with her—at least for the off season.

With Siegfried's skilled hand to guide them, Hades and June were progressing fast. Her confidence grew with every session and so did his. June taught Diego to ride. They went out on the trail nearly every day. With an entirely fenced property, they let the other horses run with them—Midus, Mari, and Oviatt. June didn't ride him. At least, not yet. She let him stretch his legs. Let him reset. She'd start him again, just not yet.

Just like that, the first Grand Prix of the season was upon them.

Qatar loomed before Hades and June, returned to the same place as that fateful night June punched a stranger in the face. Odie, who had never left the states in her life, got a passport. She and Ava were in the crowd when June entered an LGCT arena again.

Now, Diego stood beside her, hand resting on her leg as he chattered about the weather and odd concessions to dull her nerves. She smiled softly down at him.

The moment June swung on Hades, something in the air was different. He settled beneath her like he was meant to be there. Like *she* was meant to be there. The air was still, but it was far from calm, littered with promise. She could feel the electricity all around her—through her, ready to strike. The nerves of the past were nowhere to be found.

I can do this, she thought, followed by Diego's immediate answer from so many months ago. *I know that. Do you know that?*

Of course she knew that.

Acknowledgements

From the age of nine years old, I have told everyone in my life I was going to be an author. What a surreal and unfathomable experience to have my debut novel published. This book was one I wrote purely for myself because I enjoyed the story and not one I ever planned on publishing. I am so grateful for the overwhelming love and support on so many levels, both personal and professional.

I have to start by thanking my editor and dear friend Emma. When self-doubt, stress, and discouragement almost led to me not publishing Racing Hearts at all, Emma came to the rescue. This book would not have been possible without you. From correcting my horrific grammar, to double checking the timeline, to pass after pass after pass of proofreading, you have been my hero. On a personal level, you pushed me further every day. Every ounce of imposter syndrome I poured out was met by overwhelming encouragement. With each mistake, revision, and new draft, you were cheering me along. From endless editing passes, to fangirling about Diego, and diving into the world of motorsport together, I cannot thank you enough.

I'd like to thank my mom for fostering my love of horses and books. Thank you for listening to me rant about books that have yet to go to print.

Thank you to my dad for fostering my love of motorsport and racing. Even though you still prefer NASCAR, I won't judge you for it. (Maybe just a little.)

Ilo, my lovely beta reader who helped to ensure content involving professional showjumping was correct. From correcting terminology to locations, she helped to make the book feel as accurate as possible.

Thank you to every beta reader who offered me advice on the book, from the first horrifically messy draft, to the final slightly-less-messy draft. None of this would have been possible without your advice and support.

And of course, Carlos Sainz Jr., the original inspiration for Diego Cabrera. Thank you for having such perfect hair I had to write a book about it.

About the author

Jude Barnes started writing when she was just nine years old. She hasn't put down the pen since, just switched to a keyboard.

Jude's passion for horses and motorsport were fostered at a young age, with a cowgirl for a mom, and a stuntman for a dad.

In between traveling every chance she gets, showjumping on her thoroughbred Hades, and wrangling cattle on her family's ranch, she sneaks in a little time for telling stories.

www.ingramcontent.com/pod-product-compliance
Ingram Content Group UK Ltd.
Pitfield, Milton Keynes, MK11 3LW, UK
UKHW020909180825
7440UKWH00038B/649